THE COLLECTED WORKS OF MARY WEBB

*

THE GOLDEN ARROW

MARY WEBB

*

THE GOLDEN ARROW

WITH AN INTRODUCTION BY
G. K. CHESTERTON

LONDON
JONATHAN CAPE 30 BEDFORD SQUARE

FIRST PUBLISHED 1916
COLLECTED EDITION 1928
REPRINTED 1929

PRINTED IN GREAT BRITAIN BY
BUTLER & TANNER LTD
FROME

TO
A NOBLE LOVER
H. L. W.

We have sought it, we have sought the golden arrow!
  (Bright the sally-willows sway)
Two and two by paths low and narrow,
  Arm-in-crook along the mountain way.
  Break o' frost and break o' day!
Some were sobbing through the gloom
When we found it, when we found the golden arrow—
Wand of willow in the secret cwm.

M. W.

Introduction

MANY of us can remember the revelation of poetical power given to the world with the songs of a Shropshire Lad. Much of the noble, though more neglected, work of Mary Webb might be called the prose poems of a Shropshire Lass. Most of them spoke in the spirit, and many through the mouth, of some young peasant woman in or near that western county which lies, romantic and rather mysterious, upon the marches of Wales. Such a Shropshire Lass was the narrator of *Precious Bane*; such a one is the heroine, and a very heroic heroine, of *The Golden Arrow*. But the comparison suggested above involves something more than the coincidence of a county and a social type. Those two writers of genius, devoted to the spirit of Shropshire and the western shires, do really stand for two principles in all living literature to-day; and especially in all literature concerned with the very ancient but very modern subject of the peasantry. I do not put them side by side here for comparison in the paltry sense of competition. I have the strongest admiration for both literary styles and both literary achievements. But the comparison is perhaps the clearest and most rapid way of representing what is really peculiar to writers like Mary Webb and to books like *The Golden Arrow*.

There are two ways of dealing with the dignity, the pain, the prejudice or the rooted humour of the poor; especially of the rural poor. One of them is to see in their tragedy only a stark simplicity, like the outline of a rock; the other is to see in it an unfathomable though a savage complexity, like the labyrinthine

vii

complexity of a living forest. The Shropshire Lad threw on all objects of the landscape a hard light like that of morning, in which all things are angular and solid; but most of all the gravestone and the gallows. The light in the stories of the Shropshire Lass is a light not shining on things, but through them. It is that mysterious light in which solid things become semi-transparent; a diffused light which some call the twilight of superstition and some the ultimate violet ray of the sixth sense of man; but which the strictest rationalist will hardly deny to have been the luminous atmosphere of a great part of literature and legend. In one sense it is the light that never was on sea or land, and in another sense the light without which sea and land are invisible; but at least it is certain that without that dark ray of mystery and superstition, there might never have been any love of the land or any songs of the sea. Nobody doubts that peasantries have in the past, as a matter of fact, been rooted in all sorts of strange tales and traditions, like the legend of *The Golden Arrow*. The only difference is between two ways of treating this fact in the two schools of rural romance or poetry. For the pessimist of the school of Housman or of Hardy, the grandeur of poverty is altogether in the pathos of it. He is only softened by hard facts; by the hard facts of life and death. The beliefs of the peasant are a mere tangle of weeds at the feet of the pessimist; it is only the unbelief of the peasant, the disillusion and despair of the peasant, which remind the pessimist of dignity and warm him with respect. There is nobility in the benighted darkness of the hero; but there is no light or enlightenment, except from the atheism of the author. The poor man is great in his sufferings; but not in anything for which he suffered. His traditions are a tangle of weeds;

but his sorrows are a crown of thorns. Only there is no nimbus round the crown of thorns. There is no nimbus round anything. The pessimist sees nothing but nakedness and a certain grandeur in nakedness ; and he sees the poor man as a man naked in the winter wind.

But the poor man does not see himself like that. He has always wrapped himself up in shreds and patches which, while they were as wild as rags, were as emblematic as vestments ; rags of all colours that were worn even more for decoration than for comfort. In other words, he has had a mass of beliefs and half-beliefs, of ancestral ceremonies, of preternatural cures and preternatural consolations. It is amid this tangle of traditions that he has groped and not merely in a bleak vacuum of negation ; it is in this enchanted forest that he has been lost so long, and not merely on the open moor ; and it is in this rich confusion of mystical and material ideas that the rural characters of Mary Webb walk from the first page to the last.

Now we may well for the moment leave the controversy open, as to whether these works make the rustic too transcendental, or whether the works of the pessimists make him too pessimistic. But something like a serious historical answer can be found in the very existence of many of the rustic fables, or even of the rustic names. It is very difficult to believe that any people so brutal, so bitter, so stupid and stunted as the English rustics are sometimes represented in realistic literature could ever have invented, or even habitually used and lived in the atmosphere of such things as the popular names for the country flowers, or the ordinary place-names and topographical terms for the valleys and streams of England. It looks rather like bad psychology to believe that those who talked of traveller's joy were never joyful, that those who burdened their tongues with the title of love-lies-bleeding were never tender or romantic, or that the man who thought of some common green growth as Our Lady's bedstraw was incapable of chivalry or piety. The characters in the romances of Mary Webb are the sort of rustics who might have invented such names. The Golden Arrow itself would be a name of exactly such a nature, whether it were invented by the natives or invented by the novelist. The legend of The Golden Arrow, which lovers went wandering to find, " and went with apple-blow scent round 'em and a mort o' bees, and warmship, and wanted nought of any man," is a myth bearing witness, as do all myths and mythologies, to the ancient beauty for which man was made, and which men are always unmaking. But this mystical or mythological sense would not be genuine, if it did not admit the presence of an evil as well as a good that is beyond the measure of man. One of the things that makes a myth so true is that it is always in black and white. And so its mysticism is always in black magic as well as white magic. It is never merely optimistic, like a new religion made to order. And just as in *Precious Bane*, the old necromancer was driven by an almost demoniac rage to raise up the ghost of the Pagan Goddess, so in *The Golden Arrow*, a man is lured into the ancient and mazy dance of madness by that heathen spirit of fear which inhabits the high places of the earth and the peaks where the brain grows dizzy. These things in themselves might be as tragic as anything in the realistic tragedies ; but the point to seize is the presence of something positive and sacramental on the other side ; a heroism that is not negative but affirmative ; a saintship with the power to cast out demons ; expressed in that immemorial popular notion of an antidote to a poison and a counter-charm against a witch.

The characterisation in *The Golden Arrow*, if rather less in scope than that in *Precious Bane*, is sometimes even more vivid within its limits. The difference between the two girls, brought up under the same limitations, observing the same strict rural conventions, feeling the same natural instincts in two ways which are ten thousand miles apart, is very skilfully achieved within the unities of a single dialect and a single scene. And through one of them there passes, once or twice, like the noise and rushing of the Golden Arrow, that indescribable exaltation and breathing of the very air of better things ; which, coming now and again in human books, can make literature more living than life.

G. K. CHESTERTON

I

JOHN ARDEN'S stone cottage stood in the midst of the hill plateau, higher than the streams began, shelterless to the four winds. While washing dishes Deborah could see, through the small, age-misted pane, counties and blue ranges lying beneath the transparent or hazy air in the bright, unfading beauty of inviolate nature. She would gaze out between the low window-frame and the lank geraniums, forgetting the half-dried china, when grey rainstorms raced across from far Cader Idris, ignoring in their majestic progress the humble, variegated plains of grass and grain, breaking like a tide on the unyielding heather and the staunch cottage. Beyond the kitchen and attached to the house was the shippen, made of weather-boarding, each plank overlapping the next. This was lichen-grey, like the house, stone and wood having become worn as the hillfolk themselves, browbeaten and mellowed by the tempestuous years, yet tenacious, defying the storm. Sitting in the kitchen on a winter night, the Ardens could hear the contented rattle of the two cowchains from the shippen, the gentle coughing and stamping of the folded sheep, while old Rover lay with one ear pricked, and now and then a hill pony —strayed from the rest—whickered through the howling ferocity of the gale.

But now it was July, and every day when Deborah

set her mother's milk-pails upside-down on the garden hedge to sweeten, she stooped and smelt the late-blooming white bush roses. She was gathering them in the honey-coloured light of afternoon, while large black bees droned in the open flowers and hovered inquiringly round the close, shell-tinted buds.

"Deborah!" called Mrs. Arden from the kitchen, "they're coming. I see them down by the Batch Stone now. Eli's walking as determined-angry as ever. Making up sins for other folks to repent of till he canna see anything in the 'orld."

"Danged if he inna!" said John, going to the window and breaking into the wholehearted laughter of an old man who has never wilfully done wrong or consciously done right; for he was lifted by his simple love of all creatures as far above right and wrong as his cottage was above the plain. His brown, thin face ran into kindly smiles as easily as a brook runs in its accustomed bed. No one minded him laughing at them when they saw the endless charity of his eyes, which were set in a network of fine lines, and were wistful with his long gazing into oncoming storm and unattainable beauty and the desperate eyes of his strayed and sick sheep.

"Put out a bit of honey, mother!" he called, as his wife set out the old cups and saucers painted with dim and incorrigibly solemn birds, that made the dresser look like an enchanted aviary.

"Oh! John, you spendthrift! And not but a pound or two left of the last taking," said Mrs. Arden. "It's only Eli and Lil, after all."

"Well, mother," said John, "Eli's got no honey in his heart, so he mun have some in his belly, whether or no!"

Deborah had gone out on to the green hill-track, mown by the sheep until no millionaire's lawn could be smoother. Folk to tea was a great event, for here it was only in the summer that the hamlets could

2

link hands over the ridges, the white blossom flow up from the plains till it almost met on the summit, the farmer's wife on one side of the ridge walk over to see her sister on the other side.

"Well, Deborah!" said Eli, as she met them, "I see you'm going the broad road. Ribbons and fanglements! Aye! The 'ooman of Babylon decked herself for the young captains——"

"I think she looks very nice, father," said Lily, in the habitually peevish tone of a snubbed child. She took stock of Deborah jealously; detested her for having blue ribbon and a normal father; and put an arm round her waist to disguise the fact and to see if Deborah had made her waist smaller by tight-lacing. Deborah received the embrace with the unquestioning gratitude and ineradicable reserve with which she met all demonstration. Without realizing the fact, she disliked being touched; physical contact with anything larger and less frail than a bee or a raindrop worried her. At night, when she and Joe and the old folk gathered round the fire, she would draw her chair a little apart, unaware that she did so. Warm-hearted and without egoism, she was yet one of the women who are always surrounded by a kind of magic circle. The young men who leant on meadow bridges—locally known as "gaubics' bridges"—on a Sunday, when she paid a rare visit to the plain, did not call after her; when Joe's friends came in for the evening, she thought they disliked her; she wished she were more like Lily—who boxed their ears and had her feet heavily stamped on under the table and once had an April-Fool postcard with "I love you" on it.

"I suppose it's because of Lily's golden hair," she once said to her mother wistfully. Her own was brown as a bark-stack, and had the soft sheen of a wood-lark's wing or a hill-foal's flank.

"No danger!" said her mother tartly. The more

3

she loved people the more tart she was, until her husband used to say ruefully that he wished she was a bit more callous-like to him, for he felt like a pickled damson.

" What's a fellow want with nasty straw-hair for his chillun? You needna ' O mother ! ' me; folks *do* have chillun—as I know full well, as have give their first wash to a power of 'em, *and* the lambs (poor things !)—not as I wash them, being woolly, and I'd as soon bring a lamb into the 'orld as a child, for if they hanna got immortal souls they're more affectionate than most that has—but as I was saying, chillun there are, and married you'll be, and chillun you'll have, and they won't have straw thatch like Lily's, but nice cob-coloured yeads with a polish on 'em ! Dear 'eart, she's gone ! "

As Deborah came with Eli and Lily along the sward, all the sheep, newly shorn and self-conscious, arranged themselves like a Bible picture, with the three figures as shepherds. The " cade " lambs, remembering Deborah's punctual feeding, and feeling an aura of protection about her, pressed round.

" Dirty beasts ! " said Eli, sweeping them back with his stick. " Not but what that black 'un will bring a good price come Christmas."

" Dunna clout 'em, Eli ! " came John's voice from the threshold. " I'd liefer they'd come round me than find the pot of gold under the rainbow. They be my friends, as you know well, and they'm not speechless from emptiness of heart. No, sorrowful and loving they be."

" Meat, that's what they be," said Eli.

" Deb ! " whispered Lily, " isn't he an old beast ? I hate him more every day, and I wish I could get married—that I do ! "

" Oh, Lily ! "

" Not that I like sheep myself," Lily continued, " soft things ! But as for him, he's always growling

4

and grudging and taking on religious all at once."
Her lips trembled. "I hanna got so much as a bit
of ribbon, nor nothing," she said.

Deborah stooped and gathered a red rose—the
only one.

"There! that's nicer than ribbon, and Joe likes
red," she said with a smile.

Lily simpered.

"Where be Joe?" she asked negligently, hiding
her wearing anxiety as to whether Joe would be
present at tea or not.

"Haying at the Shakeshafts', but it's so nigh that
he comes back to his tea now and agen."

Colour came into Lily's pale face. Her eyes shone.
She was vital for the first time that afternoon.

"Can I come to your room and do my hair, Deb?"
she asked. "The curls do blow about so. I should
think you're glad yours is straight, and never blows
out in curls?"

Deborah was looking at a giant shadow—the astral
body of the gaunt Diafol ridge, blue-purple as a
flower of hound's-tongue — which stretched across
the hammock-like valley towards their own range
at this time in the afternoon.

"Aye," she said absently.

"Do you like these sausage-curls at the back,
Deb?" asked Lily, thirsting for female praise, since
the more nerve-thrilling male was not obtainable.

"Aye," said Deborah again.

Lily stamped.

"You never looked, Deborah Arden! I suppose
you're jealous."

Deborah awakened from her dreams and smiled.

"I was thinking that shadow was like a finger
pointing straight at you and me, Lil," she said. "A
long finger as you canna get away from. What does
it token?"

"Weddings!" said Lily, thinking of Joe and the

underclothes she would buy in Silverton, and blushing at an impropriety that Deborah would not have seen.

" Maybe — or maybe summat darker," said Deborah.

" Oh, don't be so creepy and awful, Deb ! " And Lily pulled her blouse tighter to show the outline of her figure better—a very pretty, pigeon-like outline, so poor Joe thought later, desperate at Lily's provocative hauteur.

" Deb ! " shrieked Mrs. Arden up the breakneck stairs, " take the tray and ring up Joe, there's a good girl."

" Me too ! " cried Lily, taking the largest tray.

So out ran the two maidens, their frocks flying, nimble feet scudding over the springy turf, armed with green trays painted with fat roses, beating on them like bacchanals with pokers. They were quite grave and earnest, quite unaware that they were quaint, beautiful, and the inevitable prey of oncoming destiny.

A brown figure appeared far down a cwm of the steep hillside, at first indistinguishable from the blurs that were rocks and sheep, climbing the hot, slippery hill.

Lily watched with veiled eagerness; leaning out to this new force of manhood with no thought of it, but with the complete absorption in her own small, superficial ego in face of great primeval powers which makes a certain type of woman the slave of sex instead of the handmaid of love. She was what is called a good girl, thinking no worse thoughts than the crude ones of most farm women. She was insatiably curious, and was willing to face the usual life of the women among whom she lived in order to unravel the mysteries of the Old Testament and other Sunday meat of the congregation at her place of worship. She was full of tremors and flushes—

the livery of passion—yet incapable of understanding passion's warm self. She was ready to give herself as a woman for the sake of various material benefits, with a pathetic ignorance of her own unthinkable worth as a human being. She was rapacious for the small-change of sex, yet she would never be even stirred by the agony of absence from the beloved.

Deborah went indoors like a good sister, and left Joe to his fate.

In the calm, brown kitchen, alive with the ticking of the grandfather clock, Mrs. Arden's alarum and John's turnip watch — which, when wound, went stertorously for an hour and then stopped — the three old folk, like wintered birds, sat round the board in a kind of unconscious thankfulness for mere life and absence of pain. Eli always had the robin cup, the robin being the only bird that did not rouse him to hoarse grumblings about pests and vermin. In the dim past his mother had cajoled and threatened him into a belief that the robin was a sacred bird; so sacred it was. A robin might perch on his spade while he stooped to shake potatoes from the haulm, and he only gave it a crooked smile. Any other bird he would have stoned. They drank from the cups, where the gold was worn at the rim, with a kind of economy of pleasure, as if they felt that the cup of life was slowly emptying, the gold upon it growing faint.

"Honey, Eli?" said John. "There's a bit of acid in to suit your taste!" By such mild satire he comforted himself for the heart-sickness often given him by Eli's treatment of small creatures.

"Here's our Deb," he said, with his unfailing delight in his children. "Where's Lily?"

Mrs. Arden, ever ready to further the designs of nature, kicked him under the table; he gazed at her with steadfast inquiry till the truth slowly dawned on him, and the china rattled to his delighted thump of the table.

7

"What, Joe?" he asked, and let Eli into the secret in a twinkling.

"Aye," said Eli, with a kind of sour pride, unable to help approving of success, though disapproving of youth, beauty and love. "Aye, she'm a terror with the men, is Lilian. The mother was the same." He always spoke of his late wife in the detached manner of one alluding to a cow.

"Eh, well! The dead say nought," remarked Mrs. Arden, who always had a veiled hostility to Eli.

"And that's a silence we all come to," said John pacifically. "Poor Thomas o' Wood's End's gone, I'm told. You'll be making a noration on his coffin, Eli, I suppose?"

"No. I bain't good enough for them seemingly," said Eli. "Some young chap's to come as is new in these parts. Foreman at the Lostwithin Spar Mine. Tongue hung on in the middle. All faith and no works, and the women after 'un like sheep at a gap. I shanna go."

"I'm going," said John. "He was a good neighbour, was Thomas. Stood godfather to our Deb, too, when mother took an' got her named in Slepe Church."

"Well!" said Mrs. Arden oracularly, "chapel I was reared and chapel I am. But when it comes to weddings and christenings, you want summat a bit older than chapel—plenty of written words and an all-overish feeling to the place and a good big zinc-lined font. And is the new young man married or single, Eli?"

Eli made no reply—a custom of his when a question bored him, and one so well understood by his intimates that no one dreamt of being offended.

As Deborah sat with the old people, she wondered if the strange experience that had come to Joe and Lily would ever come to her. Would she ever pluck

8

bracken as rosily and earnestly as Lily, waiting for a step—a voice? She felt rather forlorn in the staid environment, rather homesick for adventure, yet with the sense of somnolent peace that broods over afternoon services.

Out in the sun Lily pulled to pieces the small, soft fingers of the bracken with her back to the ascending Joe. A hawk hovered overhead, and the snipe that had been bleating ceased and became still. Up from the meadow Joe had left, came faint shouts; microscopic figures moved there. Joe's black hair was stuck with hay, which gave his steadfast face an absurdly rakish air.

"Waiting for me, Lil?" he asked, his delight overflowing.

"No danger!"

"Oh!" said Joe, crestfallen.

"What are you gallivanting here for, when they're haying?" queried Lily, giving him a chance for a compliment.

"Me tea," said Joe, truthfully but disastrously.

Lily was silent, surveying his corduroyed and blue-shirted figure with great disfavour.

As he had climbed the slope, there had flickered before him, pale and shaken as the nodding blue heads of the sheep's-bit scabious, a vision of fire-light and small faces, with Lily presiding over a giant teapot. For Joe's most spiritual was to some eyes grossly material. His winged desires, his misty gropings after the beautiful were clothed by him in the most concrete images. Therefore, because he loved Lily so much, the teapot of the vision was large enough for a school-treat, larger than any he had seen in the sixpenny bazaar windows last Michaelmas Fair, and the children's faces were quite innumerable. But now, near enough to touch that wonderful blouse of Lily's — a very transparent green butter-muslin made in the latest fashion by Lily and fastened with

9

pins—now the vision went out like a lantern when a blown bough smashes the glass.

" Lil, will you come pleasuring along o' me to the Fair on Lammas holiday? " he asked humbly.

Lily disguised her thrill of joy.

" 'Fraid I canna," she said.

" Oh, Lil! And I've saved five shillings on purpose."

" If so be I came, would you buy me a blue bow? "

" I would that! " said the beaming Joe; " a whacking big 'un! "

" Oh, not big—little and pretty. I don't like big things."

" I be a bit on the big side myself, Lil, but it ain't my fault, and I met be able to keep folk from jostling you—being broad like."

" If I come," said Lily, " will you bring Deb too? "

" Deb? Lord o' mercy, I dunna want Deb."

" It's not proper 'ithout," said Lil.

Joe flushed redder than he already was. The mere possibility of a state of things that could be construed as improper existing between himself and this mystery — this radiant creature that had suddenly appeared out of the chrysalis of the Lil Huntbatch he had known all his life—went to his head like home-brewed.

" A' right," he said meekly.

" And as Deb would be dull, when we went off together——"

" Aye," said Joe with much relish.

" And as she dunna like the chaps about here much——"

" I canna think why—good chaps they be, drawing a straight furrow and handy with the sheep——"

" A girl doesn't think much of that in the man she's going to wed," said Lily loftily.

" What does she think on? Chapel-going? I'll
10

go to chapel every week, Lil, if you like. I be more
of an outside prop than an inside pillar now, but——"

"It doesn't matter to me if you never go," said
Lily. "But as I said, as she doesn't like them,
why not ask that new chap that's come to Lostwithin yonder—a town chap and very smart, they
say. He's going to speak over Thomas o' Wood's
End come Sunday; you could ask him then."

Joe pondered.

"If I do, will you come to chapel along o' me and
walk back arm-in-crook and promise faithful to come
to the Fair?"

"If you like."

"What little small arms you'm got, Lil! And
shining white, like a bit of spar. I wish——"

"What?" said Lily, trembling with curiosity and
delight.

"Ne'er mind," said Joe; "come Sunday night,
when we're by the little 'ood and it's quiet, maybe
I'll say. And now I'll go round by the back and
wash me."

Lily went into the kitchen, thinking how rough
Joe was—better than her father, of course, but probably not as nice as the new Lostwithin foreman,
whom she had, with such well-laid plans, arranged
to captivate. John glanced up at her and remembered his courting days. Mrs. Arden decided
to put off pig-killing till Joe should be "called,"
in order to have black pudding at the wedding. She
also considered other abstruse questions. Deborah
felt rather like Lily's aunt, and was very motherly to
her, retiring soon at an urgent call from Joe to see
to the proper adjustment of his best tie—no mere
knot, but a matter of intricate folds of crimson silk
embellished with large horseshoes. All the things
Joe did and possessed were large.

11

II

GOING to church and chapel in the hills implies much more initiative than it does in the plain, within sound of chiming bells and jangling public opinion. Very early on the hot Sunday of the Oration John was about, milking the cows—Bracken and Wimberry—dressing a sick sheep and placing at the back door his daily votive offering of sticks, water from the cwm and vegetables for his wife's cooking.

" Be you going all in the heat, and it blowing up for tempest, father? " Deborah called from her little window, leaning out in her straight calico nightdress —for no human habitation, not even a bird's nest, commanded her eyrie.

"Aye," said John; " poor Thomas canna wait. I mun go or fail him."

There is a curious half-superstitious, half-mystic sense in the minds of some country-folk that the dead need sympathy — perhaps almost food and drink—more in the days before burial than in their lives.

" Is mother going? " asked Deborah.

" No. She's had a call."

Every one knew that when Mrs. Arden had a call it meant a small, new force in the world; and all knew the impossibility of gauging its importance, feeling that in her hands might lie the fate of a great man—a member of Parliament, perhaps, or even a vicar. So a call meant a hasty packing of homely simples, linen, and perhaps a posy; then she started on foot, or was driven by John with Whitefoot.

"I'll come then, father, sooner than let you go alone," said Deborah. She combed and pinned up her wing-like hair and took out her best frock—an old-fashioned purple delaine sprinkled with small pink poppies—and slipped it over her head. She was transformed from a pleasant girl into an arresting woman. The deep colour threw up into her grey eyes shifting violet lights, gave her transparent skin an ethereal look, burnished her hair. Dark colours were to her what rainy weather is to hills, bringing out the latent magic and vitality. This morning her dress might have been cut from the hills, their colours were so alike. Always dignified in the un-self-conscious manner of those who live in the wilds, Deborah was even queenly to-day in her straight, gathered skirt and the bodice crossed on her breast. She put on an apron and ran down.

"Mind you put a bit of mint along of the peas, Deb!" said Mrs. Arden. "I'll be back when I can."

Deborah saw her off with due solemnity, in her best bonnet and Paisley shawl—rich with Venetian reds, old gold and lavender. Joe and his bowler had disappeared. Some hours later Deborah and her father set out along the green track over the hill-top, past the little wood of tormented larches and pines that sighed in the stillest weather. Here the hill-ponies gathered in the innermost recesses by the spring that came into the open as a small, vivacious brook. They stamped and whisked at the flies, gazing without interest or fear at the other children of the wild; and John looked at them with the infinite compassion that he felt for all the beautiful, pitiful forms of life.

"What a queer day, father!—as if summat was foreboded," said Deborah.

"Aye, there's tempest brewing," John replied meditatively; "so bright as it is!"

13

"It's always bright afore storm, father, isn't it?"

"Aye. Why, Deb, how bright and spry you be yourself to-day, dear heart! The young chaps 'll be all of a pother."

"It's only my old gown."

"Aye. But you'm like chapel on Christmas night —lit for marvels."

The tesselated plain, minute in pattern as an old mosaic, seemed on this fervent day to be half-molten, ready to collapse. The stable hills shook in the heat-haze like a drop-scene just lifting upon reality. The ripening oat-fields, the already mellow wheat seemed like frail wafers prepared for some divine bacchanalia. A broad pool far down among black woods looked thick-golden, like metheglin in a small ebony cup.

As they came to the northerly side of the table-land, Caer Caradoc loomed terrific, gashed with shadow, like a wounded giant gathered for a spring. John dreamed upon it all, leaning on his silken-grey staff of mountain ash.

"See you, Deb!" he said in the tranced voice in which he spoke but seldom in a year, at which times his listeners stood silent — at gaze like the sheep before something undiscovered — until he suddenly broke off, turned on his heel, and wheeled manure or dug the garden in silence for the rest of the day. "See you, Deb! The Flockmaster goes westering; and the brown water and the blue wind above the cloud, and the kestrels and you and me all go after to the shippen with the starry door. Hear you, Deb, what a noise o' little leaves clapping in the Far Coppy! 'Tis he, that shakes the bits of leaves and the bits of worlds, and sends love like forkit lightning —him as the stars fall before like white 'ool at sheep-shearing. And all creatures cry out after him, mournful, like the o'er-driven sheep that was used to go by your grandfather's forge at Caereinion.

14

And he calls 'em — all the white sinners and the stained mighty ones, and even the little blue fishes in the hill streams. ' Diadell ! ' he calls to the hearts of them; and they follow—ne'er a one turns back—going the dark way. But I see far off, as it met be yonder where the dark cloud lifts, I see summat as there's no words for, as makes it all worth while. There's a name beyond all names, and I'd lief you kept it in mind in the dark days as 'll come on you, Deb ! For I see 'em coming like hawks from the rocks. And though you be rent like a struck pine, Deb, my lass, mind you of that name and you shall be safe. Mind you of Cariad—for that's how they name him in the singing Welsh—Cariad, the Flock-master, the won'erful one ! "

He broke off.

" Deb ! " he said confusedly, touching her arm like a child; " I mun bide a bit; I'm all of a tremble and a sweat like a hag-ridden pony."

III

Poised between the lowland and the heights and now cut out sharply against the coal-black east, like a hot ember in an oven, stood the red-brick chapel. Whatever beauty flowered within to sweeten the stark ugliness of it—creeping up the walls like swift summer vetches, reaching out determined tendrils towards the illimitable—none was visible without. It stood in a yard of rank grass where Thomas o' Wood's End lay in an open grave of baked earth. It was squat, with round-topped windows too large and too many for it, which caricatured those of Pisa Cathedral. Its paint was of the depressing colour known among house-painters as Pompeian red. The windows had black rep curtains and frosted lower panes to defend the young women in the window pews from the row of eyes that came up above the window-sills at dusk like stars, when the unrighteous outside stood on a ledge and pressed their faces to the glass. So the chapel stood amid the piled and terraced hills like a jibe. Above the door, with a nervous and pardonable shuffling of responsibility (apparently by the architect) were the words, " This is the Lord's doing."

Deborah and her father went in, he with the far look still in his eyes and his large hymn-book with the tunes in it under his arm. To him the place was beautiful, painted in the dim, gold-mixed colours of mysterious emotions, half-realized adventures. On the machine-cut patterns of the panes he had gazed while he dwelt upon the burning wheels of Ezekiel's

Vision, the Riders of Revelation. The black curtains had made a background for the cumulative
tragedy of the Gospel. The jerry-built walls were
gracious to him with the promise of many mansions.
When they prayed he was always a syllable behind
the rest, tasting each word, very emphatic, very
anxious not to stress his request for one person more
than for another. He sat now with his square, high-
crowned old bowler on his knees, his red handkerchief
spread on it, and the hymn-book open on the top,
reading " The King of Love my Shepherd is," and
seeing with a vividness denied to the lettered and
the leisured those illumined pastures and unwrinkled
waters where, simple and wise, the central figure of
the fourth Gospel presided.

Deborah looked round surreptitiously and nudged
her father.

" There's our Joe ! Whatever's come o'er him ?
Oh, I see ! There's Lil too."

Joe was broadly radiant. In his buttonhole was
an enormous passion-flower, presumably bought for
the occasion in the Saturday market; Lily had
another, which spread its mystic tracery of purple
rings, green and gold flames and blue rays on her
passionless breast with silent irony until it withered
and she threw it on the manure heap. Lily had
trimmed her hat with poppies and corn; one bunch
had come loose and drooped over her glinting hair—
loose also, and tinting her forehead with creamy gold.
She always swayed when she sang, and to-day she
looked more reed-like than ever. As the flowering
rush in the marsh with its brittle beauty cries to be
gathered, so she, with her undulating, half-ripe corn
and falling poppies, aroused in the back row of
youths such untranslatable emotions that they forgot
to place the usual pins for the dairymaids from Long
Acre Farm.

The first hymn was over, and still the preacher,

17

who was to conduct the service, had not come. Deborah wondered idly what he would be like and whether he would eat jujubes all the time, as the last visiting preacher did—a practice which, while the jujube was new and ungovernable, resulted in a private interview between himself and the Almighty, since no one could hear what he said. She remembered how, in an earnest moment, he swallowed one whole, and how the horrified silence was only broken by the sullen blue-bottles that could not understand the swing panes of the windows. There was silence now, with shuffling and coughs.

At last there came a sound of quick steps; the door flew open and a man entered—so tall that he dominated the place. His ruffled hair was as gold as Lily's; his excited blue eyes, bright colour and radiant bearing were ludicrously unsuited to his black clothes. Out in the early shadows with a fawn-skin slung from one shoulder, and a flute on which to play short, tearless melodies, his vitality would not have seemed so unpardonable. He was up the chapel in three strides, and the service had begun. After a time Deborah found herself kneeling with crimson cheeks, no breath, and the knowledge that she could not look at the preacher.

" What's come o'er me ? " she whispered to herself. She secretly mopped her face and the palms of her hands; this was observed by Lily, who knelt very straight and gazed through her fingers at things in general, but chiefly at the apparition who was praying for soberness and pardon in the tones of a lover serenading his mistress. When he began the oration, he spoke of death as a child does—quite unable to believe in his own skeleton, coolly sorry for those who were weak enough to suffer such indignity. He was full of the eloquent comfort of one who has never seen the blank wall that rises between the last tremor and the eternal stillness on the beloved's
18

face. He was so sure of himself, God, and the small shell that was his creed, that Mrs. Thomas—who had felt numb since the hollow on the other side of the bed had been vacant—began to cry. Lily also cried —from excitement, and because Lucy Thruckton *would* insert her twelve stone of good humour between Lily and the new preacher.

Deborah felt a gathering sense of desolation which, if she had been able to analyze her emotions, she would have known to arise from a new sense of dependency—a disturbance of poise. Towards the end of the service the growling in the east changed to a roar; rain came like a high tide on the black windows; the young preacher stood in a flicker of lightning as though he were haloed for glory or smitten for doom.

After the service they all crowded into the porch and waited for it to clear.

" Now, Joe ! " whispered Lily, " ask him ! "

Joe looked reverently but mistrustfully at this new manifestation.

" Mister ! " he began. " Lily wants to know——"
He paused, arrested by the rage in Lily's face. " Leastways, *I* want to know if you can come along of us to Lammas Fair and keep our Deb company ? "

" The lad's gone kimet ! " whispered John to Deborah, who was twisting her fingers in dumb misery. The preacher was surprised : but he was sufficiently educated to take a conscious interest in his new neighbours ; and he was town-bred, and very excited about country life.

" I should like to, awfully," he said, with an enthusiasm little to Joe's taste, " if you'll introduce me to the lady."

" Deb ! " called Joe across several heads, in the voice with which he " Yo-ho'd " the cattle ; " this gent's coming along of us to Lammas Fair, so you needna be lonesome." He felt pleased. The task was over; the walk arm-in-crook was to come. He wiped the perspiration of initiative from his forehead, unaware of a storm worse than the thunder which was to break on him from the united displeasure of Deborah and Lily.

Deborah, so summoned, could do nothing but come forward. With an effort she lifted her eyes to the preacher's and spoke with dry lips the correct formula: " Pleased to meet you, I'm sure ! "

He said nothing, but stood looking down at her with such frank admiration as even a bridegroom in this countryside does not vouchsafe to his bride; and with a light in his eyes that would have been considered " Most ondecent," if the onlookers could have found a name for it. As it was, they merely fidgeted, while Deborah and the preacher gazed at one another and were intoxicated with a joy new to her though not unsampled by him.

" A fortnight come Tuesday you be at Lane End at ten sharp," said Joe, quite carried away by his own *savoir faire.*

Lily raged inwardly. She was hemmed in by Joe, who could not be made to understand by all her whispers and pinches that he was to introduce her. She trod on his toes with concentrated rage; but his boots were proof against anything lighter than the hoof of a carthorse. She peered round Joe and saw Deborah as none had yet seen her—dissolved in the first tremulous rose-tints of womanhood. She dodged Joe's arm and saw Stephen Southernwood with an expression no woman had yet called up in his face— homage and demand in one. " Cat ! " she whispered, surveying Deborah again. She dug Joe in the ribs with her sharp little elbow.

" Ow ! " said Joe.

Meanwhile John surveyed the scene with impartial affection, and the dairymaids murmured seductive

20

" Don't-ee-nows " !   At last the rain ceased as at a signal; steam rose in the sudden yellow light; and they all went home down honeysuckle lanes, across the ridges and round the purple hill-flanks to milk, make love and have their Sunday tea.

IV

DEBORAH and her father returned through the hill
gate, going by tracks that ran above steep cwms
where threads of water made a small song and
the sheep clung half-way up like white flies; past
the high springs where water soaked out among the
mimulus to feed the rivers of the plain; up slopes of
trackless hills, through wet wimberries; across the
great plateaux—purple in the rainy light—that
stretched in confused vistas on every side, familiar to
John as air to a swallow. They passed the small,
white signpost that rose from the midst of the westward table-land, as others rose from various lost
points in the vast expanses—shepherds' signposts,
pointing vaguely down vague ways, sometimes direct-
ing people dispassionately between two paths, as if
it mattered little which they chose. This one was
called the Flockmaster's signpost, and stood in
gallant isolation within a kind of large crater, so
that when you had read—" Slepe "—" Wood's End "
—and passed on, it immediately disappeared like a
ship behind the horizon. At times the sheep crowded
round it with stampings and jostling of woolly
shoulders; the ponies rubbed against it; cuckoos in
the wild game of mating would alight on it with an
excited gobble and flash away again. Legend said
that somewhere here, long since, the cuckoos met in
circle before uttering a note in any field or coppy, to
allot the beats for the season. It was told with
apologetic laughter by the grandmother of a hill-
commoner that on a May night with a low moon
you might see from the Little Wood—lone on a

ridge—the grey, gleaming ring as from a stone thrown into water. Before the shadows stretched themselves for dawn you might be aware of the clap of wings; might watch the long tails steer to the four winds; might hear from orchards at the valley gates the first warm, linked notes that meant summer.

They walked in silence. John was quite unaware, now that his rare moment of vision had passed, of Deborah's psychic existence. He was subject to the poet's reaction, and he had no idea that anything had occurred except a storm which might damage the wheat. They came to the slopes of short grass from which the round yellow heartsease was disappearing like a currency withdrawn—as the old mintage of painless and raptureless peace was disappearing from Deborah's being. At the first gate of John's sheepwalk the land slid away suddenly and revealed in terrific masses on the murky west the long, mammothlike shape of Diafol Mountain.

"There'll be more thunder," said John; "it's brewing yonder, it'll be round afore dawn."

"It's raining over the Devil's Chair now," said Deborah.

On the highest point of the bare, opposite ridge, now curtained in driving storm-cloud, towered in gigantic aloofness a mass of quartzite, blackened and hardened by uncountable ages. In the plain this pile of rock and the rise on which it stood above the rest of the hill-tops would have constituted a hill in itself. The scattered rocks, the ragged holly-brakes on the lower slopes were like small carved lions beside the black marble steps of a stupendous throne. Nothing ever altered its look. Dawn quickened over it in pearl and emerald; summer sent the armies of heather to its very foot; snow rested there as doves nest in cliffs. It remained inviolable, taciturn, evil. It glowered darkly on the dawn; it came through the snow like jagged bones through flesh; before its hardness even the venturesome cranberries were discouraged. For miles around, in the plains, the valleys, the mountain dwellings it was feared. It drew the thunder, people said. Storms broke round it suddenly out of a clear sky; it seemed almost as if it created storm. No one cared to cross the range near it after dark—when the black grouse laughed sardonically and the cry of a passing curlew shivered like broken glass. The sheep that inhabited these hills would, so the shepherds said, cluster suddenly and stampede for no reason, if they had grazed too near it in the night. So the throne stood—black, massive, untenanted, yet with a well-worn air. It had the look of a chair from which the occupant has just risen, to which he will shortly return. It was understood that only when vacant could the throne be seen. Whenever rain or driving sleet or mist made a grey shechinah there people said, " There's harm brewing." " He's in his chair." Not that they talked of it much; they simply felt it, as sheep feel the coming of snow.

" Aye ! " said John, looking across the hammock-like valley; " there's more to come. We'd best keep the cows in to-night, Deb, safe at whome out of the storm."

" Aye," said Deborah heavily, like one recovering from an anæsthetic; " safe at whome out of the storm ! "

Far along the green path they saw the round form of Mrs. Arden bouncing like a ball; and they could hear the faint, tinny clamour of the tea-tray. Away behind them, against the white sky, they saw the loitering figures of Joe and Lily.

" I thought you'd got struck ! " shrieked Mrs. Arden as she approached. She had been in the house for half an hour, and loneliness was torture to her, as to all gregarious natures whose way lies in hill-country.

"Both doing well," she announced triumphantly; "only most a pity the poor child's the very spit and image of his father! They're saying down at Slepe as the berry-higgler's coming Friday. I thought to go picking to-morrow, Deb, if so be you'll come. There's a power of folk coming, greedy as rooks in the fowl yard. We'd best be early if we want 'em."

"Why, mother! What a pother you be in!" said John.

"All right, I'll come, mother," Deborah murmured, cheering up like a wet bee in sunshine under the reassuring influence of the commonplace. This atmosphere Mrs. Arden took with her, as a snail takes its shell; through its homely magic she combated the power of sickness and pain and black terror in many a stuffy little bedroom.

"The kettle's boiling and I've milked," she announced, "and all's done, only to scald the tea! And what was the new chap like?"

"No great shakes," said John.

Deborah went upstairs to take off her best dress.

"What ails our Deb?" Mrs. Arden continued.

"Nought as I know to."

"What's the chap like to look at?"

"What chap?"

"Why, the preacher! Who else? Don't I know the rest of them back-'erts?"

"Well, he's a likely lad enough."

"But to look at?"

"Long in the straw," said John slowly, "and a yellow head, like a bit of good wheat. And his tongue's hung on in the middle, as Eli said."

"Oh!" remarked Mrs. Arden comprehensively.

"Where's our Joe?" she added.

John winked.

"Bringing his girl along."

"Well!" said Patty, "Lily's a tidy girl enough, I've nought agen her—barring Eli."

25

" Talk of the devil ! " said a sardonic voice at the door. " Where's my devoted darter ? "

" Coming along, Eli."

" A good hiding ! That's what she wants, to take the Owd 'un out of her. But I'm too kind to her," said Eli. " Left the milk in the pails, she did, out in the sun. Never so much as put it in the dairy. Left it to sour."

" Laws me ! " murmured Patty economically.

" Well, well ! We're only young once," said John.

" I'll learn her to be young ! " Eli shouted savagely. " Trapesing along of your Joe and bedizening herself like the whore of Babylon."

" Now, Eli ! "

" And as if that's not enough there's my new shed, as cost me five and thirty shillings, struck ! "

" You don't say ! Anything killed ? "

" There wasn't nothing in it, or there would have been."

" Well, well ! And you one of the saved an' all ! " John's voice had a dash of irony in it, although he did not doubt Eli's state of grace.

" It inna *me*," said Eli, " it's the girl. It's a sign from the Lord that she mun be chastened. God's will be done ! " he added piously, fixing a scarifying gaze on the truant Lily as she came in.

" What about them six quarts of milk you left to sour ? " he asked.

" There, there ! " said Mrs. Arden; " dunna miscall a girl before her chap, Eli."

Lily, flushed, terrified of Eli's bitter and silent rage, had spirit enough to look at Joe witheringly and remark—

" He's not my chap. He's a great gauby."

" Laws me ! " said John helplessly. " Mother, I thought you said—— ? "

" Hush your noise ! " snapped Mrs. Arden.

Deborah, softly laying away the gown that had
26

clothed her during an experience for which she found no name, heard angry tones in the usually quiet kitchen, harshness in the Sunday peace.

"Is that you, Lil?" she called.

"Yes. Oh, Deb!" said Lily, coming up breathless and raging; "isn't Joe a great gomeril?"

"But whatever put it into his head?" asked Deborah.

"Oh, he asked me to go to Lammas Fair along of him," Lily explained carelessly, "and I thought you ought to have a bit of a randy too, so I said to Joe to get the preacher to keep you company."

"While you went along of Joe?"

"Yes. Well, Joe *is* a softie! Saying I wanted the chap!"

"Saying *I* wanted him!" Deborah added, "and I not so much as set eyes on him." She found herself crimson.

"How you do feel the heat, Deb!" Lily's voice was rather spiteful. "Now I never colour up, not if it's ever so. Being slimmer than you, I suppose. But the way he ups and says it! And the girls from Long Acre drinking it all in like brandy-cherries. And that fat Lucy!" Lily began to giggle. "And Joe so pleased with himself—smiling all o'er! It took me all the way back to learn him what a softie he was."

"Poor Joe," said Deborah.

"Lilian," Eli's voice came raspingly from below. "What saith the Book of the tiring of hair and putting on of apparel?"

Lily knew what the rasp and the text meant, and she trembled. Any bush in the rain.

"Joe," she said, running down and smiling on that crushed and sullen youth; "would you like to come along a bit of the way?"

Joe considered whether Lily with Eli attached was enough to sacrifice his hurt pride for.

27

" No, I wunna," he said flatly. He had meant so
well! He was quite sure that he had done well.
What the tantrum was about he had no idea. Deborah
seemed angry with him also, for some of the conversation had floated down. He was obstinately
determined to be dignified. It was not surprising
that he could not understand what he had done, for
his crime in Deborah's eyes was that a strange man
had made her feel " hot all o'er," and in Lily's that
the said stranger had not fallen in love with her.

From the dresser the bird cups presided over the
scene, each one a little aslant as it hung by the
handle, like a speaker leaning to his audience.

" Well, good-night both," said John, as the ill-
matched couple went out; " and God be with you,"
he added, as if he felt a need for some extra blessing.

" And with this house, leastways this small
cottage," said Eli, with the acidity of raw sloes.

" Goodness gracious heart alive ! " cried Mrs.
Arden, sitting down in a heap on the creaking sofa.
" What's come o'er the folk ? Why, you make more
ado, every man-jack except father here, of going to
meeting for an hour than Jane Cadwallader made of
bearing a man child ! Dunna fret, Joe ! She'll be
all right to-morrow-day. And Deb ! " she raised her
voice and put a twist on it so that it might negotiate
the crooked stairs, " what's come to you comes to all,
and if it didna, you'd fret."

Father and son looked at each other, mystified by
the subtleties of femininity.

" Well," said John, " I'm going to look the sheep
and see what the storm's done for me. Coming, Joe ?
Coming, Rover ? "

They tramped over the wimberries, just losing their
first startlingly bright green. John pondered.

" If I was you, Joe lad, I'd go a bit of a walk
round Bitterley to-night. I dunna like Eli's look !
and she's a little small thing—tongue or no tongue."

" Oh, aye ! " said Joe awkwardly; " I thought to go. Be that one of the last lot of lambs, dad ? "

An hour or two later, having criticized every sheep findable by Rover, they returned. John went in, grateful for the rosy firelight on the tiles, for evenings are chill here even in July. Joe stood lost in thought. Why should he go ? Sullenness came over him. But her pretty arms, her little ways, and Eli mad with her—and she had asked him so pleadingly ! Yes, he'd go ! All in a moment he felt a need of haste, wanted to be there at once. It was a good way to Bitterley—through the Far Leasowes, along Hilltop Road, down Deadman's Lane and over Bitterley Hill. He ran to the stable, bridled Whitefoot, sprang on bareback and was away with a rattle of stones amid a flying crowd of sheep before the rest of the family got to the door. He galloped furiously over the rough tracks with a heavy feeling that he could not understand, a sense that he must hasten more than he had ever done in his life.

V

BEFORE Eli and Lily had gone many steps from the Ardens', he turned stealthily to see if any one was watching them. Seeing that no one was, he stopped.

" Take them poppies and that good corn out of your hat," he said.

" Oh, well," said Lily, with an attempt at lightness, " they'm dead, anyway."

She took them out.

" Stamp on 'm," said Eli.

" But—how soft ! " Lily objected.

Eli seized her arm, twisting it slightly, and she trod on the flowers.

" Never no more," said he. " Your hat's good enough for such as you with no trimmin'. It did for your mother. And you'm not as good-lookin'. Such a figure of fun as you look—I marvel as Joe 'd think on you, with straws and old dead flowers hanging round you, and your hair all wispy, and a smudge on your nose——"

Lily began to cry.

" And that ondecent bodice ! " he went on. " You'm no better than you should be, showing yourself half naked."

Lily began to run, stopping her ears. This was worse than any of their homecomings, for her father had never before had a barn struck, and she had never been quite so daring in her attire. Eli's crafty face, with its downward seams from the mouth and nose and the two long, yellow teeth over the lower lip, was dark red with passion. His plain living, his

30

long prayers, his loud confessions of sin, his harsh treatment of himself and his unquestioning meekness to the God he believed in (a vengeful, taloned replica of himself)—all these things had to be paid for by some one. Lily and the creatures at Bitterley Fields paid—Lily with some justice, for she was quite selfish and very irritating, the creatures with none. A few times in the year, when things had gone wrong, the lust of torture came upon Eli, and the contemplation of a deferred and somewhat problematical torment of the wicked (*i. e.* the not-Eli) in hell-fire could not slake it. At these times he exhibited the subtlety of a woman in finding weak points wherein to stick pins — a subtlety inherited by Lily. The ironic remarks of everyday life—the commonplaces of rudeness—gave place to a caustic finesse which burnt like red-hot needles. He was at these times almost an artist, since he was exercising his chief gift; the secondary one of moneymaking was far below in intensity.

So they went, Lily running, sobbing, swaying, Eli following with long strides and uplifted voice.

" When we get whome," he said with relish, " there's them six quarts o' sour milk. Waste not, want not ! It mun be done summat with. Afore you go to bed to-night, you mun set it for milk cheese. You mun scald the things, stretch the muslin, lade the milk, press it. Afore that fetch the sticks, coals and water, and boil it to scald with."

" There's no muslin," said Lily in the midst of sobs, relief in her voice. She was tired out with excitement, and she knew that the work would take hours to do.

" Your good old father's thought of that," said Eli. " A father knoweth his own child. There's muslin on your back; when we get in you'll rip it and make the cheeses in that."

31

" I won't. So there ! " said Lily, for the blouse was her new, radiant, much-laboured-on treasure.

" Woe unto the disobedient children ! " Eli intoned. " I am even as the other Eli. Yea ! For I have not corrected you, and the Lord is angry with His servant for these things. You'll take it off now ! " He tore at a sleeve.

Lily shrieked, striving to elude him.

" Folk 'll see me ! Folk 'll see me ! " she screamed. " I'll be disgraced."

" You dunna mind having only a bit of muslin atwixt you and disgrace, so you met as well be without."

Lily's blouse was in ribbons. Her not very clean calico chemise, fastened with a large safety-pin, and her thin, bare arms were revealed. Part of her hair had fallen loose. They stood beneath a witan-tree on Bitterley Hill; for Lily's running had brought them nearly home. This little ash was the only one that had weathered the northern storms; it was stunted and berryless from excess of cold—like Lily's mind.

" Say you repent ! " said Eli, his eyes glittering with a frenzy of half-satisfied passion. Lily leant against the frail tree in utter abandonment.

" I repent," she said with weak bitterness.

" No. That wunna do. Kneel down and say a prayer."

Lily did so, repeating a sort of gabbled litany. If any angel or devil peered from the cavernous air upon the pigmy scene surprise must have been his prevailing emotion—surprise at the infinite ingenuity of man, the ephemeral, in finding new methods of torture for his fellows.

" And now," said Eli, " you've *said* a deal about repenting, now come on whome and let's see what you'll *do*."

Bitterley Farm was a large, whitewashed huddle of

buildings, with patches of damp on the walls. There were no curtains and the upper windows were broken. There was no garden except a potato patch and a few gooseberry bushes. A spring soaked out close to the door and the cattle had trodden it into a slough. The only beauty about the farm was a huge willow, now fleecy with white seed. Its long, slim leaf-shadows wandered up and down the ugly walls untiringly, like the hands of a hypnotist, tracing occult signs unknown to the human intellect—but guessed at by intuition. Even when its golden leaves lay like discarded raiment at its feet and the sky was obliterated with flying clouds it wove thin patterns in the sparse sunshine. It crooned for six months and cried aloud for six, saying always one thing. Perhaps the cuckoo on its top bough knew what it said, and even the hens scratching among its roots. Lily had a vague sense that it meant something, wrote some message on the bleak walls. But Eli knew nothing of it. On moonlit nights it sent a shadow to finger his harsh old face in the cheerless room : but the dream that might have come, tarried, and when he muttered in his sleep it was of vengeance, punishment and such grey negations—never of the beauty that is God. To-night the calves clustered round the door, eager for their evening meal. Inside, Lily nearly fell over the two pails of milk—she was so blinded by tears.

"Bide where you be till I come back," said Eli. Lily sat down on the floor between the pails, weary and sullen. Eli went out to the barn and fetched the sheep-shears.

"Now, take that bonnet off ! " he ordered, returning. Lily did so without comment, half dozing. Eli seized the long golden coils, all in a mass on Lily's shoulders, and before she knew what was happening they lay on the floor by her hat.

"There ! " said Eli. "That's a temptation gone.

Now do the cheeses." He turned on his heel, rather uneasy at the blaze of hatred in her leaden face. He went into the parlour and read the Bible as usual on Sunday nights. He was shaking like a drunkard, and sweating. He read three chapters instead of one, to lull his uneasiness; then he knelt and explained all about it to his God—from his own point of view. Then he fell asleep with his head on the Bible, and was awakened by the sound of his rookrifle to see Lily—perfectly white, like a corpse—re-loading.

" So you'll shoot me, 'oot, Lilian ? " he said calmly. She made no reply, intent on her work. He sat and watched quizzically. He was not afraid of death. Neither did it occur to him to question it. It was ordained. His God had said it. So be it. He had often shot a dog for not implicitly obeying him. Well, now his master was killing him. He faced Lily calmly. For the first time in his life he felt proud of her. To think of her doing such a thing—that chit of a girl ! So they gazed at each other, a kind of madness on both of them. One of the dogs howled and Eli reached for it with his foot under the table and kicked it. The room was very still, like a broken machine. Above the mantelpiece hung, rather crookedly, a painted text—" Fear God." The horsehair chairs stood inhospitably against the wall. A thick file of accounts hung on a skewer beside a shelf containing *The Auctioneer, Old Moore* and the *Imprecatory Psalms*. On the floor, not yet swept up, were the snippings of Lily's green blouse. She was ready. She straightened herself and lifted the rifle to her shoulder. They gazed at each other stonily.

VI

SUDDENLY there was a clatter of hoofs, a voice shouting " Yo-ho ! " to the calves round the door, and Joe — crimson, breathless, cheery from his mad ride—knocked the mud from his boots and walked into the passage.

" He'll see your chemise," said Eli indifferently, when he heard Joe first ; Lily's eyes flickered. Sex, a surface thing with her, but the strongest influence she knew, awoke again and overcame her madness. She fled through the door into the box-staircase, taking the rifle with her. Eli sat unmoved as he had been throughout. Joe had meanwhile fallen over the milk-pails and was in a sad plight for a knight-errant. He opened the parlour door and came in accompanied by a stream of milk.

" Where's Lil ? " he asked.

" You're in my debt for all that good milk," said Eli. " Even unto the skirts of his raiment," he added, with sour amusement.

" Where's Lil ? " Joe repeated.

" Tittivating most likely."

" There's no light upstairs," said Joe.

Eli was surprised at his acuteness.

" Maybe she's gone to bed," he amended.

" Well, I want to see her."

" What for ? "

" Mr. Huntbatch ! You're her dad, and so I try to be jutiful," said Joe, with some dignity ; " but when I come to tell her something—I tells her. I don't mouth it to other folk first."

35

" What d'you want, then? Me to call her?" Eli began to feel that Providence was not looking after him in its usual efficient way.

" Aye," said Joe; " now."

Eli called up the stairs. There was no reply.

" Lil!" called Joe, and in his rough voice dwelt an amazing tenderness.

There was a movement above, and Lily's voice, striving to be as usual, replied " Coming."

In a few minutes she came—tear-stained and limp, without the rifle and in her working dress. At sight of her face Joe opened his mouth to exclaim " Laws me!" but closed it again sharply, having suddenly grown from a hobbledehoy to manhood. He stood looking from Lily to Eli with bent brows.

Then he turned to Eli and told the only successful lie of his life with the utmost frankness.

" They want to know," he said, nodding in the direction of High Leasowes, " if you can spare Lil to go hilling to-morrow. Mother's agreed with the higgler for a big lot and we'm shorthanded. I was to take Lil back to-night if so be she'll come."

" Oh! you was, was you?" Eli was at a loss for once. He perfectly saw through Joe, and at last began to respect him as almost an equal—though grudgingly. " Well, o' course, if your mother wants her—when the ladies ask——" he began.

" Lil! Put your hat on and come along of me," said Joe. " Your father says so. You mun obey him." Slow satire pointed the words.

They went out.

" Jump up behind me," said Joe. " And, Eli!" he called back, " there's a bit of plaster gone from the wall just above your chair. I'd see to it if I was you."

Lily clung to him like a frightened kitten.

" Quiet, now, little lass!" he said. " I heerd the shot. Which of you was it?"

" Me," said Lily faintly, and they were silent.

So they came over Bitterley, trotting down the moonlit track through dark cloud-shadows to the Ardens' door. They passed the Batch Stone, a boundary mark intended to be imperishable, but worn down by the rubbing of the cattle against it until the chiselled words were obliterated. So the " thou shalt nots" of man are erased; only the great affirmatives stand unscarred, and it seems hardly worth while to spend time on negations.

Whitefoot made no sound on the turf. The grouse slept in the deep, arched glooms of the heather forest. From the spinney on the left, just before they came out of Hilltop Road into the western part of the Arden sheepwalk, there smote across them a tide of larch resin and a frothy scent from the elder-trees that stood witchlike round the wood. Out in the Far Leasowes—two large enclosures—there was a new tide of fragrance. It came from the young bracken, wild thyme, burnt grass, heather and cloud-berry bushes. With them was the austere fragrance drawn from the rock all day by the sun, and now hanselled delicately by moonlight and dew. The cattle crowded up, snuffing, very much at ease—like all animals and primitive people when nothing intervenes between them and immensity. To the west, immeasurably lofty in the flat moonlight which washed all unevenness from the ridges, stood the Devil's Chair—silvered ebony. From very far off, like the complaint of a denizen of some other world, came the cry of a sheep somewhere in the complex cwms or flats beyond the Little Wood.

As they neared the cottage a stout lamb with a very tightly curled and close-fitting coat caracoled up with heavy mirth and a long-drawn deep bass " baa ! " It looked so absurd, with its middle-aged figure, bulging forehead and awkward babyishness, that Joe burst into a guffaw. He never, as a rule, saw

D 37

either humour or pathos in the things that were his daily life. They were just " ship," " them steers," " old Whitefoot." But to-night he was strung to his highest pitch. His nerves were at last existent; he had attained in minute measure the sad distinction of the poet—who enjoys because he suffers. The lamb grunted and made off at Joe's " Haw-haw ! "

Lily awoke from a half-doze, irritated.

" Whatever be you laughing at, you great gom——" she began. No, she must not call Joe a gomeril. This was a different Joe. She was frightened of him. Also a faint and very unusual sense of gratitude dwelt in her.

The great keen air, like an eagre, not coming in several breezes, but in one soundless and indivisible force, smote on Lily's shorn head.

" Oh, Joe ! " she whispered. " I canna be seen ! My hair—— "

Joe pulled his red handkerchief from his pocket and tied it under her chin.

" Theer ! There's not a tidier wench in England," he said, with an admiration that was balm to her. She closed her eyes. Tears crept slowly down her cheeks.

Inside the house Mrs. Arden awoke.

" Somebody laughed out in the pasture, John," she said; " maybe it's the Dark Riders ! Put up a prayer."

" Now, mother ! you're too given up to them wold, unrighteous tales."

" But there is some one. Harkye ! They're taboring on the door. Maybe it's a call for me." She was up and at the window in a moment, flinging on a skirt and shawl.

" Mother ! " said Joe's voice, strained yet authoritative; " come down, 'oot."

" What's come o'er the lad ? "

" Best go down, mother," said John, beginning to dress; " and a quiet tongue is the healer."

38

Mrs. Arden went down.

" Here's Lil, mother; can she sleep along of our Deb? " asked Joe.

Lily stood at the door, white, with the scarlet handkerchief bound round her small head, her dress only half fastened in her haste. She blinked at the candle in a helpless way, like a young barn-owl.

Mrs. Arden looked over her spectacles first at Lily with solicitude, then at Joe with severe morality, tempered by primitive charity.

" Joe, lad," she asked, " is it——? Have you—— ? "

" No. It inna, and I hanna," snapped Joe crossly. " You're allus harping on one string, mother."

" Well, Joe," said Mrs. Arden apologetically, " if a shepherd dunna mind his own sheepwalk, there's none 'll mind it for him. But come you in, Lily, my dear."

She raked the fire and threw dry wood on, then hung the kettle over the blaze. The place was full of resinous fragrance and warm light. Joe surveyed the scene, standing just outside the door with his head bent to look in, his broad shoulders touching the jambs. He felt rather like he did on Fair days, when the long tramp behind the sheep was over, and they given up to their new owner, so that he could go, untrammelled and lonely, about the fair. The pride of responsibility, the stress of a necessary and difficult job were gone. He was just Joe Arden again. He took Whitefoot round to the stable.

" Well, Joe," said his father, matter-of-factly, " what about a bit of supper? "

" I dunno as I want any, father."

Deb appeared on the stairs with the little lamp that always burned by her room at night—lit by her father.

" What's the matter? " she asked.

" Nought," said Joe. " Mother 'll tell you," he added, with sublime faith.

39

Soon there was a comfortable scent of tea. Rover had never known such doings out of lambing time. He was not pleased. The light from the 1s. 11½d. "alabaster" lamp fell gently on poor Lily, sipping thankfully from the best china. Joe, embarrassed but not apologetic, consumed bread and cheese with the enormous appetite of those that come from spiritual heights. John talked of common things in reassuring tones—not understanding the circumstances, but seeing deeper, into the infinities. Deb, her straight hair falling in sweet disarray over her old shawl, sat protectingly by Lily, and Mrs. Arden, chatty, intent as a field-marshal deploying before battle, poured tea and buttered bread with the thrill of unusual excitement with which she met her many sleepless nights—a thrill which quite made up for her quiet life and her lost rest.

"There, Lil," she said, "don't you werret. Deb, you take her up now, and to-morrow we'll go hillin' and Lil 'll tell us all about it."

Her crushed curiosity spoke the "all" with relish.

Lil looked at Deb's long hair, remembered how she had once despised it, and burst into a storm of sobs.

Joe looked round accusingly.

"Nay, nay," said John, "don't take on, little 'un, we'm all friends here."

"Well, Mr. Arden," said Lil, gasping, "and Joe and Mrs. Arden"—(she left Deb out—her hair was so long, so heartbreakingly intact)—"I'm sure I'm very much obliged and—and I'll never forget it. No, I won't that."

Joe gazed at her over his large cup, with love, the white everlasting that grows in simple places, flowering in his face. He did not know that to such as Lily the snapping of flowers—even everlastings—was a matter of course. They were things to pick, use, fling away : only blossoms, not necessary to any one, like vegetables and meat. So the gospel of the grey-hearted had sunk into Lily's soul, which was meant to be a thing of colour and fragrance, but had been so frozen and stunted that only a poor little empty crevasse remained.

VII

As the grandfather clock struck five with a chary expenditure of energy, wheezing before each stroke, Mrs. Arden opened the upper flap of the door, "shoo'd" the fowls, and looked to see whether it was the man or the woman who stood outside the ornate cardboard "weather-house."

" A caselty day, father ! " she called up; " the 'ooman's out."

Soon they had breakfast and set out with baskets and large sunbonnets. John had gone with Joe to help in the hay, for it was carrying day and the winrows must all be spread to dry after the storm, then raked afresh.

John's own hay was not yet cut. The little crofts, perched so high in the cold air and the clouds, ripened late.

Sometimes it was September before the hay was safely carried; for it had to be done between storms, and storms were many. John cut it with a scythe. Spare and tall in the clear purple morning he would go up and down with vigorous, rhythmic movements, gravely followed by Rover; and a shadow-man, a shadow-dog went after them, dark and vast on the green field. Then Mrs. Arden and Deborah came and tossed the grass with a merry talking.

On the day when it was ready to be " lugged " Joe came home early. A twill sheet on two poles, reminiscent of ambulance stretchers, was piled up with hay, and carried by Joe and John as carefully as if it were really an invalid.

But if rain-clouds blew up—as they generally did—the dignified march changed to a mad rush; Rover, protestingly exchanging his stroll for a trot, was half-buried in falling hay; and, as Mrs. Arden said, it was "one pikel-full for the rick and ten for the mixen, and such a mingicumumbus as never was." They all regarded "lugging the hay" as a game of hazard played against the forces of nature, and they played with spirit.

Deborah carried dinner in a basket, and Mrs. Arden brandished the inevitable kettle; for the best picking ground was a mile away, and they would spend their noon-spell by the Little Wood.

"Real picker's weather it is," said Mrs. Arden. "Now we've got a start of the rest, let's see if we can get a tuthree quarts afore we have our vittels."

She bobbed along rosily and somewhat breathlessly, because she talked incessantly, between the two enigmas who vouchsafed few remarks. Her intuition had partially unravelled both enigmas, and she made the mistake of most people with intuition—she pulled so hard at her thread that she broke it.

"Well, Deb!" she said, after some talk of yesterday's chapel-going; "I wonder when Mr. Right's coming along for you, and I wonder what he'll be like — light-haired for sure, folks allus like their opposites."

Deborah had decided during the night that she would be an old maid. To blush as she had done in chapel was, she thought, "ondecent." If she blushed like that during a handshake, what would it be in courting? Also with Lily tossing beside her in the narrow bed—her cropped yellow head overwhelmingly reminiscent of another — Deborah was sure she "couldn't abear" marriage.

"Dear to goodness!" she said to herself; " how girls can go in for it all beats me, so it does."

She looked down at Mrs. Arden with some dignity and some confusion.

" I'll bide along of you and father and Joe," she said loftily; " I dunna like the men."

" Hoity-toity ! But Joe 'll not bide with us long. No danger ! " Mrs. Arden turned her artillery on to Lily with somewhat obvious mechanism.

" He'll be wanting them fowls' feathers I've saved—plenty of them there are, too, enough to make a nice fat double feather-bed."

Both girls looked haughtily into the distance.

" P'raps he'll marry Lucy Thruckton," Lily said patronizingly; " she'd suit him right well, both being rather full in habit."

" Lily Huntbatch ! " Mrs. Arden spoke with asperity, dropping her tact for frank curiosity. " You'm keeping a very still tongue in your head about your doings last night—a very still tongue, you be ! " She waited, but Lily said nothing.

" And it looks queer for a girl to come riding along of our Joe in the black of night with a good whome and a middling good father yonder, and me thinking it was the Dark Riders."

Silence. Mrs. Arden's charitable feelings had worn a little thin, as such feelings will when the recipient seems not only ungrateful, but unconscious of them. If Lily had thrown herself on Mrs. Arden's mercy last night, and told her that she and Joe had " gone too far," Mrs. Arden would have loved her—fought the world for her. But this cold righteousness was irritating.

" It's no good mumchancing like that, Lily ! " she continued. " You may as well out with it soon as late. As for Joe—he'll look higher than Lucy Thruckton, I'se warrant; and maybe higher than some others that'd make pretty bad wives for all their yellow hair—leaving six quarts of milk to go sour ! "

44

At this point Lily's bonnet blew off and she stood revealed.

Mrs. Arden gasped. Lily began to cry. Deborah—who had loyally promised not to breathe a word of it—whispered:

" How could it have come about ? "

" There, there ! " crooned the kind old weather-vane, " dunna take on ! It'll soon grow. But how-ever did you come to do it ? "

Lily wailed.

" It won't grow for years and years ! I've got to choose between being married looking like a ninepin in a veil, or waiting till I'm even older than Deb." The taunt was lost on Deborah, because of her last night's resolve; but Mrs. Arden crimsoned with anger.

" You ungrateful chit ! " she cried roundly. " Five and twenty's young enough for anybody—dear me, it is. A woman's bones aren't set proper afore that. It's mean little brats of chillun yours 'll be if you wed this side of twenty-five ! But you canna," she added, with a smack of the lips. " Your hair won't be growed. As you said, you'll look like a ninepin."

The humour of this suddenly struck her. She doubled into helpless laughter, slapping herself un-mercifully as she always did.

" Mother, poor Lil's very miserable; I think you met give her a bit of comfort."

Deborah was mildly reproving; she felt sorry for Lily. From her aloof height—she was at present icily self-fortified against sex—Lily's obvious sex-enchainment was a most pitiful thing. On account of it she forgave all Lily's little poisoned darts with large tolerance.

" Well, I'm sorry if I was nasty," said Mrs. Arden huffily. " But to say such things to Deb—and she Joe's sister ! And to be so high and mighty with Joe, and never to give me a word in answer ! And you

45

don't know your luck in getting Joe—a good lad as ever stepped. All I can say is, as when your time comes, Lily (as come it will, ninepin or not), and you're crying and sobbing (as you will, for you cry for nought), you'll be glad enough of me then, and of Joe too."

" I shan't. I shall hate Joe." Lily was furious. " But it won't never be," she added hastily.

" Well, time 'll show," said Mrs. Arden placably, feeling that she had time, nature and Joe on her side. " And now if we're going to get them old berries, we'd best get 'em."

They had reached the highest level. The budding heather was round them like a dull crimson sea, encroached upon by patches of vivid wimberries flecked with leaves of ladybird red. In the lustrous air all colours were intensified, and far things came close.

The Devil's Chair loomed over them—for all the distance between—like a fist flourished in the face. It was dark as purple nightshade. The cobalt shadows of clouds swept across the hills in stealthy majesty. From here there was no view of plain or valley, the plateau stretched so far on every side that it shut out everything but the distant hills. A whimbrel cried overhead, shaking its sweet, long-drawn whistle into silver drops, like quicksilver thrown on marble. The ponies drowsed in the swamps. Nothing stirred. They picked for two hours, absorbed and perspiring. Then Mrs. Arden, who had been covertly watching Lily as she ate handful after handful, remarked with caustic humour—

" You won't take many berries back for Joe's pie if you pick all the while into Eve's basket ! "

The two young women were shocked. Like most country girls they were prudish, somewhat in the manner of mediæval nuns, with a very clear knowledge of life as it is and a sense that only isolation and

46

extreme care can save from them the *mêlée*. Mrs.
Arden's frequent allusions to her "stummick" always made Deborah blush. And once at a cattle
fair, when her mother had knowingly punched a cow
in the ribs and announced with *bonhomie* to the
owner : "She won't be long !" Deborah had been
overwhelmed with shame.

"Well, it must have gone twelve, I want my
dinner," said Mrs. Arden. So they lit the fire and
filled the kettle from a wood-spring where rare ferns
touched it daintily with supple fingers. They sat
down in the short shadow.

"There's Mrs. Hotchkiss coming from Mellicot,"
said Mrs. Arden suddenly. "Laws ! Those boys
do grow. And there's Mrs. Palfrey. Fancy bringing
that mite, Willie ! It seems only a day since I was
going to and agen with him, and him nigh dead of
croup. And there's Lucy Thruckton, coming like
a sleepy bumblebee from Wood's End way," she
announced after a period of munching. She sprang
up alertly. "Well ! thank God for my good dinner,
and I'm not going to let that fat Lucy get all the
berries," she said, "so I'm off again."

The two girls stayed in the shade, chatting in a
desultory way. The pickers wandered to and fro,
lost in distance, appearing out of hollows, passing
round the white signpost like dancers in some strange
ritual. They stooped for the small, purple fruit,
wrapped in purple shadow themselves. Little box-
carts, trundled by urchins, began to fill with berries,
heaped in miniature replica of the hills. Shadows
began to climb from the cwms, and clouds came
faster. The signpost—so lonely in its ring of worn
turf—looked, with its outspread arms against the
dim reaches of heather, like a crucifix under the
troubled sky. It stood with forlorn gallantry between the coming storm and its prey. It would be
lashed by rain all night; lightning would play round

it. The pickers, as with some mysterious sense of kinship, circled about it—so disconsolately consoling it seemed, so like their own destinies. Deborah, looking at it, thought of what her father had said about "forkit lightning!" She wondered if she would ever be lonesome as it was, set up for a sign, a mark for the storm, pointing vaguely—whither?

VIII

Suddenly Mrs. Arden straightened herself, standing at gaze. A stranger was coming over the hill. He stopped by the signpost, seemed to make nothing of it, and came on towards her.

" Can you tell me the way to Lostwithin? " he asked.

" Be you him as preached yesterday? " parried Mrs. Arden.

" Yes."

She was taking him in. " A comely chap," she said mentally. He stood looking down at her amusedly, conscious of his good looks. Even his " up to date " blue suit did not spoil his supple muscularity, though it was cut absurdly. He was smoking a briar pipe of enormous proportions.

" Quite our Joe's sort ! " commented Mrs. Arden.

" Joe's sort " was, of course, young manliness personified, just as " Deb's sort " was perfect maiden-hood, and " John's sort " something that brought tears to her eyes when she sat and thought her own thoughts in chapel.

" The signpost doesn't say much," he added.

" Oh, that ! " she commented, with much scorn. " Nobody takes no notice of that. You canna go by signposses here, you mun go the way the hills 'll let you. But them posses," she added, " they do for the counting councils to be busy about, painting the names and that. Else who knows what they'd be doing?—for a more mischievous set of men there never was ! Besides, poor things, they want to seem to be doing something for their money like other folks."

He laughed.

The two girls by the wood jumped, looked and sat mute, expectant.

" And the way——? " he reminded her.

She had made a resolve.

" Now, it being so hot," she said persuasively, " what'd you say to a cup of tea ? "

" Well, I'm sure I'm much obliged, but——"

" Come you on," said she, with authority. " Come you on and set you down."

" Well, to goodness ! " breathed Deborah. " Mother's bringing him here."

Lily skilfully made the most of her front hair under the bonnet. She would see if she couldn't cut Deb out, although her curls were gone.

" Gawls ! " shrieked Mrs. Arden, while yet a long way off; " here's some one as you both knows."

For the second time Deborah's eyes met those of the stranger.

" Lily," said Mrs. Arden, " run and get some sticks while I fetch the water, there's a good girl."

She hustled Lily into the wood.

" And so I've got my second chance," said Stephen Southernwood.

Deborah was silent.

" I never saw a soul except you in chapel," he continued.

Deborah twisted her apron into a rope.

" My name's Stephen; might I ask yours ? "

He had more ease of manner than any one she knew, although he had not attained the absence of self-consciousness which the Lord of the Manor down at Slepe had gained (not without tears) at Eton, and which Joe had always possessed as a birthright. At present he was going through a strange experience; he was meeting his primitive self for the first time.

50

It was a very shadowy self so far : but it was something quite different from " the nice young man "
who had caused such a stir among the ladylike
drapery assistants in Silverton.

What had caused the change he did not know; was
it the hills, the storm, the clear, still face beneath the
darkened chapel window ?   Since yesterday Deborah's
face—vital, yet unawakened—had come before him
in flashes, vivid and transient.   This transience had
stirred desire in him; he was ever for the fleeting
rainbows of life, and what was denied he must
possess.   Her evident capacity for large life fascinated him, and the veil of sleep that was upon her
fired him to a wakening onslaught like the sun's upon
a dim country.   Life ceased to appear as a neat,
correctly docketed arrangement of a little football,
a little Huxley (to improve the mind), a little Sherlock
Holmes (relaxation), a little religion (respectability).
How it did appear he would have been ashamed to
say.   The drapery assistants had made him feel
smoothly romantic.   They themselves were smooth
in manner, and they saw to it that in their presence
life had no rough edges.   The utmost propriety, the
utmost glossing of facts was necessary in order to
pass muster with them.   They were cool, collected,
conventional.   He suddenly hated them and their
smoothness.   They had smoothed him also as a
rolling-pin smoothes dough.   They had deferred this
curious, electric, mad meeting with himself.   He had
sampled the pleasure of a kiss fairly often; but his
world had been far removed from the forcible kisses
of desire, the indecent snatching of the starving for
bread, the hot struggle for existence.   He had been
detached and impersonal about the great facts of
life; now they were hot and clamorous in his ears.
He looked swiftly at Deborah, and immediately all
that he had ever read about the embraces of lovers
came into his mind as a poignant, personal matter.

She turned her head away, for the look in his eyes was like a strong clasp of her. His thoughts galloped. He dragged at the reins, intuitively feeling such thoughts to be indecent in Deborah's presence : but they were not to be stopped. They rushed on through the whole of human experience; it lay open to him as the countryside below did—vast, delicate, savage. Kissing ceased to be a game. It was a key to intenser life. The act of speech was no longer merely for courtesies, expressions of opinion, pleasantries. It was for demanding joy from the world, surrender from women. The hearthfire, little houses, night, took upon them the magic that they wear for lovers. For the first time in his life he realized Death—the murderer of ecstasy. Rapture, relentlessness, force—these ceased to be words. They were manhood; they were himself. Tears, tenderness, pain—these were woman; these the woman who loved him would be and suffer in the glory of surrender, in the birth-pang. All these things—dim and half understood—flashed through his protesting mind, while Deborah sat, constrained and afraid to look round, gazing into the melting distance. A voice far down in Stephen's being answered the whimbrel that called above. It summoned Deborah peremptorily; it shouted defiance at the hills, the world beyond, the intangible and therefore terrible depths of blue air. Out of the muddle of half-understood ideas, small wishes and conventions that had concealed Stephen Southernwood from himself sprang a creature direct and impulsive as the old gods—who took their way unknown and unhindered, claiming with a nod the love and tears of the witless daughters of men, themselves recking nothing of a love that is pain, only knowing a swift desire, shattering to the desired. So he entered into half his heritage—the physical glory of man. The other half was so far undreamed of.

" Why do you look away all the time ? " he asked.
She turned her head with an effort.
" Where d'you live ? " was the next question, direct
to rudeness.   Yet she felt a delicious homage in it.
She nodded sideways.
" Upper Leasurs."
" Can I come to Upper Leasurs ? "
" Aye—no."
He laughed.
" You funny little girl ! "
She had never been called little.   She was indignant
for a moment.   Then she found it sweet.   She felt
happy and humble-minded as she did when they sang
in chapel of sin and forgiveness.
" I tell you what," said Stephen, " I shall come to
Upper Leasurs and the rest of 'em whether you say
I can or not."
Deborah's apron was a long, creased rag.
" You've not told me your name yet ! "
" Deborah."
" Shall we go for a stroll in all that green and red
stuff, Deborah ?   What's it called ? "
" Wimberry wires."
" When they call us we won't go."
" Mother 'll holla till we do," said Deborah, matter-
of-factly.   But she went with him.   For the first
time in her life the heather was only a carpet, the
sky only a roof.   She walked between them in a
shaken world, to a sound of shaken music.   The
whimbrel's cry fell there like broken glass ; and
in her soul the crystal of her pride shivered into
fragments.
Lily, who had been listening behind a stunted
may-tree, stamped with rage, and was what Mrs.
Arden called " almighty imperent ! "
" Why should I call them, Lily Huntbatch ? "
" It looks bad."
" Not as bad as you looked, in the dark of night,

along of our Joe, with your dress only half done up."

Lily was silent, but she thought ecstatically how she would try and capture Stephen, throw Joe over and be quits with Mrs. Arden.

"Here they be, friendly as calves o'er a gate," said Mrs. Arden, forgetting her annoyance.

"He's a deal taller than Joe," said Lily; "head and shoulders."

"That he's not! Joe'd be above his ear. I've notched him and Deb year by year on the door, and I know."

Lily watched Stephen.

"The chief among ten thousand!" she murmured, with the cheap emotion of her kind—often mistaken for love, altruism, religious fervour.

"You're the chief of all gomerils, Lily!" said Mrs. Arden. Then she surveyed Deborah.

"Took for matrimony," was her comment.

"I think it's very vulgar," Lily remarked, "to talk about marrying and kids all the time like some do. I can't see why a chap can't talk to a girl without such things being thought of."

"No more do I. Only they dunna, you least of all. And as for vulgar, if such things be vulgar, then you and me and the greatest in the land, aye! even the ministers of God's vulgar—for they're all the signs that such things came to pass. And come to that," she added, rising to metaphysical heights; "come to that you'd call the Lord Himself vulgar, you wicked girl! For didn't He plan it all out from the first kiss to the last christening? Answer me that, Lil Huntbatch!"

She gathered breath as Deborah and Stephen came up.

"This is Lily Huntbatch, that's walking out with our Joe," she announced.

The look Lily gave her was venomous.

54

" Do you like walking out, Miss Huntbatch ? "

" Depends who with." Her bewildering smile was lost; he was looking at Deborah.

" Your safety-pin's undone, Deb," she snapped, " and your belt's crooked."

" Here's Lucy—after some tea, I suppose," said Mrs. Arden. " She's terrible earnest for victuals, Mr. Southernwood, and she does credit to 'em."

Lucy bore down on them.

" Well, you *are* hot," said Lily, welcoming a victim for her anger.

" I be that."

" And red in the face."

" I allus am."

" Your hat's all collywessen."

" It do get like that."

" And your brooch is coming off."

" If I loses 'im, I loses 'im," said Lucy calmly.

Lily gave it up. If Lucy was too inert to mind about her brooch, given her by her only admirer at the age of twelve, with " Mizpah " on its moonlike surface, she was invulnerable.

" There, Lucy, my dear, you shall have a nice cup of tea." Mrs. Arden spoke protectingly.

" Thank you kindly," Lucy replied, rapaciously and gratefully. " I'm sure I'm ready for bucketsful, the sweat's poured off me till I feel right thin."

At this remark Stephen was seized with uncontrollable laughter.

" And he stuffed his handkerchief into his mouth," Mrs. Arden recounted to John afterwards, " and he rocks to and agen like me with the colic. I never seed any one laugh like what he did. Eh ! I like good laughers. Ill they may do, but they're not bad-hearted—not if they laugh till it hurts 'em. And then Deb started to laugh, and I couldna help but join, and Lil—as had been sitting all the while like an owl with the face-ache—began to say ' hee-

hee !' very mincing-like, and poor Lucy (never knowing what it was all about) opened her mouth and bellowed, and the old whimbrels set up a din of laughing round about. You never heard such a noise in your life, father ! and then all of a sudden the thunder came on and we were all in a pretty taking. And Stephen (he says I'm to call him by his given-name) remembered as he ought to have been at Lostwithin hours ago. He'd stayed the night at Wood's End along of the storm. And he ran one way and we the other, and poor Lucy went lolloping whome, frittened to death. Deborah went awful quiet when it came on to thunder; and she says 'Good-evening' very stiff to Stephen, as if she'd minded something agen him; and when we were coming back she says, 'Mother, there's summat foreboded.'"

"Aye, she said that yesterday."

"Well, better go the way of 'ooman, whatsoever's foreboded," said Mrs. Arden. "Why, goodness ! There's Eli trapesing through all this rain. He's come for Lil, sure to be."

IX

Eli had passed a very irksome and busy day; for he managed to get a great deal of work out of Lily, feckless as she was. He had been obliged to strain the milk, light the fire and get his own breakfast. He had forgotten to feed the young turkeys, and three of them had passionately and poetically died—to spite him, as he said. The cow Lily always milked had kicked him, objecting to his hard hands. He had cut himself while peeling potatoes. Altogether he emerged from his single-handed contest with inanimate matter and what he called " brute beasteses " somewhat battered. Also he had been again troubled with a curious sense of admiration for Lily, realizing that if she had spirit enough to behave as she did last night, she could do most things that she chose.

" She could make a darned sight better butter nor what she does," he grumbled, " if she could shoot her feyther."

He had felt rather startled on coming down in the morning to see the long golden locks on the floor.

" I've bin a fool," he said. " When 'll she cotch a husband now as she's nothing to take the eye ? "

Altogether it appeared to him that it would be a forgiving and dignified thing to go and fetch her back again.

" The prodigal daughter ! " he thought, with a wry smile. " Well, she wunna get much but husks at John's. Poor as a winter feldefar ! No yead for business. Keeps that great strapping girl of his eating her head off at whome and doing nought. Work 'em and marry 'em, I says. Keep 'em hard at it and they unna kick."

He suddenly remembered that Lily *had* kicked, and was displeased.

"Gerrup!" he shouted at old Speedwell, his brown pony, now sprinkled with white. She moved away slowly, and he threw a stone after her.

"Worth twenty women, that hoss is," he murmured—apparently to the Almighty, to whom he spoke frequently and familiarly.

"Never say die, her won't."

He threw another stone. He could not throw at the Almighty or Lily, and he had a need to throw. Yet he was fond of Speedwell in his knotty and sapless way.

He put on his old, round felt hat, very high and pointed in the crown and broad in the brim, and set out. He felt that he was under an obligation to Mrs. Arden for Lily's board and lodging for the night. This hurt his pride. "And me with all that money!" he said. A present was the thing: but what present? He did not intend to give anything for which he had, or might have, any use, nor anything for which he could possibly get any money. It was very awkward: everything he saw was of use, or might be. The gooseberries were over-ripe; but Lily could make a pie—the Ardens should not have them. There were some chickens with the gapes; but he could, no doubt, cure them. No: he would keep the chickens. But he must take something. He looked round the parlour. His eye fell on the MS. volume of imprecatory psalms—copied out by Lily on Sundays during her childhood under Eli's tight-mouthed supervision. Yes, he would take that. He came out, and tumbled over the prostrate bodies of the three dead turkeys. He would take them too.

"May as well be handsome while you're at it," he said. "They can make a pie. It won't be no worse than young rook pie, and that great gawk Joe 'ull be glad of summat to fill his belly."

So he set out with the psalms under his arm and the turkeys bunched in his hand.

"Summat for you, missis!" he said grandly, as Patty came to the door. "Take 'em! A free gift they be—free as the Lord's pardon. And I want that darter of mine. The prodigal darter, she is; and her loving father's come all the way to fetch her. Say she's to look sharp."

It was late, and supper was laid. Joe and his father had just come in, and were washing in the back kitchen. Lily was in Deborah's room, reading an old fashion paper. She sprang up when she heard her father's voice, looking wildly round for a way of escape. Mrs. Arden called her. Lily put on Deborah's sun-bonnet—a blue one that suited her; looked in the glass; decided that she was not attractive enough for her object, and turned in the collar and a little of the front of her dress to show her white throat. Then she very softly climbed out of the low window, and dropped on the turf.

"Joe!" she whispered through the back door, when John had gone to speak to Eli.

"Aye?"

"Don't let him take me, Joe—not to-night!"

"Right you are."

"And, Joe——"

"Aye?"

"Will you come out along the hill a bit when he's gone?"

"I will that!" said Joe.

"When be she coming?" asked Eli from the door. "Supper? No. I wunna take any victuals off you, poor things!"

Mrs. Arden sniffed.

59

" Say she's to come this instant minute," said Eli.

Joe loomed over him.

" A word with you, Eli," he said.

" Hark at our Joe calling him Eli ! " said Mrs. Arden to Deborah. " Did you ever hear the like ? It's always been ' Mr. Huntbatch ' afore."

" What is it now ? " asked Eli crustily, moving off with Joe.

" She's not coming to-night."

" Well, of all the imperence ! She's got to come."

" Not to-night."

" And what good 'll she be in the market when she's bided two nights along of you ? " snarled Eli.

Joe's hand was heavy on his collar.

" None of that, Eli ! " he said.

" Loose me be ! And what 'll she please to do after to-night ? "

" I dunno."

" Will she come whome to her loving feyther ? "

" I shouldna think so."

" What, then ? "

" Mayhappen she'll marry me—if she'll take me."

" Oho ! And what 'll you give me to make up for the loss of my dairymaid ? "

" I've nought to give."

" Oh, yes, you have—you've got bone and muscle, and you can ride. If I give my loving consent to this here 'oly estate, will you give your written word to round up my sheep when I ask you ? "

" Maybe that'd be every night," said Joe drily.

" Only now and agen," Eli reassured him ; " and a bit of help at sheep shearing."

" Well, I dunna mind that ; but nought in writing. And I don't know if she'll take me yet."

" Ho ! Listen what I'm going to tell you. She'll drop into yer arms like a blighted apple. Anything to get away from her devoted parent."

"But all as I do for you is done on one condition," said Joe; " you say nought about last night."

" Well, I dunno as I want to."

" On your word of honour ? " continued Joe. " No, that's no good—on your credit as a moneyed man."

" I swear ! " said Eli solemnly.

X

W<small>HEN</small> he had gone Lily crept out of her hiding-place in the wood-house and met Joe on the hill. She had no idea that he was going to ask her to marry him, and so, by the irony of things, she spent more time and energy luring him on than she had ever spent over anything.

" My, Lil ! You do look pretty. Why don't you allus turn your dress in ? "

Lily smiled.

" What was it you was going to say about my arms on Sunday, Joe ? "

" As I wanted to touch 'em."

" Well—you can."

Joe's hand went gingerly up and down one arm.

" D'you like me, Joe ? "

" Like you ? Oh, laws ! "

" Well, then, would you like to—put your arm round me ? "

" Let's sit down, Lil." Joe was quite overcome. He had always thought " askin' to wed " was as difficult as catching sparrows in open weather. And now here was Fate playing into his hands. It seemed too good to be true.

" Shall I be on your knee, Joe ? " asked Lily confidingly.

Joe had the sensation of home-brewed very strongly. He was conscious that he must not have much more of this heady delight.

" You *are* big ! " Lily's flattery was obvious, but sufficiently subtle for Joe.

" You're a bit of honey, that's what ! " said Joe
rapturously.

" Like to kiss me, Joe ? "

There was a short silence.

" You don't like kissing, I can see," Lily commented
disappointedly.

" Not like it ? " Joe gasped.

" Well, you kiss as soft as a hen pecking bread."

" I'll show 'ee if I like it."

" Oh, dear ! You've knocked my bonnet off. My
hair ! "

" It's all right—all curly like a young lamb, and
shining."

This was sweet to Lily as homage to a king de-
throned. She leant back against his shoulder. He
kissed her again. They were in the Little Wood.
Her eyes sought his bewitchingly as she lay in
apparent abandonment to the sweetness of the kiss.
She was wondering how many more hints she must
give him before he would speak. Joe kissed her
throat. Then he put her on the ground roughly.

" We'd best go whome," he said.

" Why ? " She was petulant, not having as yet
attained her object.

" I want to do right by you, Lil; and you're so—
I canna remember ought when you're like you be
to-night."

" How d'you mean ' right ' by me ? "

Joe took a deep breath.

" I mean will you wed me, Lil, my dear ? "

" Well ! Why ever couldn't he say that before ? "
thought Lily. She smiled.

" I might."

" Soon ? "

" Maybe."

" Come on whome, Lil. The devil's in this little
old wood."

He walked furiously down the track, Lily half

running, not understanding the fires she had kindled so carefully.

" When ? " asked Joe, slackening speed as they neared home.

" I dunno."

" Next week ? "

" Well——"

" Saturday next as ever is ? "

" Oh, Joe ! "

" Saturday it is, then ! And no more Little Wood till then. For you're like home-brewed, Lil." He gazed at her in puzzled and admiring wonder.

" And you remember as it means no going back to your feyther if you marry me quick. See ? "

Lily did see—had seen all along with a clearness that would have startled Joe.

" There's a cottage at Slepe, not set; I'll take it. We only want a few chairs and a table and a mangle to begin with, and a double bed——" He stopped. " My tongue's hung on in the middle," he muttered.

There was a short silence.

" I dunno as it *can* be Saturday, after all," said Lily at last.

In Deborah's small, whitewashed room with " God is Love " over the mantelpiece and a bunch of mimulus in the window, the two girls tossed all night.

" What a craking them two keep up, like calves in a strawy calfskit ! " Joe thought. An intolerable sweetness came over him as he let his sleepy thoughts wander on to next Saturday.

" There's surely no harm in thinking of it now, it being all settled up," he reasoned; " besides, I mun get used to it, or I'll never remember all the things I've *got* to remember ! "

" Hark at those girls ! " said Mrs. Arden to John. " They're both in love."

" Or it met be heat lumps," John suggested.

" Dear sakes, what a man ! "

Mrs. Arden would have her romance.

Lily was faced by the necessity of a decision—a thing she hated. There were three ways open to her, and she must traverse one of them, since she could not stay where she was. All were equally detestable to her. She could go home, be a dairymaid, or become the mother of Joe's children. She writhed at the idea of physical endurance. She did not love, and it is love that makes all pain, all privation, a crown of everlastings. The lover knows that the reward is greater than the hardship. To Lily, who had never cared for any creature, it was not so. She had always supposed that some time she would have children : but now that the vague future had come near it was a different matter. So much for Joe, then. But could she go home ? No. The dairymaid's situation remained.

" Not if I know it ! " she said. " Work, work, day in, day out." She came back to Joe. An idea struck her. With a pathetic mingling of naïveté and selfishness she decided that she and Joe could be " brother and sister." As she had not divined anything of Joe's nature or his dreams—for intuitions do not come to the self-centred—this resolve was not so heartless as it seemed.

Having come to a satisfactory decision, Lily curled up to sleep like a kitten.

Deborah half awoke.

" He's coming to High Leasurs," she thought, " to see me ! Me ! Not Lily." She was astonished at his blindness—Lily was so pretty. She was glad with a boundless joy. Already on the horizon of her life flickered the immortal fires, darting strange rays, changing the world.

" Stephen . . . Stephen Southernwood ! " A dart of pride ran through her as she remembered that Lily had not lured his eyes from her once.

"Stephen!" she said aloud, half asleep.

"Keep your silly names to yourself, can't you?" grumbled Lily. But Deborah was asleep.

"Stephen," she murmured again.

"Oh!" cried Lily, much irritated. "Joe! Joe! Joe! then, if it's got to be said!" She cried from sheer vexation.

XI

" Your Joe's gone off his chump, seemingly ! "
said Mr. Shakeshaft to John.   " Down at that cottage,
day in, day out—missing good wages all for a wench.
How bin the mighty fallen ! "

" They've kept company a goodish while," said
John, primed by Patty, who did not want it to seem
" a wedding as had to be."   " It's not a sudden-
thought-of thing," he added anxiously.   " Don't go
for to think that."

" Whoever did think it ? " said Mrs. Shakeshaft.

" What's Deb say to it ? "

" Oh, Deb ! " John smiled broadly.   " Well, Deb,
you see—Deb's in—oh, I wunna to say ! "

Down at Slepe the small, empty cottage echoed.
Joe whitewashed, hammered, forked the garden,
brought home a small recalcitrant pig, and finally
went to Silverton and bought the furniture with his
modest savings. Lily went with him, and they
took the road past Bitterley, stopping to interview
Eli.

" Well," said he, " I give you the blessing of the
Lord freely—freely. But I've nought else to give.
Still, you wunna lack.   He feedeth the young ravens
that call upon Him.   Get out, you fowls !—always
running after me for sharps ! "   Joe hoped that he
and Lily would not be kept as short as Eli's fowls.
Lily went indoors, and came out with a small parcel—
the severed locks. Mrs. Arden, confronted with a
sobbing Lily who could only ejaculate " Ninepins ! "—

had set her wits to work, and remembered the ladies' papers in the People's Dining Saloon at Silverton market.

"Why, Lil," she said, "it's as clear as cider! You go in along of Joe when he goes after the furniture, and you take in your hair and get a switch made. It's quite the thing. The advertisements say no lady should be without one. Then you just pin it in among them curls, and coil it round, and there you are."

Lily, having got her parcel, set herself to work on her father's pride, and finally squeezed thirty shillings out of him. Her small, rather forlorn heart was quite lit up by the joy of the shopping in store.

A ready-made white dress, a veil, a piece of artificial orange blossom, cotton gloves and the long-desired set of ribbon-trimmed undergarments—all these were at last stowed away in the trap, while Joe wandered from jeweller's to jeweller's, looking at such a multiplicity of rings that he became hopelessly confused.

"Whoa there, lad!" he apostrophized himself loudly, to the astonishment of the passers-by. "Where's that little small one that I seed but now?"

Finally they went to choose the furniture in a whirl of haste and embarrassment, while a cool and dispassionate shop assistant yawned and wondered when it would be closing-time. Then they had tea. Joe's "Tea and ham for two" was full of the tones of love, pride and ecstasy: but Lily was surreptitiously absorbed in her ribbons, and the waitress, like Gallio, "cared for none of these things."

The ostler at the "Drover's Rest" had a good deal to say as he piled things into the trap and let down the back to accommodate the iron bedstead.

" You're lugging home the furniture and the girl
and all, seemingly," he said, surveying Joe's best
cap with a piece of honeysuckle stuck in at the side.
" But I hanna seen the pram yet—no, I hanna."

His face was convulsed with wrinkles of laughter.
Joe looked at Lily out of the corner of his eye as they
drove out of the cobbled yard. This was " Something
like ! " he felt. Such things were the small change
of the marriage festival, and made him realize his
fortune.

" Funny chap, eh, Lil ? " he ventured.

" I don't like that sort of fun."

" Of course not," said Joe, much dashed.

They spoke of where the furniture would stand,
and wondered if the weather would " keep up," as
they jogged home. They went through the great,
golden plain of corn, set with jade-green meadows of
aftermath, blue-green turnips and the black-green
secrecy of woods. They had to pass through four
little villages besides Slepe in the long twelve miles
of quiet road. At each one, as evening drew on, the
young men leaned against a wall or over a bridge,
smoking, the day's work done, and setting up a
hearty cheer when the trap hove in sight.

" Oh, dear ! " said Lily. " I feel all of a shake,
like Quaker's grass."

" Well," Joe replied, with what was meant for
comfort, " it's nothing at all to what getting married
is. But never you fret, Lil—it'll be o'er, soon or
late, and you and me all by our lonesome in that there
little place for good and all."

" Look at them Wyandottes over there ! " said
Lily hastily. Joe was momentarily interested, and
they fell back upon slight things until the long climb
from Slepe began. Then Joe said—

" I think you met let me kiss you now."

" A' right."

" And I'm going to put my arm round you too,

tight. For we'll be man and wife the day after to-morrow."

They came silently up the steep, half-obliterated track in the heather. Joe was quiet and soberly happy, Lily trepidant, very curious as to the new Joe who was appearing; she kept at arm's length the picture of the future, as conjured by Mrs. Arden's remarks. Mentally slipshod, she had none of the rare, sad, godlike faculty for seeing the end of a thing in its inception. Deborah possessed it in large measure.

XII

THE wedding eve came on with unhurrying prompti-
tude, and Joe's last preparations were made before
noon. He lit the fire, put the kettle on the pothook
and laid the tea with the new china. He surveyed
it all with a man's unbounded pride in domestic
work, remarking, " It do look summat odd ! " He
felt that it was worthy even of Lily. He ate his
bread and cheese, washed and waited. Lily was to
slip away in the early afternoon and come to see his
work. He sat on the doorstep, and the honeysuckle
round the porch dropped its limp, spent flowers about
him—with the one broad petal lolling back like the
tongue of a faery hound in age-long chase of a death-
less quarry. The scent was thick in the garden, in
the dusty lane, in the house. Joe drowsed and knew
that whatever happened to him in the future he
would not grumble—not even if he died in the work-
house, for this waiting was sweeter than the honeysuckle. The dense thickets of delight before him—
thickets with no notice-board up, to which even the
church pointed him on with kindly finger; the little
faces (he rose here, and went to look again at the
large brown tea-pot, marked 2s. 5½d. cash); the
years to come, with more and more of the tonic
sweetness of nature in the little house day by day—
all these shone before him in summer colours. He
thought of to-morrow, with the gay walk to church,
the walk back, the homely tea at Upper Leasowes,
the loving comprehension that meant home for him.
For it seemed to him that there was nothing about

his thoughts unknown to his father; nothing about his hopes and fears with which Deborah did not sympathize; nothing about his bodily welfare that his mother did not forestall. All these emotions were quite dim and unexpressed; but they were none the less real to him. Then he thought how, when the rooks began to go home and the shadows to steal out of the hollows, and the first star sat like a bird on one arm of the Devil's Chair, he would cease to be only " the lad," and " our Joe," and " owd Joe of Upper Leasurs." He would be a woman's all in all, and on his strength of hand and clearness of eye would depend two fates—perhaps many fates. They would walk down the path, " just ordinary," they would come to the village, pass beyond it, pass the wicket. He would shut the door.

" Joe Arden," he apostrophized himself, " you mun mind to give Lily a cup of tea, and you mun mind to leave her to settle a bit while you go and see to the pig. For even a cat wants to look about a bit in a new whome, and she's got a vast of strangeness afore her."

He thought of Lily, and as he pondered on how his future peace and his to-morrow's rapture depended solely on her, were bought entirely at her cost, the sharp sweetness of human life—in which pain is the honeysuckle round the door—came over him in a rush.

" Such a little small thing as she be," he thought. " I canna make out why she took me. Women be won'erful."

But, seeing that she had taken him, it never occurred to him to doubt for a second that she would sit down meekly in the shadow of the honeysuckle and be all a wife should.

The gate clicked and she was there. She had never looked so frail, so provocative; she had never been more purposeful or less desirous of admiration. They went in. Lily was genuinely pleased; after the rambling ruin at home, impossible to keep in order even for more industrious hands than hers, the compact, neat little home was delightful. She thought how easy the work would be. She was not meant for the hardy magnificence of manual labour. She should have belonged to the professional or tradesman's class, had a small " general " to bully, and been able to say with pride to her friends, " Oh, no, I never do any work, but I know how it should be done." But here she felt a decided impetus in the direction of domesticity, because for the first time it was picturesque; for the first time she saw herself in a romantic setting of shelves, cupboards, clean paint and flowers. She had a vision of the vicar's wife alluding to her as " Joe Arden's pretty wife who makes such good jelly."

" It's real nice, Joe—dear."

There was quite a little rill of affection in her voice. She had never been loved, and his deep thought for her, so quiet and unceasing, had touched her. It had wakened—as the prince did in the fairy tale—somewhere amid the dragon-like scales of her egotism a very sleepy, very illusive princess, who might, if all went well, sit up and rub her eyes and become a queen.

They looked at the pig, the geraniums, the apple-tree. They had tea for the first time out of the cups that had gold on their rims. It seemed to Joe that a flaming mist hovered in the kitchen. He bethought him of his responsibility as head of the house. He could no longer sit in silence and leave his father to do the honours and " make things go." No. The radiant, regrettable fact was that his father would not be here; *he* must crack the jokes and quote the wise old saws.

" Lil," he said archly. " What'll your name be this time to-morrow day ? "

"Lilian Arden," she replied, as sweetly as a small bird chirping.

"What else?"

"Mrs."

"Aye. That means as I needna be feared of the little old 'ood."

Lily puzzled over what he meant, till he suggested that they should come and see the rest. Up in the low-ceiled bedroom she understood.

"Oh, Joe! Oh, *dear* Joe!" she sobbed. "I canna—I darena."

"What's come o'er you, Lil? What's frit you?" Joe was quite dazed. Into the sunny room a shade had come, deep as the thunder-cloud shadows on the hills. He sat down gingerly on the bed, patient, mystified.

"I canna tell you—I canna!" said poor Lily. "And oh! what a dear little room and all—and roses on the jug! Oh, dear—it's cruel hard."

She ran to the window and knelt by the sill.

"I wish I was Deb," she wailed. "Deb's such an everyday sort. She never thinks of things like what I do. And so she dunna mind. She said to me on'y to-day as I was a lucky girl—and so I am, only—only——"

"It's all a jumblement to me, what you're saying, Lil—like them anthems when they try who'll sing fastest. You tell me straight out, and it'll be clear as the Christmas star."

Lily knew it would not. Even her own mind was not clear. Fear struggled there with curiosity, and fatalism brooded over all; she was like a clock without a mainspring, like a road with no signpost. Love would have taken away all need of thought, all curiosity, all fear. Where it led would not have mattered. The ways of lovers are many as the sheep-tracks on the mountains; but they all lead into the shadow-blue distance; into beauty; into rest; into stress and blessed grief and godlike laughter.

74

" Well ? " Joe spoke with benevolent patience and large comfort. His benevolence, which took away the fire from his face for a while and left it as it was when he warmed the half-frozen January lambs, encouraged her.

She rose and came towards him, and for the first time in her life real feeling, not overlaid by any pretence, was in her face. She sank by him on the floor.

" I canna go through," she sobbed, " it's—your mother said—about—this time next year."

Joe understood.

" There, there ! " he said, " don't you werrit, my dear. Things just comes, you know. We'm just got to keep loving and read the Book a bit and it's all easy."

" Not for me ! " In her voice was the primeval cry of woman when sex comes upon her without the nimbus of love.

" No, I know. And I'm main sorry. And I'll do all I can to be a good chap, Lil. I swear I will. I'll cook for you and wash for you, and I wish I could do all for you; but I canna," he said sadly.

" Joe ! " she trembled. " Couldn't we be just brother and sister ? "

Joe stood up.

" Daze my 'ounds—no ! " he shouted.

He knew nothing of other ways of love than his own—he never dreamed that lovers could be at once spiritual, passionate and childless.

" No ! " he repeated tensely. " All or nothing, Lil."

Lily sobbed.

" Oh ! I dunna want to be married and have chillun, and I dunna want to give up this nice little cottage and the veil—and all," she moaned.

Down below, transfixed with wonder, Mrs. Arden stood with the little last gifts she had brought. She

75

turned and crept out by the back way. They must never know what she had heard.

As she climbed home, like a very stout bluebottle in her print dress, she panted: " Well, Joe mun find his own road now. Poor Lil—it's bad to be like that, well, well ! "

She surveyed the landscape — huge, primeval, towered over by vast, fawn-coloured clouds which, in spite of its hugeness, were much too big for it.

" So long as they're fond on each other," she murmured, as the swallows darted by with excited little snatches of song, " nought matters. Not trouble, nor sickness, nor chillun, nor the lack of 'em."

And with this speech, surprisingly tolerant considering her profession, she nodded at immensity as if she knew a thing or two not altogether to its credit.

Three hours later, out on the hill at the Leasowes, Joe waited for Lily.

" Well," he asked, " have you reckoned it all up ? "

" I canna reckon anything."

" Well, what's the word—all or nought ? "

" Oh ! It *canna* be nought, Joe."

" All then ? "

" I s'pose so."

" And the berries are worth the picking ? "

There was anxiety in his voice. " For certain sure ? "

" I s'pose so."

" Come thy way in, then," shouted Joe uproariously, " for I want my supper summat cruel, being that uneasy. Mother ! Mother ! give us a bit of summat to eat, and give Lil a drop of cider. Sit by me, Lil," he added, holding her hand under the table. " I'll do my best to suit you, Lil," he whispered, " and you shall set the pace."

Then silence fell between them, while Deborah machined the seams of Mrs. Arden's wedding-dress, and Mrs. Arden explained that it had to be " loosed out."

" For I never wore it atween the wedding and the christening," she explained, " and so it didna need altering."

She saw Lily bite her lip.

" Lil, my dear," she said, filled with a large and beautiful pity, " I hanna given you much yet, and I was thinking maybe you'd like a tuthree of the bird cups. Now you just take your pick."

So she gave her treasure without a second thought.

Lily's eyes filled with tears; her tired face lit up. Somehow to-night Mrs. Arden, whom she had never liked very much, was more protecting than Joe. She went to her and leaned on her chair, looking across at Joe's face—still a little stern from the conflict and the possibility of losing her—and a new sense of pride in him sang like a finch in her heart. But to-night Mrs. Arden, with her large charity, asking nothing, giving all; John, with his glance from which the hardness of youth had long passed; and Deborah, with her unruffled virginal absorption in the outside of the ceremony, were more comforting to Lily than all the length and breadth of Joe's love, all the mingled wine of passion. She chose the cups with childish delight, and as Mrs. Arden wrapped each one up, a second spark shone in Lily's heart, and she kissed the old woman of her own accord.

XIII

THE day had come, clear and multiple-tinted, full
of the sound of bees in the heather, and crickets
at their endless spinning. Deborah was gathering
her three tall lilies in the dew, with the pathetic
generosity of sensitive temperaments that deny
themselves a cherished beauty for the sake of a
recipient who does not even see it.

"Dear Joe!" she thought; "dear Lil! they'll
only be married once; let them have the best of
everything."

Then, in a more mundane mood, she reflected
humorously that she would now have her bed and
her favourite blue sun-bonnet to herself, and no
Lily to dog her footsteps when Stephen came.

She took the lilies upstairs.

"Just right for you, Lil," she smiled.

"Does my hair look all right?" asked Lily
absorbedly.

"Aye. Not a soul would know."

Joe, on his way downstairs, knocked loudly and
asked if he could come in.

"No! No!" they shrieked with much laughter.
"Get off with you!"

"Well, you come out then, Lily, and gie's a look
at you. There's some one coming over the hill
from Lostwithin way, Deb; best hurry up with
your own tittivating."

Lily came out. If she was never to have another
triumph, she had one now. Joe gazed at her with

78

a long, humble, adoring look and said nothing at all.
So much can a few shillings do for a woman!

Deborah, fastening her own dress at the back with
great difficulty, had the air of a little girl who is
showing off a doll, until she suddenly felt in the way
and closed her door gently.

The lilies lay caressingly on Lily's arm; her white
frock fell softly about her; the veil flowed from her
small, corn-coloured head. It was a pity the lilies
in her heart had not been tended. She flushed
under Joe's look, and her eyes were like chicory-
flowers.

"Lil!" said Joe softly, "be you quite sure about
what I asked you?"

Lily pouted.

"I'm not going to be asked questions on my
wedding-day," she said. "Maybe it won't be for
you to say 'all or nought,' so grand and solemn,
Mister Joe! but to take what you can get." She
ran downstairs with a delicious consciousness of
power. As she stood in the doorway athirst for
admiration, Stephen came up. She gave him a
long, slow smile and wished she could change bride-
grooms; but his eyes were on Deborah, who came
down in her delaine gown.

"For goodness' sake, somebody fasten me! I'm
squeedged as a cuckoo in a sparrow's nest!"
cried Mrs. Arden from the kitchen.

They started for church in great mirth, after an
earnest discussion between Mrs. Arden and Deborah
about the oven damper. They were accompanied
by all the lambs—stout, close-curled, ego-centric—
but this escort fell away by twos and threes.

"Our Joe looks grand! Such a man and all,
the very moral of his father!" Mrs. Arden whispered
to John.

"Now, mother! There's the making of a better
man than me in him."

79

"And young Stephen?" queried Patty; for in spiritual matters and in the winding of the clock John spoke with supreme authority.

"Well, he's got a goodish way to go; and it's a dark road to the heart of God when you grope by other men's lights; but at long last he'll be a fine chap—if he comes through—a fine chap."

"I've taken a dislike to the marriage service," Stephen was saying to Deborah. "I can't stand being tied to anything, can you?"

"So long as you're tied where you want to be," said Deborah impersonally, "I don't see as it matters. You'd stay there anyway."

"But who knows where he does want to be?" he asked restlessly.

"The wings of a dove," John murmured; he was watching a pigeon against the dark profundities of the hills, and looking with tenderness on the four who had life to face : "The wings of a dove, to flee away and be at rest." But he meant something quite different from the smooth longing in congregational singing — something vast and dark as the hills themselves and as all-satisfying.

"Yon's the Devil's Chair, Stephen!" said Deborah. "Some say the ghosses go Thomasing there, to choose 'em a king. But they canna see him as they choose, for the mist; and the tale goes that when the ghosses see who's king it'll be the end of the 'orld."

"I shall go to the Devil's Chair," said Stephen, "and find him."

XIV

WHEN they reached home again two wedding-guests were sitting on the wall—Eli and Lucy Thruckton.

"As the hymn says," Eli remarked, "child and parent meet again. Well, well! Now I suppose you'll be setting to in the manner of Genesis with the multiplication table, though there's fools enough and to spare as it is."

Joe and Lily went in hurriedly.

"John," he continued, "those calves you bought look mighty bad. You're easy took in!"

John was ruffled. He was very sensitive about his business faculty, not having any. He also went in.

"Patty," said Eli, "I've brought these two fowls to grace the groaning board. They're no good for market, being of the black-fleshed kind."

Mrs. Arden was put out at having more cooking to do when everything was ready. She thanked him somewhat hastily and took the lean little birds indoors.

"Well, Deborah!" The incorrigible old man turned to her next. "Well! You're peart enough to-day, but what saith the Book of them that laugh? What did the daughter o' Babylon become?"

"And who have we here?" He nodded mockingly to Stephen.

"A very silly, jealous old man," remarked he succinctly, and went in, followed by Lucy.

"He's stuck as many hard words into me while

you was at church as cloves in a Christmas apple," observed Lucy.

Eli turned to Rover, who watched him kindly but with dignity, as well-treated animals who have an assured position always do.

" If you was my dog," he said, " I'd give you a good hiding ! "

Then he went in and sat down sourly to wait for tea.

Lucy had brought a large red flannel pincushion made by herself in the form of a very fat heart, fastened with coloured pins, with a large " L. A." also in pins.

Joe took upon himself to thank her, speaking of putting it " on our chessun-drawers," at which Lily blushed and whispered to Deborah—

" Where *shall* I look ? "

" At Joe," replied Deborah amusedly.

Mrs. Arden dearly loved a festivity. Flowers, pretty colours, " company manners "—these were dear to her as land to a sailor. She saw much of the dark side of life in her nursing of labourers' wives, women on lost hillsides, wandering gipsies. She sat now in the shady room with the window open on the purple outside, pouring tea from the bright pewter pot and pressing food on every one until Lucy said—

" Well, I'm as full as a tick ! "

Whereat the young men roared, and Lily murmured, " Vulgar thing ! "

After this the young ones wandered about the hill, and Stephen and Deborah strayed away. The plateau was drenched in gold light, splashed with grape-coloured shadow. A few berrypickers came and went on the skyline.

" Deborah," said Stephen, " d'you know that you are most awfully pretty ? "

"Oh, no! I've only got straight hair, not wavy like Lily's."

"Is it long?"

"Pretty fair. What be you doing?"

"Just feeling it."

"Oh, you munna! Eh, dear! It's all coming down!"

He laughed, holding up a handful of hairpins.

"Suppose they see!" she cried.

"Come to the wood, then."

"I don't like to."

"Come!"

She went. Her hair fell in long, smooth tresses, touched with copper here and there by the sun. She was very much confused.

"I've never done such a thing!" she said.

"*You* haven't let it down, *I* have. And you're the prettiest girl in the world."

"Oh! whatever be you doing?"

He had picked up a long strand, putting it to his lips.

"Oh! you munna!" Deborah's vocabulary seemed to consist of exclamatory negatives.

"Why not?" asked Stephen.

"It's not right."

"Everything's right if we love each other," said Stephen, expressing a truth by accident.

Deborah was overwhelmed.

"You do love me, don't you, Deborah? I love you *madly*," he said boyishly. He stooped and kissed her.

"I don't know."

"Well, think! Quick! I've never seen any one a bit like you, and I want you, Deb!"

He flung himself at her feet on the pine needles, and lay looking up at her—flushed, triumphant, admiring.

"Now!" he said, "I shan't give you these pins

back till you say, (1) If you'll come to Lammas Fair.
(2) If you'll come to what-d'you-call-'em's chair.
(3) If you'll sit on my knee now."

"Well!" was all she could say. Such a wooing
was different from anything she had ever dreamed of.
Where were the conventions of the countryside, the
" walking-out," the gradual intimacy, the slow ritual
of embraces? Once more she had a sense of inse-
curity, lack of poise. He was like a storm. He got
up as suddenly as he had lain down, and sat by her
on the log.

" Well, are you going to promise, or shall I chuck
'em in the stream? "

" Oh, dunna! Father and mother'll think I'm so
flighty if I go back with my hair down. And I'll
never hear the last of it from Eli."

" Then promise! "

This new self was a pleasant person, he found,
albeit queer. His pulse was hammering; he was
more excited than he had ever been.

" There goes one! " he said.

Deborah was distressed. Lammas Fair was all
right; but she had a superstitious fear of the Devil's
Chair, and as for sitting on his knee—why! they had
only met four times. How could she?

" There goes another."

" I'll come to Lammas Fair."

" Yes! Go on! "

" Not the rest."

" There go two more, then. Only five left."

" Oh! it won't stick up with less, it's so heavy! "

" Well, then——"

" I'll come to the Devil's Chair."

" I'll save you the trouble of the last," said Stephen.
And behold! she was on his knee.

" Will you come and live with me, Deb, right
away, so that I can always pull your hair down and
kiss you? "

84

"I mun think," she said tremulously; "I mun be away from you and think a long while. For there's more to it than pulling hair down, Stephen, and kissing."

"I know," said Stephen, his face on fire.

But Deborah was not thinking of passion—the existence of which she barely guessed. She was thinking of the demands of a love that should possess her whole life, wondering if she dared enter upon it.

Flushed, confused, but firm, she emerged from the wood, doing up her hair as best she could.

"Well!" said Lily, superior in her dignity as a married woman, "I think Deb's carrying on awful. Look at her hair! Any one can see as he undid it, look at his face."

"I'll undo yours to-night," Joe remarked, and Lily's new-found dignity collapsed.

"Let's have a song!" suggested Mrs. Arden when they went in; "what d'you say, Lucy?"

Lucy never gave an opinion of any kind. She called it "useless argufying."

"Let's!" said Stephen enthusiastically.

So they sang glees till supper, while Eli sat with his mouth tightly shut, silent and sardonic. After supper, at which the fowls appeared veiled in sauce, John proposed a hymn or two. It grew late, and Joe nudged Lily.

"Just one more!" she pleaded.

"Let it be the Golden Arrow," John suggested. "It's an old song, Stephen, and it's about an old ancient custom. In time gone by the lads and wenches in these parts was used to go about Easter and look for the golden arrow. It met be along of them getting sally-blossom for Palm Sunday as the story came; but howsoever, they was used to go. And it was said that if two as were walking out found the arrow they'd cling to it fast though it met wound them sore. And it was said that there'd be a charm on 'em, and sorrow, and a vast of joy. And nought could part 'em, neither in the flower of life nor in the brown winrow. And the tale goes that once long ago two found it in the sally-thickets down yonder. And they came through Slepe singing, and with such a scent of appleblow about 'em as never was—though appleblow time was a full month off; and such a power of honeybees about 'em as you only see in summer-time. And they went like folks that want nought of any man, walking fast and looking far. And never a soul saw them after."

" Good riddance to bad rubbish ! " said Eli, very bored.

" But every year," John continued, " when the ghosses go to the Diafol, them as found the arrow come two by two, merry as whimbrels in a fine June. And every time St. Thomas comes round, there's a tuthree more of 'em, for there's allus some finds the arrow in the worst years. There's a good few old women as come first, in the tale; like wold ancient brown trees they be, groping and muttering, some saying, ' Accorns for the pig, faggots for the fire; but we missed summat.' And some saying, ' We lived 'ard; we supped sorrow; we died respected; but we'm lonely.' Then they all set up a cry like a yew-tree on a windy night : ' Out o' mind ! Out o' mind ! ' Then the ghosses stir like poplars, all grey and misty-like in a ring round the Chair, and there's no sound but sobbing."

" An owd ewe with a hiccough, more like," said Eli.

" Maybe there's more than the sound of sheep coughing on a wide mountain, so close under the power of the Lord," John replied. " Howsoever, in a bit there's a noise of singing, and in come the lovers, very gladsome, standing among the grey 'uns

with a rosy light on 'em. And they one and all
speak for the Flockmaster to be king—him as lights
shepherds whome and carries the dropped foals."

"What I allus say and allus will," said Mrs. Arden,
"is that them grey ghosses as died respected are
more to my liking than a gang of unruly folk with
apple-blow, sheeding petals all o'er the place for
Lord-knows-who to clean up."

"Apple-blow," remarked Eli in a heartbroken tone,
"as met have set into good cooking apples at seven
shilling the pot."

Lucy, who had been opening and shutting her
mouth in a lethargic effort to speak, began in her
circumstantial way—

"My Aunt Martha says as when she was a
gurld——"

"Time out o' mind," said Eli neatly.

" —there was used to be a waggon wi' three carthorses to lug 'un as went up a valley over yonder on
Palm Sunday when folk went after the arrow. And
whatever d'you think was in it, Mr. Southernwood?"

Stephen was duly expectant.

"Sugar-plums!" said Lucy ecstatically. "Sugar-
plums and oranges full to the top. Eh! I wish they
did it now!"

"Now, folks," said John, "take parts and tune up."

"We have sought it, we have sought the golden arrow——"

They sang to a grave and wistful air with a lilt in
it that enriched the words. Joe kept up the bass
with great industry.

"Laws, Joe," said his father, "you din like a
cuckoo on the chimney!"

"Let the lad be, father," whispered Patty; "dunna
you know the proverb—

'Sing loud when you'm wed,
    You'll sing soft enow on your jeath-bed'?"

Lily's clear soprano rose above the rest. She was so happy and excited that she sang with more emotion than Deborah, who felt the symbolism while Lily felt nothing. She was so pleased to be admired in her new dress that she had quite forgotten her fears. She went down the hill with Joe, chattering like a cricket.

" Early on Monday I'll be here," said Stephen to Deborah at the gate, " and on Monday I want your answer."

" What answer ? "

" About living with me always, every day and every—year." His new self had nearly said "night."

" No backing out ! "

" That's not in my line," she said rather haughtily.

" Thank you for me," Lucy Thruckton was saying earnestly; " it's been grand—tea *and* supper. Good-night all ! "

" Well," growled Eli, " I never saw such people ! Wasting good victuals and drink to persuade four young fools to do what they're only too ready to do without ! "

He slammed the gate and departed in the deepening shadows—a hunched and grudging little figure in the frank and splendid hills.

XV

JOE and Lily ran down the path like children.

Below, in a purple cup brimming with golden moonlight and covered by a lid of sky—jewelled like the cover of a wassail-cup—lay the small, huddled village of Slepe. The church tower—grey, square, knowing all winds, all rains, all snows, and regarding them but as the beating of small birds against its massive walls—rose out of a tall rookery. A farm or two, the vicarage, the school where Deborah and Joe learnt all their less useful knowledge, the post office and a few cottages—these were all the human outposts between the empty valley and the lonely hills. When Joe and Lily reached the bottom of the cup they saw that even the bedroom windows were all dark; they heard cows breathing inimically behind hedges, while the stream (broad here with a sheen as of tapestry mirrored in armour) spoke with bated breath to the rook-burdened elms. They felt like conspirators.

"If the dog at Low Levels barks, I shall skrike," said Lily.

They crept by the church. The clock ticked with loud, measured sounds over the intense rich quiet.

"Isn't it a randy?" said Lily. "It feels just as if we was doing wrong."

"Aye."

Joe spoke with relish, then added, "But we're not; for we're taking the bitter along with the sweet. It's folks that want all ale and no work that do wrong."

" Eh, dear-a-me ! Why did you go for to damp it all ? "

Lily began to cry under the sense of reaction, the remembrance of yesterday and the knowledge that she could not—as she had always dreamed—take her hair down and stand like a hair-oil advertisement before her bridegroom, but must surreptitiously and ingloriously take it off.

She hated her father; she mistrusted God; she edged away from Joe.

The soft night, like a moth, flitted on over the bloom and dust of the world.

" There now, Lil, don't take on," said Joe. They came into the precincts of the honeysuckle. Joe unlocked the door.

" Laws ! the old fire's out. Ne'er mind, Lil. You see how quick I'll start it and get you a cup o' tea."

Lily sat by the stainless, new kitchen-table in the dark and sobbed. The pig outside set up a yell for supper. Joe went to the back door.

" Hold your row," he shouted. Then he poured such a generous libation of paraffin on the embers that there was a terrific roar. He was feeling very much of a householder, and very full of admiration for his father in bearing up so well for so many years.

" Now, Lil," he said, " look's a blaze ! kettle will boil in no time."

Lily was slightly consoled. She lingered over the tea, crumbling cake, drinking cup after cup, until Joe suggested that it was time to turn in. He locked up and lit the candle. Lily did not move.

" I'm comfor'ble here. Canna I bide here ? "

" No," Joe answered shortly. He, too, was tired, and it seemed so unlike his dreams.

" Come on this minute, Lil ! "

She went.

90

Upstairs a bat flew round and round the room. Reality came upon Lily unbearably. She remembered the funeral of a girl friend and her baby.

" Oh, there's a bit-bat ! " she wailed. " It's a sign, Joe. I'm feared. Leave me go down to the kitchen ; I want to go on as I be. Why should I slave and get ugly and sickly for the sake of brats I dunna want ? What's the good ? What was I born for ? Look how father treats me. I want to enjoy myself. I dunna want to do things nor put up wi' things—not for you nor anybody. Oh, why did I ever take you, Joe Arden ? And me so young and all, and you so set ! "

She flung her cotton gloves on the chest of drawers and threw Lucy's pincushion out of the window.

The shepherd's vast, vicarious sorrow came like a cloud over the midsummer passion in Joe's face. He looked more like his father than ever.

" Now, now ! " he whispered. " You're tired, little 'un. See here, let's get these fanglements off and this pretty hair down——"

" Off," said Lily hysterically.

" And then you'll have a good long sleep, and be right as a trivet."

He helped her as his mother might have done, with the sexless solicitude that love brings when the beloved cries from the dark. He patted her as he did the lambs.

" There ! " he said, " now for that pretty night-gownd. Where is it ? "

" Top of my box." Lily spoke with small sobs.

" That's it ! Now you go to sleep. We'll have a rare day to-morrow."

" Sit by me ! " implored Lily, " and dunna let the bit-bats come."

This confidence in him was the sweetest thing life had yet given him. Sitting on Lily's box through the long hours with the small, ringed hand in his he was content. He watched Lily's face growing clearer as dawn came up in pearl armour from beyond the ranges. The honeysuckle scent surged in at the lattice; his arm grew stiffer.

" It'd be a poor thing if I couldna watch with her one hour," he murmured, unconsciously scriptural.

" I mind what father said, and what I never saw till now—for I'm a gawk and that's the truth—' if there's any one in the 'orld besides Him that first said it as can say—this is my body, broken for you— it's a woman to the man she's set her heart on.' "

Joe was unaware that Lily had barely begun to cultivate a heart.

XVI

"WELL, I wonder what they're doing down at Slepe," said Mrs. Arden, as they sat down to breakfast on Monday morning. "My word, Deb! You *be* togged up—you've waved your hair!"

Deborah blushed.

"I won't say as it dunna suit you. You look real nice—not like yourself at all," she added with maternal candour. "But I do wonder if they're hitting it off all right down there."

"Well, mother," said John slowly, "since we can't know why do you werrit?"

"Hark at him! 'We can't know!'" Mrs. Arden spoke tartly, for she felt flat after the festive week-end, and irritated at all the accumulated washing-up with no Deborah to help her. John's placidity brought down a storm on him.

"Hark at him! 'We can't know!' Speak for your own ignorant self, John, as can't see a thing nearer than the colour on the farthest-off hills, and that's not real, for it goes when you come up to them. Don't speak for me, as maybe knows a tuthree things you dunna!"

She snapped her lips and thought of Friday at Slepe.

John met this squarely, as he met all storms.

"Well, well, mother," he said, "if I help you to dry them plates by and by, no doubt my ignorance'll mend. Rover!"

He was gone—straight, lean, dreaming on the far heights. The sheep, on their lawns near by, left

93

their grazing to follow, pattering after him with an increasing sound as stray ones joined the flock, until he walked in muffled thunder of little feet and looked from a distance like one pursued by large snowflakes.

" Well, mother, I'll be going now," said Deborah.

Mrs. Arden looked at her face—lit, as John would have said, for marvels. She felt a crisis in the air.

" Deb," she said, bringing from her store the best wisdom that she had, as she would have brought her cranberry jelly, " dunna give till you're asked—aye, asked many and many a time—and then only through the gold ring, and chary-like."

Deborah went out, overwhelmed that her secret had been discovered—ashamed, ecstatic, with a stress of joy in the high places of her being like the galloping of the ponies on the high sky-line. She had no more of the recommended chariness in her than there was in the bloom of the hills, the burning sunlight, the eternal song of the rock-springs that never failed.

She reached the signpost an hour too soon and sat down beneath its white arms, merged in rolling seas of heather.

Down at Slepe, just as she reached the signpost, Joe awoke, filled with a great new sense of well-being.

" Lil ! " he whispered; " it's gone seven. We'll be late ! "

Lily slept on. Joe looked at her pale face, blue under the eyes, at the brown lashes still bright with half-dried tears. He looked at the lilies in the jug— the tallest of them was snapped, and rested its faded head on the soap-dish. He felt that he was to blame for it. If he had known the word, he would have called himself an iconoclast. He crept softly downstairs and lit the fire, pottering up and down with cups and bread-and-butter till the kettle boiled.

" I didn't ought to wake her, and she worn out," he

thought. " All my fault too. But there ! Deb'll
be that cut up if we're not up to time."

He hesitated.

" My lad ! " he adjured himself, " turn your back
to the storm. For if Lil was tetchy yesterday, when
I'd sat up all night along of her, what'll she be now ? "
He heaved a sigh of foreboding. But he had much
to learn. On Lily's tired face, when he apologetically
woke her, broke a smile so bewildering that he
blinked.

" Why, Lil ! "

She continued to look at him softly.

" Lil," he said, " d'you feel bad ? "

" No, Joe."

" Be you sleepy ? "

" No, Joe."

" Be you wishing you was back along of Eli ? "

" No."

" What then, Lil ? "

" I dunno."

" Well," said Joe, basking in the unexpected
warmth and doubting the great doctrine of retributive
reward and punishment; " well, all I can say is,
whatever you're thinking, it suits you, Lil. And
now here's your breakfast, and then we must be off.
And we've got a whole day," he added delightedly,
" a whole day afore us."

" I wish we needn't go," said Lil.

" Not go ? Why to goodness not ? "

" I—don't know what to talk about to Deb," Lil
replied. " Girls' talk is so dull."

Joe laughed till the teacups rattled in their saucers.
And by nine o'clock (when they should have been two
miles away) they started.

XVII

UNDER the white cross on the hill sat Deborah and Stephen : he was voluble, she was silent.

" Well, if you won't, you won't," he was saying. " But why you consider it wrong for me to kiss your arm when I've kissed your mouth, Lord only knows."

He threw sticks crossly at a huge green caterpillar crowned with gold that was crawling in the short grass.

" Dunna hurt it, Stephen ! "

Stephen saw his chance.

" I'll stamp on it, if you don't let me kiss your arm."

" Oh, well——"

Deborah spoke wearily.

" Oh, stop ! There's Joe and Lil."

" Hullo, Joe ! " shouted Stephen. " What's that about the newly wed ? "

Joe sang out the rest of the couplet with enjoyment, to the discomfiture of Deb and Lily.

They took their way through the solitudes, where innumerable sheep-tracks crossed and recrossed. Joe leading unerringly. The two girls dropped behind.

" Well, Lil ? "

" Well, Deb ? "

Sheep cried through the clear air; the two young men tramped in front—full of the pride of life, whistling, mimicking the sheep—quelled, when they paused for the girls, by a " Get along, do ! "

" Well, Lil ? " said Deb again, after a long silence.
She said it pleadingly, insistently. She was like
one that sets out on a long journey, and waylays
other travellers to ask for short cuts.

" Well ? " echoed Lily, blandly and with an aggravating pretence of denseness. She remembered
Deb's quiet scorn of her " carryings on." She was
enjoying herself.

Deborah sighed.

" I thought," she said sadly, " as being friends
and that, and me lending you my blue bonnet, and
being Joe's sister and all—you'd have told me——"

" Well, Deb," Lily replied, with icy superiority,
" I never thought you was one of them prying,
curious girls."

" Oh, no ! " cried Deb hurriedly, " only——"

" What ? "

" You know I've thought time and agen of being
an old maid."

Lily laughed.

" Well, shall I or no ? "

" You softie ! "

" But I want to decide, Lil ! "

" *He'll* decide," answered Lily concisely.

" Oh ! "

" You needn't worry your head."

" Oh ! "

" All that'll be left to you is——"

" What ? Let's sit down, Lil."

" You'll know all in good time," said Lily.

" Are you two coming, or are we to come and
fetch you ? " shouted Stephen.

" Coming," cried two voices hastily.

" Now then," said Stephen; " you old married
folk trot on in front."

" I like that ! " chuckled Joe. " And what about
you ? "

97

" We follow at our leisure," replied Stephen.
" I bet you do."

They had begun to descend. The interminable,
winding valleys lay beneath in broadening vistas.
Their steep sides were clad in amethyst, blue, gold,
amber, crimson, copper—infinite colours, overlaid
by the violet gauze of cloud shadows. All down
their way stood foxgloves, and Stephen fitted a
flower on each of Deborah's fingers. With them
went a stream, rocking on its swift waters the yellow
cradles of the mimulus, where tiny shadows slept.
The hills closed in round them; the far prospect
was gone, then the near view, then the ramparts
in front; finally nothing remained but their own
narrow way—multi-coloured, cricket-haunted, with
a roof of blue sky laid across the hills above like a
sheet of paper.
" Deb," said Stephen, " let's sit down. I want
to talk to you."
The atmosphere of joy round Joe was too much
for him. He pulled the mimulus to pieces.
" Deb, I want to ask you a big thing." She shut
her eyes, and the sun fell on her calm face as it falls
on a field of ripe wheat.
" I want to ask you, Deb," he went on, his voice
trembling a little with suspense and eagerness, " if
you'd live with me without——" He paused. The
enormity of the thing in her eyes and in the eyes of
her people suddenly appeared to him; but he was
not of the kind to hesitate.
" Without marriage," he finished.
Deborah lay back, motionless.
" You see," he went on, very anxious to explain,
" it's such a mockery to me now, this last week—
all that. I don't believe in it, and it seems such rot.
And I always did hate fuss and promises and to be
tied down."

98

His eyes took their restless look. "Sooner than that, I'd shoot myself!" he added, with the rash certainty of one who had never touched a gun.

"If you'll take me, Deb, I swear to you here and now that you'll never repent it. I'll love you far more than wives are loved, and be faithful to you for ever and ever—what the hell's that?"

A loud, raucous, mocking laugh, rather like Eli's, had rung out far above them.

"Only the grouse," said Deborah.

"What a din! It startled me."

He was rather ashamed of his superstitious fear.

"Well, what do you say, Deborah?"

"Oh, I dunna know. It's all dark, Stephen."

"But it's no different really. If people love each other, they stay together, whether they're married or not. If they don't, they don't."

Deborah saw that clearly. What she did not see was his temperament—his way of shifting as the wind does before a stormy night, of striking out wildly, here—there—like a giant in the making; of dashing after every butterfly of a new idea as a poet does in his crude youth.

"Oh," said Deb hopelessly; "it couldna be. There's father and mother——"

"What do they matter, if you've got me?"

He stood there in stately youth, like a sapling by the water.

"And Joe——"

"What does Joe matter? He's got his own boat to steer."

"He'd liefer see me dead."

"Why?"

"Well, about here, you see, we set a lot of store by marriage. Wed, and grey's white. Dunna wed, and white's black."

"Of course, if you think more of Joe than me——"

"Oh, you know I dunna."

99

" Well, then ! "

It was his own incorrigible reasoning.

" And the neighbours—Mrs. Shakeshaft and all—"

" We'll go off together, and let them say their silly say."

" And Eli——"

Her face grew quite rigid, as she thought of his creaking voice upbraiding her, calling her a sinner.

" Damn Eli ! "

" And——" Deborah took her courage in both hands—" and me."

" You ? " he questioned.

" Aye, me. I'm like other women, and I want what they want—a ring, and to be ' Mrs.' "

Her lip trembled.

" Well," he said with young egotism, " if I'm not enough to make up for that, I'm sorry."

He turned away.

" Oh, dunna go, Stephen—dunna ! Let me think a bit ! "

" I don't like half-hearted givers," said Stephen coldly, for he was very eager and her hesitation tortured him.

" I'm not, I'm not ! " cried Deborah, deeply hurt —for generosity was her strongest instinct. She stood up, very straight and gracious in the blue delaine. The tower-like hillsides became a mere background for her, the colours grouped themselves behind her like meek waiting-maids. She stood like the goddess of some rich land. Her eyes were tender, agonized and haughty.

" Stephen," she said, as he looked at her with bent head and both hands out towards her; " Stephen, I'm no niggard. If I give, I give wi'out stint and of the best I've got. But the heartbreak and the sorrow as you're bringing on them I love, is a'most more than I can bear. Do you love me true, Stephen Southernwood ? "

100

" Yes, Deborah."

" Will you love me on to the last turning and the end of the road ? "

" Yes," he said rather impatiently.

" Do you want me so bad that you're lost without me ? "

There was a note of wistfulness in her voice.

" Of course. Oh, Deborah, say yes ! "

" Stephen," she said, with her father's unhurried utterance ; " are you certain sure ? "

" Before God, I am ! " he cried—with truth, for he was at that moment. But he did not realize that he was dynamic, while she was static, and that the crash of such temperaments is wilder than the crash of worlds.

" Then, Stephen," she said, with a clear look at him, standing in a pool of shadow ; " then—you can ask me."

He flung himself at her feet.

" Will you be my sweetheart, Deborah Arden, and my mate, and the love of my life ? "

She put out a hesitating hand and touched his hair, damp on his forehead.

" What a lad you are ! " she murmured, motherly.

" Answer, Deb ! " he said passionately.

" Aye. I'll be your sweetheart," she said softly, " and your mate, till I lie in the daisies, and the love of your life, while life lasts."

A wandering seed of thistledown drifted slowly across the cwm, very high up, from one steep to another without descending, as if it walked on an aery bridge to an aery destiny.

" And now," Deborah said, " let's go on to the others, for I've no more to give and no more to say for a while."

" But, Deb ! I was just going to kiss you."

" Not now—not just after that. I'd as lief kiss in church. It's a new road we've started on, Stephen," she added, with the sense of desolation creeping over her again; " a new road, and it may be a waidy one. Never loose my hand, lad ! "

" Never ! Not for all the old devils up yonder," said Stephen, nodding in the direction of the Devil's Chair—hidden from them now, but set high above the country like a black pearl in a troubled sea of mist, for the thunder had come round and muttered in the west. The grouse laughed again.

XVIII

" Yo-ho ! " came Joe's voice from far down the path. " Well, you laggards ! " he bawled, as they came up.

" The path's so twisty," said Stephen.

" The path's straight enow." Joe looked at Stephen contemplatively. " There's nought wrong with the path," he added, " but maybe you're a twisty walker, Southernwood."

Deborah sighed.

As the last valley widened and the hills swung back, they heard the distant, plaintive music of the merry-go-round at Shepwardine—like a bee in a jam-pot. They came down the quaint street, by the old market, where fruit was set out so temptingly that Joe bought two enormous melons, which he carried under his arms. The street was full of country folk, interspersed with visitors who hoped to attain the peace of the countryside without its toil. Strings of hill-ponies went by, droves of bullocks, sheep with red letters on their shorn bodies.

Joe steered for the merry-go-round, and Deborah saw above the crowd, above Joe, above everything in the world, she thought, Stephen's bright head and keen face, eager for joy.

" Good morning, Mrs. Arden ! " said Lucy Thruckton primly. She was sitting on the grass with a bottle of ginger-beer.

" Hullo, Joe ! " shouted various friends. One

irrepressible from beyond Lostwithin, seeing the melons, called out—

" So you've brought the twins ! "

" If you *be* market-peart, Charlie Camlin, you needna blazon it."

" Be you coming, Lucy ? " asked Deborah, as they took their seats on the merry-go-round.

" No. I'm thinking it's a toil of a pleasure."

Deborah thought that many pleasures were like that.

Eli came up. He was here to look for a house-keeper, and had been treated with contumely by two ladies upon stating his terms. He was annoyed.

" Turn ye, turn ye ! " he intoned, coming up to them just as the hobby-horses started.

" We be ! " said Joe, amazed at his own wit; " as fast as ever we can."

There was a roar. They began to move to the tune of " Oh, where is my lad to-night ? "

Eli stumped off.

Stephen's eyes were ablaze. He loved quick motion, music, colour. He had an arm round Deborah, and the more excited he was, the more like iron it grew.

" Oh, Stephen ! " she pleaded; " loose me go ! "

But he was beside himself with excitement, the fulfilment of his emotional and poetic love of beauty, and crude life.

" I won't," he said.

" Oh, do 'ee, Stephen ! You're hurting me."

The merry-go-round was in full swing, racing madly, the music at its loudest and quickest.

He bent down.

" Deb," he shouted, with his mouth close to her ear, his eyes holding hers, dominant, flashing blue fire; " Deb—when ? "

" You're hurting me, Stephen."

" Then, say ! "

" Oh, Stephen—and you said you were fond of me."

" I tell you it's *because* I'm fond of you." He spoke in a hard voice, holding her tighter. His logic seemed unanswerable to him. He was without Joe's dumb apology for the ways of nature. His arm never slackened, though the tune did. He had no idea where he was; he was so intent on his desire.

" Say when ! " he repeated.

" I dunna know what you mean."

" That's a lie ! "

He jumped from the roundabout before it stopped, and disappeared.

Deborah felt faint. She had no compass to help her in this extraordinarily stormy sea, and she was frightened.

Lily immediately alleged that she felt faint, too.

" Dear sakes, what a gawk I am ! " said Joe. " I'd never ought to have let you go on."

" By the faintness o' young women," said the roundabout proprietor with cameraderie, " the chapels is filled."

He nudged Joe in the ribs.

" Some folks have no manners," said Lily.

Lucy Thruckton gaped in happy bepuzzlement.

Lily was annoyed at her air of being above all these things, possessed of herself alone.

" Lucy," she asked sweetly, " should you like a lover ? "

" Aye."

" And a wedding ring ? "

" Aye."

" And a veil ? "

" Aye."

" And a cow to give you quarts and quarts of milk ? "

" Aye."

" And children to do the work for you ? "

105

" Aye."

" Well," said Lily, with a foxlike snap of her small teeth, " you won't never have none of them—so there, you fat thing ! "

Deborah sat drearily with Lucy, while Lily and Joe wandered about. At last she saw Stephen in the distance. He was coming towards her. Both his hands were full of roses—such roses as she had never possessed, for it was cold on the hills. He must have spent half a week's pay on them, she thought, horrified. He flung them—crimson, honey-coloured, pink—into her lap, and himself on the ground.

" I'm a beast," he said; " a frightful beast ! I won't do it again, Deb—I'll be a good boy."

He looked up with humility in his eyes.

She found the humility delicious.

" There, there ! " she said. " It's all right. Only do get up," she added, surveying him with almost jealous pride; " folks are staring."

He got up.

" And now," he said, selecting a fat, red rose and presenting it to Lucy with a kindly little smile, " here's one for Miss Thruckton."

He had noticed Lucy's clouded face; perceptiveness was one of his gifts. He could not bear that any one's joy should be dimmed. Joy was so fleeting, he felt, so easily missed, and night came down so fast on the fair.

They went home through the dusk. Before they reached the little wood, the sky was seeded over with dim stars like pearls. Stephen smoked, bit his pipe-stem, kicked at boulders and was silent. He had constituted himself the gaoler of his desires and he did not like the post. Deborah made little attempts at conversation; but they were both beyond such palliatives of a crisis. They had come

106

to the point where emotions are crude and huge—
like a naked land of beetling rock. They reached
the place of Deborah's morning promise. Joe and
Lily were ahead. Deborah looked up and smiled,
forgetting in her joy the pain that went with it.

" It's the secret cwm," she said, " where the arrow
was."

The smile, so sweetly lavish in the faint light, was
too much for Stephen. He caught her hands.

" I want that kiss."

" I'd liefer not."

" Well, of all the——! D'you love me ? "

" Aye, Stephen. I love you true."

" Well, then ! I kissed you in the little wood.
Didn't you like it ? "

" Not all that. It made me feel queer-like."

Stephen was exasperated.

" Look here," he said, " we'll have this out.   D'you
know what marriage means ? "

" I'd liefer not talk of such things yet."

" Oh ! Well, I choose to, so I shall. Do you know
what it means ? "

" Aye."

" Well, living with me will be the same."

" Aye."

" So if you can't even do with kissing——"

Deborah was in despair. She had her code, she
had summed up life; marriage and all its cares,
griefs and joys came into her sum of things. But
passion was new, terrible. She had not realized the
feelings involved in it. She had thought of herself
as a wife, with the same emotions, the same poise,
as she had in her maidenhood. To many women
marriage is only this. It is merely a physical change
impinging on their ordinary nature, leaving their
mentality untouched, their self-possession intact.
They are not burnt by even the red fire of physical
passion—far less by the white fire of love. For this

last Deborah was prepared; she had felt its touch
without shrinking. But when Stephen kissed her
in the wood, a new self awoke in her. She was
horrified; she needed time to fuse the two fires, to
realize that in unity they were both pure. She gazed
into the dusk with averted head. Stephen still
had her hands.

" How did you feel when I kissed you? "

" Canna we go on, Stephen? "

" Not till you say how you felt."

" Fainty-like."

" What else? "   The merciless catechism went on.

" And—as if I was—no better than I should
be," she whispered, too honest to prevaricate, too
genuinely simple to realize the provocativeness of
her words.

Stephen bit his lip.

" And yet you didn't like it? "

" No."

" Well, it's time you learnt to. So I'll take what
I've a right to."

She held herself stiffly under his kisses, then
drooped in spite of herself with the sweetness of
them.

" Now," he said, " you shall go on."

He walked with his arm round her.

" When can I come and fetch you? " he asked,
with the wooer's instinct to seize the moment of
weakness.

" Oh, Stephen, dunna ask me yet! leave me a
bit! "

" Why? "

" To get them used to it at whome—and to get
used to it for myself."

Suddenly indignation awoke in her. She disen-
gaged his arm and confronted him, dignified and
determined.

" If you dunna do as I ask—aye, do it quick and

108

eager—you dunna love me, Stephen. And if you dunna love me—beyond kissing and that—there's no right road for us but the parted road. I'll do without a ring and a bell, I'll bear with the black looks of all and the trouble of them at whome. Aye——" she gave a little sob—" I'll give up the name of wife for you, Stephen, if you say so. But——" a scarlet flush surged over her—" go to an unhallowed bed I won't. I'd liefer die. Love hallows all," she added softly—" the kind of love that gives, and asks nought."

Stephen looked at her ashamedly.

" But I can't give up—I can't go against nature," he said helplessly.

" I know you canna," said Deborah. She was slowly, but surely, attaining the new balance which she needed, the larger wisdom.

" I know you canna," she repeated. " I'm not the woman to wed a man that could. Only "—she sought about for an illustration—" only you'd ought to feel like mother and father feel to me, and like the flockmaster would feel to the lambs, as well as what you feel as my man."

Stpehen laughed to hide his awkwardness.

" A regular family party ! " he said.

Deborah frowned. Then she forgave his flippancy and smiled.

" Aye," she said. " And when you feel like all of them——"

" Well, what ? "

" I'll maybe give in about kissing."

" I feel like them all now," said Stephen, " and more."

" Then you'll do what I ask you," replied Deborah composedly, " and leave me be."

" All right. But I want my answer. When can I come and fetch you ? Will you tell me on Sunday, when we go to the Devil's Chair ? "

Deborah pondered.

" Aye," she promised.   " Come Sunday, I'll say."
They went on up the cwm, parting at the signpost.
The Devil's Chair loomed across the valley, blotting
Hesperus from the glimmering sky.

XIX

WHEN Deborah got home her father was lighting the lamp outside her door. In spite of Mrs. Arden's remonstrances he had always done this since Deborah fell down the sharply turned stairs as a child. Punctually, like a sunset bell or a watch light, it shone at nightfall; equally punctually Mrs. Arden's voice was vigorously raised about " spendthrift ways." The lamp comforted Deborah now.

She followed him about dumbly all the week, finding his calm strengthening.

" Deb's mased, I think," said Mrs. Arden to John. " She doesn't do a hand's turn for me. I shall give her a bit of my mind."

" Never cut love, mother," he replied, in his wistful way.

On Saturday night Deborah suggested that they should sing " Lead, Kindly Light ! " So she and John sang it in the scented night, while Mrs. Arden— who called it " that miserable, miauling thing," and disapproved of hymns on a weekday—washed up remonstratingly in the back kitchen.

" The light leads through queer ways, Deb, time and agen," said John; " bogs and suchlike. But it takes you somewhere at long last. It's no marsh-fire."

August had come on the land like a flame. Only primary colours were left. Day by day the Devil's

Chair shook in the heat haze as though it would fall. Opposite, by the Little Wood on the Wilderhope range, the shepherd's signpost, blistered in the sun, confronted it whitely. Between the ranges lay the valley, shadowed alternately by each. All round was the restless plain.

On Sunday Deborah had the basket packed, with matches for Stephen's pipe, when he came to the door.

" So you've come all the way only to go back to Lostwithin again ! " said Mrs. Arden.

" It's worth the walk." Stephen looked at Deborah —flushed and radiant.

" So you're off picnicking." John spoke meditatively. He never treated trifles lightly, because he saw their hidden meanings.

" A wild-goose chase I call it." Mrs. Arden surveyed them amusedly, but indulgently.

John looked steadfastly at Stephen.

" She's all we have now the lad's gone," he said.

Stephen fidgeted.

" Aye ! We miss the lad." Mrs. Arden shook her head as she packed the breakfast things on the tray. "He says to me, 'I'll be up every day, mother !' But I knew he never would. It's not in nature."

" Shall I carry that tray ? " asked Stephen; " it's heavy for you."

" I've carried more than that in my time, thank you all the same, lad, or where would your sweetheart be ? "

" Now, mother ! " John cautioned.

Stephen looked round to see if Deborah minded : but she was in the garden, leaning on the gate, gazing at the signpost far along the hill.

" Well, we'll be off now," said Stephen, taking

command with his usual decision. They started; John and Patty waved to them from the gate.

" Dunna be late," they called.

It was all unbearable to Deborah.

" Hark at the pigeons breaking their hearts in the wood," she sighed, as they descended into the valley. " How can I tell 'em at whome, Stephen? "

" Lord ! you'd think it was a black crime."

" So it be to mother. Maybe not so much to father. He sees out an' beyond things."

They walked apart. Stephen was genuinely repentant, ashamed of his new self. Deborah was withdrawn in the gloom of foreboding. He did not touch her; his look was comradely. They talked about trees and birds, and the changing seasons that she knew like a rosary. She became more at ease.

Stephen was a strange anomaly.

He was too perceptive for a ploughman, too vital for a gentleman. His mind was at present a confused mass of other people's principles, non-principles, creeds, negations : but beneath them lurked a poet.

They began to climb towards the Chair.

" Your old fellow's damned hard to get at, Deb ! " Stephen mopped his face.

He gave her his arm up the steepest part, and was immediately overwhelmed with longing to kiss her.

Deborah stopped.

" Can we go back, please, Stephen? I've ne'er been here afore, and I don't like it."

The Chair had begun to loom large on the sky.

" Rather not," said Stephen.

" Please ! " She was sweetly feminine in her manner of asking. She was one of the women who depend on their own charm and dignity for what they want from their men—not needing legislation. She was not often refused.

"All right. But I'm beastly disappointed."

Stephen turned round with depressed shoulders and a most forlorn expression.

Deborah felt selfish.

"We'll go on, if so be you want to," she said.

So on they went.

On the cold northern slopes round the Chair the heather was hardly in bud. Cranberry buds of most waxen whiteness hung against the rock like tears. Not a creature was visible. Stephen climbed out of the shadow beneath the throne on to its jagged masses, and called to Deborah to follow.

"Oh! No—no—no, Stephen."

"Don't be silly."

"It's black harm for us both."

"Now what harm can come to us, when we love each other so?"

His words dropped into the silence and were swallowed. In the intense quiescence of the place one might almost have imagined mockery.

"Now, Deb! See how good I've been! I've never once taken my rights as your lover."

"Rights?" said Deborah faintly. She had always belonged to herself completely, always been reserved, poised like a windhover. She looked up at him, standing on the top of the Chair with a kind of easy mastery about him. Was it a symbol? Could he shield her from harm, as he said? He was very strong. She supposed he could.

She climbed up; he stretched his hand out.

" Hold hard on to me," he said cheerfully, " and you'll be as right as right."

"I allus will," she answered.

The stone under his foot slipped, and he fell on to the flat rocks that made the seat of the chair. She

114

swayed, but recovered by loosing his hand. He laughed; but to her it was a portent, and she would stay there no more.

They wandered down the northward slope, where a row of blasted trees stood like a broken-toothed comb. Beneath them was a partially ruined cottage.

" We might live here if it was repaired," said he, delightedly, " as Lostwithin is only just down there— it would be nothing of a walk."

Deborah shuddered.

They had their meal, and lingered in the shade until a little breeze sprang up.

His mood had changed.

" May I put my arm round you, dear? " he asked.

" Aye."

" Do you like it there? "

She smiled.

" Maybe, Stephen."

" Very much? "

" Aye."

" Then may I kiss you? "

Deborah gave him her lips. He kissed her throat, pulling her blue bow aside.

" No," she said flatly.

" Only just under the bow ! "

" Not till we'm wed. Oh, dear ! I forgot."

She gazed at him in distress.

" We'll count that we're wed now, Deb."

" Oh, no ! things must be done decent."

She had an innate mistrust of the swift gratification of wishes.

" Well, I can't wait for ever, Deb ! "

He had quite forgotten that he had only known her for a fortnight.

" We must decide things, you know," he reasoned.

"Not yet awhile."

"Yes, to-night. On the way home."

"You're so hasty, Stephen."

"Well, would you be pleased if I wasn't? I shouldn't be if **you weren't so** pretty, Deb!" His arm tightened.

"No, Stephen."

"I'll be good all **the way** home, and talk about silly birds and things," he said, laughing.

"We'll go back now, then."

He strove very hard to come up to her demure standard all the way; but his eyes were so pleading, he helped her over stiles so carefully and brought her flowers with such a depressed look that she felt as if she had done wrong.

He was silent most of the way.

As they neared High Leasowes, he said—

"Well?"

"What?"

"When is it to be? When will you come?"

"I dunna know."

"I can't go on over yonder without you. I shall chuck it and come and live at Slepe."

"But you canna leave your work!"

"Oh, hang the work!"

"But look 'ee, Stephen! I've got to tell father and mother, and I dunna know how to."

"But as you must, it may as well be soon as late."

"Aye."

"Well then, when?"

They reached the door. Pinned to it was a paper. Written on this in Mrs. Arden's large hand was "Had a call to Black Cwm. Father will wait to bring me back in the morning. Go to Joe's if lonesome."

Deborah had a swift intuition. She snatched

116

the paper from the door, and crumpled it in her hand.

"I've seen it," said Stephen, "over your shoulder."

They looked at one another, while the light slipped from the valleys.

XX

" ARE you going to ask me to stay to supper, Deborah ? " he said steadily.

" If you've a mind to."

The surge of joy and foreboding in her heart nearly stifled her. She turned with relief to make up the fire and lay the table. He ran to-and-fro in his shirt-sleeves, fetching things for her. He brought coal and made his face black. Then his collar came undone.

" There ! " said he, " that's how I look at the mine."

She looked at him admiringly. How young he was to be a foreman ! How tall he was ! What a way he had with him !

They laughed about his black face.

" You can wash you in the back kitchen, while I go up and do my hair," she said. Half-way upstairs she stopped. There was the lamp, lit. It must have been lit hours ago, ready for her. It was like a glance from her father. And she had to tell him—! The price was too great, she felt. Yet how could she give Stephen up ? It never occurred to either of them that he might have sacrificed his principle—or whim. At present his opinions, though short-lived, possessed him entirely. It did not occur to him that Deborah was sacrificing all—he, nothing.

After supper they talked softly, he on the hearthrug at her feet.

" I'll get you a window-full of geraniums," he said, " for our cottage. And we'll have red tiles, like these, and a chiming clock, and a roaring fire."

Deborah forgot, in the warm picture, the darker side of her love-story.

" And an armchair for the maister," she said.

" Oh, you darling! But I shall want to sit at your feet."

" You'll soon tire o' that," said Deborah, amused.

It was strange to see him there, so bright and eager, when she was used to her father and mother and Joe, with their quiet ways and sober looks.

" I've got something for you," he said. He opened a little box, and there lay a ring.

" For me? "

" Yes, I didn't see why you shouldn't have your ring."

" But how did you get it? "

" Walked to Silverton."

" Walked all that waidy road? "

" Yes, for you. And now, when can I put it on? I shall make you a vow when I do."

" Oh, I dunna know."

The look she was beginning to know came into his face.

" Let it be here and now," he said.

" No, no."

" Deborah, I might die to-morrow. I might get crushed in the mine." He spoke without the least abatement of vitality.

" Oh, hush! " she moaned.

" And think how you'd feel."

" Don't 'ee! "

" Well, then "—it was the inevitable, unanswerable argument.

He took her hand, which hung limp by her side, and put the ring on her finger.

" Deborah Arden," he said, " with this ring I plight you my troth forever. I worship you body and soul. Amen. Now, Deborah, I shall consider you my wife."

119

The years to come, with their mighty, hollow thunder, beat upon Deborah's brain. The past, with its round completeness of kindly intercourse, rippled behind her like a lilied lake. Only the present she could not realize. He was the present. He was the future also—eternity. Should she grudge him a golden hour? She thrilled to feel his arm round her, hard as it had been at the Fair. What a man he was !— her man. What a lad !—hers.

The wind rose and fingered the windows, trying the door, feeling for a crevice.

" The time's so short for enjoying ourselves, Deb."

" I know it be."

The more she hesitated, the more unbearable he found any hesitation.

" You don't care about me a bit ! " he cried at last. " You don't know what love is. I'd better go."

" Maybe you better had," said Deborah sorrowfully. She went to the stairs door and opened it.

" Look at that lamp ! " she said. " Lit for me, nights—never a one missed for three-and-twenty years. And you say I dunna know what love is ! Can you say you've done as much for me ? "

" I will do as much—more."

" Maybe."

" Well, I must say ! " He was in a towering rage. The more he longed for Deborah, the more angry he became. He flung his coat on.

" Good-night ! " he said bitterly. " Now you can go to Joe's."

She suddenly had a vision of him lying somewhere at Lostwithin—silent, with shut eyes, never to ask her anything again. Suppose such a thing happened ! Such things did. There he was now—alive, loving her, wanting her—now, to-night. Any other night might be too late. She clung to the door. Her hands were cold, her lips dry. Life would be no good

to her without him. And here they were, warmly
shut in together from the world.

" It's as if it was to be," she thought. And now—
she was sending him away.

He turned at the gate with a tragic look.

" We might have been so happy ! " he said
accusingly.

She ran to the gate.

" Oh, come back ! " she cried, sobbing and pulling
his sleeve like a child ; " come back into the warm,
and don't 'ee talk in that awful way about dying."

She clung to his coat. It was the only way to
fight the horror that had come on her at his words.
She pulled him in and shut the door.

" And now," he said, smiling at her in complete
unconsciousness of the agony of mind he had given
her, " come and sit on my knee."

She sat on the arm of his chair.

" Why, Deb ! Your hand's trembling."

" Oh, no ! I'm never one to tremble," said Deb ;
" I can skim as clean as anybody."

" I'm a beast. Oh, Deb, forgive me ! But you're
always forgiving me," he added, hitting his forehead
with the unmerciful thoroughness of an actor—but
without affectation, for it was natural to him to make
his emotions pictorial.

" Of course I be," said Deborah.

His young self-absorption was pierced for a moment,
like thick woods by early sunlight. He looked up
at her solemnly.

" Deb ! " he said, and there was a kind of dull
terror in his voice—" Deb ! If ever you stop forgiving
me, I shall be done for. Never stop forgiving me,
Deb ! Stick to me, Deb ! "

He besought her like a child in the dark.

" I will that ! " said Deborah, with her warm,
maternal smile.

From without, somewhere on the empty table-land, came a long, shuddering cry; in its trembling ferocity it was like the curse of a hag.

"It's only the owls saying 'what ails you?'" said Deborah.

"I don't care about these old hills of yours as much as I did," he said uneasily; "you've got such dammed funny birds here."

But Deborah was still following her previous train of thought.

"I couldna stop forgiving of you," she said softly, "it's so mortal sweet—unless you stopped wanting me to."

"That I never shall," he answered with certainty, and nestled his head against her arm.

"You're tired," said Deborah.

"Oh, no! I'm never tired."

But his flush betrayed him.

"It's time you went to sleep," said Deborah, motherliness driving out all other feelings. Her tenderness, the vague, illimitable love in her—vague as rings in water, widening eternally—touched a chord in him that had never yet sounded. Within the rather tinny, meaningless music of his untried youth this hint of manhood struck out a presage of grandeur. It was Deborah's justification for her sacrifice.

He stood up, his arm among the brass candlesticks and pewter pots on the high mantelpiece.

"Deborah," he said, in a voice that enraged him by the way it went up and down. "Deborah! I'll sleep out in the shippen to-night. Rover and the cows are good enough company for me," he added, with a little forced laugh.

He turned impetuously to the door—dreadfully disappointed that he should feel so flat after doing so great a thing.

"Beastly stale," he cogitated, as he surveyed the

inside of the shippen with great disfavour; " beastly
stale doing the decent thing. Here! get out, you
old dunderhead!" he apostrophized Wimberry;
" put your fat self between me and the door, for the
Lord's sake—or out I shall go. Ouf! What a
stench! . . . And Deb never said a word!"

Deborah had not been able to say a word. She
had never seen him look so splendid. He seemed to
tower in the little place. It was her nature to see
the beloved's small, plain doings as noble. For her,
when Stephen was most mundane, a nimbus was
about his head. When he was angry—when he was
cold and selfish—still more in those mad moments
at the Fair and on the way home, when he was
masterful with a cruelty that was (though she would
not confess it) intoxicating as the first mad autumn
winds to her, at all these times she determinedly saw
in him only the greatness. Now in these few moments
there had really been only greatness. A profundity
she had not dreamed of, had not asked for, had shown
in him. It was like coming to a sudden splendid
valley, full of deep colours, after walking a bare hillside. Renunciation was to him like stopping a runaway cart downhill. She dimly felt that he was not
made for it. She rocked herself softly in the firelight.
" Glory and honour and power," she murmured.
" Aye! them's his by rights. And he does so mislike
the smell o' cows." She smiled at this in spite of
herself.
" And for me," she thought, " Deborah Arden of
the Upper Leasurs, with straight hair and no book-
learning, he's gone to the shippen along of the
cows."
She thought of a carol about " a kingly stranger "
and a stable. There seemed to her nothing incon-
gruous in associating him with it.
" And it inna as if he only wanted to stay along of
123

me *a bit*," she thought, with a lift of the head. " No ! He wanted to stay more than anything in the 'orld."

Colour surged over her. Her hand was on the little bow at her neck. " I wouldna let him touch it this afternoon," she murmured in a sudden confusion of pride and trembling. She hummed to herself the roundabout air—" Oh, where is my lad to-night ? "

A great rattling of cow-chains from the shippen set her smiling.

" There's allus summat doing where he be," she thought.

Then she went down, with John's little lamp in her hand, into the dark warm night, and stood within the shippen door.

" If so be you're tired of Rover and the cows," she said with a touch of dignity, " you're very kindly welcome—to bide wi' me."

XXI

THE hours flitted over the grey cottage and the shadowy hills—silent as the bats that hung at dawn from the beams of the shippen. Out of the east, from beyond the signpost, came day like an iridescent dove. Out of the west came storm like a hawk. Just at dawn the storm broke over the Chair and swooped across the valley, lashing the cottage.

"Gi' me a bit of comfort, Stephen," whispered Deborah.

"Aren't you happy, my little love?"

"Aye. But them that's happy wants comfort most. Them that's got nought canna lose it."

"I know, Deb."

It was his own intolerable nightmare now, this mist that might come across the flowery way at any moment, with its impalpable, inevitable "no more."

"Tired?" he asked anxiously, as Joe had asked Lily. For to the comely and the awkward, the poet and the plodder, come the same unheralded majesty and frenzy, the same sweet backwash of tenderness and penitence. And Deborah replied as Lily had, as women in the primæval forest replied, with a weary, ecstatic, bewildering smile. Only her smile was to Lily's what hill breezes are to the spent air of the plain.

"And you have to go to work through this!" she said later.

She was making him some tea. When he went away he turned up his collar and faced the storm joyously.

"This evening," he called, "I'll come and help in the telling."

He squared his shoulders and tramped on, singing every song he knew, accompanied by a rush of wings that rose up before his coming and fled through the rain on either side with flapping and whirring and the long-drawn query of plovers.

He passed close to the Devil's Chair, entering the cloud that was round it, close and clammy. From near by a covey of grouse rose with their quacking laugh.

"Damn those birds!" he said, feeling hemmed in and pursued by something invisible.

He began to run, silent and shivering, down the northerly slope to Lostwithin.

At ten Mrs. Arden got home.

"Well, Deb!" she called, with her usual assumption that the world waited for her news with bated breath; "both doing grand, and all over nicely afore the doctor came."

She sat down beaming by the kitchen fire.

"Bless the girl! No more notice took than if I said ''tis raining!' It's high time, Deb Arden," she sent her voice into the recesses of the back kitchen, "it's high time you gave over thinking there's nought in the 'orld but flowers and birds and such. It's time you was serious like Joe's Lily, and saw as there's only three things as matters to a good 'ooman —the bride-bed, the child-bed and the death-bed."

Deborah went silently to her room and drew out from under her pillow a pearl ring. "Pearls for tears," she said. Then she stroked the pillow. She was one of the women who see on to the end of things, to whom the commonplace is transparent as glass— revealing the interior of life. She saw, with a vividness that would have surprised her mother, the philo-

126

sophy of her last sentence. On her pillow she saw the shifting shadows of the future; round her little bed she heard the years rustle like falling leaves. It was no longer a mere part of her furniture; it was an apocalypse of love. The night just gone had set about it an immortal radiance for her. She shut her eyes and saw a day to come when a pillow should be pressed by a small head beside hers. She saw further—saw her own face quiet on the hard pillow of death.

" I be ready, Stephen," she whispered; " ready for all. I'll go with you gladsome in wet weather or in shiny; and lie quiet in the daisies knowing we loved true."

" Deborah ! " came Mrs. Arden's voice.
She went down.
" What an old fire ! It must have been alight hours, Deb. Whatever for ? "
" I thought to set the bread to rise."
" That's a good girl. Has it ris ? "
" I forgot it after all, mother."
John came in, shaking the rain from his coat.
" There must have been a gad-fly in the shippen last night," he said, " for the mingicumumbus the cows have got the straw in is a disgrace to any cow."

The day dragged on for Deborah, while her mother lay down in her room and John chopped wood outside. The rain was a steel wall between her and Stephen. Would he come this evening ? Surely not, through this. Surely yes !
In the bleakness of absence one rapture filled her— she had done all she could for him. Nothing could take that away. She had loved him, given him of her best. So the ultimate bitterness of parting was not hers; she had the peace of those who know, when the beloved is gone, that they spent themselves and

127

crumbled the stuff of their being for him while he was there.

All Stephen's sweet words, his stormy kisses, the pride of her womanhood in being desired so much by such a man—desired so that he forgot to consider her, she reflected triumphantly—these things were small beside the fact that she had made him happy. She had stood in the immortal company of those that have it in their power to give joy and do not miss their chance, crowning the beloved early with untarnished gold and morning flowers.

" What else matters ? " she thought.

XXII

THEY were sitting over tea in the fresh evening, when a shadow fell across the floor and Stephen stood on the threshold.

" Well, Stephen," said John; " a cup of tea ? "

" I will, thanks, Mr. Arden, for I didn't wait for any after work."

Mrs. Arden became conscious of " summat in the air." A man did not go without his tea for nothing.

Deborah looked imploringly at Stephen.

" You begin," she said.

" Mr. and Mrs. Arden," said Stephen impetuously, " I've come to ask for Deborah. Only we don't want to be married, because "—the objection seemed rather foolish when John was looking at him so earnestly; he therefore emphasized it more—" because I don't approve of it."

" You bad, wicked, ne'er-do-weel of a fellow ! " cried Mrs. Arden, in a rush of fury—" to try and take my girl's good name off her ! "

And she boxed his ears.

John, for all his trouble, smiled. Deborah was frozen with wrath and distress.

" Mother," said John, " be silent ! Leave the lad to say his say. Now, Stephen."

Stephen had remained commendably self-possessed, though flushed.

" Mr. Arden," he said, " though we shan't be married, I swear to you that it will be just the same."

John was gazing away through the window to the

129

far distance beyond it, into things that are not of this world.

"I love her," said Stephen impulsively, "with my whole soul——"

John looked at him.

"And body——"

Mrs. Arden blinked interestedly.

"And I will love her till death."

Deborah's eyes had never left him.

Feeling them all so focussed on him, he was embarrassed. He clinched the matter.

"I love her better than myself," he finished.

"Well, then, you're different from most of 'em," Mrs. Arden burst out, "or where'd the chillun be?"

Stephen frowned.

"Mother!" said John sternly, "this is not a time for such talk. Deborah, what do you say to this?"

"I say as I love him and I'll follow him through the 'orld."

"Not without a ring, Deb?" cried Mrs. Arden, horrified. "A ring hallows all. Not without the ring and the bell and the register, Deborah! Not while I live!"

"Mother!" said John, in mild rebuke. "Well, Deb?"

"Whatever Stephen do say."

"And you'll give all for nought?" cried Mrs. Arden.

"He's chosen me out of the 'orld," said Deborah, with pride. "Nought else matters."

Stephen looked at her. Mrs. Arden intercepted the look and at once became preternaturally silent.

"Father," she said afterwards, "it's no manner of use. She's his'n."

"So long as we're all in all to each other, it's just the same," said Stephen.

"So long," John assented.

130

Stephen disliked his look of kindly pity more than Mrs. Arden's scolding.

" Marriage makes things no better, if you're sick of each other," he continued.

" Never a bit."

" Well, then, Mr. Arden——"

" But," queried John, with his straight, keen glance, " are you sure you're man enough to keep a woman safe, Stephen, my lad? It's a long road and a winding, and she'll be footsore, time and agen."

John was thinking of the lambs he carried—four or five sometimes, when they went long journeys—with their small, palpitating bodies and their pathetic eyes.

" Are you man enough to carry her, though you'm weary, Stephen, and tramp on, though all the powers of darkness be agen you, and smile at her still, when you're nigh done yourself? Think, lad! "

" I am," replied Stephen, without a moment's hesitation.

" Think what you could give up for her, Stephen."

" Everything."

" Health and happiness? "

" Yes—but there's no need."

" Your longing after her? "

" Of course not. I love her too much."

John smiled sadly.

" Your principles, Stephen? " He said it with a kind of forlorn humour. " Your principles about not marrying, eh? "

" No. I mean yes—if she asked it."

" She never will," said John. He turned to Deborah. " Well, may God be with you and light your candle, Deborah, my child—this night and all."

It almost seemed as if he fell back upon God to light it now that he could no longer do so himself. It was his silent comment upon Stephen.

" And when did you think of—going ? " he asked Deborah.

She looked at Stephen.

" I've got a cottage," he said. " The one by the Chair—there's no other empty. The landlord's begun the repairs to-day. He seemed pleased to let it—and surprised. It'll be ready next week, Deborah—when will you come ? "

" When you come for me, Stephen."

" Well," Mrs. Arden broke out, tried beyond bearing; " a more miserable business I never see ! No jokes, no walking out, no asking in church, no best dress, no party, no wedding, no cooking till you'm all in a sweat, no nothing ! " She threw her apron over her head, and cried loudly.

" And what poor Joe 'll think, and what he'll say, and what he'll do, and what Lily 'll say, and all their chillun, when they come (as they will, right as right, in spite of what I overheard unwilling and not eavesdropping at all), I'm sure I dunna know ! " she cried in crescendo.

" What Joe and Joe's great-grandchildren will think," said John, with a wry smile, " is one of the great quantity of things that dunna matter, mother."

XXIII

STEPHEN slaved at the cottage, as Joe had slaved at his. He was in a frenzy of eagerness, tenderness. Beneath other emotions was the flame of desire which burns all obstacles from a young man's path and takes him and the woman he loves for its fuel—licking up in its course tears and pity and fulfilling the unseen purposes of God.

Deborah and Lily—different as they were—both looked for it in their lover's eyes; wept when they found it; treasured it beyond the joys of heaven. This kinship just at first was stronger even than Lily's sense of superiority and respectability. Though she had a good deal to say when Joe told her the news, when she saw Deborah she made a great effort and was silent. She had only been married a week, and she was still primæval, as a bride is once, a great woman always.

She and Joe had come up to tea on Sunday, the day before Deborah's departure.

" Well, Joe, lad ! " said his mother; " you'm twice the man you was."

She looked at Lily with approval, seeing that the measure of Joe's well-being was also the measure of Lily's lassitude. She saw a new, minute line on Lily's forehead, and, as her manner was, to show her sympathy for Lily, she rated Joe.

" What's the good of standing there, grinning like a turmit-lantern ? " she cried, " when you ought to be down on your bended knees, thanking me and

K

Lily for making you what you are—not as you're much at the best of times ! " she added, with intense pride in her eyes. " You seem to think," she continued, glad to find an outlet for her anger against the absent Stephen, " you seem to think, as you stand there with your long, useless legs and your twelve stone six of do-naught, as you made the 'orld and all in it in seven days, like the Lord Almighty. Instead of which there you lay in that wold cradle, no bigger than the dolly in the tub, and if it hadna been for me, where'd you have been ? And now it's not enough but Lily must give up her days to feeding of you, and her nights of nice sleep as well. I'm ashamed of you, Joe Arden ! "

" Well, mother," said Joe, with a slow smile, when the storm abated; " it do sound awful, I know. I'm fair ashamed to be that sort of chap. But I didna make things how they be, and there it is."

John came in with his brushing hook and hedging gloves.

" Goodness me, mother, what a craking you do keep up ! " he said; " like a bird-frightener and a dozen of corncrakes all at once. I could hear you in the far leasowes."

Mrs. Arden was still indignant at his command of silence with regard to Deborah's concerns.

" If you listened to my craking a bit more than you do, John, it'd be better for us all," she said. " Lily, you go up and lie down a while, and Deb'll come and have a chat."

Deborah and Lily gazed out of the window. There was a new freemasonry between them.

" Who's been dropping a tie-clip under your chessun drawers, Deborah ? " asked Lily. " Joe's got his'n. I'd put it away, if I was you."

" I didna know it was there, Lil."

" Where be all your pride now, Deb Arden, and your high and mighty ways to me about my bits of
134

carrying on? But there—I won't go on at you. Can
I lie on your bed? D'you mind how we knocked
about, them nights last week, Deb? My! what a
time ago! It's to-morrow you go, inna it?"

"Aye."

"Make the most of to-night, then," said Lily.

There was so much wistfulness mixed with Deborah's
confusion that Lily heroically reserved all her criticism
for a future time.

"Joe's in an awful taking about it," she confided
to Deborah. "He says he'll give Stephen one for
himself, when he sees him. I'd warn Stephen."

"Oh, he won't be afeard."

"Joe's awful strong."

"But Stephen's bigger."

"I never did admire them lamp-post fellows."

Mrs. Arden came in.

"Tea's ready," she said, "and father and me want
you to open your present, Deb."

Downstairs was a large box, containing a tea-set.

Beside it, with—"From Father"—very firmly
written on its white paper, was a large brass lamp
with a rose-coloured shade.

Tea was a somewhat strained meal, Joe being sullen.
Finally he burst out—

"Well, Deb, I didna think you'd do such a thing.
All the fellows are grinning behind my back—wish I
met catch 'em at it. You needna bring the chap to
my house."

"Joe, Joe!" said his father; "never cut love,
lad!"

"You're welcome to bring him to *my* house,
Deb," said Lily.

Joe was much put out, and muttered, "I shall
have a few words to say to you, by and by."

"You can say 'em and welcome!" Lily replied
pertly, for it was a long time before they would go
home, and she lived for the present. "You can say

135

'em and welcome, so long's you dunna say 'em with your mouth full."

" I'm glad you've met your match, Joe," Mrs. Arden said, when the laughter subsided.

Joe good-humouredly passed his cup for more tea, for Lily's laughter rang little bells in his heart.

Deborah looked round them all wistfully. They seemed too small and bounded for her needs.

" Father, can I look the sheep along of you ? " she asked.

" Surely you can, my dear."

They went out into the cool colours of evening.

" There's a sheep gone astray over yonder," Deborah said absently; " hark at her crying."

She was not thinking of the sheep, but of the ridge on the west, where Stephen was making ready for her.

" Aye, Deb," said her father, answering her thought and not her words; " he'll be putting a tuthree last touches now, no danger, so as to come for you bright and early."

" Thank you kindly for the lamp, father," she said, " and for all."

" It's nought, it's nought, my dear."

From the house Lily's voice rang out in " The Golden Arrow," with Joe's bass, humming like a huge bee, and Mrs. Arden's cracked but enthusiastic treble.

Deborah and John looked at each other with the wordless glance that defies fate.

Above them in the invisible heather the top of the signpost caught a last sunray.

XXIV

THERE was no room for grief in Deborah's heart
next morning. The first mad gale of early autumn
set the ponies galloping over the hill-tops; the sky
was like a garden of lilies and delphiniums; she knew
that Stephen was coming to her with long strides—
coming to fetch her, to rule her days, to depend on
her for his comforts, to kiss her again.

"Here he comes," said John, who had been staring
mournfully out of the window since he got up hours
ago.

Stephen kicked the wicket open.

"A grand day, Mr. Arden! I say, may I call you
father now?"

"Aye, lad."

Patty heard him.

"I'd liefer you called *me* by my marriage name,
seeing as I'm no relation—not so much as mother-
in-law—on account of stuff and nonsense in folks'
brains, that stops 'em being married right and
proper." She nodded with *staccato* emphasis.

"Right you are!" said he affably.

"What about Deborah's things? Shall I bring
them with Whitefoot?" John asked, wistfully aware
that Stephen was now the first authority for the
disposal of Deborah's things.

"Oh, I can carry them," said Stephen, and shoul-
dered the box.

"But you'll come with Whitefoot, and bring me
the lamp and the tea-set, father, wunna you?" said
Deborah. "To-night?"

"Not to-night," John answered, to Stephen's relief; "mayhappen to-morrow."

"Come and send us, father!" said Deborah.

"Just a few steps, then."

At the last gate of his sheepwalk he stopped.

"Well, well—you'll be wanting to get along home and make her a dish of tea, Stephen."

With this long-planned hint he turned homewards.

When he got in, Patty was rocking to and fro, wailing, with her apron over her head.

"Why, mother, whatever's took you?"

"It's the chillun," cried Mrs. Arden. "I'd never gid 'em a thought before, poor mites. The chillun, the poor little things as'll be baseborn!" she sobbed.

"Mercy me, mother! I never thought of that. I was so busy thinking of our Deb. What a fool I be!"

"You be, John."

"What'll we do, mother?"

"Do? Why, make him marry her, of course."

"How?"

"A word here and a word there, and a good yammering time and agen, and Lil and Joe can say summat, and you can put in a word, solemn-like. And Eli!" She suddenly had an inspiration. "Aye, Eli! Let Eli go along and mouth his old tex's—maybe they'll do some good for once."

"But Stephen'll be neither to hold nor to bind, and that'll vex Deb."

"Well, and ain't that better than the other thing? The lot of a love-child inna roses."

John pondered. He could not see his way at all clearly.

"Well," he said at last, "it's more in your line than mine, mother. You'd best go about it as you think right and proper."

"There's a sensible man!"

Stephen and Deborah went through the deep lanes, where the air was heavy with meadow-sweet, breast high in the ditches, curd-white, like garlands for an elfin bridal. In a little spinney Stephen paused.

" Come, I must kiss you."

They lingered a long while.

At last she said, " Shan't we be getting on, Stephen? I'm fair longing to see the cottage."

" Yes, yes! I can kiss you then as much as I like. Come on! "

He went so fast that she was almost running.

" Oh, stop, Stephen—please! "

" Come on! " he cried. " I'll help you."

He pulled her up the hill by her wrist till it ached; then flung his arm round her waist at the top, and ran down the slope.

She laughed.

" Oh, Stephen, you *be* hurryful! "

They came to the cottage, standing wide-eyed, facing the Devil's Chair. The dark paint over the upper windows was like raised eyebrows. Over the lower windows and the door he had painted a broad red band, barred with white—" To liven it up," he said. No other cottage was in sight.

Stephen set the box down. It had bruised his shoulder, but he was unaware of the fact.

" Now then, Deb! Here's the garden. I planted all those things. Here's the kitchen."

" Eh, how nice! "

She wanted to examine everything, but he hurried on.

" Here's the parlour."

" Oh, Stephen! How pretty! And is that your harmonium? "

" Yes—for you to learn to play. Come on—upstairs now. Here's our room."

Deborah stood mute—so beautiful it seemed to her.

The walls were pink; in the window stood a geranium; on the bed was a rose-patterned counterpane.

" And you've thought of it all and done it all in these few days—I canna think how ! "

" No sleep ! " he said, with satisfaction at the effect of his words.

" You mun sleep well to-night," she said, in a maternal way.

" We, Deborah."

" We."

" This may as well be supper," he said, as they sat at tea in the parlour. " Gracious me, if she hasn't got that aggravating bow on again ! "

He pulled it off.

" I be so untidy without it, Stephen."

" Who cares ? "

" Oh, Stephen—dunna pull my hair down ! I did it so careful. Eh, dear ! some one's sure to come."

" Never a soul ! "

They pondered on that.

" Stephen ! "

" Well ? "

" I canna sit in the window like this."

" You can if I say so."

" I'm going to tidy me."

" Right ! " said Stephen unexpectedly.

" And, Stephen——"

" What ? "

" I'm so awful tired with the walk, and—last Sunday——"

" Well ? "

" And I was wondering——"

" Well, what a time you take ! "

" If you'd do summat for me, seeing as I came out to the shippen for you."

" Out with it, then ! "

140

Stephen spoke irritably. He was tired, excited, on
fire, and Deborah seemed so unimpassioned.

" Oh, I'll tell you after," she said, surprised at her
own temerity and suddenly terrified at the knowledge
that her whole life was irremediably his.

" All right—go on then, and I'll lock up."

" It's not but half-past seven yet ! I was only
going to tidy me."

" Well, you needn't bother to."

" But I want to wash up."

" I don't."

She was dismayed at his curtness. She heard him
fastening the door.

" Locked in wi' love ! " she whispered. Suddenly,
in the midst of all her joy, she began to cry. She was
very tired. She had been too excited to eat, and the
parting with her father had worn her.

" What in hell's the matter now ? " asked Stephen,
coming in. He spoke with the entire lack of sentiment
that passion brings.

" Oh, Stephen, I'm so tired."

" So am I," he said, seeing whither her pleading
tended.

" I lost a lot of sleep last week."

" So did I."

" Oh, canna you see, Stephen ? "

" See what ? "

" What I'm asking."

He flew into a rage.

" I suppose you want me to go out to the
shippen again. A fine sort of bride you are ! I love
you a great deal too much to do anything of the
kind."

She accepted this without comment.

" Dunna hold me so tight, Stephen, please ! I
canna get my breath."

" I can't help that."

" Your arm's so hard."

141

She had said this before; she tried to remember when. Suddenly it came to her, and with it came the vision of Stephen's face at the Fair, perfectly hard, his eyes looking into hers as they were now.

" I suppose he'll be sorry to-morrow," she thought, " and bring me flowers, like then."

She gasped for breath.

" Oh, Stephen ! "

He kissed her on the mouth, effectually stopping speech and breath. He took no notice of her pallor.

At last she fainted.

When she came round, he was bathing her face miserably, cursing himself under his breath. She smiled at him.

" Don't, Deb ! "

" What ? "

" Don't smile at me ! "

He was inconsolable. He would not share the unthinkably black tea that he made her. He stormed at himself, tramping the room.

" I'm not fit — your father was right — I'm a brute."

Now that his arm was not round her, Deborah forgot everything but pride that he loved her.

" I'd not have you different," she said.

" Don't, Deb ! I shall be the same again ! I can't stay in. I'll go for a walk in the dark."

" Dunna go ! "

A flicker of laughter came into her eyes.

" Pick up my things, do ! " she said.

Her hat, coat and bow, which he had flung on the floor, were reduced to a crushed and trampled ruin.

" I'll get you some more, Deb. I'll walk to Silverton and buy them. I won't get any baccy for six months, and then I shan't have wasted any money," he added, with ferocity towards himself. " Now, Deb—finish your tea ! Back soon."

142

" Where be you going? "

" I don't know."

The old restlessness was in his voice.

" Bain't you tired? "

" No." '

" But, Stephen——"

She looked round the room.

" It be your room as well as mine."

" I don't deserve to share it."

" There—there ! "

" I never listened to you."

" Ne'er mind."

A sound outside arrested them. It grew on the air like an incoming tide. It was under their window. He looked out.

" It's a lot of sheep," he said, " coming from by the Devil's Chair, running away from something. They've gone down the hill now, into the mist."

" It's from the Chair as they're running. Folk say they're often like that."

" What rot ! "

He had forgotten his penitence.

In the morning, Deborah was too tired to get up. Stephen had gone before she woke. She lay watching the Chair all day while he was at work. She looked at the white clouds drifting behind it, driven on to vague destinies. She thought of the sheep last night, driven by vague terror. She thought of herself—weary, beseeching the man she loved for rest and being unheard. She felt like the clouds—the sheep.

" Having no shepherded," she murmured.

A picture rose before her of the white signpost and her father—very careful, very absorbed—carrying a newborn lamb and encouraging the mother to follow. She fell asleep and dreamt that it was Stephen and not her father who carried the lamb.

She awoke to hear Stephen calling her. He was in a quiet mood, feeling the reaction from yesterday. They strolled on the hill after tea in the clear blue air of a stainless evening. Afterwards she had her first lesson on the harmonium.

XXV

" Now then ! Work the pedals, pull out a stop, press the notes and then play."

Deborah was in despair. She did not even know what stops were, and did not like to ask.

" Oh, there's some one at the door ! " She got up with relief, and went to open it.

" Behold, I stand at the door and knock ! " said Eli—quite unconscious of any blasphemy.

" It's Eli," said Deborah, pale with fear.

" When you've enjoyed your new character as much as you want to," sang out Stephen, in great spirits, " walk in, old party ! "

Eli came in.

" Thou art the man ! " said he.

Stephen was amused.

" The woman has tempted thee," he went on. " Flee from this place !

" Not much ! Have some wedding cake ? "

Stephen spoke with irritating pleasantness.

" I will neither eat bread nor drink wine until I have turned the hearts of this people."

" Your loss ! " Stephen retorted.

Eli was annoyed. Religion was his hobby, and he was much in earnest about it. He was accustomed to see people quail before his utterances. Deborah did quail, as he was pleasurably aware. Not so Stephen.

He surveyed Stephen, half in and half out of the only easy chair, looking particularly lithe and pleasant in his working corduroys and blue shirt with the sleeves rolled up. His air of youth and well-being made Eli very wrathful. He detested youth.

He began to speak in a creaking, lugubrious tone. Stephen lit a pipe.

"When them there bones o' yours be layin' in the soggin' wet ground——"

Deborah moaned.

"You'd be the death of any religion," Stephen remarked.

"And them two eyes with pennies on 'em——"

"Here, dry up!"

Stephen was angry.

"And nought but a poor, white skellington left——"

"Drop it!" shouted Stephen furiously.

Eli saw that he must change his course or go. He did not want to go yet.

"How is the faithful city become a harlot!" he cried. "Deborah Arden, I proclaim you before this man, and will proclaim you in the parishes of Lostwithin, Slepe and Bitterley, unless you get in my trap and come whome with me, weeping and gnashing your teeth——"

Stephen laughed. This enraged Eli.

"I will proclaim you," he said, "with your slow smile and your brazen ways and your body as is giv' to lust—I will proclaim you a whore."

No sooner had he said the last word than his mouth was full of blood. Deborah caught Stephen's hand as it descended for the second time.

"Oh, no!" she cried; "no, Stephen! He's an old man."

Eli blinked malignly, standing his ground. He raised his hand.

"By Jehovah, in whom is justice and no mercy, I curse you both, root and branch, in your lying down and your rising up, and——"

His mouth was becoming extremely painful and was swelling.

"May you burn everlastingly! Whoso sinneth against the Lord——"

He spoke with one side of his mouth.

"Dunna laugh at him, Stephen!" Deborah whispered. "It only makes him worse."

"Whoso sinneth against the Lord, let him be utterly cast down!"

It did not occur to Eli that he might be sinning against Love himself. But Deborah, remembering it all afterwards, thought that he had been taken at his word.

"Here, I say, get out, you old gramophone!" cried Stephen, and he pushed Eli down the step.

Eli had never been so angry. He had never yet been laughed at. He stood up in the trap and hurled his Bible, which he had brought in order to read texts to the weeping couple (he had not a doubt that they would weep) straight at the window. The glass cracked from side to side.

"Oh, it's a token!" wailed Deborah.

Stephen flung himself at the gig, but Eli howled and flogged his horse, old Speedwell, until she broke into an unwilling gallop. He drove like a fiend— up hill, down hill, shouting texts, cursing, jerking at the reins and always flogging.

People stood at their doors and watched him, appalled.

He came through Slepe. Lily was leaning on the gate, and he lashed at her with his whip.

"Whose rick's afire?" Joe asked, coming to the door.

"It's father, drunk or crazy—lashed me across the face."

"I'll round up no more blasted sheep for him," said Joe.

Eli felt that every one was against him. There

was his housekeeper—insisting on three good meals a day and beer. Beer! He was an abstainer himself; it was so economical. And she wouldn't get up before five or stay up after eleven. Six hours' sleep out of his day! And Lily sitting there as pert as could be! And that Deborah! When he thought of Stephen, he became a murderer in everything but fact. His mouth was hurting him abominably. The more it hurt, the more he lashed.

Speedwell shuddered so that the trap shook as she went up the last hill. When they reached the yard she fell down in the shafts.

" You've murdered your only friend!" said the housekeeper; " aye, she's met her fatal."

He came to himself. He reeled. Blood ran down his chin: he took no notice, but bent over the horse. They had gone to market together, to the fairs, to lug turnips, to carry hay, all Speedwell's life—and she was old. She had taken his curses as none else did, listened to his texts, pricked her ears when he declaimed his next Sunday's address on the way to town. The cattle and sheep, the dogs, came and went: Speedwell stayed. His wife died—well, no matter. She had been a great expense: Speedwell could exist in the poorest field. Lily left him— he was relieved. He did not like Lily—she was so young: Speedwell was old and ill-favoured. When people gave back his vituperations or would not listen to him, and he needed sympathy, he would say to himself, " Me and Speed 'll dunna hold with such ways." When he had failed to think of a lacerating remark at the right moment, he made it to Speedwell, and felt that her " roaring " was sympathetic. She was worth nothing, so he felt her to be a permanence on the farm. She was without any desire to amuse herself—this pleased him. All these things, gradually accumulating in his mind, had built up a regard for her, a unity of idea, a thing which stood in him for

148

love—though others would have hardly called it so. And now she lay in a heap in the yard, and her eyes accused him. He ran for water, but she would not drink. With the generosity of the tragic moment which is too late, he brought out corn from the bin—corn that she had sniffed afar all her life and never had. She could not eat it.

" There ! " said the housekeeper, with an eye to herself; " that comes of starving folk; they get as they canna eat, not if it's ever so."

" 'Oman ! " shouted Eli in a terrific voice, " fetch that there brandy as you keep in your bedroom and drink be stealth."

But when the brandy came, he could not make Speedwell take any. She desired peace, and having done her long day's work, she took it. When Eli saw that nothing availed, he flung himself down beside her, and wept. The housekeeper was so terrified at this that she took her most valuable possessions and ran for the nearest village, never looking back.

Eli tried to pray : but he had prayed for so many things that he did not want, that he felt prayer to be too offhand a thing for real need. He lay there in the dark, and the old mare slept away her last hours. A thought occurred to Eli. John was a great hand with animals : John might get her to take something. But no !—not John : he was so poor-spirited, and such a bad business man, and Eli had sneered so often at his kindness to animals. But then— ? There was no vet. anywhere within ten miles. Speedwell groaned. He rose, hesitating no more, and began to run over the rough hill in the dark toward Upper Leasowes. His face was very swollen, and he felt giddy. He caught his feet continually in rabbit-holes. He clasped his head in both hands, because it ached, and ran on—a small, toiling figure in the vast night. Tears trickled

L

down his cheeks; the sweat poured off him; he gasped for breath. At last he could run no more; he walked; then he crawled. Finally he reached John's in a state of collapse. All the time, back in the yard at Bitterley, Speedwell was dead.

He knocked.

"Whatever's the matter?" called Mrs. Arden. "Is that you, Eli? Dunna come here at this time o' night with your texes and your hell-fire, for goodness' sake!"

"John!" said Eli faintly.

In the croak John recognised the same cry that he heard in the lamb's bleat, the young bird's chirp. He had never heard it from Eli before. He went out.

"Speedwell!" gasped Eli, in a heap on the step. "Her means dying. Come over and help us."

John gave him an arm back over the hill, and—when they found all over—strove to comfort him. But he would not be comforted.

"Out of my sight!" he said. "Leave me and my sin to the hand of the Lord, and let Him deal with me as He thinks well."

He went in and shut the door.

XXVI

THE markets at Silverton round about Lammastide are great days. Then you may see faces that you never see for the rest of the year—faces with quietness on them like a veil. To go into the market is to step back into multi-coloured antiquity with its system of the exchange of necessaries, and the beauty of its common transactions.

Fruit from deep orchards by lost lanes, from the remote hills; flowers from gardens far from any high-road; treasures of the wild in generous baskets— all these are piled in artless confusion in the dim and dusty place.

The Saturday after Deborah's departure to Lost-within was the great wimberry market. The berries were brought in hampers that needed two men to lift them, and the purple juice dripped from them as in a wine-vat. Other fruit lay in huge masses of purple, gold and crimson. The air was full of its aroma. There were cheeses from dairies beside the great meres, that joined their waters across the fertile fields when the snows melted. There were white frilled mushrooms from pastures where the owl and the weasel lived undisturbed. These were gathered in the morning dusk, when dew made the fields like ponds, by barefooted young women with petticoats pinned above their knees—a practice that caused many a detour of young farm hands on the way to work. There were generous, roughly cut slabs of honeycomb from a strain of bees that were in these parts when Glendower came by. There were ducks with sage under their wings as a lady carries an umbrella. One stall was full of sprigged sunbonnets, made after a pattern learnt in childhood by the old ladies that sold them.

These simple things, all recklessly cheap, gave to their sellers something of the large dignity of Nature herself—who gives in full measure out of unfailing storehouses. Beauty was everywhere, except in the meat market. There slow bluebottles, swollen and unwholesome, crawled and buzzed; men of a like complexion shouted stertorously, brandishing stained carving-knives; an unbearable stench arose from the offal, and women with pretty clothes and refined manners bought the guts of animals under such names as " sweetbreads " or " prime fat kidneys," and thrust their hands into the disembowelled bodies of rabbits to test their freshness.

John was taking some wool to the stapler and a calf to the auction. Joe had some bullocks to look at for Mr. Shakeshaft, and Lily had offered to sell wimberries for a neighbour in order to go to town. She pinned some honeysuckle in her dress, and tied a pink ribbon round her hat. She would have other admiration than Joe's to-day. Joe was nice, of course; but he was not eloquent. She sat between the two men, who bulged over the sides of the cart like half-grown swallows from their nest. When Joe swayed the others did too.

" You're crushing my dress, Joe."

" Well, ain't that what it's for ? " A large hand crept round her waist. She was busy making calculations about a lace collar she coveted. She must have it, but she had no money. They jogged on. The calf, looking in its sack like a baby in a headwrapper, lifted its red and white face and gave a prolonged moo. Then, having made its protest against things in general, it nestled into the sack of wool and went to sleep.

"You met help me along with the calf, Joe, if Lil can manage the berries."

Lily was delighted. She set out her goods with a consciousness that her hair was as bright as her bunch of yellow lilies.

The youths of Silverton were alive to their opportunities.

"Hullo, Gertie !" "Morning, Miss !" they called. She sold all her flowers as buttonholes.

She still had the berries to sell.

"Bother Joe, being so long," she thought, for she wanted a cup of tea.

But Joe had not been long. He was standing just inside the door of the market, watching her with enormous pride—delighted to see her admired. When he heard her chaffing them, he slapped his leg delightedly, till a butcher, who was pounding steak, said—

"If you *must* pun meat, pun mine !"

A wholesale fruit-dealer, with a roving eye for a pretty girl, and an hour to wait for his train, came up to Lily.

"Five shilling for that lot and a kiss, miss—and a cup of tea thrown in."

Lily wavered. To get rid of the wimberries and have a cup of tea was a pleasant prospect. "What's a kiss ?" she thought.

"A' right," she replied.

They went to the People's Dining Saloon close at hand. It had a long trestle table, where the market-folk sat with noses nearly touching, like parrots in a cage.

"I must do some reckoning first," said Lily, who had begun to repent; she also wished to doctor the accounts before Joe appeared. She put the butter down at one shilling a pound, and took sixpence off

153

the wimberries. This gave her enough to buy the collar. "Easy as easy!" she thought.

They had tea and ham. The dealer was very pleasant. Lily felt that the kiss would really not be disagreeable. Only two diners were left, and they were counting out eggs.

"Look here, missis!" said the buyer, an old man with hair as stiff and long as a pony's mane. "Look here—eleven a shilling's my price. Now that's over a penny each. Now I counts out twelve—see? Eleven for me and one for you. Now agen."

The curious manner of his arithmetic confused the seller.

"It's all Welsh to me," she said. "I've got five young chillun and you'd ought to treat me fair."

"I *am* a-treating of you fair," said the ancient, and he began to count the eggs again. At each dozen he placed one in front of her.

"But I don't want any back, I want to sell 'em!" she wailed.

"So you can sell 'em when you'm got a dozen there—leastways, eleven!" shouted the buyer, exasperated.

The dealer looked at them scornfully, and turned to Lily.

"Now, for the reckoning, miss!" he said, and took his kiss.

Lily's horrified eyes beheld Joe's face flattened rosily against the plate-glass door, with its superannuated legend—somewhat disconcerting on this broiling day—

"Christmas Puddings piping hot."

Lily was piping hot.

Joe came in.

"Seems to me," he said, " as there's a little fellow here that 'd be better not here."

"How should I know the little lot was yours?" said the dealer.

" Come on out of this, Lily ! " commanded Joe.

John, sitting at his stall, with his blue gaze and white hair and a bunch of delphinium, selling Patty's butter, saw them go and was concerned.

" The lad's looking mighty set," he cogitated.

" Well, well—I munna meddle." Watching his patient face, full of a love that had to control its generosity, it was possible to believe in a Divinity who stood aside from the world's madness not from indifference, but for some great end.

Joe and Lily sat by the river in a deserted corner.

" Now, then ! " said Joe.

" Wunna you kiss me, Joe ? "

" No. Not till I've got to the bottom of this business," Joe replied, with a new-found wisdom. " Besides, I've got no tea to give you for it."

Lily began to cry.

" Best begin," said Joe. " Here we stop till you do, if it's all night."

She knew that he would. She was in despair.

It seemed so bad, and was so slight.

" It was them wimberries."

" Eh ? "

" He bought 'em off me."

" Oh."

" Only if I'd kiss him. And he threw in a cup o' tea. It inna my fault if I'm pretty," she added petulantly.

Joe looked at her thoughtfully.

" It be," he said, with perspicacity. " I dunno how it is, Lil, but you make your clothes look, when you've got 'em on, like them women in the papers— ondecent. Now, our Deb never does. And," he added with decision, " if you want to look ondecent, you can look it at whome—to me."

The prospect caused a relenting expression which Lily saw.

"I sold the things pretty well," she remarked.

She was rather dismayed when he asked the prices.

"The butter was too cheap," said Joe.

"It's gone down."

The interview was over. She bought the collar while Joe went to see if his father was ready. They drove home in great content, and all clouds seemed to have blown away. Lily registered a black mark against Deborah for the propriety of her dress.

When they got home, she rushed upstairs to try on the collar, leaving the paper on the table. Joe picked it up.

"I thought you'd no money?" he called. "Where's this from?"

He frowned as the explanation dawned on him.

"You lied about that butter," he said, ascending the stairs. "The second mean thing to-day. You're different to Deb. Look here—next time you want money as bad as that, ask for it."

His voice rose.

"And I'll not have strange fellows paying for the tea and ham of the 'ooman I sleep with."

"Oh, Joe, if I'd allus lived along of a fine chap like you," sobbed Lily, with great *savoir faire*, "and not along of a stingy monkey, I'd be different."

A second black mark went down against Deborah; another little tap was given to her destiny.

XXVII

" Deb ! " said Stephen, waking her at four on
Monday morning, " it's an A1 day. Up you get !
We'll go and see the sun rise from the old chap's
chair."

" It's mortal early," said Deborah. She felt
selfish to dash his pleasure, but she had only had
two hours' sleep.

" You *are* lazy," he laughed. " Why, if I was a
ploughman like Joe, you'd have to get up at this time
every day. You *do* make a fuss."

He felt particularly well himself ; he could not
understand her lassitude, and it irritated him. By
the irony of things Lily, who had given herself meanly
from mean motives, was considered by Joe, regarded
as respectable by the neighbours, and admired by
herself. Deborah had given in large measure, like
the land of great hills and wide pastures whose child
she was ; and she had none of Lily's privileges.

" Couldna I just have one more nap, Stephen, and
you go on without me ? "

" No, it's getting light, and we shall miss the best
of it if we're not quick."

He looked at her long, soft hair, her clear face,
and his mood suddenly changed. " We're too late
now, in fact."

His arm slipped round her.

" I'll be very quick," she said hurriedly.

" So you're even ready to get up to avoid me."

" Oh, dunna say that, Stephen ! "

He was really hurt as well as offended. He was

157

so entirely unable to control his new-found capacities
for emotion (kept under until a month ago, and never
trained or pruned) that he rushed at things like a
calf just turned out in a field—hurting himself,
indignant, all afire to grasp every joy. Because so
many normal joys had been denied him he was all
the more voracious for pleasure. He had cultivated
so many principles, quoted so many texts, preached
so fervently, lived in such a grey atmosphere—all
without real conviction; and now that, in his extraordinary renaissance, the body and not the soul
awoke first, he was like a drunkard. Had he loved
Deborah with all his being they would have been safe.
But he loved in the manner of many civilised people,
and not in Deborah's way—for she was primæval,
and her realities had never been sponged away.
His had. He regarded her as his best possession,
but the idea of sharing every thought, every hour's
work with her would have made him laugh. Joe
would have laughed too, but he had the virtues of
his narrow view of life; Stephen had not. He had,
in fact, no definite ethic of his own as yet. He had
not had time to think it out since he threw the ready-
made code away. Deborah's love was the sweetest
flowering of which humanity is capable, because it
was primitive and spiritual. To give—to be with
her man—to be so utterly at one that no explanation
was ever necessary—to work, laugh, sleep and watch
the splendid seasons together, being in other things
than sex free and equal, and in sex so mutually
generous as to forget self and rights—such was
Deborah's idea of love. This idea, though vague,
made her feel glorified and not lowered by giving
herself to a lover.

Her eyes were full of tears.

" How can 'ee say such things, Stephen ? "

Anger awoke in her. She had given him her
independence—and she had been strong in her

self-reliance as a mountain fox. She had given him her flawless health, her day-long tramps over the hills, the solitary hours, dear to her as to her father. She had given him—more than all—the sense of right, respectability, which is deeper in her type of character than in any.

Her dignity flamed into words that stung him to fury.

" You love an 'ooman like a lad loves cake—till there inna nought left. And you think of Stephen Southernwood a deal more than's good for you."

He had enough greatness to see the truth in the words, not enough to own it. He shook her.

" It's time you learnt that you're my woman and not my great-grandmother ! " he said.

He would have been funny if he had not been so grievously mistaken.

" You're mine, d'you hear ? It's not for you to criticize my way of love."

" I'm no more yours than you're mine."

" Yes, you are."

" Not if we're lovers as well as man and woman. Stephen, shall we go and see the sun rise now ? "

" No. I've changed my mind."

" Oh, Stephen ! Canna you be like it says in that nice hymn — lover of my soul ? Just this morning ? You've been the other kind of lover all the while——"

" Would you like it if I wasn't ? "

" No, only I wanted the other as well."

" You shouldn't have taken up with an ordinary chap like me."

" You bain't ordinary, Stephen."

" Yes, I am, thank the Lord ! I suppose you're sorry you took up with me now ? "

" Oh, Stephen, you know I love only you in the 'orld. Only I want——"

She hesitated, unable to find words to express the
159

fact that although, like most women, she was fascinated by virility, curbed virility claimed her whole-hearted adoration.

"If you love me, you must want what I choose, and when I choose," said Stephen shortly.

He reached the mine late, with shame in his heart.

"Damn you, Southernwood!" snapped the manager.

"Damn *you!*" said Stephen.

"A month's notice!" said the manager.

But at the end of the day the aggregate of work that Stephen's bad temper had produced was so large that the manager shouted after his departing figure—

"You can stop on."

After Stephen had gone, Deborah walked slowly to the hilltop, and sat watching the distant signpost—like a white pin in a large purple cushion. Below, in the plain and in the valley where Slepe lay, corn was being cut and bound in stooks. Little figures moved about, far down, and the reaper passed across the field with no sound. The hills lay under the noon sun like ripe plums in a huge basket.

From the yard at the spar mine came weird, plaintive sounds, as the rock-crusher ground the body of the mountain to fragments. These sounds were so wild and eerie that they might have been the forlorn music of fairy players sitting, shadowy and huge, in the dim rock-foundations, fiddling madly of nameless terror, fluting of unreachable beauties and rocky immortalities, harping on their own heartstrings to the deaf ears of men. Deborah listened and thought of Stephen down there, with his shirt-sleeves rolled up, his nostrils a little expanded with excitement in the giant work he controlled, his nod bringing a fresh trollyful of rock to be ground up.

Suddenly he seemed to her like the rock-crusher, but with no regulating hand. Hers must be the regulating hand—yet she felt only like the crushed rock. The music rose; Stephen was working like a demon to-day, and the men cursed as they sweated. The mountain, a thing beautiful with such majestic and static beauty as only a lover or genius can reach, lifted its voice in a passionless death-song.

Deborah attained the beauty of the summits. She sat down on a rock at the foot of the Chair, and gazed towards the mine.

"He'm eager," she pondered, "and he canna stop to think of me no more than the rock. He chose me out of the 'orld." She smiled. "It inna his fault as he'm eager. So long as he'm for me and me for him, nought matters, and I dunna complain." She looked around the reaped country, the gashed hillside, and spoke aloud as if Stephen were with her.

"So long as there's aught left of me, Stephen, you met crumble me—if you've a mind to."

The sound of the rock-crusher rose again on the still air.

"Only never leave me, Stephen!" she cried, and a great terror came on her, so that she clung to the rock till it hurt her hands.

"Don't let it be for naught, lad—don't 'ee!"

The music died.

She remembered that Stephen would be coming home for his dinner—and there was no dinner ready. She ran down the slope. The cranberry flowers, open now, showed more like tears than ever on the scarred face of the rock.

The fire was out, the sticks wet. She had not yet coaxed it to burn, when she heard his step.

"Oh, Stephen!" she cried in a panic; "you'll be right vexed—I hanna got your dinner ready."

He stood on the threshold and looked across at

her, as she poured paraffin on the coal. He had run up the hill without his coat or waistcoat, and was clammy with sweat, tired, hungry, and ruffled by the sullenness of the men. Deborah thought the look in his eyes was one of anger, and she sat down on the salt-box and began to cry.

Stephen crossed the room and knelt down by her, resting his head against her shoulder. He said nothing whatever. It was the second purely noble moment of his life—the second outward sign of the possibilities that John had seen. He made no apologies, no effort to be picturesque, no attempt at self-justification. He forgot his hunger, the men, his tiredness. He forgot self. Without a word they remained so until the clock struck two, and the dinner hour was over. He went out, giving her a long look and still having foregone the luxury of words. Many such moments, and Stephen would belong to the small company of men who hold the world back from the beast—the self-givers, the lovers, in whom the flesh and the spirit burn together with a steadfast flame, and light the earth. But he had so much to unlearn, to give up, to suffer. He was like the mass of stone that is to be a great statue, and how long the statue would be in the making none could say.

XXVIII

WHEN Stephen came back to tea, Deborah had the place glowing with comfort. In the afternoon she had done a day's work; only so could she express her joy. After tea she sat on his knee like a happy child. He told her tales about his work; he wanted the reassurance of her laughter. She looked up at him in the fading light.

" Poor Lily ! " she murmured; " with only our Joe."

His mouth twitched.

" Don't, Deb ! " he said. " Joe's a decent chap. But I'm on the mend." He laughed rather unsteadily. " Come to our room a minute—I've something to show you, Deb."

On the floor were a blanket and pillow.

" Good enough for me," he said.

" But, Stephen——"

He was immovable. He slept on the floor for three nights, caught a bad cold and still kept on. He sang with a new joy as he went to work, though he was tired from the unaccustomed hardness of his bed. Deborah acquiesced, as she always did when he was what she called " set." Her pride in him strengthened when she peered over the rosy counterpane and saw him restlessly asleep there with his greatcoat for a blanket.

At the mine he continued to work feverishly.

" Well, if he do sweat us, he sweats himself first," said the men. They liked him in spite of his hastiness and the tales they heard of his religious and moral shortcomings.

If other lives could have been hindered from impinging on those of Deborah and Stephen, they might have worked out their destinies in the swift way of great lovers. But Mrs. Arden with her definite morality, Joe with his obstinate and straitened view of sex, Eli with his ranting dogmatism, Lily with her petty spite, and the world in general with its terror of nonconformity—all these came round them as stealthily as the tide round a promontory, and (some of them with the best intentions) brought about tragedy. The only person to utter no word was John, for he had no moral code. Those that dwell in the lands of the sun do not need fires.

" Thou shalt not " was mere foolishness to John, who was always so occupied in loving—the great affirmative—that he had no time for such negations.

When he came on Tuesday, he looked at Stephen in his long, earnest way, and when they wandered round the garden together while Deborah was busy in the kitchen, he patted him on the shoulder.

" Deb looks fine," he said.

Stephen walked on for a space. Then he replied—

" I'm doing my best—now."

" Aye."

" I didn't—at first."

" No."

" How d'you know? "

" The lamp's not been alight in your face all that long, lad."

Stephen was embarrassed. He edged away from the subject.

" Like to see over the house, father? "

They were upstairs before Stephen remembered the blanket and pillow on the floor. John saw them. He had the mystic's complete grasp, on necessary

164

occasion, of the commonplaces, the vitalities, the realities of life. To say nothing would have been to create a tacit understanding that something was wrong. He looked out at the day, full of cool colours.

"I shouldna wonder," he remarked, "if we had the first bit of frost to-night. I dunna know as there's anything so bad to bear as a frost in August, when the country's all full of lusty life. I see you'm a bit of a self-chastiser, lad."

He smiled as he had not yet smiled at Stephen.

"And I don't think the worse of you for it, nor "— he looked at him with kindly understanding—" nor for the cause."

"You two men, come on!" called Deborah. She was so happy to see affection springing up between her father and Stephen that she had made enough toast for a choir tea.

"If you dunna eat it every bit," she said, with a tyrannical nod and a radiant look at Stephen, "I met cry—so there!"

"I wouldn't have that for anything," said Stephen, coming round to her chair and remembering with shame how she had cried on Monday morning. There was a pause, during which John was ostentatiously interested in Deborah's sewing-machine.

"Oh, dear-a-me!" he said after an interval, "I've broken your machine seemingly."

He held up the handle with a guilty expression. Since he hated machinery as Eli hated youth, Deborah and Stephen laughed.

"I'll put it on in a jiffy," cried Stephen. "Look— you just turn this crank——"

But John was not as interested in the crank as in Stephen and Deborah.

"I wish," he said, just before he ambled off on Whitefoot, "that you could come along some evening

M   165

and lend Joe and me a hand with Eli's sheep, Stephen. You can ride, I daresay ? "

" A bit."

" I was thinking it 'd be in your line. How you ever come to be doing the preaching in black coat and weskit beats me," said John amusedly.

" I've had enough of it; you can't stick at things for ever."

The restless look came into Stephen's eyes.

" Why are you going to see after Eli's sheep, father ? " asked Deborah.

" Well, since the owd mare died, he's good for naught, poor chap. He sits in the house like an owl in a tree, and when I go in, he says, ' The Lord's dealing with me. Take your silly face outside, 'oot ! ' And, of course, the animals and that must be seen after, so I thought to myself, if Joe 'd borrow a horse and you'd ride Whitefoot, we'd soon round up the sheep."

" Which day ? " asked Stephen, wondering how much speed could be got out of the venerable Whitefoot.

" To-morrow ? "

" Right."

" You and Lily mun come along, Deb, and mother 'll bring tea, and we'll have a bit of a randy."

He rubbed his hands. To do a kindness and make several people happy as well, was his idea of bliss.

XXIX

" I DUNNA care to have much to do with Stephen,"
said Joe sulkily, when John called at Slepe. " And
I told Eli as I wouldna round up any more of his
blasted sheep."

John looked at him.

" But still," Joe amended gruffly, rather discon-
certed by the look, " sin' you want me to, I'll come
this once."

" That's a good lad.   And Lil ? "

" Well, of course, I dunna hold with Deb's ways,"
Lily remarked, with her nose in the air, " but still—"
she thought of Stephen, whose admiration she coveted
because it was withheld, " still, as it's my own father
you'm giving a hand to, it's my duty to come."

" Duty's a word I've no use for.   But if you'll
come that's all right."

On Wednesday evening, Eli, sitting far back in
the dreary kitchen, presumably being " dealt with,"
blinked with surprise at seeing a merry party come
over Bitterley Hill.

" Three baskets, John, two wold horses, my darter,
that gomeril Joe, John's old 'ooman (a bad 'ooman
that—a sharp-tongued 'ooman), and that blasted
Stephen," he ruminated.   " Now, what'n they after ?
My apples ? "

His one tree of wizened cider-apples would hardly
have justified a raid.   He watched every movement,
his head moving backwards and forwards like a cat
watching a fly-catcher.

167

"They'm making them some tay. What the land's coming to I dunna know—the way folks drag their victuals out o' doors, like a cat drags meat off a plate, and chaws 'em along with the beasts that perish. I'd like to throw another Bible at that Stephen—wish it met grind him to powder according to the good and gracious promise."

"Now, then, you young chaps!" said John, when tea was over, "let's see what you can do with them ship."

"Be very careful, won't 'ee, Stephen?" Deborah implored.

"Rather!" He dug his heels into the astonished Whitefoot and was off, shouting like a madman. He and Joe galloped over the hill, round the hill, up sheep-tracks, over heather, whistling, shouting—Stephen lithe, Joe dogged—both enjoying themselves mightily. They forgot their dislike of each other in the comradeship of physical effort.

"Fetch up that owd ewe with the cough, 'oot, Stephen?" sang out Joe, and Stephen was off down a slope nearly as steep as a roof. He was palpably the best rider. This annoyed Lily, especially as he had not given her a single look of admiration. Also there were the black marks registered against Deborah on Saturday.

"Dunna he look a handsome chap?" asked Deborah, with clasped hands.

"Handsome is as handsome does. I'm fair surprised at you and him living in sin," replied Lily. "The Slepe folks say there'll be a curse on you, and they dunna care to have much to do with you."

"They needna." Deborah spoke with outer calm and inner misery.

"And," said Lily, annoyed by the calm, "if we have children, I shan't care for them to 'sociate with yours, cos yours'll be baseborn."

Mrs. Arden, who had been absorbed in pride of Joe's horsemanship, was brought back to the spot by the last word and by Deborah's low wail.

"Lily," she said, with her extraordinary acuteness for the adversary's weak point, " it's early to talk of your chillun yet, afore even the morning sickness has begun! There, Deb, dunna take on. He'll marry you if you ask him, right enough. Do it for the little 'uns sake, as may come."

"Ki-i-i-i!" yelled Stephen in the distance, galloping to and fro. Deborah thought what the sons of a man like Stephen would be.

"Eh, what lads!" she said to herself, with radiant eyes. "They shanna be shouted after by Lily's brats."

She determined that, if she could, she would sacrifice Stephen's views to these bright, wonderful visions that glanced at her out of the future with his eyes.

John was counting the sheep, standing in the pen of iron hurdles with the woolly bodies round him, saying, "There, there!" when they came in panting after a long and nimble chase.

"Only two short now," he said.

A raucous voice was uplifted.

"Get off my land, Joe Arden, and you, Southern-'ood! I'll summons you for trespass, breaking fences, sheep-worrying, sheep-stealing and cruelty to animals. And" (he glanced balefully at Stephen) "I'll summons *you* for stealing my Bible. Oh! you met laugh, you backsliding and perverse generation, you met laugh! But the Lord 'll deal with you, as He's dealing with me, one of these fine days, and you wunna like it. Not as *I* mind," he added hastily, "for I am with Him as His own familiar friend, and what I did is betwixt me and Him; but you wunna like it, you young rapscallion with your kept 'ooman."

" Get into your hole ! " said Stephen, " or I'll twist your neck."

" Man, man ! " John interposed, " we'm getting in your sheep for you. You're in the situation of one as is receiving a favour," he added in amused explanation.

" I'm in the situation of wanting my farm and my pasture and my flocks and my herds to myself."

And Eli undid the hurdles, letting all the sheep out.

" I'll be blowed ! " said Joe.

" Well, well, Eli ! I thought to see to their feet and look over 'em thorough for you—but as you will." John was somewhat nettled. " I thought they'd get straying," he added.

" I like 'em to stray."

" And get fut-rot."

" I like 'em to get fut-rot."

" And they met die, if they wunna seen to."

" I like 'em to die."

He stood there, a ridiculous, squat old figure, and John could have wept for him. Joe and Stephen only saw the humour of it. They lay on the horses' necks and roared, helpless, Joe slapping his leg at intervals and Stephen imploring him not to.

" It sets me off again, you fool ! " he cried. " Look at the sheep ! "

They were sedately returning whither they had been brought with so much labour; even John was obliged to laugh at the prim jauntiness of their departure.

" Now," said Eli, " you've had your bloody picnic. Get off my land ! "

He went back into the house and slammed the door.

" If I was you, Steve," advised Joe, still comradely, on the way home, " I'd put soft ideas in me pocket, and get married. It inna partic'lar pleasant to have Deb called a kept 'ooman."

"Oh, shut up!" said Stephen. But he pondered on it.

"What puzzles me," continued Joe, whose strong point was not tact, "is you doing such a thing when you're a preacher."

"I've given all that up ages ago—a fortnight ago," Stephen replied.

"You're a bit of a quick-change artist, bain't you, Stephen?"

"Well, if I wasn't, life's so short that I should never get anywhere. I suppose you don't want to, though?"

"Not partic'lar."

"Well, I do."

XXX

On the next Monday Deborah inaugurated her first washing-day. Stephen fixed a line for her between two of the dead trees in the garden hedge.

"I'd liefer they came down, Stephen," she demurred.

She found the views of them from the east—against the sunset sky, and from the west—against the Devil's Chair, equally depressing.

They seemed, with their boughs and trunks like bleached bone—their loss of the elasticity of life—their cant away from the Chair, to speak of some terrific happening up there. So did the desolate acres of burnt heather, each bush charred and left as a skeleton above the black-strewn ground. There had been a great summer fire here, years ago; the dry heather had been heated to a smouldering glow; a spark had leapt up; the hill-top had been wrapped in flame.

There were some that scouted this explanation, and spoke of voices—wordless shouts—the sound of feet that passed and came again in the stillness of an August noon. They said that the Chair shook in the heat-haze and a tongue of flame leapt from it like a flung torch.

Stephen laughed when Deborah told him this; but it made him dislike the charred slopes and the trees.

"I'll have 'em down when it's cooler," he reassured her; "they'll make good fuel."

He came home to-day before Deborah had finished bringing in the clothes. She was taking them from the line, rosy and full of energy. He went and helped her. He thought as he watched her gracious figure, with the white apron flying in the breeze, its bib sweetly rounded, that such necessary work gave a woman beauty.

"Isn't it soft, Deb, the way people think a bit of work's a disgrace?" he said.

"It's only poor feckless things that think it, surely. There's nought like work for health, and good health's the flower, inna it, Stephen?"

"Yes. Enjoyed your wash?"

"Aye, the first since we were——"

She was going to say "wed."

The emotions of the past few days rushed to her lips.

"Eh, Stephen! Couldna you bring yourself to it?"

"What?"

"Wedding me."

"I don't know."

"You met put notions—not as I'm saying aught agen *your* notions—second."

"Second to what?"

She could not bring herself to speak of those visionary boys. She must wait, she thought, until they were "quiet like."

She felt that they must be comrades, in some mood of calm communion, before she would have courage for that. To-day he was too purely masculine; his eyes too openly acclaimed her a fair woman.

"Second to me," she said. But she had never thought less of herself.

"Who's been nasty to you?"

"Lily."

"Damn Lily."

173

" But everybody's the same. No one's been to
see us."

" Good thing too."

" Only—well, mother's the same."

" H'm."

" And Joe."

" Joe ! what's he matter ? "

" Stephen, would you mislike it all that much ? "

" Yes. I hate to be tied."

" But we're bound faster than books and rings can
tie us. It'd be no different to us. I'm yours now,
for certain sure."

Before the sudden flame of masterful joy that her
words woke in his eyes she looked down.

" Mine ! I don't need an old fool's mumbling to
get the woman I want—nor to keep her. Besides,
I hate to give in. They'd think it was their doing."

" But it won't be. It'll be me."

He was in the mood to listen to her—a peculiar,
uplifted mood of which he was capable—a state
known to people of a certain calibre, such as the saint
in his long fasts, the genius in his timeless agonies of
desire for unattainable beauty. Stephen had been
stern with himself during the past week, and had
suffered in proportion to his capacity for joy—which
was extraordinary. He was full of a white exaltation,
and was ready—if the truth must out—for the next
downward plunge.

" We'll talk about it to-night," he said.

" Be you——? "

" Well ? "

" I took that old rug away. The week's up,
Stephen."

In his gratitude to her for so easily forgiving him,
his young delight at the ending of his self-imposed
hardship and his intensified passion for her, he
whispered just before they fell asleep—

174

" Will you marry me, Deborah Arden ? "

" Aye, Stephen," she murmured in a glow of happiness; " and thank you kindly, lad."

Outside, the Chair reared itself haughtily above the cowering land. Around it, as the August night drove on, and the mists stood in the plain to the tops of twenty-foot hedges like water in deep bowls, rose and moved in silence impalpable tenebræ. They swept round it as if in a dark incantation, with beckoning arms and stealthy haste, passing across the dim waste of burnt heather in lost eddies.

Deborah woke in a panic, dreaming of Stephen's face distorted with anger as he flung a snapped wedding-ring at her feet. He was sleeping with his hand under his cheek, his hair fluffy and damp, and an air of boyishness mingling with traces of passion on his face—a look that arouses in a woman a storm of love, feminine, wifely, maternal.

She kissed him softly. Her evil dream had fled.

" Hullo, Deb ! " He stretched with a vigorous enjoyment that made what she called " a puzzle-garden " of the bedclothes.

" When am I to go and get that gold ring, Deb ? "

He had not changed his mind, then. She rejoiced. It was summer in the land as yet; the year had not spent all her maiden glory. Still there was gold in the fields—purple on the hills. The apples flamed in little orchards. Deborah's cheek fired with delight and content of the future. It never occurred to her that it is not the generous, splendid moment that wears on a nature like Stephen's, but the long, feature-less months with no special credit or romance. She did not know that the only thing that could hold such a man when he was young and crude was the

175

sense that nothing held him except his own will; for restraint drives such natures mad, and they will be over every fence. She did not know the restlessness of his nature, the underlying melancholy that might spring out at any moment when the glory was off the hills and gone from the fields, when the largesse of the year had been given and the hardness of winter had come. Then, when the bloom was gone from his first passion for her, and she had given all she could, it would be her turn to dip into the wells of his being for comfort and tenderness.

She did not know that under his new-found materialism lurked a superstition more powerful than hers, because unplumbed by him. This was partially the outcome of the dark doctrines he had been taught as a child; it was partly inherited from a race that had come of the soil, as Deborah's had; it was also the primæval instinct of the poet and the savage, who find in rock and flower a fearful alphabet. He had no idea that this existed in him, and he had not the conscious poet's safety-valve of expression.

It was impossible to say what would happen if this superstition awoke before his mind had worked out its views of time and eternity and his physical passion grown to calm maturity.

Already, when the wind mewed in the chimney like a great cat, and the early autumn storms trod the hill like crazy giants, and the ebb-tide of colour set in while evenings darkened, he would feel an unpleasant sense of vacancy and eeriness. At these times he felt a faint homesickness for lighted towns— a momentary irritability. It was so fleeting that Deborah did not notice it. She herself rejoiced in thinking of the long warm evenings when they would hear the storm howling, and smile at one another in the cosy lamplight—shut in from all storm, all cold.

176

"When'll those may-trees on the slopes get their leaves again, Deb? They're nearly off," he said sadly; "I want to see them in flower."

"It met be June," said Deborah; "the thorn blows late hereabouts."

XXXI

On Deborah's wedding day the wind raged over
the vast, rolling plain in the west—a plain utterly
different from that on the other side of the two
ridges, which was flat except for a few round hills
between the rose-coloured turnip-fields and the diaper
of stubble and grass. But the smallest hills to the
west would have been striking features in an ordinary
countryside; the valleys were chasms, the flattest
lands a switchback. It stretched away, broken by
sudden mountainous masses, like a stormy green sea,
where the ridges were breakers and the woods black
froth. In the centre of the semicircular horizon,
blue with distance, fronting the Devil's Chair like
the throne of a rival potentate, was Cader Idris; on
either side lay mountains like cones, like clenched
fists, like recumbent goddesses and crouching beasts.
Above was a grey and white welter of shredded cloud,
massed here and there like fleeces of giant sheep, but
mostly strewn like dove-coloured and lavender
feathers till the sky looked like the eyrie of a bird of
prey.

Below Stephen's cottage, and much farther from
the menace of the Chair, the hamlet of Lostwithin
clung to the slope of the hill with frenzied tenacity;
the cottages looked like small stones taking part in
a huge landslip.

Stephen and Deborah walked along the hill-top,
where black rocks were piled in grotesque heaps, as
though for a rockery in the gardens of the ancient gods.
On nearly every rock were carved by the chisels of

the seasons faces like gargoyles, heads of beasts, profiles distorted as if with unthinkable agony. They passed these and went across the hill to the top of the first gorge to gather foxgloves for Mrs. Arden. The hill was gashed for nearly its whole height, and a tide of foxgloves rolled sheer from top to bottom like arterial blood.

In the intervals of hot sunshine masses of purple shadow, acres wide, raced across the country. The wind raved, plucked at Deborah's hair and dress, tore at her arm which was linked in Stephen's.

" Hold me tight, 'oot, Stephen ! " she cried, standing with her white dress wrapped tightly round her by the wind.

He thought her adorable.

" I will that ! " he replied. " Now and always."

He held her so closely that she could scarcely breathe. They picked the foxgloves—a strange, elfish bouquet for a bride, with their gaping mouths and spotted lips and the queer nodding of the shut buds.

" What a strong scent they have," said Stephen, as they passed on; " sleepy, somehow."

He was curiously sensitive to all scents. It was true that there was something anæsthetic in it. It was almost malevolent.

They turned south.

" Mother 'll be right pleased with them," said Deborah, " and with our tidings."

At Slepe the vicar was waiting—beaming, benevolent, ready to let the past fortnight be a bygone now that they had done as they should.

" Well, Southernwood," he said, shaking hands cordially; " glad you've come. You won't regret it, my lad."

Stephen was bored. Comment on any action of his annoyed him.

When they were married, the vicar patted Deborah's shoulder. He had christened her and prepared her for confirmation.

"God bless you, Mrs. Southernwood," he whispered. Deborah's heart sang. She had followed every word of the service with thrills of joy. Stephen had yawned, watched the flies in the east window, yawned again, rumpled his hair in a way he had when his mind was not sufficiently occupied, and made the responses condescendingly. She did not notice it. She looked up at his sunburnt face, just thin enough for its firm contours to be visible, and she was wrapt in blessedness.

They took the path for Upper Leasowes. In an ash at the foot of the hills swallows were clustering for departure, with small cries and short, excited flights, and much preening of underwings, and low singing in the intervals of sunshine. As they climbed up to the Ardens' cottage, Stephen was fighting against a sense of extreme flatness; he felt even more irritable, more overwhelmed with bathos, than he had done when he went out to the shippen. It was to his credit that he tried not to let Deborah know.

They crept up to the door stealthily, flung it open and rushed in. Mrs. Arden shrieked. She was making jam in her working dress—print, with a large black apron, and one of Joe's caps rakishly pinned on her grey hair.

"Laws me! What'm you doing away from work, Stephen?"

"Getting married."

She sat down on the chair on which she had previously placed her wimberries, amid peals of laughter.

"Well, well, dear sakes! I be glad. Not but

180

what you'd ought to have done it a bright bit ago, Stephen."

It irritated Stephen to be treated like a naughty but forgiven boy, when he wanted to feel like the grandiloquent hero of a drama.

" It's nothing to do with me," he said. " Deborah wanted it."

" For sure she did, and quite right, too, and I'm glad you've done it in such good time."

" Good time for what, Mrs. Arden ? "

" Never you mind, my lad. But you met be calling me mother if you've a mind, seeing as you've done as you should."

She wiped her eyes in a great fluster, looking, as she emerged from the basket of wimberries, like a stout Bacchanal.

" John ! John ! Wherever is the man ? Never about when he's wanted, and under my feet, like the chickens, day in, day out, when he inna. John ! "

" Coming, coming ! " replied a muffled voice from the wood-house.

" Didna I tell you, John, when you made such a Bob's-a-dying about these two, as it'd be all right ? Well—it be. They're better-for-worsed as nice as nice, and they're man and wife for none to put asunder."

The irrevocability, thus emphasized, irked Stephen. He stirred Rover with his foot, and frowned.

" Well, mother," said John, " I didna think it was me that made the fuss, but I'm pleased that you're pleased, and I'll wish 'em both all good." He smiled at them.

" And now, what about a bit of dinner, mother ? They'll be clemmed."

As they were finishing dinner, Eli knocked. He presented a letter to Mrs. Arden with a scowl.

181

"Who's it from?" she asked.

"Me. You needna think it's a merrymaking nor yet a tea as you're invited to in that. It's nothing like them things—of the earth, earthy."

"Well, Eli, what is it then?" asked John, coming to the door and leaning against the post, pipe in mouth.

"It's me," said Eli, "the miserable sinner as you see afore you—but not such a sinner as some I could name."

He placed one eye very close to the crack of the door, and watched Stephen as he surreptitiously kissed Deborah.

"An evil and adultrous generation — I see yer, Southern'ood. Where's my Bible?"

"Maybe you'd like to know, Eli," said Mrs. Arden stiffly, "as they're married, right and proper."

"The words of the wise," said Eli, "that's to say, of me, have shown 'em the error of their ways."

"Nothing of the sort, you old Jack-in-the-box," muttered Stephen.

Eli's appreciation was a very bitter draught. He stood for everything that Stephen hated and feared.

"You met as well come along to chapel on Harvest Thanksgiving day—three prompt—and get saved, Southern'ood," said Eli patronizingly. "I be going to preach, very special."

"What about?"

"Never you mind. You come, you and the woman God's give you."

Eli looked at Deborah as if he thought the gift of doubtful worth.

Stephen felt very emphatically that he had obtained Deborah by his own personal efforts. He got up.

"Well, we must be off, Deb."

" Good-evening, sinners ! " said Eli. " Be you going through Slepe ? "

" Yes, we can."

" Well, you can take this here invitation to Joe and that darter of mine. It'll save me, and get some of the lust of youth out of you.''

XXXII

As they neared the cottage at Slepe in the early evening, under a sky of ink and gold, the sound of Lily's raised voice and hysterical sobbing came through the window.

"I *shall* keep it. I told the man I would—and pay two shillings a month."

"It's to go back, straight," replied Joe's voice obstinately.

"I *won't!*" screamed Lily. "It's a lovely locket, and dirt cheap. I was going to put some of your nasty black hair in it——"

"Pack it up! Lockets—on sixteen shilling a week?"

Lily broke out crying afresh.

Deborah hurriedly knocked.

There was a startled silence. Then Joe appeared at the door, very dour and perspiring.

"Being as you've come," he said, "you met take a parcel for me to the post. Lily, bring that locket down when you come."

"Joe, we thought we'd come and tell you as we'm married," said Deborah.

"You don't say! Well, Stephen, I think the better on you. I do that, marriage—aye, a grand thing."

Joe caught a smile on Stephen's face, which had a clenched look. He stopped, wondering how much of their quarrel had been overheard. There was another silence.

Deborah produced Eli's letter.

"Well, he *is* a funny old bird," said Joe, opening

184

the letter as he would open a poultry basket full of hens.

" ' Eli Huntbatch has pleasure in announcing ' (is he having a sale, Stephen?) ' as he intends to speak at three prompt, Sunday, on Sin. His own in especial. The Lord wishes you to attend ! ' "

" The old fool's mad," said Stephen.

At this moment Lily came down. She wore a green blouse, made low in the neck, and in the opening hung a locket made of a large imitation emerald. The brightness of the green glass set off her delicate complexion, and she was rather flushed from crying. Stephen looked at her with quite a spark of admiration and a sense of sympathy; for he, too, loved bright things—the glimmer on the surface of life. But he loved them because they concealed the black depths below; Lily loved them because they were all in all to her.

" They'm come to say as they're married," said Joe—addressing the alarm clock, it seemed.

Lily was taken aback, put out. She had always felt and seemed so very righteous since Deborah's departure with Stephen. Now she had no such pleasure. It was scarcely worth while having children, she reflected, if they would have no advantage over Deborah's. For (she looked admiringly at Stephen, disparagingly at Joe) " if mine take after their father, they *will* be plain-featured," she said to herself.

" Well, Deb, I'm sure I'm glad to hear it," she said. " There couldna be any blessing without the holy estate, could there? " She looked at Joe again. " The sweat's made streaks down your black face, Joe." Her voice was like a knife. " If you don't wash for your wife, you met for company."

Joe departed to the wash-house, not, apparently, overweighted with the blessings of the holy estate. Presently he put his head in.

185

" Come and see the pig, 'oot? " he asked Stephen in a non-commital manner.

They sat down on the bench where Joe cleaned the boots, at the other side of the cottage from the parlour window.

" Come and I'll show you my lace collar," said Lily, when the men had gone. They went upstairs and sat down on the bed.

Deborah admired the collar; she was feeling pitiful towards Lily, because of her tear-flushed face and the smallness of her joys and sorrows. It seemed to her that Lily, whether safely married or guiltily unmarried, was cut out for small failures in love. She wondered why.

" I'd pack up this locket, if I was you, Lil," she advised.

" Oh, you *was* listening, then ! " Lily was bitter.

" I couldna help it, Lil."

" H'm ! Well, I want it. I'm fond on it."

" But you're fonder of Joe. Poor Joe ! You'd liefer please him than have bits of jewellery."

" Hush ! Hark at 'em down there ! "

From under the window came Stephen's voice—

" I thought, if you'd care for a bit of a loan, Joe, and surprise her—— ? "

" No. Thank 'ee kindly, Steve."

" Jewellery's a lot to women," said Stephen, out of the depth of his experience among the young ladies of Silverton.

" It shouldna be more than their chap. It inna to Deb, I swear, and yet you're getting good money."

" Well, then—— "

" No, Steve. It's right kind on you, but she mun learn to do on what I get. If she canna now, what about when the little 'uns come ? "

" Good Lord, man, you're not thinking of kids already ! "

Stephen's voice was full of surprised amusement.

" Aye."

" Well, I'll be blowed ! "

" I calc'lated it all up afore I axed Lil," said Joe, " of course. Who else would, if I didna ? "

" Calculated what ? "

" Wages and insurance and how many kids I thought to have."

" And," said Stephen, with the unevenness of laughter in his tone, " what's the reckoning ? "

" Six."

" What ? "

" Well, it's a good middling number. How many d'you want yourself ? "

" O Lord !—none ! "

Stephen desired to be exactly the opposite of Joe, and was much too amused to be serious.

" But why do you want six, man ? " he continued.

" To do my duty."

" Who to ? "

" King and country."

" And Lily ? "

" Lily mun do hers."

" But, Joe," said Stephen, who already possessed a few qualities of a lover; " but, Joe, I should have thought you'd want to make Lily happy."

" Eh ? chillun's what makes women happy. And is it the first thing you think on, day in, day out, making Deb happy ? "

" I try to."

" Oh, well, as I said, you're a quick-change artist— all one thing one minute, and all summat else the next. I plods on the same. The girls we've married must take us as they find us."

So they groped, like two half-blind men, among the great ripe orchards of life, picking up only such apples as they fell over—Stephen picking up most, because he stumbled oftenest.

Upstairs the two girls gazed out of the window at

the ebony clouds, solid, crenellated, cut into curious
capes and peninsulas, like huge maps of unknown
lands. They elaborately avoided looking at one
another.

" Six ! " whispered Lily, and she fidgeted so
feverishly with the locket that she broke the clasp.

" You're lucky, Deb ! Your Stephen's worth a
hundred of Joe."

" None ! " thought Deborah, and a mist came
over her. Also she had a vague sense of something
being out of joint in that Stephen should talk to
another man—to any one but herself—in this way.

" Fancy him wanting to give me the locket ! "
Lily said. Present joy, pleased vanity, curiosity as
to whether Deborah would be jealous, elbowed away
the shadow of the future.

Deborah was not jealous. Stephen loved her, she
thought. Soul and body, they were all each other's.
To her the fact that Stephen had asked and taken all
that she had to give—spiritual and physical—was
the absolute proof that he loved her. And if he
loved her, he felt to her as she did to him. Anything, therefore, that he might do or be to others was
charity. Could her perfect peace have been shaken,
and a doubt dwelt in her, still there would have been
no jealousy; for, if she had doubted his love, she
would simply have resigned all claim on him, become nothing to him. Lily could not understand
her.

" I hope Joe 'll let him," Deborah said.

" Joe's that busy doing his duty to a man as
never so much as saw his soft face, that he's got no
time to think of me," said Lily, with acidity. " If
he dunna give me bits of things, who will ? I'll only
be young once. I'll only be pretty for a bit, and
wanting to enjoy myself—but the wold country as
Joe's so set on, it's always the same." She clenched
her hands. " I hate it ! " she cried; " them old trees
188

and the hills as'll be just as blue-coloured when I be dead."

"There, there, Lil!" said Deborah. "Joe dunna really care for them things more than he does for you; it's just men's silly way of talking," she added, dismissing with maternal amusement the whole school of masculinity summed up in—

"I could not love thee, dear, so much " . . .

"Hark!" said Lily.

"I wonder where those girls are," came Stephen's voice. He had an uneasy intuition.

"In the parlour, where we left them."

That they should exhibit initiative was evidently not in Joe's mind.

"Let's go and see."

Upstairs there was a moth-like flutter; downstairs a heavy crunching of gravel. In the parlour, when Joe and Stephen entered, sat two exemplary wives, deep in the perusal of Lily's new cookery-book.

XXXIII

As Deborah and Stephen walked home in an increasing tumult of wind, under clouds like froth in a tide-race of black water, Deborah waited for him to tell her of his talk with Joe. She meant to confess her unintentional eavesdropping, and she thought how amused Stephen would be. She wondered if Stephen would tell her that he only said " none " for the sake of differing from Joe. She thought how sweet it would be to speak softly about the future—to know each other's mind to the depths.

But Stephen said nothing. He had forgotten all about it. Had he remembered he would have thought it rather an improper subject upon which to enter with her. In the society he had known it was not considered decent to talk to a woman about any of the physical necessities of life except eating. A woman who was to give herself to a man and bear his children was not consulted in either matter. A tacit understanding was the nearest approach allowed.

Stephen walked on moodily. He was thinking how dull the country was getting, how forlorn. For the colours were withdrawing with what seemed to him the terrible leisureliness of fatality. They would soon be gone as the willow-wrens were gone from the woods below Lostwithin, as the cuckoos had long been gone from hill and field. The density was gone from the shadows; scent dwindled daily; the stars were like scimitars instead of silver flowers.

As they reached the hilltop a late mountain moth
wandered vaguely over the heather—shining whitely
here, for, from some accident of soil, it was never
purple, but of a bleached pallor, for acres round the
Chair. When they stood a moment by Cranberry
Rock, which was like a lesser throne for some digni-
tary, an owl cried with its long, laughing shudder
from the ragged holly spinney down the southern
slope.

"It's saying—'What ails you?'" said Deborah.

"What a vile bird it is—and what a shake it puts
on '*ails*,'" said Stephen, "like the stop on the
harmonium. Autumn's beastly. When I was going
to work yesterday I saw a regular gang of swallows
in an ash, getting ready to go. All the corn'll be in
before long too, and the heather dead."

"Aye. But the turn o' the year'll come agen
afore we know it."

"Not for nearly half a year. We might be dead
before it."

"Oh, Stephen!"

"Well, we might. It's just luck. How do we
know, if there's nobody to look after us? We might
be like frozen bees any day—not a bit of us left
except a carcase for the mixen."

It was the outermost fringe of his hidden grief; the
pity of it was that he only showed her the fringe.
He was afraid to look at the thing himself, and so
it was like a beast behind undergrowth. He did not
regard her as a being who might have helped him.
She was the weaker—he her protector. A deep
reciprocity of sympathy and strength between lovers
had never occurred to him. With a mixture of
cowardice before the problems of immensity and
mistaken manliness towards Deborah he crushed
down all his questionings, fears, horrors, and was
silent.

191

"Oh, Stephen!" said Deborah now; "I be sorry you feel that—but we mun hope things is better'n that for us. I'm thinking there's good beyond it all."

She had not made herself a philosophy; she had lived in such simplicity that it had not occurred to her. Now, faced for the first time by a grief that her love told her needed comfort, she searched in the recesses of her being and found this intuition there like a rosy flower.

But to Stephen—used to people who said much and meant little—her words seemed cold, conventional, empty. He said no more.

The heather screeched, the rocks moaned and whined as the wind probed their crevices. The Chair was obscured at intervals by low, driving clouds.

"Don't let's go nearer to it than we can help," said Stephen, "it's so beastly." He laughed constrainedly.

They went by a smaller path lower down.

"When I'm feared of it," said Deborah, "I think of Wilderhope and the Flockmaster. I dreamt I saw him standing by a white cross—by the signpost—with a lamb in his arms; and his face was your face."

"Mine?"

"Aye. Only terrible sorrowful-like."

"Hope the dream won't come true, then. Who's he supposed to be?"

"I don't know. Father learnt me the tale. He said it meant as there was love about, going to-and-agen in spite of Devil's Chairs and all. And he said"—Deborah puckered her brow in thought, as she put back long blown ends of her hair—"he said there were plenty of little crosses in the world, as some folk took to be only posts, but they were crosses sure enough, and love hanging on 'em—'forever
192

martyred and forever gladsome '—that's his very words."

"Oh! Christianity-talk. I can do that myself—could until I chucked it."

"No. Not chapel nor church Christianity. Just home-brewed," said Deborah. "I allus seemed to believe in them things, when I was in chapel, like you believe in flowers in winter. But when father talked of 'em, I *knew* 'em. It was like cowslips in your hand. Keys of heaven, cowslips be called."

"A pretty name."

"Aye."

"Shall we go after cowslips together, Deb? Next June?"

"Aye."

"And now let's go in and light the fire and the lamp and cook a bit of supper and play something lively," said Stephen.

He was determined not to think, since thought opened the door to such horror. What if there had never been a grain of truth in any creed, and everything—all the beauty, the goodness, the effort, the achievement—were purposeless as dust in the wind, fortuitous, annihilated now, to-morrow or in an æon? What if he were no more than the moth, flickering for a moment in imbecile activity on the bleak mountain in the cold night wind? Such thoughts, like chained bloodhounds, awoke often unexpectedly, and lifted their voices; howling for his soul. What if one broke loose? What if it followed with irresistible, unswerving pace till he was in its grip?

He shuddered. He knew that then joy would be dead. And joy was air and water to him. He clenched his hands. They should not get loose. He piled on wood and made a roaring fire, made toast, pulled Deborah on to his knee, and made love to her in his own inimitable way, with his eager face and eyes full of vitality, his mouth—which could be grim or tortured—now pleasant with laughter.

The idea of going in among those kennelled hounds of thought, braving them, and either being consumed by them or taming them, never occurred to him. If it had, the idea would not have appealed to him; for he had physical, not moral courage.

They sat in the fire glow, ringed in an impalpable peace and joy until the glow should fade.

" Oh! I say, Deb! I made you something coming from work yesterday."

He felt in an inner pocket and pulled out a long chain of scarlet beads.

" Rose-berries! And on a string and all!"

He put it over her head. She laughed with pleasure. The berry-colour was repeated in fainter tints in her cheeks; her eyes shone.

The long necklace hung down over her dress like a rosary.

" Now, out with the hairpins!" said Stephen.

" Oh, you're allus doing that!"

" You're always looking so pretty! There! My word, Deb, you *are* ripping."

Deborah took courage from this.

" What did you and Joe talk about?" she asked.

" His beastly pig."

" What else?"

" Nothing."

" Eh, Stephen, what a fib!"

" A fib? How?"

She shook her hair over her face.

" I heard."

" Oh."

A humorous thought made him forget propriety in laughter.

" Did Lily hear old Joe's programme?"

" Aye."

" What a lark ! "

" Not for Lily."

" H'm. No. I daresay not."

" Stephen ! "

" Well ? "

" It wasn't only Joe that said things."

" Did I put my foot in it too ? Well ? Out with it."

She was silent. He remembered suddenly, and was embarrassed.

" That ? I had to say something. He was so solemn."

" You said it to aggravate Joe ? "

" Partly. But don't let's fag about it. It seems a funny thing to talk to you about."

" Who else so right ? "

In her question was the sense of injury that she felt because he talked to Joe with a frankness he had not shown to her. She sat with the firelight flitting over her, wistful, with the lit look which came from within, and which would have singled her out of a roomful of women for a man's love. Yet the essence of her being, the unique thing which caused that look was what he least understood in her.

" Who else ? " she asked again with more insistence. Pride conquered her girlish shyness. He did not answer; he was looking at her with a return of his first passion.

" Who else should you talk of your children to but the 'ooman as'll bear them ? " she said, and her voice shook with sorrowful indignation. " Who else should you tell your wishes to, and your sorrows and looking-forward, and the way you mislike the wind, nights ? (and that I know along of you covering your ears). You dunna tell me any of them."

She stood looking down at him with a dignity

seldom found in civilization—almost always among savage tribes.

"Oh, damn!" cried Stephen, springing up, so that her height diminished; "d'you suppose I can *talk* to you when you look like that? Give us a kiss, Deb!"

"Eh, dear!" Deborah shivered suddenly. "There's a thorn in your necklace, Stephen!"

XXXIV

A week later a sudden hard frost blackened the geraniums in the garden. Stephen detested the look of them. He found this enforced intimacy with every mood of Nature, this impossibility of getting away from stark realities, very wearing after living in a town. He did not realize that half the content of his past town life was owing to his unawakened state.

A town to him now would be little more restful than the wilds. Reality was after him; go where he would he was its quarry, because of the greatness in him. There are some who, like the white hart in old Welsh tales, are forever hunted while small game goes free. If he had escaped from the lost, vindictive cries of the storm, the starved garden, the neutral colours, the heavy pressure of the huge night on his heart, with its mute " whither ? " he would still have had to face plaintive cries from dark houses, tormented faces in the street, the dumb terror of animals driven to slaughter. He did not know this. He put the blame for his keener vision, his new, unwelcome capacity for acting as a receiver for these messages out of hidden mysteries, upon the gaunt horizon, the huge knife-like ridge on which he lived, and the opposite ridge that broadened into mountain plains, shadowy in the early autumn mornings as the fleeces of cloud that swept over them. Lesser men dwell in impregnable castles of content in the most lonely, the most populous places. Greater men set forth on quests against all the agony and mystery of life, and win their peace or go into a madhouse. But Stephen

o

was too clear-sighted for the first, too much the bondsman of joy for the second. Therefore he lived at present in vivid sunshine—like a butterfly between two night-frosts, a poet between two portents.

Every day the reaches of plain, the ridges and rock-masses, the glittering spar and the men that tore it from its bed with such reckless expenditure of their little share of life, were more hateful to him. The woods that he went through on his way to work grew spectral; cold mist swirled there; dead leaves hung on the boughs like rows of weasels and magpies before a keeper's house. A cold presence moved among the sad perspectives of the larch and oak boles; sinister, inimical to joy, the Dark Keeper went his rounds—strangling life, hanging the shrivelled corpse of beauty in the bleak air derisively. Stephen felt his presence; saw his snares laid for men; began to feel that all humanity was but a poor line of rotting leaves and blackening corpses before the hollow house of death.

One day, as he walked in a gloomy reverie, a sudden noise behind him made him start. He looked back; there in driven, protesting, panic-stricken hosts came all the leaves of the summer—all the tongues that made soft music night and day, all the silken curtains under which pigeons had crooned, over which rain had slipped laughing. They came like a driven sandstorm, some a yard or more high, swirling in the eddying wind, others in a thick mass low down. They came round him—hitting him as terrified birds hit a window; patting, stroking him, till he felt as if he were fingered by corpses. Their stiff helplessness horrified him. They passed on in a frenzy of nothingness, feckless with the coming of corruption.

"Damned things!" he muttered. "I won't come this way again."

Fear crept over him as he reflected that he, Stephen Southernwood, the strong and happy, was afraid of

198

dead leaves. He thought his sanity must be threatened. The hollow scraping sound of a fresh company of leaves swelled behind him. He ran uphill to the end of the wood.

He looked through the gathering dusk toward the cottage, and saw the one window red as a poppy. She was there waiting for him; she would not fail him. Only he could not tell her. He laughed unsteadily.

"Blessed if a chap could tell a woman he was in a funk at some dead leaves!"

Night by night he came home a little sooner, was a little more flushed with haste.

All day long the picture of the red-curtained kitchen with the round table set for tea, the steaming kettle, and Deborah—neat and bright in her new berry-coloured dress—making tea, were to his mind what the Sacrament is to a Christian. The evenings were happy times, radiant as those last autumn days when the spendthrift gold shines with the strange intense lustre of fleeting things.

Only in his passion for her could he forget everything —even the predatory whine of the wind. He felt immune as a god while in its aura. Should she fail him, he thought one night when the storm shook the cottage and she lay asleep in his arms, he would be a beggar—a prey for every despair. He wished more and more as September slipped by that he had never taken the cottage. The whole countryside was acquiring in his eyes something portentous, apocalyptic. For the personality of a man reacting upon the spirit of a place produces something which is neither the man nor the place, but fiercer or more beautiful than either. This third entity, born of the union, becomes a power and a haunting presence—non-human, non-material. For the mind that helped to create it once, it dominates the place of its birth forever. Hence came the troops of mediæval saints and devils. Hence came folk-plays, nature

199

poems, sonatas—the heights of vision, the depths of melancholy.

Stephen could have made these ridges and valleys immutable in lyrics or elegiacs, painted them in radiant atmospheres, liquefied them in symphonies. But he had not the technical training for any of these. He only had the capacity for pain. He had not the safeguard of expression.

" Deb," he said one day, when the first light snow powdered the dawn-cold hills, " couldn't we go away somewhere? I do hate this place."

" Go away? Oh, Stephen ! "

She had no key to his state of mind. He had told her nothing of his feelings. It seemed to her simply a freak.

" But the work? And it's so scarce, and winter coming and all ! "

She did not want to move, to disturb the warmth and peace of their home. Doubts, fancies, wonder had come upon her lately. She wanted to be anchored here, in the hills of home, near her father.

" You brought me here, Stephen," she said pleadingly. " Dunna root me up agen."

He said no more. Every day he pulled his collar up, shrugged his shoulders and set his mind to endurance of things so impalpable that he could not express them even to himself—but none the less real for that. He forced himself into some of the moral courage he lacked. His personality grew. The men felt his presence more, though he said less.

Towards the end of the month was the harvest thanksgiving in Wood's End Chapel—the day of Eli's extraordinary invitation. Deborah wanted to go.

She saw less of her father now, for ways had grown almost impassable. The homely associations of the harvest service and the tea—never missed from childhood—made her anxious to be there, if Stephen would go.

" Would you mislike going, Stephen ? " she asked longingly.

Any festivity, anything that meant light, colour, human merriment, appealed to Stephen; it helped to keep the other things at bay.

" All right, I'll come. I'll make you a new berry necklace, too," he promised, his spirits rising. " All the fellows will be jealous, and Lily will be green with envy."

" Why ? "

" Jealous of your prettiness."

He had summed up Lily in a way that would have surprised her.

" It's a goodish walk," said Deborah, wondering if she could manage it, for she had felt tired lately.

" Oh, nothing to people like you and me, Deb ! Lazy girl ! Suppose you want me to hire a trap, h'm ?"

" Oh no, Stephen ! I can walk right enow."

She was troubled, none the less, at finding that when she went to meet him in the evenings (which he had asked her to do after the dead leaf episode), she flagged, and could not keep up with his stride.

" I'll go and see old Nancy Corra," she reflected. " She'll give me summat to take off the sick feeling and the tiredness. She's got stuff for 'most everything."

She also thought that Nancy could give an authoritative opinion on the suspicions, fears and hopes that had possessed her lately.

" She'll be at the tea, Sunday; I met fix a day to go then," Deborah decided.

XXXV

NANCY CORRA was always to the fore in camp
meetings, revivals, services where conversions took
place, and teas. She lived at a hamlet half-way down
the ridge, at some distance from Lostwithin, called
the Clays. Huge heaps of lead refuse rose in unwholesome whiteness, like mounds of rather dirty sugar,
round the deserted mines. Grey water trickled
stealthily between them. Somewhere here the
Romans mined for lead.

"Wold ancient mines they be," Nancy would say,
"and a vast of lead's been took from 'em, time and
agen."

Her small cottage stood among the white mounds,
with a strip of garden at the back where she grew her
"yarbs." Here were horehound, tansy, pennyroyal,
balm o' Gilead, all-heal, mallow and a hundred more.
She had trouble with them, for the soil did not suit
many. She would plod up into the larch-woods with
an old bucket and shovel and bring back leaf mould
for them; and they survived, though their leaves
were often strangely spotted.

"There be a curse on the place," people would say
as they passed at dusk, and they would shiver and
hurry on. It certainly had an unkempt air, and the
house a wary secrecy. Nothing could be brought
against Nancy, yet the police in the neighbouring
villages eyed her unfavourably, and now and then
one would watch her house. That is to say, he would,
with much trampling and clambering, hide in the
deserted engine-house and go to sleep there. He

was watched in his advent and departure by a satiric Nancy.

"Wise as sarpents they sim to theirselves, and harmless as doves they be," was her comment on the police force. She knew that her secrets—secrets that might possibly have cost her life and certainly would have gained her several years in prison—were safe. Yet they were spread over the countryside, in the keeping of gipsies, wives of labourers, barmaids at small taverns on untravelled roads, women who tramped, pedlars and unmarried girls of all classes. Her unacknowledged patients were few. Her acknowledged patients—old folks with rheumatism, rickety children, field workers with a gashed hand or a whitlow, drunkards' wives with bodies covered with bruises—she prescribed for with surprising efficiency; her cures were simple, often drastic, usually very sensible. But her real patients—those who made her income—came in the evening, closely shawled. They crept up to her shut door and curtained windows through the colewort and butterbur at the foot of the gaunt mounds, when they were terrible with inky shadows. They would tap the window, and the door would open softly, revealing old Nancy's extraordinary figure. She wore her thick, grey hair hanging to her shoulders, cut square like Raphael's portrait of himself, and she scratched it with suspicious frequency. Under this thatch her aquiline nose, lead-coloured cheeks and cunning mouth were unpleasant; but when she looked up suddenly at people they started with surprise at her beautiful eyes. How such eyes came to light such a face was a mystery—one of the curious instances of compensation which make optimists of people who see life as a whole. They were Cymric eyes—kin to the Gaelic, but less merry, less melancholy. Keen, far-seeing, mysterious, sardonic, they were of a clear periwinkle grey, with lashes that seemed as long and dark on the lower as on the upper lid. They seemed too large, too lustrous, for her face. They were spacious enough for the wistfulness of a saint.

" Eh, Nancy Corra, if you'd give me your eyes, he'd marry me to-morrow," she was told sometimes.

Mrs. Arden, if any one spoke of Nancy in her presence, flew into a rage.

" Eyes ! Aye, she'm got eyes. Got 'em off the devil down the wych-elm spinney in among the dead-men's-fingers ! " she would say. There was a deadly feud between them. Yet their professions did not clash. Nancy was never called in by Mrs. Arden's cases. " She'd o'erlook the child," the women said. Most people shared Mrs. Arden's belief that Nancy had gained her mysterious knowledge from the devil. Whether, in her interference with natural laws, Nancy did unmixed evil, or whether she helped to right the balance of punishment between the sexes for the sin of " going too far," was a puzzling question. But it was quite clear that she was in herself an arrant hypocrite.

Deborah knew of the feud between Nancy and her mother, but Nancy lived near and had won quite a reputation by her cures of small ailments; also it was a long way to a doctor in Silverton.

XXXVI

THE harvest thanksgiving day was clear and mellow. Under the low grey sky the rooks went cawing to the stubble fields; blackberries were ripe; and in the quiet woods Deborah and Stephen saw the bird-cherries flaming with red leaves, and witan-trees burning with scarlet berries. The purple had nearly gone from the plateau round the signpost; but the wimberry leaves were of an intensely bright red. They came to the chapel slowly, for Deborah was tired and leant on Stephen's arm. She wore her berry-coloured dress and the necklace. Within, the chapel was decorated with corn and wild apples, heaps of fruit, yellow fern and nuts. Eli had sent a quantity of eggs, which was thought very generous until a decorator broke one. Mrs. Arden had sent her usual giant loaf, and Mr. Shakeshaft his usual miniature haystack, made by himself, Joe and the farm boy.

Deborah and Stephen met a fire of critical observation, for they were romantic, wicked, repentant and well-favoured all at once.

Mrs. Arden, in a flutter of excitement—for she was to officiate as a pourer at the head of a table, and she wore the famous gown—beckoned them to sit by herself and John. Then Joe and Lily came in, Joe very red and smiling, Lily self-possessed. Eli, sitting at the top of the chapel, surveyed them all inimically.

Lucy Thruckton entered, and the two young brides surveyed her, the one with pity, the other with scorn.

Deborah noticed that Nancy was there, very splendid in a tartan blouse. Lily managed to sit between Joe and Stephen, and observed Stephen's keen profile and slim, muscular hand with much approval. Stephen was remembering the last time he was here, how glibly he talked of death, how absolutely impenetrable he was then to the reality of it. He stared at Eli in order not to think, and Eli stared back at him unblinkingly. Joe was answering various winks and nods of young men friends in kind, Lily was looking satirically at Lucy, who appeared in her balloon-like white dress like a cow in muslin.

In the hymns—which depressed Stephen because they were all about harvest being over and the final harvest of death—Joe boomed like a foghorn, and Nancy, who had an extraordinarily metallic and powerful voice, annoyed Mrs. Arden extremely, and reminded Deborah of her coming interview. John looked round them all with his usual benevolence, and Eli rasped with fervour—

> " Whatever, Lord, I lend to Thee
> Repaid a thousandfold will be,
> Therefore I lend my all to Thee ! "

It was a hymn he liked. There was a cheerful compound interest about it.

Later on he preached his sermon.

" The Lord's druv me to it," he said, " now listen what I'll tell you."

He discoursed at great length and with real emotion about Speedwell, and how he had " overdruv " her.

He was stirred to eloquence, and they all thought him " touched "—except John.

" I be a great sinner," he said, and they all thought he was posing, except John.

Then he grew weary of reality and preached in his

usual ranting style, and they all thought what a grand preacher he was—except John.

As he ranted, Stephen sat immovable, seeing Christianity, every religion, the bedrock of all religions —belief in some great purpose, some pity at the back of things—all these, caricatured as he had never seen them before. Blankness fell on him. He felt that Eli, Eli's sermon, Eli's God, were frauds. The devil seemed to be Eli's intimate friend—well, there was *no* devil. God seemed to be in Eli's confidence. " Well," said Stephen to himself, with passion, " there is *no* God."

No anything. No immortality.

Here the horror deepened so that his head swam. Those bloodhounds—his thoughts ! At last the feared disaster had happened, one of them had broken loose—was on his track.

It was the horror of emptiness, utter negation— that modern ghost, more ghastly than mediæval devils or the ancient gods of slaughter.

Any god—however mutable, however cruel—he thought, would be better than this nullity. Suddenly the whole thing was summed up and symbolized for him in the Devil's Chair—an empty throne. There it was; no devil, no angel, no god ever was there, ever would be there, nothing. There was no court of appeal, there was not even any one to defy, curse, be tortured by; just vacancy and the insect-like lives of himself and the other millions in the world, all going nowhere for no purpose except extinction.

He shuddered at the appalling picture. He could not get the look of the empty throne of black rock from his mind. He crushed Deborah's hand until she whispered " Stephen," white with pain.

Eli's voice droned on. The sleepy flies in the ugly windows droned. Joe, wrapt in rosy and health-giving slumber, gave little snores and was violently poked by Lily.

Lucy Thruckton beamed when Eli painted hurriedly in grey tints the joys of paradise, and still beamed during his half-hour's digression on hell. It became obvious that she was so tightly laced that her face must crease in some way, and so good-natured that it creased from ear to ear.

John was lost in contemplation. He was thinking of the radiant mornings on which he had felt— as some felt in Galilee a while ago—a Presence near him, and, as they did, " wist not who it was." He smiled at the remembrance of the transcendent beauty of the hills on those days, the wistful meaning in the cry of the sheep, the quiet messages in the rain.

Eli saw the smile.

" Cursed are they that smile, for they shall weep," he said, adroitly transposing the text.

" An' all they that rejoice shall be utterly cast down. ' When the silver cord is loosed an' the golden bowl is broken——' "

Stephen gave a smothered groan and stood up, with his hand to his head. He could sit there with his thoughts no longer—he went out into the air.

" And Judas went out an' it was night," said Eli patly.

" Only it ain't," said Joe under his breath. " We'm not 'ad our teas yet."

Deborah looked at Eli with flashing eyes; she had never been so angry; she followed Stephen out.

He was sitting on the wall resting his head on his hand.

" Oh, Stephen, my dear, what's come o'er you ? " she asked, with a hand on his shoulder.

" Only a bit of headache."

" You'll come back to the tea ?   A cup of tea 'll do you good."

" I can't.   That old devil——"

" Eli ?   He's done prating now.   If he starts on you agen, I'll give him a bit of my mind.   Do 'ee come, Stephen."

" All right."

" Not if you'd liefer go home ? "

" No.   It's all right."

They went back.   There was a great bustle of moving benches and carrying in tables for tea.   The two women who had been preparing it in a side room came in with tablecloths.   Every one ran about with plates, except Lucy, who sat in pleasurable anticipation, remarking—

" Naught done's harm to none."

At last all was ready, and Mrs. Arden, Mrs. Shakeshaft and Mrs. Prior of Long Acre took their places at the head of the tables.

" Lord, Stephen ! " exclaimed Patty, " you look as if you'd seen a ghost."

" My old man," said Nancy, from another table (she always mentioned this fictitious gentleman with great emotion), " seed a ghost just afore he was took for dyeath."

" Dear now ! " commented Lucy, with her mouth full of cake.   " It was a bad day for him."

" It'll be a bad un for you, if you gulp all that cake so fast," muttered Eli.   " You're too kind to yourself, young 'ooman.   If you was my darter——"

" Well—what, father ? " Lily asked, amused to see Lucy subsiding in self-conscious blushes.

" If her was my darter," said Eli slowly, so that all eyes in the room were focussed on the unfortunate Lucy, " I'd give her a good thrashing twice a day, and get some of that there fat off'n her."

Having reduced Lucy to tears, he rubbed his hands and turned his attention elsewhere.

" Spare the rod and spoil the child. Now, look at my darter—a respectable young married 'ooman—and all because I didna spare it."

Lily crimsoned and looked appealingly at Joe.

" Hush your row, Eli ! " he muttered.

" And look at others I could name—the darter of a soft-hearted man here present. What's it brought her to ? "

Here he swallowed the bread and jam, which he was charily eating, in one extravagant mass, as he reflected afterwards with regret. Stephen continued to shake him until his head rolled about.

" Say another word, and I'll knock your beastly head off ! " he cried, all his misery finding an outlet in rage. Eli's teeth chattered with the shaking, but he was undaunted.

" Gi' me back my Bible, you young thief," he said, " or I'll summons you."

" Now, now, Eli and Stephen," said John. " You'm spoiling the party."

Mr. Shakeshaft started an elaborate conversation with Joe and another man about the merit of two sheep-dips.

Mrs. Arden, elegantly pouring out, turned to Eli and remarked—

" If I was you, Mr. Huntbatch, I'd make the most of the time, since you'll pay no more if you chaw till nine."

There was a general titter, Eli's economies being well known.

" John," said Eli, portentously, " yer taste in religion makes me afraid for yer, yer taste in cattle makes me sorry for yer, but yer taste in women makes me heave."

Stephen seemed cut off from the rest, stamped with

a peculiar mark, ringed by the infinities. Homely scenes, kind faces, the four comfortingly commonplace walls, even Deborah had receded, the whole world had rolled up like a drop-scene and left him facing blank nothingness.

He could not get his spiritual experiences in touch with real life at all. Life ceased to be real. It was a hum of insects round carrion. All these people—himself—had acquired a vagueness, a fleetingness; only the thing he had felt was true; negation was the only fact—the rest, dreams.

He thought of books, of how eagerly he had read them to find the truth when he was a lad at the college.

But there was no truth, seemingly, nothing to find out.

He thought how he had striven to keep straight, how fiercely he had repented and punished himself when he had sinned. But there was no sin—no goodness—nowhere to get to by going straight. The system of reward and punishment had never appealed to him; herein had lain the originality of his crude, rather mixed preaching. But the idea of continued existence after death had been to him a sufficient reason for all effort, a sufficient reward for all hardships.

It seemed perfectly useless to him to make any effort, if the grave were all. This sense of negation drugged every faculty, and his vitality struggled against it unavailingly. He looked across the table, steamy and fragrant with tea, at John's calm face and eyes like cwm-water. He wondered how John would look and what he would say, if he could make him understand his state of mind.

Every one at the tea, all the world of men outside seemed inchoate, purposeless, like the swarming, slimy, minute life in stagnant water. He felt sick.

211

" Stephen, lad," said John in his voice which was quietude, " you met drink a sup of tea, and you'll feel better." He leaned across the table amid a buzz of talk. " And, lad," he said, " there's an answer to every question, and at long last the light shines."

Stephen was startled. How did John know? Ah, well—what matter? He and John and the rest were nothing—a few midges, humming for a day. It did not matter what they thought or were. Yet John's words, his look, remained at the back of Stephen's mind, and he wondered idly now and then whether John had had any experience to warrant them or whether it was the usual kind of cant.

" Well, Mr. Cadwallader, so you've got a son ! " said Mrs. Prior.

" Ou? Aye." The proud father indifferently munched a pie.

" And it's mother doing well? "

" Ou? Aye."

" And I hear he's like his father."

" The very moral of him, poor lamb ! " broke in Mrs. Arden, with a sympathy quite lost on the father, who ate largely and with the efficiency of a chaff-cutter. All the women surveyed his knobby head, huge mouth, minute nose and batlike ears, and felt intense sympathy for Mrs. Cadwallader.

When tea was over, Nancy slipped up to Lily.

" And how are you, my pretty? " she asked.

" All right, thank you."

" Now you tell old Nancy all about it."

She edged Lily into a corner. Deborah, coming to speak to her, heard Lily arranging to go and see her.

" Come along of me, Lily," she said.

They agreed to go on the following Saturday, as Lily had reasons of her own for wishing to go when Joe was at market.

"And what about All Halloween?" Mrs. Arden said suddenly, mindful of future festivities now that this was nearly over. "We mun have a bit of a randy for it, no danger! There'll be the accorns, and the nuts and the apples to sort, and I could do with a bit of help. So suppose you come, Deb and Stephen, and stop the night over. Joe and Lil, you come and have a bit of supper, and you, Eli, and Lucy—if there inna too much weather for coming so far."

"Oh, I'll come, weather or no weather," said Lucy.

"Aye, her will!" said Eli. "Her's like a young duck—always hankering. 'Whose god is their belly'!"

"Manners!" said Mrs. Prior, majestically.

"And I'll get some nice pippins ready, and cobs and that, and we'll play All Hallows games."

"I wunna play never no wicked games," said Eli. "Now listen what I'll tell you. Such games is cursed in Leviticus, Tobias and the rest of the prophets. Witchcraft, they be. I wunna come if you have games."

"Stop away, then, and good riddance!" said his son-in-law heartily.

"On second thoughts I *will* come," snapped Eli, "to keep you from selling your souls too cheap."

"Well, it'll be four weeks to-day," Mrs. Arden announced, "and mind you all come. Not but what it inna much use to play them games when we're all married."

"Except Lucy," Lily giggled.

Lucy flushed, remembering what Lily had said at the fair.

"But still," Mrs. Arden reasoned, "there's things as we can still be interested in, if we *be* married."

Nancy laughed sardonically.

Eli rose, remarking, " Well, we mun be going to our happy whomes. We've thanked the Lord for six mortal hours for the worst corn harvest there's been for years, so let's hope He'll do better with the roots."

He slammed the chapel door behind him,

XXXVII

As they walked home it suddenly seemed to Stephen that Deborah was holding him chained to the ridge by virtue of the marriage into which she had persuaded him. As he thought it, a blight fell on his love for her, and it flagged, instead of flowering, as it might have done, and filling the world and making all questions unnecessary. He strode on doggedly and did not speak. She kept up as well as she could, and made breathless little remarks to which he gave no reply.

When they reached Cranberry Rock, she was so exhausted that she sank down and began to cry. He went on, oblivious of her absence.

" Stephen ! " she called frantically. " Stephen ! " He turned.

" Hullo, what's the matter ? "

" I canna go any further. I mun bide a bit."

" Not tired, surely ? "

" Aye, mortal tired."

Before her tears, her helplessness, he forgot his sense of injury. The lover in him came to the top.

" Poor little girl ! " he whispered. " There, I'll carry you."

He carried her down the steep slope, dodging the flat, white stones that lay about. He thought they were like tombstones with no name, no date, no word of hope, fit (as he bitterly reflected) for the nameless, dateless dead, beasts and men, who had gone into the silence of annihilation. A horror of them came on him ; there were so many ; one would surely be spared to crush his own life, his own joy which he wanted. Suddenly he caught his foot on one, and stumbled.

" Leave me walk now, Stephen ! " said Deborah. " You're too tired and it's too steep."

" No, I'll carry you."

" Oh, *please*, Stephen ! "

He went on, still carrying her. He felt that only her weight, her nearness, kept him from flinging himself over the rock-wall that dropped sheer to the plain away on their left. Deborah gave up the argument, inwardly delighted at not getting her way.

" How strong you be, Stephen ! Don't your arms ache ? "

" No."

His heart did. He felt that he was doing his duty to Deborah. He was acting up to what he had promised. The thought that it was his duty took away the charm. His love for her, which had been slowly growing from the mere desire of the young male for the female that is his mate, and might in time have become an all-inclusive passion, was checked like a plant in drought.

" What a God-forsaken place this is ! " said Stephen, in the irritation of overwrought nerves, when they reached the cottage, crouching there like a white mouse petrified with fear.

Deborah leant against the doorpost. She had no vitality left to spend for him, but she smiled.

" For goodness' sake, let's go in," he said in a fever. " Here, I'll light the fire. What in hell we went to that awful affair for, I don't know."

She said nothing, and he thought her unsympathetic and cold.

At last the fire blazed, and things looked better.

" There ! Now let's sit here, and have a good supper and hot drinks and a game of cards—or something."

" But, Stephen—can't we go to bed? "

" You can, if you like. I shan't."

He instinctively felt that the first edge of things must wear off before he dared trust himself to sleep.

" But why, Stephen? "

" I'm not tired. It's a good fire, and I want to sit by it."

" I'll stay along of you, then," said Deborah heroically. But she fell asleep in her chair as she said it, and Stephen helped her upstairs. The cold air and the loneliness after he went down struck sleep from her, and she lay and cried, too tired to move but not too tired to feel. She thought she had offended him.

Below, by the dying fire, Stephen sat and brooded, read a week-old paper, nodded, tramped to and fro, and brooded again. The hours went by as silently as owls. Frost tingled outside; stars perched on the Devil's Chair, like goldfinches on a black stump, and flitted west.

The Chair looked dark and gigantic, and not so much like a saddlebag chair as it did from some places, but more like an embattled castle where no torch shone.

In the morning Deborah, coming down early after a restless night, found Stephen asleep, with his head on the table. She stole about lighting the fire and making tea; then she kissed him, holding the cup invitingly before him. He woke stiff and exhausted.

" I dreamt——" he said; " oh, no! it wasn't a dream."

A weary look came over him.

" Ne'er mind what it was, dear lad! " said Deborah. " Draw up to the fire and have this—it'll hearten you up."

She cooked some bacon and toast, and the little room grew reassuringly comfortable.

" You make things so different, Deb," he said gratefully.

" You're not angered with me ? "

" Of course not."

" Then naught matters. We're together, and that cures all. Naught can part us—not even dying."

Her face lit up.

" Don't ! " said Stephen.

" Oh, you mean it's bad luck to boast. Well, I'll touch 'ood. That's a sure charm."

" I didn't mean that."

" Only I wish as we could be together more," she went on. " Not you down there and me up here. When you go, mornings, I stop living till you're back."

He could not understand this.

" And I get thinking—I canna stop—of all the things that met come to you, Stephen. It's like watching your own heart taken off you, and wondering if they'll put it back or no."

" That's morbid."

" No, it's only love of you, Stephen. Folks inna frit of losing their second-best brooch, but they keep fingering the best one. I shouldna think as Eli ever loses sleep, longing after God Almighty, like father's done many a time. And Lily never reckons the time till Joe comes back; she's her own best treasure, is Lily—and Eli's his own God. But you—Stephen— oh, Stephen ! I'm feared when I think as you're more to me than father and God put together. Every time you're away, out of my sight and hearing, I'm frost-bitten. Then you come in, and it's summer. But I've *been* frozen. I knew what it would be, if you stopped away long—the cold going deeper, till it was one of them black frosses, till it went right in, and I was dead. But any minute, if you came back, there'd be summer agen."

" For goodness' sake, Deb, don't talk like that ! "

" I only wanted to say, Stephen, dunna you think you met some time get a bit of a sheep-walk or some-

218

thing—and be at home, like father is—and look like I dreamt I saw you by the little signpost? A grand flockmaster you'd make, Stephen—so big and kindly and all."

"But what for?"

"So's to take away the daylong sorrow."

"What sorrow?"

"Being away from you."

"But I'm back at six."

"If you was back an hour after you'd gone, the sorrow'd be the same while it lasted. And there's always the fear."

"What of?"

"Everything. All the 'orld's agen you, if you're fond of your man—when he's away. There's thunder and machinery and runaway horses and a slip on the hillside—it turns me sick. There's so many things set agen lovers."

"But such things don't happen."

"Aye, they do—every day. They met happen to you, and me not there. If the rock-crusher——"

She shut her eyes, ghastly pale, then went on with an effort.

"If it caught you, Stephen—how could I get caught, too, when women's not allowed in?"

"Get caught?" he said mazedly.

"Aye."

"You don't mean——?"

"I mean I'd take the only thing left as I wanted."

"What?" asked Stephen, in a horrified whisper.

"To be as you was. If so be we'd wake agen, we'd wake together, and if not—what'd it matter?"

He stared at her. This way of loving had never occurred to him. He knew people did it in books sometimes, but it seemed out of place in real life.

"I wish you didn't feel like that," he said.

"So do I."

"Then don't. Stop it. Cure yourself."

" When a man or an 'ooman feels like that," said Deborah, " they're not to be cured, not this side of silence. Whether it's God they're in love with, or a child, or a man, it's the bones of them and the blood of them. As soon cure folks of breathing."

Stephen's load grew heavier. He felt tied hand and foot. He was bound to Deborah—and to this place—both because he had married her and because of her way of loving.

He went to work feeling like an old man. From the arms of the trees, as from air-crumbled mummies, had fallen the gorgeous raiment; of all the beauty there remained only grey bones in the chill sarcophagus of the October sky.

Down at the mine the work grew more and more irksome to Stephen. It was too mechanical, too easy. He had long ago mastered it in every detail and it left his mind free. It began to give him the sick distaste, physically exhausting, that abhorred and enforced labour always gives. He worked harder than he need, but the manager would have preferred him to work less and glower less on receiving orders. He was left with one point of light in an infinity of darkness. Joy in work, pleasure, the desire to learn, the sensuous delight of colour, the impetus to righteousness, eternity, God—all these were fallen away like the golden leaves. There remained something stark and cold on which he dared not look.

In all this Deborah's lit window was his only hope—rosy in the night as he climbed desperately towards it, regardless of stumbles and cut knees. And sometimes it came upon him with horror that even for this a black wing waited, ready to fan it into nothingness, as the leathern wings of the Banshee of Wales fanned the lives of men. Whenever he remembered that he and Deborah were tied by an

220

oath by law, he heard the wing rustle like a bat in the rafters of his brain. And now a second bond was on him; he must stay with Deborah every day, every hour, or he would murder her soul. The wings in the rafters rustled again. Deborah might not be able to keep the light shining. If it flickered— if it went out—what then? It was all he had. That gone, nothing would be left to him but panic flight, out of this place, these thoughts, maybe out of this life altogether, or else——? He shuddered, as all sane and healthy people do before the prospect of the gradual chafing of the cord of reason till it should fray to a thread, and at last snap.

Every morning, when Deborah woke him with a cup of tea, made on her little spirit lamp, he saw the sun come like a threat from behind the Chair; every night, as he fetched sticks from the lean-to woodhouse for the morning fire, he saw the stars fall beyond the black horizon like shot birds into water.

XXXVIII

ON Saturday afternoon Lily called for Deborah, as it was only a little further to come this way from Slepe to the Clays. She came too early in the hope of seeing Stephen. She and Deborah went arm-in-arm along the ridge, past the brown foxglove stalks which rustled stealthily in the wind, down the wide, bare pastures, through the dark larch-spinney, and into Nancy's garden—now dank and full of stagnant, aromatic scent. The yellow afternoon sunlight of mid-October struck flat on the drawn red curtains of the kitchen and the hills of slag—white without purity. When they knocked, Nancy looked from the upper window.

"Oh, it's you. You can come in. Bolt the door after you."

They entered the hot, dark kitchen, and Lily clutched Deborah's arm.

"And now, my pretty, what can I do for you?" Nancy inquired of Lily, who appeared likely to be the best customer, being more malleable than Deborah. "Aye, aye, quite private we'll be. You come along upstairs, one at a time, and there's the Word of God for the other to pass the time with, bound in morocca, without money and without price, for I got it off'n a raffle, so I did."

From above, the muffled sound of their voices came down to Deborah as she sat and looked at a text made of cut whisky corks on the opposite wall. The room was so close that she wished Lily would be quick, and half thought of going without seeing

Nancy. At last they came down, Lily scared and
pale, Nancy brisk.

"Now that'll be five shillings, my pretty," she
said, "and that's counting the stuff you'll take
whome. And now for you, my dear?"

When they had gone, Lily looked round the
kitchen, found a half-pound bag of lump sugar, and
began to crunch it.

"Oh, aye," said Nancy, when Deborah had talked
a while, "it's as plain as sin—the family way."

Deborah thanked her, radiant, and rose to go
immediately, very much to Nancy's dissatisfaction.

"The one downstairs is a sensible girl," she said,
"and you're a softie."

She whispered in Deborah's ear.

"No," said Deborah flatly.

She went down.

Nancy turned her attention to Lily.

"And you'll come again next week?" she coaxed.
"And when you've took that stuff and some more,
you'll not be so wissen-faced."

"Thank you," said Lily faintly.

"Dunna you take it—leave it here!" Deborah
cautioned her.

Nancy was much annoyed.

"It'll be five shilling for you, without the stuff,
and you'll be worser and worser and worser afore
you're better, and you'll wish you'd come to old
Nancy," she remarked.

Deborah paid her, and they went out, leaving her
muttering soft vituperations.

"Well, Lily," Deborah said, "I'm thinking it's
maybe the same kind of gladsome day for both of
us."

"Gladsome? Miserable, I call it."

"Naught's miserable, if you and your man's fond
of each other, and if you inna, living along of him's
a disgrace."

" Everybody dunna have such queer ideas as you,"
Lily replied, rather nettled. " Whatever will Stephen
say, after what he told Joe ? " she added spitefully.
" Stephen 'll say what's right to be said."

The picture of Stephen thus conjured was attractive to Lily. How romantic, to be married to
Stephen ! But there—she must make the best of
things.

" What'll Joe say ? " asked Deborah kindly.
" Mighty pleased he'll be."

" They allus tell their husbands in whispers in the
novelettes, dunna they, Deb ? And then the husband
says, ' Ah, my dove ! ' or summat, and the writer
says the rest's too sacred, along of him not being
able to think of any more to put."

She wondered what Joe would say. To be like
the heroine of a novelette would be pleasant. To
hear Joe say, " Ah, my dove ! " would have a thrill
of newness in it. Yes, she thought she would tell
him.

" Not as I'm going to have a brat," she cogitated,
" being as Nancy's so clever. But I can easy tell
him afterwards as I was mistook."

She looked at Deborah rather wistfully.

" Stephen 'd say, ' My dove,' certain sure, Deb."

" That he never would."

Lily was taking away some of the glamorous
atmosphere that had lain on all things for the past
half-hour, that had swept away every thought and
left only a flood of light. The reminder of what
Stephen had said only a few weeks ago disturbed
her. She had meant on reaching home to go and
put on the berry-coloured dress and then, sitting in
the rosy firelight with Stephen's hand in hers, to
bring him with simple words into the light where
she now dwelt. She had thought that there would
be a long silence, as bits of charred stick fell softly
into the white ash under the grate, and the soup

bubbled on the fire. Now she was not sure if she had better say anything. She must wait until just the right moment, for if Stephen received her news churlishly, it would be too terrible. She quickened her pace; she was so longing to know if he would be in the right mood.

" Come a bit of the way with me, Deb ! "

Lily remembered that the shortest way—down Coldharrow Lane—was lonely.

" I wanted to get back," said Deborah, " or Stephen 'll be back afore me."

" You're soft about that chap ! Can't a man be left a minute and get his own tea ? "

" Stephen's not ' a man.' He's my man. And he's my lad, and my friend "—Deborah's voice shook a little with suppressed emotion. She searched for a way of making Lily understand. " And the lover of my soul," she concluded.

" That's blasphemy, Deborah. It's a hymn."

" If your man inna the lover of your soul," said Deborah, as she went with great self-sacrifice down the lane with Lily, " you've missed the honey and only got the empty comb."

" Empty nonsense ! I'd liefer a man was in love with me in the old-fashioned way. It's a deal more exciting."

" It's a deal more exciting *my* way," insisted Deborah, " for it's only when a man's the lover of your soul and wants you so as he's nigh beside hisself, as you're his 'ooman, right and true. I'm thinking it's only then as you've a right to be called his wife and sleep along of him."

" You talk very indecent, Deborah, to my thinking."

" It inna talking straight that's indecent; it's smiling and sniggering and colouring up over things."

Lily remembered that she must be pleasant, or Deborah might turn back.

" Lucy colours up awful in chapel, if there's any-thing about births and that. Nasty-minded thing ! " she said.

" It's queer that folk never blush about dying," said Deborah, amused. " It's a deal more indecent than being born."

" Would you keep this hat of mine all green, if it was yours ? " inquired Lily, who had become bored during the last remark, " or put some red on for the winter ? "

" Aye, a nice warm colour is red—berry red."

" It dunna suit you, Deb," said Lily, who had seen and been annoyed by Deborah's unusual and successful daring.

" Stephen likes it, so I dunna mind."

" You think of never a mortal thing but that chap."

" Of course."

" Selfishness, I call it."

Lily, being a past mistress in the art of selfishness, felt qualified to judge. Deborah was amused.

" Selfish folk are folk as do things for others except Lily Arden, I suppose. I allus thought selfishness was thinking of yourself, and I'm that busy thinking of Stephen that I canna. Night and day, there's no rest but doing things for Stephen, and naught but fears when he's away."

" What a miserable life ! "

" That it inna ! But if it was, I'd sooner be miserable and have Stephen than be happy and not have him. Seems to me, loving's like the Golden Arrow—bright and sharp, and him that finds it'll keep it against the 'orld. There's not a many do find it."

" Such softness, going hunting for old arrows ! "

" Well, I mind you was used to be glad enough of an excuse to go along of a chap on Palm Sunday and look for the arrow. But you never found it. I wunna looking for it, and I found it. Well, good-night, Lily! I'll be turning now."

"Take care the arrow dunna prick you!" Lily called after her acidly.

Deborah hurried home up the dim lane, where ghostly honeysuckle waved long tentacles against the cloudy sky, and along the dark ridges, where ever-moaning winds were deepening their lament. She felt that it was all wrong to be unselfish to others at Stephen's expense. If she didn't put him first, who would? It was dreadful that he should have to wait outside, with no tea ready. She almost ran home.

When she arrived, all was dark and silent. Before she reached the cottage, she thought she heard Stephen's voice somewhere near the Chair. She called, but there was no reply; then, before she had time to call again, there was a tremendous explosion and the rattle of falling rocks from the Devil's Chair. She was frozen with fear. Then, with a cry of "Stephen!" she began to run uphill straight towards the terror, all fear gone from her.

227

XXXIX

Down at the mine that morning Stephen had heard a thrush sing above a bed of early autumn violets in the manager's garden. He had gone for some order sheets while the manager was at breakfast; and, while he waited, the thrush played on his heart in the yellow wistful light. The idea of death, which every day of autumn had seemed to voice more insistently, which had haunted him since he had been flooded with the sense of nothingness, fled for a moment before the bird's voice. Stephen suddenly knew why he loved lights, colour, spring, song; why men built themselves warm houses and planted orchards; why women made their windows bright with geraniums and clean muslin; why mothers delighted in their babies and young men delighted in football and the zest of love. It was because all these things kept away the idea of death—the knowledge of future intimacy with it; because they built up around the fleeting moment the sapphire walls of immortality. Stephen did not put it in this way, but he remembered how he used to feel sometimes on a holiday, when he and a friend would come on some long walk to an inn at nightfall, and would sit there in the comfortable firelight with a sense of leisure and rest, at home for the moment in a kind of timeless glow, quite forgetting the coming journey in the dark. So the thrush and Deborah's kitchen, and young leaves, and a gallop made him feel. He stood tranced, listening to the sad, tentative music, the aftermath of spring. Then it snapped, as the

228

bird's life might snap before another spring, and only some rusty oak leaves fell on the apple-green violet bed with its few purple buds.

Stephen woke again to a grey world and the voice of the manager, who was talking more pompously than usual because his mouth was full of bread and bacon.

That evening Stephen went home faster than ever. In the woods no colour lived but the sad green of the pines. The tongues of fire that had streamed up the hills when all the larches were golden were now almost extinct. At the gate he looked up. There was no light. The cottage looked little more than one of the strewn rocks from so far down; above, like a fortress on the bleak sky, loomed the Chair— unexpectant, imperturbable, sinister.

Stephen loathed it. He knew all about quartzite and its enduring nature; he knew that for thousands of years the Chair had fronted everlastingness while men died like flies, and would front it and partake a little in its quality for thousands more after he himself was dead. He wanted to partake of ever-lastingness himself—was he not better than a mass of quartzite that he could reduce to powder in the rock-crusher? Yet there stood the rock, smooth, weather-proof, ancient with an age that no other strata for hundreds of miles had attained. It was harder than steel, impervious to fire. It kept in its dark heart secrets of porphyrite and silver. The shapes of the bits of sky that shone here and there through windows made by the laying of one rock across two others had not altered by more than a fraction since the Romans mined at the Clays. Such pieces as sometimes broke off and crashed down the slope were only, compared with the pile, like marbles dropped from a palace window. The hills all round— especially the common sandstone—were being worn away : but this wore so slowly that many centuries would do no perceptible work on it. All the way home, in the midst of wondering why Deborah had not lit up, he stared at it with the fascination of horror. And the craftsman in him, the practical manual worker, grew enraged that mere rock should have any power over him. He forgot that material conquest usually means spiritual defeat.

" If only I'd got it down at the mine," he said to himself, and felt desperate when he remembered what a span of time would be cut from his life before any appreciable portion of it was destroyed. It was not for him, he felt, to lay low such a monument of years. It seemed to him rather, as he looked up at it, as if it were a huge, smooth doom-table on which the death-day of every man in the plain and on the hills was engraved—his own with them. The idea would probably have struck him as ridiculous in daylight or when he was with other men. But those that have dwelt in the majestic reserve of wild places—intolerable to natures that have not as yet found themselves, and being the peace passing understanding to people like John—will know that intuitions come there which cities call madness or genius.

Stephen had, through a curiously timed mixture of circumstances, fallen from the surface of life into the foundations; he awoke in dark, hard reality. Loneliness made a mist around him. He stumbled on in the dying light with bent head and clouded youth, to all appearance a vigorous, sane, though labour-tired man going home to his well-earned rest : but in reality he was one of the few on whom has come the ageless, brain-wracking necessity to look into pain, evil, death and the deserts beyond death for himself, with his own eyes, not through the safe and rather misty glass of ready-made dogmas or
230

legends. What would happen to him none could tell; but some chance as vast and mysterious as the metamorphosis of sandstone into quartzite must come upon him. He would find in the advancing gloom on the appointed day either madness or God. He might run away from the place where these things had come upon him, but he did not know that the things were no longer dependent on the place.

He thought of Deborah. She seemed to belong to this country of mountains; he could not imagine her anywhere else. He could not leave her; yet how could he stay here, in hell?

He rounded the last shoulder with his usual sensation of pushing everything back with both hands and fighting his way to the door that meant refuge. It always stood open to welcome him, making a golden patch in the dusk.

To-night it was indistinguishable. There was no light. He quickened his pace. Every hound in the kennels of despair was on his track, he felt; every black bat of horror in his brain was astir, with leathern rustling. But once inside——! He came to the door. It was shut and locked. No one replied to his knocking. He set his shoulder to it and pushed; set his teeth and flung himself against it. The stout hinges gave at last; he got in. When he had searched he sat down on the stairs in a kind of stupor.

Deborah had failed him.

No matter-of-fact explanation occurred to him; he was too much strung up for that. He sat there until the silence of the cottage maddened him. He went out and the Chair confronted him. If Deborah had been to him all that he was to her, strength and peace would have come to him from their perfect communion even in absence. But his love for her was as yet small and bounded; it had little kinship

with the infinities. When she called him the lover
of her soul, and included in that phrase all that a
man can be to a woman, she was wrong; for although
he was of the few to whom this is possible, he did
not yet, and might never love in so godlike a way.
The intensity of his desire for her was simply the
passion of an eager nature for one of the most beautiful things in the material world—a woman's body;
but the fierce, indestructible, white-hot passion which
desires the body because of the beauty it sees in
the soul was not yet his. Therefore when her
presence was withdrawn, she became non-existent to
him. Now, for the first time, the thought of flight
began to take definite shape in his mind. He saw
Deborah in one scale and freedom in the other. He
had not allowed himself to think, during the past
weeks, what life would be away from this place.
Now he began to do so. He thought of the sea, of
countries where colour rioted, of all the scintillating
world, of adventure and forgetfulness.

Then he remembered what Deborah had said of
absence, and sickened at the thought.

He looked up at the Chair.

"Damn you!" he shouted. "I can neither go
nor stay, and you know it. You know the whole
hateful business——" He broke off. "There's nothing there!" he whispered. "I'm talking to an
empty chair."

He went into the house again, but he could not
rest.

"If I go on like this," he said, with the pathos of
the common phrase in the tragic moment, "I shall
go off my nut."

An idea occurred to him. He went out to the
woodhouse and brought from a safe hiding-place a
small cartridge of dynamite. He had brought it one
day to show Deborah, and in the stress of his thoughts
lately he had forgotten it.

" I'll blow the old rocking chair sky high," he said to himself, " and see how it'll look then."

Something practical to do put new heart into him. He climbed towards the Chair. At the back of his mind, so shamefacedly hidden that he did not even own it to himself, was a curious new hope. What if some presence—however evil—did really lurk there as some people imagined? He wished that it might be true, for it was the Chair's emptiness, the impersonal element in the world, that overcame him. He thought : " Well, if you throw stones into a lion's den you find the lion." The primitive element, the underlying superstition of the human mind came to the surface in Stephen. He went as the first sentient man might have gone to wake and brave the unknown gods. He told himself that he was only going to " knock the old Chair to blazes," because it annoyed him. But the other reason was the true one.

He clambered up the rock and chose a crevice for the cartridge at a point which he judged to be the extreme end of one of the arms seen from a distance. He packed in the charge and tamped it with powdered soil and small stones. His height was dwarfed by the rocks, so that he moved under the dark clouds like an ant on the face of the mountain, and the rocks stood up in ironical massiveness above his impotence.

He clambered down some way and lit a match.

" Now we'll see if you're everlasting ! " he said, and, stretching up, lit the fuse and ran over the rocks.

" Oh, Stephen ! Whatever's been doing ? " cried Deborah, as they met. " You'm not hurted ? "

" Hurt ? Of course not. I was only putting that dynamite charge out of harm's way, Deb."

From the hilltop, where they had been wheeling and alighting since the explosion, a covey of grouse rose with their mocking staccato laugh.

" Let's go in," said Stephen. " Those birds are devilish. Wherever have you been ? "

" To get a tuthree things at the Clays. I be so sorry to be late, Stephen."

She judged that her news must wait, and, in her present need of sympathy and the communication of her joy, she thought she would go across to her mother's on Monday. Stephen said no more about his doings; but in the morning, as soon as it began to grow light, he went to the window. The Chair stood exactly as it had always done. He could not detect even a nick in it from this distance. All his trouble had not altered it in the least. When he went later to investigate, he found that although he had dislodged quite as much rock as he could expect, he had made little more difference in its appearance than a woodpecker makes to the tree on which he hammers.

Superstitious tremors began to make themselves felt in Stephen's nerves; and because he had neither Deborah's naturalism, nor John's deep, pantheistic Christianity, nor Joe's stolidity, nor the indifference of a shallow nature, he had nothing with which to combat them.

XL

On Monday, when Joe came back from work, Lily planned her novelette scene. She had spent the day in visits to the cupboard, where she had hidden Nancy's bottle. She had taken the cork out, smelt it, and returned it to the cupboard. It was doubtful if she would ever take any, for she was one for whom future evils paled before present discomforts. She always took the way of least resistance.

" Why, Lil," said Joe, half-way through tea, " what ails you ? You're like a duck in thunder ! "

Lily was offended. It took the rest of tea for her to recover her dignity. When they had cleared away, and were sitting by the fire, Joe smoking with a sense of great well-being, Lily thought the moment propitious. She whispered. " Well ! " said Joe, all in a beam, and without the faintest tincture of novelette. To show his delight he became arch in the customary manner of the countryside.

" I could have told you that ! " he said.

It was too much for Lily. " A duck in thunder " and " I could have told you that " ! Where was the romance ? Where was the " Ah, my dove ! " She bounced off his knee and began to cry.

" There, there, Lil ! What's took 'ee ? " asked Joe, feeling rather like a duck in thunder himself.

" And that's all you say ! " cried Lily vehemently. " And much you care—selfish beast you be ! All I've got to go through, and never a word of thanks, nor anything ! "

She quite forgot, in her interest in the pose, that she did not intend to go through anything.

" Now, Lil," said Joe, " you know I'd liefer go through it for you. There's nought I wouldna go through to keep you from sorrow."

" That's only talk."

" Lil, you've no call to say that. It inna my fault the way the world's made."

Lily took no notice.

" And there I'll be," she went on, on rising accents, " groaning and clutching the bedpost, and maybe going mad with it all——"

" Stop it, Lily ! " shouted Joe miserably.

" And you sitting here, and smoking by the fire as pleased as Punch ! "

" Oh, Lily, you'll drive me crazy ! Dunna you know as there's no tarment I wouldna go through for you ? "

" Prove it, then ! "

Joe looked round the kitchen slowly. He was always slow. Then he rose and put the poker carefully between the bars of the grate.

" What's that for, Joe ? "

" Never you mind."

He watched it redden and whiten. Then he took it out.

" Now, Lil," he said, " I *will* prove it."

He slapped the poker down on his hand, so that it made a weal across it.

" Damn ! " he said, and withdrew it. It was beyond human nature to keep it there : but he slapped it down again in a second.

Lily watched him, fascinated. He put it in the fire again.

" Lil," he said, " I be a poor weakling, seemingly, and I canna keep it there. But I'll go on *putting* it there till I've proved what I said to you, and till you've giv' me your promise not to talk like

236

that, for I can't a-bear it, Lil, and that's the truth."

The sense of power this gave to Lily was very sweet. She said nothing. Joe continued his self-inflicted torture. He was beginning to feel rather queer.

" A'most think I'll sit me down," he said.

" D'you feel bad, Joe? "

Something in his face stirred the better feelings in Lily. She ran to him.

" There ! " she said. " You've proved it right enow. And where's the oil? "

" And you wunna talk like that? "

Joe spoke anxiously; he was determined to go on until she promised, and he was becoming eager to put the poker away.

" A'right. But look at your hand ! Where's the oil? "

" I'll get it," said Joe.

Lily rummaged in a drawer for rag. From the doorway suddenly came Mrs. Arden's voice.

" What an awful smell of scorched meat ! Dear sakes, Joe, what's gone of your hand? "

Lily observed with horror that Joe had brought Nancy's bottle instead of the oil.

" That ain't oil," said Mrs. Arden, sniffing it and looking at Lily.

" I'll fetch it," she said.

" Joe," whispered Mrs. Arden, " I've come down that hill as I never did afore. I mun have a word with you, afore I go back. And as for that—fling it on the mixen ! "

" Whatever for? "

" Because I say so. Take and do it now."

" But it's summat o' Lily's. It seems queer to break Lily's bottles without her leave ! "

" When you've heard what I've a-come to tell you, you wunna think so."

Joe departed with the semi-sullen air that he used to wear as a chidden small boy.

"Well, my dear," said Mrs. Arden adroitly, when Lily returned in a fluster, "so I hear there's grand news for me. You'll be thought a deal of in Slepe, I know—and a pretty child it'll be, if it's like its mother, so it will, and John's got summat put by for the eldest granchild. I've brought you summat for luck; it's early days, but time soon passes."

She produced a small, lace-trimmed gown.

"Joe's!" she announced, with pride and a consciousness of the impossibility of any one believing her. "There, put'n away, my dear, for I hear him coming lumbering back. Like carthorses, the men be, inna they?"

Lily was mollified, pleased, comforted, glad to hear Joe spoken of unfavourably, sorry for his hand, delighted with the frock, and quite unconscious that Mrs. Arden knew anything whatever.

She bound up the hand.

"Well, you be a great baby!" said Mrs. Arden. "Burning yourself, as if you wunna useless enough already."

Joe was silent. His dark eyes, full of dumb eloquence, sought Lily's as she tied up his burn unskilfully.

"Lil," he whispered, as Mrs. Arden poked the fire, "gi's a kiss!"

Lily gave it silently.

"Come and send me, Joe!" said Mrs. Arden.

"Maybe Lily wants me," replied Joe, looking at Lily longingly.

"Now you leave Lily to a bit of rest. Always hanging around, the men are, Lil!"

She carried her point.

"And the long and the short is," she said, after talking to Joe, without stopping, for ten minutes,

238

" as, if you dunna look out, there's no knowing what'll come to pass."

Joe was dazed.

" But sure*ly*," he said, " Nancy 'd never dare——!
And Lily 'd never have the heart——! "

" That's a kind of goods Lily dunna keep, no more than her father."

" Mother ! "

" What ? "

" You mun keep your tongue off'n Lily, or you'm no mother of mine."

" Your mother I be, and ever shall be 'orld without end—most the pity, say I—but I like you all the better for it, lad, and your father 'd have said the same. But the truth is, Lily's one of the poor in spirit."

" Mother ! "

" Well, I only called her what's supposed to be a great thing in the Bible."

" But she said to me—— "

" Listen to the gauby ! What's it matter what she *said ?* "

Joe groaned.

" I canna believe she'd tell lies to me."

He suddenly flared up.

" Deb's a tell-tale ! "

" Deb's no tell-tale. She only said, innocent-like, as they'd been to Nancy's, and I came down, all in a fluster, to find out, and there was the bottle—in mistake for the oil."

Joe looked at his hand. It came over him slowly that Lily had let him burn it to show his sympathy with pain which she never intended to undergo. She had played with him.

" Well, I be damned ! " he said—so suddenly that his mother jumped. She noticed the concentrated passion on his face, as she stood on tiptoe for him to kiss her.

239

"If you'm angered when you're talking to her, lad," she said, "mind you of your wedding night."

The mention of his wedding night was unfortunate. The irony of things pressed on him. He went home with long strides.

"Lily!" he called.

She came, bright-eyed from some of her favourite literature.

"What were you doing with Nancy's bottle?"

"How d'you know it was Nancy's?"

"Dunna bandy words with me! Them as has knocked about the 'orld, like me, knows about such as Nancy."

"It's nought but rhubarb."

"I'll learn you to lie to me!" shouted Joe. "And I want to know the meaning of you letting me grill my hand like a rasher, when you meant all the while—what you did mean."

"I didna mean nothing," said Lily, with some truth—for she never did.

"I'll learn you!" said Joe, in a towering rage, "to come kissing of me, and whispering to me to make me the gladsomest man in Slepe, and all the while—you're a damned lying 'ooman."

"Oh, Joe!" cried Lily, terrified.

"Did I or didna I say 'all or nothing'?" queried Joe.

"Aye."

"And what did you say?"

"All."

"Well, all it shall be."

He slapped his burnt hand on the table, and was silent with surprise at the pain.

"Now," he went on practically. "You promise me never to take no more of Nancy's stuff, and never to tell no more lies."

Lily looked up. In her distress, and her flickering love for him, which always burned higher when he

240

was angry, the shallowness of her face was momentarily obscured. She was almost beautiful. Joe looked at her, and was pacified in his own despite.

"Dunna you want to have little 'uns sitting around with their mugs?" he asked.

"No."

Lily spoke in a heartfelt tone. She was thinking of washing the mugs.

"Well, I'm——! Anyway, you mun promise."

Lily did so, with some relief as she thought of the unpleasant smell of the bottle.

Joe melted.

"Look here, little 'un," he said. "If you'll go on nice and proper this time——" he drew a deep breath——"I'll let you off'n the other five. I thought to have six," he added regretfully, seeing his dream-picture fading.

"Was it for you to think, without asking me?" said Lily pertinently, but ungratefully.

"I dunno."

"And was it for you," she continued, seizing her advantage, "to go and talk to that Stephen about it, and not to me? Not but what Stephen's a fine chap, and taller than you."

Joe was dumbfounded.

"So you knowed as I wanted six?"

"O' course. Duty to king and country, not to speak of yourself."

Joe flushed.

"I suppose it might have seemed queer-like. I'm right sorry, Lil."

Lily thought that this was much better.

"I'm awful fond of you, Lil, and I'll do the work for you, evenings, when I get back, and borrow Whitefoot to go drives——"

"And buy me the locket?"

"And buy the locket, by hook or by crook," said Joe recklessly. "Only no games, Lil! and I'll stick to what I said."

Lily never even saw the genuine, hard-won unselfishness of this.

Joe stroked her hair.

"What'll I be this time next year, Lil?" he whispered.

"A donkey," said Lily, whose spirits had risen at the hope of the drives and the locket.

"Gi's a kiss!" said Joe, who was tired with unwonted emotion, but happy, because in some mysterious way Lily was dearer then ever before.

Lily was happy also, but quite untired, for emotion had as little effect on her as rain on a plant under glass—neither breaking nor renewing.

Neither Lily nor Joe, nor Nancy nor Mrs. Arden noticed that their respective weakness, doggedness, lack of principle, plethora of principle, tragedy and comedy, had left things just as they were; that with their will or without it the courses of life flowed on to their undreamed-of endings, from their mysterious source.

XLI

"John! John!" shrieked Mrs. Arden on All Hallows Eve—"wherever *is* the man? Never in the quarter he's wanted in, like the weathercock in winter. John! There's the nuts and the apples, and the logs to fetch from the wood'us, and water and dear-knows-what! And you mun move them accorns now, for I go tiddly-bump o'er 'em whenever I go across the bake'us."

The acorns were arranged on the floor in a large semicircle round a fire lit especially to dry them. In their tight husks and their look of crowded civility they were like an attentive lecture audience.

"Whatever be you doing?" shouted Patty.

John was deliberately filling, trimming and lighting the little lamp that he continued to put on the bracket at the turn of the stairs by Deborah's door.

He went up the six stairs and placed it there in silence.

"Well, of all softness!" complained his wife, "and she a married 'ooman as'll have her own chillun afore long; and you putting a lamp as if she was a baby! And her not here neither! You'll come to want, John Arden, and see your wedded wife in the House afore you'm done—playing such May-games with the money at your time of life!"

She went up and put it out. She was much ruffled by preparations and by her last week's interview with Nancy, in which, she could not help feeling, the honours had not been all hers.

"Mother!" said John, striking a match and re-lighting it; "dunna do that again."

"Well, well!" said Patty, who knew where to draw the line; "play with your silly toys if you mun, but dunna get in such a passion over it."

"Mother, how can we say 'Lead, kindly Light,' if we dunna light our own bits of lamps? How do we know as the bit of love we give our Deb metna be all as she'll have one of these days? And if the Maker of the sun and the flocks of stars could say so homely—'I will light thy can'le—' canna we poor creatures light them each for other?"

Patty wiped her eyes stealthily. John's eloquence always made her cry. She was intensely proud of him—he was her Bible.

"Well, anyway," she said briskly, after a pause, "you met fetch the logs and the water and the apples and the nuts and the——"

"Now, now, mother! One at a time. Dunnat o'erdrive the willing horse."

"It's me that's o'erdruv!" She forgot that the festivity was of her planning. "With Stephen and Deb coming for the night and all."

"Why did you ask them then?"

"Bless the man! would you let your own girl, as you're so busy lighting a useless lamp for, trudge the roads past midnight—and she three months in her time?"

"Eh, you dunna say!"

"I say and I know. And now you mind what you're after, father, and not go blurting out nothing unseemly. For your tongue's hung on in the middle and oiled with nonsense."

"I didna know as more than one tongue in this house was like that. Well, well, to think of my little lass——"

"Your little lass'll want some water to make her

244

a cup of tea more than her'll want you to stand mumchancing, John."

John departed. Mrs. Arden made up the fire, looked at the soul cakes—very rich and generous successors to the original plain oat cake—put the kettle on, laid tea and went to change her dress.

Soon Joe and Lily arrived—Lily radiant, wearing the green locket, Joe ponderously careful that she should be out of draughts and by the fire.

" Well, lad," said John, when Mrs. Arden took Lily to change her shoes, as it was raining; " any news for the wold father ? "

" There met be." Joe took out an enormous handkerchief, patterned with horseshoes.

" Queer thing, father," he said, " as being gladsome makes you sweat so."

" Aye, aye. Better'n nitre."

John's one remedy for all ills was to take a dose of nitre and pile on the bedclothes. He would then get up next morning and go out in a north-easter without discomfort or any ill effects. They sat on the settle, smoking contemplatively.

After five minutes Joe said—

" How'd you like being a wold ancient grandfather, an' you so spry and all ? "

John rose and went to the old corner-cupboard, with its inlaid door and large brass hinges; he took out a small box of antique shape, lined with a bit of old newspaper on which could still be read extracts from " Mr. Pitt's speech on Saturday." He brought it to Joe.

" Theer," he said, with the concealed ecstasy that giving always woke in him. " That's for your eldest, Joe."

" Well, thank you kindly, father, I'm sure. Laws me ! it's full of money ! "

" Aye."

" But you've got no money to part wi', father ! "

" Seems like it, don't it ? " said John.

The years of loving sacrifice in scraping that boxful without letting Patty go short were amply crowned for John by this one moment. He sat down again in the corner wrapped in beatitude.

" Well," said Joe, who had enough of his father's penetration to understand the greatness of the moment—" Well, he'll be a rich mon afore he's born ! Leastways she. Leastways I dunna know which to call it. I mun show Lily."

" Best wait till you're whome, lad."

" Why ever ? "

" She metn't like for things to be said afore me," said John.

He knew how much more Joe would enjoy the surprise in private.

There was a knock, and Lucy appeared, breathless, but good-humoured.

Close on her heels came Eli.

" Well, well, the party's in, I see ! " he said; " leastways the tuthree poor, foolish folk as dunna know better'n to be waddling through the muck, like goslings for a scrap of meat."

" Well, well, Eli ! " said John, " if you be a gosling, come and cackle by the fire."

Lily came down, very pleased at having done her hair in a new way.

Eli stared at her frowningly, remarking, " Well, of all the scar'crows I ever see, you'm the worst. Who'm you been clipping, to get that there fangle-ment ? A poor scrannel chap with sixteen shillings a week canna buy it you."

At this point Joe's elbow found itself in Eli's chest, and Eli sat down suddenly. Joe smoked on imperturbably.

Lucy, whose emotions were as transparent as she was opaque, giggled.

" If I wan you, Lucy Thruckton," Eli said grimly, " I wouldna get no fatter. It dunna look respectable."

" Why, Lil," John exclaimed, as Lily ensconced herself between him and Joe, " what a picture you do make agen the old settle ! "

Joe leaned forward and surveyed Lily from every position, as if she were a work of art just introduced to him. Lucy gazed at her with awe and envy. Lily felt that the evening was a success.

Stephen and Deborah came in, and were whisked off to put on dry things. Deborah came down in an old gown of her own, and Stephen in John's best coat and a scarlet handkerchief tied round his neck.

" Laws me, Stephen ! " cried Mrs. Arden, with great admiration; " that bit of red just sets you off."

Lily thought so too. She and Deborah both sat and admired Stephen's bright, crisp hair—Deborah because it was not like her own, Lily because it was.

Stephen felt a kind of comfort in wearing John's coat. He knew that it had lain above a heart full of mysterious peace, that its worn sleeve-edges had brushed the book-rest when its wearer travelled into regions where thought stopped. Peace breathed from it, as from all John's small possessions—the three ties in his drawer, carefully folded, lying between the handkerchiefs Deborah hemmed for him last Christmas, and the gilt tiepin Joe bought with his first earnings; his prayer-book, which lay on his father's old tool-chest and held in its turn his mother's workbox and a bead mat made by Mrs. Arden, even the simples he kept in the outhouse seemed friendly, and Deborah had been known as a child to rush out there after a scolding, and come back hugging his old tin can of sheep-dip, from which she appeared to gather a store of consolation.

"Well, you gallus young whippersnapper!" said Eli combatively to Stephen.

"Well, you sour old great-grandfather!" replied Stephen patly, for Eli always roused him to repartee, in whatever mood of joy or sorrow he might be.

Mrs. Arden suddenly cackled with laughter, slapped herself and cackled again.

"You seem amused," said Eli.

"To think of you——!" She mopped her eyes.

"Mother," John cautioned her, "what did you say to me afore the party come in about oiled tongues?"

"Deborah," said Eli, seeing that he could get no change out of Stephen; "you look married all o'er."

"Well, Eli," Mrs. Arden put in, "she's tired after the waidy walk. She'll be better for a cup of tea. And maybe, when folks have had their teas, they wunna nag so."

"Paid for!" shouted Eli suddenly to Lucy. "She's been doing 'trust' this half-hour, with eyes as big as them soul-cakes with longing after 'em."

"Well, Deb, my dear, is your tea putting some heart into you?" asked Mrs. Arden. "The roads be long in the dark."

"The roads be long in the dark," echoed Stephen, half to himself. He was sitting next to John.

"Stephen," said John in a low tone, "our travelling's a circle. Whether we're outward bound or homeward bound dunna matter; we're just as nigh the sun."

Stephen made no reply; he felt grateful, but, in the darkness where he was, all comfort seemed futile. He was momentarily happy now, in the light and the chatter which kept thought at bay. He was thankful to be spending a night away from Lostwithin and the Chair, and he felt more than ever, after this taste of freedom, the longing to be away.

"Mother says," said Lucy ponderously, "as when

248

they give a soul cake to folks in time past, they was
used to say—

> ' God have your soul,
> Bones and all.' "

"How beastly!" said Stephen.

"If you're too high and mighty to want the Lord
to get your soul, what'n you do when the devil gets
it?" asked Eli.

"There is no devil," replied Stephen.

"Why, there's his Chair, close agen your cottage."

"Empty!" said Stephen, in a voice of such curious
quality that even Joe stared.

Eli slapped the table hard—also Mrs. Arden's hand,
which happened to be on it at the moment.

"There *is* a devil!" he cried, as one might say in
winter, "There is summer!"

"An eye for an eye," said Mrs. Arden, slapping his
hand smartly.

Eli did not notice.

"I know there's a devil."

"I wish there was."

Stephen was unaware how they all stared in surprise
at his heartfelt tone.

He had come through vicissitudes of horror and
despair to a state when everything seemed unreal,
himself more than all. Sometimes, as he sat in this
warm, curtained room, with laughter round him and
the spread table before him, the sensation verged
upon catalepsy. A kind of crackling emptiness
seemed to envelop him. He had grasped life, and it
had given way in his hand—like a lizard's empty skin
or the shell of a blown egg. It was a great relief to
be away from Lostwithin, but—he must go back
to-morrow. He shuddered. The place had become
for him the embodiment of his own mind. It was
seared upon his being—the dim plains, with their rich
249

colours of wood and tilth and orchard, were like his own youth; in the midst rose the gaunt and knife-like ridge, with its ever-empty throne—like the negation that now dominated him. And now Deborah seemed ready to fail him. She had not come to meet him for three days; she had seemed tired, and had not cheered his forlorn mood. To sit in their cottage all evening with Deborah, pale and absent-minded, opposite him, with the wind pawing at the window, trying the door, hooting in the chimney, and with nothing to distract his thoughts from the insistent, unanswerable cosmic questions that seemed to hoot in his ears with the wind—this, he felt, was more than he could bear. Any place, any person, even Lucy Thruckton, whose adipose deposit fronted abstract questions with comfortable equanimity, was a plank to cling to in the flood.

Outside, from somewhere up on the first plateau, broke out a sudden bleating of sheep, contented yet eager.

Every one listened, silent.

It broke out again—a wistful cry, full of a longing which seemed fulfilled and yet ever renewed. Coming down the dark slopes in the clear, chilly air, it set the imagination on fire.

"Aye!" said John, in a hushed voice, "'tis Allhalontid. Year in, year out, I hear the sheep cry, nights. But never as they cry on Allhalontid, Christmas Eve and Midsummer night. And on those nights, if so be you was up by the signpost, that makes the shadow of a cross in the light of the moon, you'd see the sheep clustering, all turned one way and not afeerd. And I'm thinking they see him there—the Flockmaster himself, with his worn feet and his eye for sorrow and the wideness of his pity. I'm thinking I'd liefer be there then," said he dreamily, "and hear him call across the little hills and the high mountains, than gather the treasures of earth and heaven."

"There'd be no one there," said Stephen scornfully and wearily. Yet he, of all those present, could most understand John. For the man who affirms nothing is kept away from the ready-made faiths, not by their tax on his belief and their wildness, but by their lack of wonder.

"Heh!" said Eli, with concentrated scorn.

"Who's being superstitious now, John?" asked Patty.

Deborah was silent, basking in the comfort of her father's presence. She kept wishing she had told Stephen her news, then being glad she had not. Day by day she put it off, and if it was a great mistake it was an excusable one, for Stephen was curt, distrait, melancholy.

"You little pest!" Eli exclaimed suddenly. "I'd wring your neck if you wunna made of chaney." He glared at the bullfinch on his cup. "Vermin," he added.

"There's no vermin in my house," said Patty, "and you met leave the bird alone, Eli, seeing as its never lived and never will—let alone its tail feathers all being scrubbed away, with my mother being such a thorough woman."

"D'you like my locket, Stephen?" asked Lily, with a fascinating glance. She was bored with John's talk of flockmasters. But Stephen had forgotten ever having said anything about the locket. He looked back at her with the long, preoccupied gaze that was becoming habitual to him, and made no reply. She flushed under what she thought (and hoped) was his first look of admiration and passion. She returned his look with a little smile and half-closed eyes.

"Well! you two'll know each other next time."

251

At Eli's remark Lily hastily removed her eyes.

" A penny for your thoughts, Mr. Southernwood," said Lucy, with laboured pleasantry.

" Better pay a thousand pounds not to know them," Stephen muttered.

" Laws, Stephen ! What ails you ? You binna going to get like Eli, never happy unless you're miserable."

" No, no, mother," said John. " The lad's only thinking out summat in the machinery line. Them things take a power of thinking to keep up with their tricks."

" Well," said Joe, who had noted and entered for future inquiry Lily's provocative look at Stephen, " if we'm going to play the fool with them apples, mother, let's begin of it, or we met be playing other kinds of fools."

" To be sure ! Well, everybody's got to peel one without breaking, and throw the peel o'er shoulder, and it'll make the initial."

" Who of ? " asked Lucy rapturously.

" Your husband as is to be—or wife. But when you're married it'll make the initial of the first——"

" Mother ! " said Deborah. " Can I have a better apple than this 'un ? "

" Aye, you can, my dear. There's none deserve it so well."

" Who'll it make the initial of if I do it ? " asked Eli.

" If you do it," said Joe, conscious that he was making the cleverest utterance of his life, " if you do it, it'll make the initials L.S.D."

Lucy was peeling a large baking apple with her mouth open and her tongue following every movement of the knife.

" I shouldn't put yourself about, Lucy," said Lily. " It'll only make a big, round nought."

252

"Now then, Stephen," said Joe; "as we'm all got to play this soft game to please mother, I'll race you with that there russet, and see which cuts ourselves first."

"Joe, Joe!" cried his mother. "You've sliced yours like a turmit cutter."

"Oh, well! Let's roast the chestnuts," said Joe.

"I think so, too!" remarked Lucy, almost with animation.

"Hark at her!" said Eli, sternly divesting his apple of its skin. "And her only just got outside that raw baker!"

"Stephen's done his better than anybody," said Deborah. "Throw it, Stephen!"

"It's a N," said Lucy.

"N for nothing," commented Stephen, and relapsed into silence.

"Wish I lived here," he said after a time, looking across at John. "There's no beastly black Chair."

"If you only look you can see all colours in that black rock," said John; "all colours and sparkling white."

"What makes you think things like you do?" asked Stephen curiously; "about the Flockmaster and all that. How d'you make up such things?"

"I dunna make 'em up. I say 'em like that for lack of better ways. I've seed him lead out his flock ath'art the sky. I've seed him lead the spring flowers down the pastures; I've harkened at his voice in the heather. And what's wonnerful in that? Look you, Stephen! Those little small berries of Deb's are so mortal uncanny, with the life in them and a rose-tree in every one, after them the queerest things seem naught."

"But everybody knows rose berries 'll end in rose trees; there's nothing in that."

253

"Everybody knows what marrying ends in, but they'm took all of a heap just the same," said Mrs. Arden briskly, "as you'll find, maybe."

But Stephen's thoughts had gone back into their grey, grinding treadmill, and he did not hear. Deborah made dumb and unnoticed signals for silence to Mrs. Arden.

"And for once in your life, John, you'm said a thing with sense in it, for it's what I'd have said myself. Joe, what'n you grinning at like a turmit lantern?"

"Father," said Joe, "did you hear as Mr. Prior's sending fifty shorthorns to America?"

"No! Bless me!" said John, quite dazed at business on such a scale.

"Aye. And as nice a lot, they do say, as ever gadfly went after."

"Well," put in Mrs. Arden, "they'll be glad enough of some good Shropshire milk in America, no danger! Poor things!"

"Only," Joe went on, not intending to give up his tale till he had finished it circumstantially, "only he canna get a man to go along of them—not for love nor money seemingly."

"And no wonder!" said Mrs. Arden. "To fly in the face of the perils of the deep, only to be where you dunna want to be, goes agen common sense."

"He's going to give good money, mother."

"No money'd send me among icebergs and Injins and skyscrapers and Bible-pedlars," said Mrs. Arden, who had an extraordinary gift for distilling the essence from a continent.

"What sort of man does he want?" asked Stephen indifferently.

"Oh, a handy chap—honest and that. He says, if he don't hear of one come Christmas he'll advertise."

254

" Fancy ! " said Mrs. Arden.

Such a tremendous step is seldom taken in these parts.

To be out at sea—to be in the zest of storm and change—to be away from here ! So flamed the thoughts in Stephen's mind. Then he looked at Deborah, and the thoughts died like sparks in rain. But they came afresh.

" I suppose he'd give good wages ? " he asked.

" Why, Stephen, d'you know any one likely ? " asked Deborah.

" I know one chap. But he may be—tied."

" Christmas 'll soon be on us," said Mrs. Arden. " Scarce two months till St. Thomas."

" The longest night," said Deborah, with a thrill of inexplicable foreboding.

" Why d'you say it like that ? " asked Stephen.

" I dunna know. Maybe it's along of the ghosts meeting on Diafol mountain on the longest night—to choose 'em a king, like I told you."

" All the ghosses in Shropshire ! " said Mrs. Arden complacently.

" A wild night it is, most allus," John murmured; " a night to lose sheep on."

" Grandmother says," remarked Lucy oracularly, " as in her young days you could hear the ghosses going across the fields, high up, setting in to the Diafol like a tide, she says, and skriking soft one to other like gilly-owlets."

" Your grandmother ought to be among 'em for a wold lying witch ! " said Eli. " If she was *my* grandmother——"

" Well, what would you do, father ? " asked Lily suddenly, an intuition telling her that he was stumbling into a pitfall.

Eli pulled himself up just in time. He looked at her like a quizzical ferret.

"Love, honour *and* obey the owd mouldiwarp!" he said crisply, "as the Word says grandchillun should, likewise chillun. But they dunna."

"Well, well!" said John. "It's fine to have the young folk round us at the fall of the leaf, when we're minding us of the rising wind and the dark night setting in; and the green leaves that was so soft, brown and hard as a bark-stack—and we only like little brown leaves on the tree, little brown leaves!"

"I ain't no brown leaf!" said Eli pugnaciously, looking extraordinarily like one, with his wizened face and air of futile obstinacy.

"'Little blind mice,' we called 'em when we was chillun," said John.

"Deb and Lil! While I mind, there's some paper patterns I've got for you. Come up and get 'em," said Mrs. Arden.

"Blouses?" asked Lily.

"Little frocks?" thought Deborah.

"Blouses! Allus dizening yourselves like popinjays," snarled Eli.

"It inna blouses!" Mrs. Arden broke into one of her laughs.

"If you laugh so lungeous, 'ooman, you'll break a blood-vessel one of these fine days."

"Now then, you four men, get the lead ready for telling the future while we're upstairs," commanded Mrs. Arden, ignoring Eli's remark.

"Why," said Deborah, "father's lit my lamp!"

"And would you believe," complained her mother, "as he does it night after night, as obstinate as a clockwork mouse, though I tell him about the wise virgins and the saving of oil."

"But the wise ones put oil in their lamps," Lily

corrected. She had always taken prizes at Sunday school.

" Well, that dunnat alter his softness, dun it ? " said Mrs. Arden.

Deborah's eyelashes were wet. When they went downstairs again she sat by John.

" Well, lass ? " he said.

" I see the stairs be as light as ever," smiled Deborah.

John returned the smile.

" It dunna take so much oil," he explained apologetically. " Seems to me it's worth a few pence a week—the kindly light."

" Now then ! " Mrs. Arden organized the revels. " Get the lead martyr-hot, Joe, and dump it in the basin of water."

" A sinful game as I 'unna play," said Eli, who had a horror of the hot lead spurting up into his eyes.

" What have you got, Joe ? " inquired Lily, when the lead had sizzled into a shape.

" Laws me ! It dunna look like nought.."

" It looks," said Eli, drawing cautiously nearer. ".. like a piece o' lead."

" You old spoilsport ! " Mrs. Arden scolded. " Now, Stephen, you try ! Dear heart ! It's like a ship, masts and all ! "

" That just shows," said Deborah, " that there's nought in the game. For we're never going on the sea, be we, Stephen ? "

Stephen was looking at the lead, dumb with surprise and feeling rather superstitious, for it was remotely like a ship.

Lucy solemnly tried her luck.

" A lump ! " said Eli, " and that's what it should be."

When Deborah's turn came, Mrs. Arden exclaimed—

" It's like a cream-mundle ! No ! An arrow."

" The golden arrow," Deborah murmured; " you try, Lil."

" She's got a cradle ! " Mrs. Arden announced delightedly. " One of them plain sort."

Joe bent over and looked at it so intently that his pipe fell out.

" So it is ! " he said. " Dunna that show ? "

" It shows nought," Lily cut him short.

" You met as well call it a coffin as a cradle," remarked Eli.

" You nasty old beast ! " Lily shrieked, white with superstitious terror, and blazing with hatred of his grudging spirit.

" Now, now, Lil ! Dunna miscall your poor old father," said John.

" He hadn't ought to be any one's father ! " wept Lily. " And how he ever came to be passes me—for he's no more heart than a wold stump, and no more looks than an Aunt Sally."

Joe guffawed.

Eli was taken aback. He had, for once, said something more unpleasant than he meant.

He blinked like an owl in lamplight.

" Like to shoot me, Lil ? "

" Yes."

" With my rook rifle ? "

" Hold your row," said Joe. " You'll want some sheep rounding up after Martinmas."

" And the cattle," Eli added; " and some ponies fetched ready for the fair."

After supper John suggested a hymn.

" That's the first righteous word I've heard to-night ! " said Eli. " And that's only a poor measly 'un. We'll sing ' Day of Wrath ' ! "

" That we won't ! " Stephen contradicted, suddenly full of life and animosity.

258

"We'll sing 'Lead, kindly Light'—and please all," John said pacifically.

"That's Deb's favourite."

"The Golden Arrow first," Mrs. Arden suggested; "it's a grand tune."

"And neither sense nor godliness in the words," snapped Eli.

The quiet kitchen, with its colours of old medlars and wild geranium, its bright copper and dim china, and the faint, worn tick of the clock, was suddenly full of melody. Deborah's voice endowed the song with strange meanings. Lucy gasped her words out, "All blow and no tune," as Eli said.

John swayed a little as he sang, dignified as a bard, with nothing harsh in his rather faded voice. Stephen did not sing until he saw that Eli also was sitting silent, trap-mouthed and sardonic. Then his voice rang out so masterfully that Deborah quite forgot to sing herself. Rain soused on the window, the leafless roses knocked against it with urgent little taps, as though Destiny forged the lives within with small, relentless hammers. From the shippen came the contented rattle of cow-chains. John listened pleasurably.

"They seem pretty comfor'ble," he said. "But I never can think what took them that night you was alone, Deb. It was just as if some one had been chivying them summat cruel."

"Maybe there was frittening," said Deborah, with a sweet, remembering flush and a glance at Stephen. He came out of his reverie and smiled back. She was so rose-like and gracious, and the stolen joy they had shared held such glamour.

"There's most awful frittening, now and again, isn't there, Deb?" he said, and they both laughed.

Lily, who was annoyed that his eyes should caress another woman when they were so alight, so deliciously

259

merry and masterful, cut into their warm silence with a suggestion of the hymn.

The wistful notes—groping like blind children for something tangible to cling to—filled the firelit room and died.

The second verse began. Eli had a powerful, extremely raucous voice, and he was emphatic.

"They loved the garish day!" he sang, with a comprehensive look at the two young couples.

Into John's voice crept the ardour of the lovers of God. The room became an audience chamber, and his strange, uplifted joy touched some of the others to a kindred, though lesser fervour. Joe sang with restraint, which showed how religious he was feeling.

"O'er moor and fen—" Deborah sang, with presage in her heart and a sense that not Stephen, not God, but her father's little lamp on the stairs would be her guide.

"O'er crag and torrent—" Stephen's voice rose in sudden joy at the picture conjured up.

Lucy wept at the line about angel faces, and Eli sang it in complete forgetfulness that the only "angel face" he had lost was his wife's, which he had been wont to call in her presence "an o'erdone baking apple." Mrs. Arden, having judiciously saved her voice, came in on the "Amen" with emotion.

"Theer!" said Joe, after a little silence. "Now we're all good chillun, dad, and we'll be off whome."

"Aye, lad," said John, with his radiant smile and his right hand still shut, as if on the finger of God; "and the Lord bless us and keep us," he added, with dreams still lingering in his eyes.

Even Lily was impressed.

"I see, John," said Eli, "as you're one of the chosen, in spite of yourself."

He went out. But he put his head in again.

"One of your cows has got an awful hoost," he said. "She means dying."

"I'm frit of the ghosses in the 'ood," said Lucy, hinting broadly that Eli should accompany her.

"No ghost 'd tackle such a roundabout thing," said Eli, who was determined not to do so.

John said he would walk with her—an offer of great unselfishness, for it was a night of nights with him, having Deborah under his roof, and he wanted every moment.

"You'll be up when I come back, Deb?" he asked wistfully.

XLII

As Stephen sat by the fire with Deborah and Mrs.
Arden, he puzzled over John. What was it that he
could not gauge in him? Deborah partook of it
also, though it showed itself differently in her. He
rested his cheek on his hand, staring into the fire,
looking so comely and so sad that Deborah stroked
the other hand and Mrs. Arden said—

" Well, Stephen, lad, what'n you dwining about?
Be you thinking o' your sins or is it the colic? Them
eyes o' yours wunna meant to conquer wold sins, but
young wenches."

Deborah was pleased. It was the second compliment her mother had paid Stephen this evening.

After a time John came in.

" Untoert weather," he said. " God help all poor
folk benighted."

Deborah felt a peculiar sweetness in being back
in her little attic, with the bunch of late chrysanthe-
mums put on the dressing-table by Mrs. Arden. It
seemed so familiar and safe; and there was such a
thrill in remembering her lonely maidenhood passed
under its sloping roof, and comparing it with the
present. She decided that when she had blown out
the candle, so that the keen wind could plunge in
as of old, and the stars glitter in the square of sky like
dew on a dark flower, she would tell Stephen her news.
But Stephen was tired out in mind and body, for he
was hag-ridden by thoughts, longings, despairs, and

he had done a day's work and a long walk after it. He fell asleep before the light was out, wrapped in the strange peace that had laid its hand on him all evening; for once he neither tossed nor dreamed. It would all come back to-morrow, doubtless; but to-night there was a truce. John's personality, music, change and good-fellowship had made for him a surface peace above the black tides. But Deborah could have given him the deep-sea peace that no wind stirs, had he loved her—not as most men love their wives, but as a few men (eccentric, unsociable, selfish, the world calls them) love the woman who is one soul with them. Deborah, because she loved him in this large way, was invulnerable to all trouble while she was with him : but parting—even for a night—was a thing unthinkable to her; herein she paid the lover's penalty, for the very thought of absence from him set her shaking.

To the lover it is not the reason or the result or the duration of absence, but just absence itself that is the deadly thing. If you cut a man's heart out, he would not bother about reasons or results or the length of time it stayed out, because he would be dead. So it is with the lover. The pulse of life stops at parting. Stephen did not know this love, so he had one advantage over Deborah. Although he was afraid of many things that a lover meets with courage, he shared with the mediocre herd the indifference at parting which the world calls sensible.

" Want to be with your husband all day ? " exclaimed the manager's wife in her call after Deborah's marriage. " How very extraordinary ! " Those who knew her husband would have understood her remark. To a crass world it does appear extraordinary that two beings who need each other desperately, and who do not know how soon they may be wrenched apart, should treasure every golden moment.

For such love as this comes unseen and passes

unknown, like the doom of pain and the impulse of spring.

Only a few reach out strong, yet trembling hands for it; for only a few care to drop their small treasures, and the hands that reach for it can hold nothing else.

Deborah was bitterly disappointed when she turned and found that he was asleep. She denied herself a good-night kiss in order not to wake him, and lay gazing out into the illimitable night, finding it small. With wide grey eyes she contemplated the suns and planets wheeling to their age-long destinies in their intolerable silence, and she felt them to be pitiful, easy to understand as a child's secret. Their vastness did not daze her; she dwelt in it now, since Stephen came. Their fires did not frighten her; she was fire. The stillness that broods upon the cosmos and is not stirred by the swing of the constellations, the deep reserve and mystery of it all—these did not trouble her. Stillness was upon her also, and she had her key to the secrets of life and death. The lover dwells like leaf and flower—quiet, incurious. He does not question of God. He is content to abide by the laws of life, whoever ordained them, for they have given him his treasure. He is not anxious about his beginning or his ultimate destiny, for he shares in a Sacrament that is without beginning or end.

But when it happens that the passion of one lover is godlike, and of the other not so, the blackness of the tragedy is impenetrable.

Deborah lay and smiled in the darkness, her hand laid lightly on Stephen's. The new life that was coming to her did not mean quite the same to her as to most women, who often long for some one on whom to spend love. But Deborah wondered how she would find time for the new-comer. It was not for the baby's self, not in the usual tide of mother-love that she rejoiced — it was because the child would be Stephen's, because she now had something to do and bear for Stephen.

" Pain for Stephen ! "

Her eyes grew bright as the stars outside. For the lover is the eternal martyr, the eternal reveller. He has found the arrow, sharp and golden, the desire of all time; he clasps it to his breast with fierce rapture.

Stephen was muttering in his sleep. " America—" she heard him say.

" It's queer-like, how folk talk in their sleep of things as they've never so much as thought of in the day," she said to herself.

A fox barked in one of the near woods, and down a cwm an owl cried, with its mirthless laughter and long tremolo—making the middle word five syllables—

" What ails you ? "

XLIII

AFTER the first excitement of the locket and the drives was over, Lily began to find Joe very unsatisfactory. She thought of Deborah with increasing envy. She thought of Stephen's long gaze at her on All Hallowe'en, and almost persuaded herself to ascribe it to love.

By love she meant admiration and desire.

The more she thought of him, the more uncontrollable grew the wish to see him and to be seen by him. So the pose which had begun in a desire for romance, a dumb longing for beauty, grew into hysteria. She saw herself as a beautiful but unappreciated wife, cruelly obliged to bring up a family for a man she did not love. She went further, and imagined Stephen thinking of her, finding Deborah dull.

"Stephen and me was made for each other," she remarked to her looking-glass. "Why canna we be together, when he loves me, and me him?"

Stephen had, in fact, awakened in her an emotion slightly nearer to that selfless absorption than any one else had, so that there was a particle of reality in her artificial feelings. These grew all the faster for their necessary concealment; she never, as a rule, concealed an emotion. Slepe seemed duller and duller as the winter days drew in. Lostwithin became a magnet.

At last, one morning when Joe was at a distant sheep-fair, she set out to walk to Lostwithin. It took her a long time, but she reached the woods above the mine before the dinner-hour. She knew that Stephen had his dinner at the mine now. She sent a child with a message, and sat down on a tree-trunk under a larch that still held a few yellow needles, pleasantly conscious that her hair outshone it. She felt delightfully alarmed and tremulous. She was as steeped in her pose as an actress in her interpretation of a character. She felt exalted, interesting, noble. She patted her hair and arranged her dress. She was cold, but what did that matter?—it was for Stephen's sake. Time went on, and she grew very cold, and forgot that it was for Stephen.

" Stupid ! " she exclaimed. " Dawdling so ! "

Annoyance began to conquer romance. But when he came suddenly round a corner, romance returned.

" Oh, it's you ! " he said, rather bored. " What's up ? "

" Sit down, 'oot," she coaxed.

She sat close to him, and saw to it that a strand of hair brushed his shoulder. He always felt a little sorry for her, so he was comparatively patient.

" Well, Lily ? "

" I come o' purpose——"

" Well ? "

" To see you."

" What about ? "

" He's nigh as slow in the uptake as Joe," she thought.

She tried a new tack.

" I'm awful cold, Stephen. Could I have your coat round me ? "

" H'm ! All right," said Stephen grumpily. " But for the Lord's sake don't be long, or I shall catch a cold, and get it hot from Deb."

" I meant—a bit of it. Put it on agen. There ! "

" It looks rather—I hope no one 'll see us," said Stephen nervously, " or what'd Deb say ? "

Lily was encouraged by proximity.

267

" Deb ! " she cried, in the voice that seemed to her
suitable, and made Stephen jump. " What does
Deb matter to you and me ? "

Stephen raised his eyebrows.

" Well, she's my wife, that's all," he remarked
curtly.

" Not by rights," Lily went on, beginning to enjoy
herself; " by rights it should be me."

" Here, drop it, Lily ! " Stephen said crossly.
" Who are you getting at ? "

She put her head on his shoulder and began to cry.

" Oh, Stephen ! dunna be so——" she was going
to say " soft," but substituted " hard " instead.
" Canna you see ? "

" I see you're making me look a fool. Do get up ! "

With an instinct to dare all at once, she flung an
arm round his neck, and kissed him.

He sat perfectly silent. She suddenly wished that
she had not done it. She no longer felt elated—only
shy, and very much aware that her face was scarlet.
She got up suddenly and stood with her back to him.

Stephen was touched by her silence as he had not
been before. He had seen the blush. He saw her
as a comely and desirable woman; though he person-
ally did not wish for her love, he felt that some expression of gratitude for it was necessary. He got up
and put a hand on her shoulder.

" It's very decent of you to—like me, little 'un,"
he said. " But it won't do, you know. What about
Joe ? "

" What's he matter ? "

" Well, you know, he'd be vexed," said Stephen
mildly.

" We wunna let him know ought. We'd go off
together. Oh, Stephen, take me off with you !
I'll do all the things I dunna like—darning and that.
And you've got golden hair, like me, and we both
like randies. Say you'm fond of me, Stephen ! "

Stephen began to find the situation unbearable.

" Of course I like you, Lily," he said, to soothe her.

" Then—kiss me, Stephen."

" No."

She began to cry again. He detested tears.

" Do stop crying ! " he besought her. " The place is miserable enough without that."

She saw his evident pain.

" I wunna stop unless you kiss me."

He walked up and down.

" You ought to be ashamed, Lily. Go straight home this minute ! "

" I wunna ! " cried Lily, rising to the height of tragedy. " I'll drown myself sooner."

Stephen's nerves, already frayed, gave way at this. He did not know Lily, and he thought she meant it. His face twitched, and he implored her to stop.

She delightedly perceived her power, and went on. It was almost like a retributive punishment for the way in which he had once lacerated Deborah.

Lily continued, crescendo.

" If you wunna kiss me this instant minute, I'll go straight and drown myself in Lostwithin Pond. And you'll see me floating on the top, with my golden hair all draggly."

She was enjoying herself, as she once had when tormenting Joe in like manner.

But she had a different man to deal with now. Stephen, turned sick by this vivid picture of the corruption which he feared and loathed, and which seemed to thrust its leprous face into his at every turn, sprang forward and shook her savagely.

" Stop it, you little beast ! " he shouted.

Then rage and the sight of her face—frightened, flushed and pretty—woke a new emotion in him.

" There you are, then ! " he said. " You asked for it—now you shall have it, and a few extra for your trouble."

He kissed her so hard that she struggled.

Then she suddenly remembered all the black marks that she had put down against Deborah from time to time. She was having her revenge now. Here was Deborah's model husband kissing her—Lily—with the frantic kisses of a lover.

She ceased to struggle. The moment she did so, Stephen came to himself. He sprang back, and stared at her dazedly.

" Get away in the name of decency ! " he said hoarsely.

" Where to ? "

" Anywhere. Drown yourself, if you want to ! "

" I dunna want to. I want to live along of you," said Lily, with unblushing directness.

Stephen was amazed. He was himself so ashamed that he felt he could never look her in the face again. He did not want ever to see her again.

A look that Joe had never seen came into Lily's face. She had, through stages of admiration and fellow-feeling, come near to loving Stephen. She let her poses slip from her. She stole up to him and put her hand on his arm.

He shook it off.

" Let me bide along of you, Stephen," she pleaded. " I dunna want nought else. I only wanted it a bit, before you kissed me, but now——"

She stopped, chilled by the extreme dislike in his face ; and made the only renunciatory speech of her life.

" But if you'd liefer not, ne'er mind."

" I would ! " said Stephen heartily, wiping his hot face, " much liefer not."

She stooped and kissed his hand, with a gauche little movement. Then she turned and went away through the wood.

Stephen sat down on a log.

" Well, I'm blest ! " he said.

He decided, on the way home, that he could neither tell Deborah of the incident nor stay in Lily's vicinity. This half-hour had given him another push towards flight, another reason for hating Diafol mountain.

XLIV

Martinmas was over, and nights encroached more and more on the days. It was pitch dark when Stephen started in the morning and long before he came back at night — grim and tortured. In the wilds, away from theatres and lit streets, men turn to the tavern or to their wives for warmth, colour, excitement. Stephen did not care for the bar parlour, he found it dull. So all that made the days worth living through was in the bright kitchen and the moonlit room above. And now it seemed to him that even this joy was tarnished. Deborah sometimes forgot to have a bright fire; sometimes forgot to talk; seldom answered his passion with her long, mysterious looks of tender passivity. She had become remote of late.

On the last morning of November he plunged straight into an impenetrable white fog when he stepped from the door, where stood a forlorn snowberry bush, bare of all leaves, looking like a worn birch-rod. Deborah was terrified at his going, for the hills had as many gashes and fissures as an old tree—one especially, where there had once been a cloud-burst, went almost sheer to the level of the plain. She lit the hurricane-lantern.

" And whatever you do, dunna go to leave the path, Stephen," she implored. " Dear heart, I canna let you go ! "

" There, it's all right," he said irritably. " I'm not a stupid sheep. I know the way."

" There's been some as lost their way in the dark of a white fog," she said, clinging wildly to his arm. " Oh, stay with me, Stephen, my dear, just to-day."

" Why to-day? "

" To-day we're sure on. To-day's ours. We're not sure on any other day."

Stephen looked out, past the rime-grey bush where drops stood like a cold sweat. Then he looked back into the rosy kitchen, where the fire roared and the brasses shone. Yes; it was very tempting. He looked again into the impalpable blanket of nothingness—at once imminent and impenetrable, like death. The Devil's Chair was hidden, like some black altar when curtains are drawn for an unholy rite. Because it was hidden it was all the more present with him. He felt, in his cottage in the fog, as if he were some minute insect in a fruit which some one was slowly crushing. No; he could not sit idle all day and look at the white window, be conscious of the clammy mist enwrapping him like a woollen burial robe.

Deborah was looking up, tears in her eyes, a smile of hope beginning on her lips.

He kissed her hastily.

" I must do my work, you know, Deb. Don't get silly ideas. I shall be as right as a trivet."

He was not aware that if he had knocked her down he would not have caused her as much pain as he did by those words.

" Then you'll go? " She spoke hoarsely.

" Of course. Why not? "

" Only to-day—I canna bear it. Dear sores! I canna. The Devil's Gully in all this fog? What's the work matter? I'll starve along of you, Stephen, sooner than you go in danger. What's the sense of it? It's like taking a pauper's penny and throwing it to and agen o'er a pond. I've nought but you, Stephen, in the 'orld. I want nought else. Stop to-day, Stephen. If you get notice gi'ed you I'll ne'er complain, whatever we come to. But if so be you go outside the wicket, you'll be out of sight, and me not know till six—all them mortal hours—where you be."

" Deb! Don't be so silly. You're not like this generally, you're quite sensible."

" That I'm not," said Deborah, with a sense of insult. " I'm *never* what folks call sensible. I try to put a good face on things, but I'm like this—allus like this—inside. And it wears on me. And if ought went amiss with you, Stephen, in such a forgotten kind of place, you met be there—oh! " She covered her eyes with her apron and sobbed.

" I shall be late," said Stephen, sorry for her trouble, though mystified. He did not know that love, in the most momentary absence, is tortured with every vision of horror.

" You'd feel the same if it was me," she cried desperately.

He just stopped the negative on his lips.

" I should control myself," he replied, as the non-lover and the semi-lover always can reply.

" You couldna—no more than if you got caught in a thrashing machine."

His hand was on the gate. He opened it and picked up the lantern. He thought her unreasonable, but he kissed her again.

" Back at six. You have a nice time and read a bit by the fire."

" To be comfor'ble with you away," said Deborah, searching for words, " is like being in hell."

" Oh, well! " he said, feeling injured, for he had thought himself very unselfish to suggest comfort for her when he was going out into the cold; " don't, then ! "

He was gone.

" Stephen! Stephen! " she called; but her voice was like a muffled bell. She leant on the wicket, regardless of the bitter, still cold, and strained her eyes to see his lantern. A leaden grief was on her.

" It's a foretokening," she murmured. She stayed there till she thought he must be at the mine. Then she went in and laid tea—nine hours too soon. She spent the day cooking things for tea, warming Stephen's shoes, looking at the clock, going out to listen for sounds from Lostwithin. To see the tea laid for him was reassuring.

" Of course he'll be sharp set and want his tea," she murmured again and again. The idea that the tea might be spread in vain was so horrible, so fiendish in its sickening torture, that her mind refused to hold it. She forgot to have any food. She forgot the little white boots with pink ribbon that she was making surreptitiously. At three it was quite dark and the silence grew denser. Not a bird nor a sheep was abroad on the hills. Not a breath of wind touched the bents. When she stood at the gate, two hours before he could possibly come, the fog stole in at the door, stealthy as a company of ghosts, making the kitchen dark.

Twice she started to meet him, but remembered that she might miss him on such a day, and not be home to welcome him.

She never thought of the Chair, of her superstitions, of possible tramps, or that she was helpless and alone in a great waste. She was clear of all terrors but the one. The air of the roundabout came back to her, with its wistfulness in the midst of the crazy revelry, that was like the lament of sensitive spirits amid the unthinking lustiness of life—" Oh, where is my lad to-night ? "

XLV

THE sense of being reduced to nothing by an unseen force grew on Stephen as he went down the hill. To the gayest heart, the most securely grounded in optimism, fog is deadening, and on a solitary mountain-side it is nerve-racking. To Stephen, with his desperate need of joy, his craving for immortality and his agonized conviction that no such thing existed; with his desire for some one to worship and his grey certainty that there was no one; with his lust for clarity and certainty and his finding of gloom and stark negation—it was an unbearable witness to his worst fears. He wanted, as he could not get free of his desperate spiritual ill, opiates of some kind to deaden it. Here were no opiates — only reality. The mist wreathed about him like seaweed round a derelict ship. It towered above him, when the feeble lantern light struck it, like prison walls. The dry, dead heather dripped with it; the rich plain, the hills, the blue sky were all dissolved in its colourless uniformity, as this world and the hope of another had dissolved for him.

It would be easy to finish it all here and now, he thought. But he was too near the precipitous side of the hill to think of it long, for he had the healthy young animal's shrinking from pain and death. Nor could he face the complete annihilation that death meant for him now—could neither face it nor believe in it nor deny it. So he trudged on through the sigh of the heather, browbeaten, miserable, morose.

"'Arf an hour late!" said the manager when he arrived—and he said it in the way that always exasperated Stephen, through a yawn, during which he played on his teeth with his fingers, as on a keyboard.

"When I was a young chap," he continued, "I was at work 'arf an hour afore time—day after day."

Stephen looked him over appraisingly.

He was a small man, and very sensitive about it.

"If people's righteous overmuch, it stunts their growth," said Stephen slowly and pleasurably.

"If you're late again," said the manager, with pent-up hate in his tone, "it's the sack."

Stephen made up his mind on the spot to take Prior's cattle to America. It was the match to a fuse long ready. He said nothing; he was too much occupied with his thoughts of freedom. He loathed the manager, the men, the look of spar; he loathed and despised Lily; he was beginning to hate even the work and the machinery. Had it not been for Deborah he would have given notice twenty times. Now his nerve snapped. The place had been too much for him in his crisis. In his characteristic way he wanted to rush off at once, but he must wait for his wage day so as to leave money for Deborah.

"Three weeks more!" he thought hopelessly. But the end was at least in sight.

"Well, best get your coat off and do a bit, now you've been so kind as to come," said the manager. He went off, blandly conscious that he was "licking Southernwood into shape."

All day Stephen pondered. He would get his wages, leave them all with his insurance policy and his savings-bank book for Deborah, and go on December 21 to Prior's, starting for Liverpool that day with or without the cattle. He would send a note to John by Lucy Thruckton, who lived next door to the Priors, and he would send another to Deborah by a boy. She would be provided for. He could send her nearly all his wages; and if anything happened to him she would have his insurance. He crushed down the knowledge that this would make no difference to her. He would not remember that material needs are only a secondary thing to some natures, though in his preaching days he had been very fond of the text : " Man doth not live by bread alone."

He toiled back at night up the rime-whitened hillside, like a gnat on a huge, sealed hornet-comb.

As he came near home, the mist thinned on the hilltop and the moon burned through—ghastly, coppery, huge. She hung above the Devil's Chair, giving no light, fierce without warmth.

Unwholesome in the icy fog, she was, compared with the bright, beneficent harvest moon, what a poison-gourd is to a melon. It was as if on the barren hill, in the unfruitful miasma, had sprung an immense, livid fungus, rotten and worm-eaten, the essence of all the brooding harm that Stephen found in the place.

If he stayed here longer it would be too late, he felt. Even in three weeks it might be too late. No—it should not be. He would cling fiercely to sanity, now that freedom was so near. If he stayed, he was sure that the result would be the Devil's Gully, the asylum, or one of those horrible, nerve-caused double tragedies that are sometimes heard of in lonely places. He breasted the last hill, meeting the rising wind. A few lines now marked his face, that had been smooth as a lad's. He looked older, rather thin.

The lamp was in the window, the curtains drawn back to show the inside of the kitchen. At the gate stood Deborah, white with cold, but all afire with joy that he was home.

"At long last!" she murmured. "Oh, lad, dear heart! It's been a waidy while! Come you in and warm you."

In her low voice was the essence of all homes, the security that laughs at death. She pulled him in and bolted the door.

"Shut in wi' love!" she said.

The snowberry bush at once began to tap urgently, threateningly. Later, when the wind strengthened, it tapped the window also. From the three remaining dead trees and from the acres of heather came through the night a low, long-drawn whimper like the gasping "ah—ah!" of a woman in pain.

"Half a minute!" said Stephen, when the tapping had gone on for some time. He fetched the axe from the wood-shed and hacked determinedly at the bush till only a stump remained.

"There, that's better!" He returned to the fire, his nerves quieter.

But now that the tapping was gone, a smaller, weirder sound was audible, the low, thin "Phe-e-ew!" of the wind in the keyhole. Stephen got up and stuffed paper into it. But the wind whined in the eaves, in the window-chinks, in the chimney.

"Just as if it wants something—or somebody!" said Stephen superstitiously.

"The way it is hereabouts," said Deborah, "was used to make me glad, nights, as the cows was safe in shippen and the sheep folded. Father and mother'll be by the fire now at Upper Leasowes, and father'll be mixing sheep ointment against lambing time."

"I expect they miss you."

"Aye—Joe gone and all."

279

" You'd rather be with your father than any one, wouldn't you, Deb? "

" I was used to. Now I ne'er want to be along of any but you."

Stephen frowned and hastily changed the subject.

" I suppose he'll be busy with the lambs soon? "

" Aye. Nights, when he was used to be out in the lambing shed, I ne'er slept."

" Why? "

" There wunna no peace. When them you're fond on goes out in the storm, it lets the rainy wind and the whoar frost in. Neither fire nor can'le's any good then."

Stephen began to walk up and down, into the scullery and back again, knocking his head every time against the lintel, and oblivious of it.

" You'm restless, my dear! " said Deborah anxiously; " your poor head'll be all of a bruise. You work too hard. You'm not feeling bad, be you? "

" No."

" You'd tell me ought you felt, wouldna you, Stephen? "

" Of course."

" Mind and body, there's no secret atwixt us, be there? "

" Oh! " said Stephen in an overwrought tone, " damn that wind! Damn it! "

" There! there! " soothed Deborah; " what's the wind? Nought! It met cry and cry, but it canna get in, nor yet do nought agen us. There's no door ajar in our two lives to let 'un in. We'm shut in wi' love, like I was used to be under the seynty tree in June; we call it golden showers about our way, from the shine of it. We'm got our own seynty tree now, you and me."

Stephen quickened his step.

" For the Lord's sake, stop! " he broke out.

280

Deborah looked at him anxiously.

"Stephen, lad," she said; "you'm not heart-well!"

He laughed suddenly—tragically.

"Oh, I am!—never better," he said.

"Well, then, Stephen, there's no call to stamp about when you'm trudged all day, and bang your poor head, as is the comeliest in the 'orld. Give o'er tramping, and let me stroke your hair."

His head ached, his throat was parched. He flung himself down and rested his head in her lap. He began to pull bits out of the rag hearthrug—a present from Mrs. Arden with "Good Luck" in red flannel on a green background.

"There, now rest you!" said Deborah, more radiantly happy than ever in her life before, since she was tending him and he was depending on her.

"Now you're my little lad!" she said, smiling archly, "for all your maistering ways." She ran her fingers through his hair. "It wunna for nought as I found one of God Almighty's ladycows on my gown the day I saw you first," she went on, "for they token gold and luck, and you're a golden lad, and you've brought me luck and no mistake!"

He was silent, striving not to see the tragic irony of all she said.

"In the old tale of the Arrow," she said, "there's a mort of wold ancient women as come in, and they say: 'Accorns for the pig, faggots for the fire—but we missed summat!' And in a while the lovers come in, triumphing-like, and say they've missed nought. And no more have we."

He turned restlessly.

"Stroke more!" he said imperiously, "and sing! Don't talk."

She began to sing in a hushed voice, while the firelight stole up and down the walls, and the

281

wind lashed itself into the yelping fury of starved hounds.

" We have sought it, we have sought the golden arrow !
   (Bright the sally-willows sway)
Two and two by paths low and narrow,
   Arm in crook along the mountain way.
   Break o' frost and break o' day !
Some were sobbing through the gloom
When we found it, when we found the golden arrow—
Wand of willow in the secret cwm."

She looked down in the silence afterwards; he was asleep. She took up the small woollen boots. She would be doing them when he awoke, and he would ask what they were.

She smiled.

" I know right well what he'll say," she thought. " He'll say : ' What the devil are those doll's leggings ? '—for he allus calls my stockings leggings and my nightgown a shirt, him being such a manly chap, and nothing of the 'ooman in him, thank goodness ! "

She crocheted in a maze of delight at this thought and at the prospect of telling him her news.

But when Stephen awoke, he only wanted to go to bed, and never noticed the boots. It is the tragedy of the self-absorbed that when the great moments of their lives go by in royal raiment with a sound of silver flutes, they are so muffled in self and the present that they neither hear nor see.

XLVI

St. Thomas' Day, like a mildewed rose, died before it flowered. In the dark morning Stephen looked at Deborah's sleeping face in the candle-light, and wavered in his resolve. Snow was falling; the flakes flattened themselves like soft berries flung against the panes. In the curious mock daylight, which even a light fall of snow gives to a morning, Stephen could see the Chair looming coal black on the east. It stood against grim, white clouds through whose impenetrable layers the sun would never rise to-day. Snow was a new variation of the capacity of this country for wintry gloom. Stephen hated its aspect even more than the fog. It lay, deep and inscrutable, over gaunt hill and dimpled meadow. It took away the beauty and the cruelty of the land, leaving mere sterility. It had come softly in the dark, like a lingering death. Only in the sky a few frail colours bloomed—the sole emblems of vitality in a dead world. They were delicate and alluring as the desire of youth for youth, of a clear soul for God. Stephen gazed at them, finding them friendly in a world of animosity, and longed to follow them beyond the horizon. His resolve was stronger than before. In the last three weeks he had been hard pressed by despair, and had sunk into gloom and morose bad temper. Now the day of the breaking of all chains had come for him; at this moment the cattle-boat would be in the Mersey. Life had a glow again. He did not know that this was only a false dawn—that the new life would be as dark and haunted as the old, until he conquered or went under.

Should he go while Deborah was asleep? He thought not. He would not deny her or himself the last kiss. Not that he regarded the parting as final. In a vague way he thought of coming to fetch her some time, when he had made a new home. He did not know at this time that a lover would sooner lie in the hedge-bank than be left alone while the most splendid home is built, since the first alternative is life and the second, death. " Deb," he said, waking her with a kiss; some timeless sorrow had brooded on her sleep; she woke to his smile with the air of a frightened child. Out of her half-dreaming state she looked up dazedly, and said, with the strange, unconscious voicing of fate to which human beings are sometimes doomed—

" The longest night be come ! "

Stephen hurried over breakfast, a feverish flush on his cheeks, a horror of what he was doing in his heart. He was afraid that Deborah might say one of those heart-wringing things that she did say at times, and so foil his purpose after all.

She wondered at the wildness of his kisses when he left her, at the way he turned round so often— lately he had forgotten to turn at all—and waved his hand. Then he disappeared in the wandering snowflakes, and she turned back with a lagging step.

It was four o'clock when a small boy from Lost-within came up the path with Stephen's note, and Deborah's heart seemed to stop.

She ran to the door.

" Not hurted? " she cried. " He's not hurted? Quick—quick ! "

She shook the boy.

" What'n you after, shaking me ? " he said, dodging her. " Is who hurted ? "

" The foreman—my man, Southernwood."

" Hurted ? No. He give me this to give you."

" You'm sure he's all right ? "

" Didn't I say so ? "

" Would you like an apple ? "

So she rewarded with the best she had the
messenger of horror, as one might bring out wine
and delicate fare for the Black Reaper himself.
The boy ran off, and Deborah opened the letter.

" DEAREST DEBORAH—I am obliged to go away.
Have asked your father to come for you and take
you home. Forgive me.—STEPHEN."

She did not faint. Her only sensation was one
of surprise that she was not dead. Hour after hour
dragged by. The letter was burnt into her brain.
Still she was not dead, she thought.

" Obliged to go away."

She knew that was not true. Nothing could make
him go unless he wanted to. And above all—not
alone.

" Have asked your father to come and take you
home."

But Stephen was home.

" Forgive me."

Forgive what ? She could not be forgiving or un-
forgiving, angry or loving, cold or passionate; she
could never be anything any more.

" Stephen." She stood where she had opened the
letter, incapable of any motion, for a long time.
And she continued, with dazed pauses, to say over
and over, in every tone of love—

" Stephen—Stephen ! "

Yet she had not realized anything. When five
o'clock struck, she suddenly said, " His tea ! " and
ran to re-light the fire. Then she looked at the
letter; and slowly as the massing of thunderclouds

for a storm that will devastate the plain, or the first glissade of rock for a landslip that will sweep away a mountain side, the real meaning of it began to come upon her.

Stephen did not love her.

It was perfectly dark. The cottage was hushed as a tomb. A mouse began to nibble in the wainscot. The wind moaned and blew eddies of snow in at the open door.

Stephen did not love her.

The finality of this she never questioned.

Something akin to hers might be the emotions of a Teresa confronted with incontrovertible proof that Christ never lived, or of a mother, not yet free from the pains of childbirth, told that her baby is dead.

She looked round. All was pitch dark; but she saw with agonizing vividness scene after scene of her life with Stephen. Again the weary surprise came on her that she was not dead. She groped for matches, thinking, " I be in a nightmare. I'll wake afore long."

She lit the candle.

" Neither lamp nor can'le," she muttered, " after this."

Then she went upstairs and brought down an armful of letters and Stephen's clothes.

" None met see. None met know. None met set hand on 'em," she murmured.

For the priest will burn his church and his sacred chalice rather than that the holy things, which have grown mysterious with darting light from beyond the horizon, should fall into bestial hands.

All hands that were not Stephen's seemed bestial to Deborah now. With the sense that, life being over, things must be put away—as one tidies a room at night—she went on carrying out the chairs, the crockery, her sewing-machine, everything, until her back ached—though she did not know it.

286

The snow thickened.

She went to and fro, enlarging the pile outside the door.

" The longest night is come ! " she said.

The wind raved in the pinnacles of the Chair, shrieked in the dry heather, threatened the dead trees, tore at her dress, blew down a picture from the wall with a crash of glass. Deborah was dragging out the little oak table, when suddenly Nancy Corra stood in the doorway.

" A queer night to be out," she grumbled; " I was at Lostwithin, along of a young 'ooman that's bad. And now I durstn't go whome in such weather. Met I bide in your kitchen to-night ? "

At the word " bide " Deborah had a vision out of the glinting past.

She stood and smiled at Nancy with such exquisite sweetness that Nancy was taken aback.

" You'm very kindly welcome," she said, " to bide with me."

" Whatever be you doing ? " asked Nancy. " What's that bonnyfire ? "

" Gi'e me a hand with the dresser ! " said Deborah.

It suddenly came to Nancy, as she saw of what the bonfire was composed, and looked at Deborah's face, that she was with a mad woman. She stole away while Deborah's back was turned.

" No," said Deborah. " You mun help me."

Nancy was obliged to come back. They went on carrying out the furniture in the blinding snow. At intervals it was fine; a powder of stars came out over the Devil's Chair.

" The longest night be come ! " said Deborah.

" Aye. No doubt," replied Nancy slavishly.

" And all the ghosts in Shropshire are coming here to choose 'em a king."

" Aye. It's snowing bad," Nancy answered, anxious to keep off ghosts.

"Now bring the mangle." Deborah caught her arm. Nancy shrieked.

"Did you hear that devil yonder?" Deborah said. "In the little coppy, it was."

"Oh, dunna!" cried Nancy, in a cold sweat.

"Playing bo-peep along of another — by their voices," said Deborah. "But there's no leaves now for 'em to hide in. Nought but dead leaves now — like little blind mice on the tree. Little blind mice! There! Didna you hear that? 'Howd yer! Howd yer!'"

She sang the words as a wagoner sings them, high on the first, with a fall on the second.

"Lugging stones, they be," she added, "for the Devil's Chair."

"It's only the wind," said Nancy; "only the wind, my dear."

"Hearken now!" cried Deborah. "There's another. 'Haw-woop!'—that's what he said. And there go the Dark Riders."

Nancy, torn between fear and greed, managed to conceal some spoons in her apron.

"Now, you come down along of me, my dear," she pleaded, despairing of getting away alone, "and see what a nice cup o' tea I'll get you."

"There's a child crying up at the Chair," said Deborah. "They'm strangling it."

"It's only the wind," Nancy reiterated.

"It's a love-child," said Deborah. "Hark at them, all the devils, shouting, 'Come-by-chance! Come-by-chance!'"

"But yours wunna be a love-child," said Nancy. "You'm married all right and proper now."

"Left—left!" moaned Deborah, with depths of unplumbed agony in her voice.

Suddenly she began to sing—

"Oh, where is my lad to-night?"

"If I ever get out of this," said Nancy privately to the hotch-potch of malice and might which was her conception of God, " I'll gi'e up the paying job."

"They're strangling that child. Hark at him skriking," said Deborah.

"I hear nought."

"Canna you hear the ghosts shuffling and whispering soft-like?"

"You come down, Deb Southernwood."

"Never no more, never no more."

"Look'ee," Nancy implored, feeling desperate; "let's be going, it's an awful night."

"Aye. A night to lose sheep on."

Deborah fetched out paper, and stuffed it round the base of the bonfire.

"You munna light it!" cried Nancy, stirred by such waste of good furniture, though not concerned at the waste of a soul. "Whatever'll your husband say?"

"I be no wife—a kept 'ooman."

"What? I thought you was married."

"Stephen," Deborah explained—and at his name she was shaken with long, terrible tremors; "Stephen dunna love me."

This reasoning was beyond Nancy.

"'Accorns for the pig, faggots for the fire,'" murmured Deborah, "'but we missed summat.'"

She began to sing "The Golden Arrow"—

"Some were sobbing through the gloom
When we found it, when we found the golden arrow—
Wand of willow in the secret cwm."

Nancy, frozen with terror, listened to the ghastly music.

Deborah stood gazing into vacancy.

"Shut in wi' love!" she whispered, and then, hoarsely and without emotion—

" Gone—gone—gone for evermore ! "

The things were all brought out. The house was bare, cold, awful.

Outside, towering up with a little cap of snow, was the pile of furniture.

Deborah looked straight before her.

" Do you love me true, Stephen Southern'ood ? " she asked.

" Do you love me so bad that you'm lost 'ithout me ? Are you certain sure ? Then I'll be the love o' your life while life lasts, and your mate till I lie in the daisies."

She turned to Nancy.

" They've chose their king. Hark at 'em ! " she said. " Him in the Chair. The Flockmaster's dead. Hark at the devils laughing ! And hark at that voice, full of trouble and trembling—' The thorn blows late.' "

" It's only an owl," asseverated Nancy.

" Well, good-night to you," said Deborah. " I'm going to light it now."

" What a wicked waste ! He'll come back and want the things."

" Never no more—never no more ! " said Deborah.

" Where be you going, when you've lit it ? " asked Nancy, in order to take care to go the other way.

" The other side o' silence."

" What softness ! Why not stop the child being born, and go free ? "

" What child ? "

" Why, yours that's coming. Yours and Southern-wood's."

The swift destruction that had been going on in Deborah's brain was arrested for a moment. He was gone, he did not want her, but she could still bear his child.

" Summat to do for Stephen," she whispered.

She advanced on Nancy with fury in her eyes.

290

" I'll learn you to try and rob me, you thief ! " she cried.

Nancy fled, dropping the spoons.

" 'Twas only three, and there they are ! " she said.

But Deborah had identified her with the fate that had thieved her all; it was well for Nancy that she fled.

Deborah poured paraffin on the fire and struck a match.

From the bitter loneliness on every side came shrieks, sighs, bellowings, threats, as the wind rose and fell. The air was full of snow, driving, whirling; and what with its eddying round the Chair and the falling of stones, and the strange sounds as of laughter and sorrow that came thence, it seemed as if the old tales were true and the ghosts had indeed come in like a tide.

The fire blazed up. Deborah watched it.

" The kindly light," she said. " God help all poor folk benighted. God keep Stephen—for I canna, I canna ! "

She rocked in the agony of the thought that she did not know where he was, that she could do and be nothing more for him. No living creature stirred in the waste but the two women—one running over the ridges, hounded by fear, the other beyond all fear, having suffered till feeling snapped.

Stephen, turning into his berth, tired after a busy day, had no inkling that his rather cursory preparation for her welfare had been brushed aside by circumstances.

Beyond the Wilderhope range at Wood's End Lucy Thruckton snored. She had in her usual ponderous manner failed to get under way with Stephen's letter to John until very late, and had then turned back, afraid.

" 'Twill do as well to-morrow-day," she said, and did not know that on her flat-footed movements two lives might depend.

At High Leasowes John lit Deborah's lamp, as usual. As usual, Patty scolded. They went to bed, and, as on every other night, John prayed—kneeling at the old, knobby chair in the window—for those he loved, adding, as always, with a swift feeling of selfishness, " And all other poor folk."

He gazed out through a small, clear space in the frosted window-pane.

" May love bless 'em all and keep 'em all," he concluded, " now and for ever."

He was unaware that his own love, his little lamp, was the one thing between Deborah and death.

Above Lostwithin the fire licked the black night with red, forked tongues until a glare lit the brooding sky. Down in the plain women who were awake late shook with fear and woke some one to keep them company.

" The Devil's Chair's burning," they whispered. " Maybe it's the end of the 'orld ! "

Still Deborah stood and watched the fire, until it began to pale. Then such a horror of loneliness came upon her that she ran, stumbling, away from the place. She was too worn and numb to reason any more. She had no purpose left—either to live or die. She had even forgotten Stephen's child. Blindly, as the bird over the seas, she went—sometimes falling, always without consciousness of direction—down the hill on the Wilderhope side, through the black woods, along lonely lanes, to the foot of the Wilderhope Range.

" The kindly light," she said with a gasp, as she began to climb.

Hours passed. Slowly and with growing feebleness she went on. She reached the farthest gate, where John had been to " send " her on the day when she went away with Stephen. She reached the second gate, and saw, small and softly bright in the infinite blackness of the night, the light of the lamp shining through the open door of her old room and through the uncurtained window.

John, coming down at five to attend to the cow with the " hoost," found Deborah on the doorstep—unconscious.

XLVII

IT was Christmas Eve. Joe and Lily were coming
to tea to-morrow. Mrs. Arden had ordained that
Deborah must be "took out of herself." She had
lain in a state of semi-coma since the black night on
which she came home. Sometimes she called for
Stephen with low, terrible iteration. Only John's
presence seemed to make an atmosphere of partial
peace around her. He sat by her hour by hour,
silent, breathing out love. In his eyes lay the
anguish of a great lover confronted with pain that
he cannot cure.

Mrs. Arden was wildly, concealedly jealous. She
had not hitherto loved Deborah nearly so much as
Joe. The fraying of feminine on feminine in daily
life often has this effect on mothers and daughters.
But if a cataclysm comes, as it had in Deborah's life,
reality comes to the top. Mrs. Arden loved Deborah
now with complete self-abnegation and with the
jealous devotion that such love brings. She slaved
from morning till night; and whenever she saw—or
thought she saw—that John's silent presence was
more valued than all her labours, she cried with her
loud, hiccoughing sobs away at the end of the garden
by the rhubarb. Then she would return and give
the patient John "a bit of her mind." At all times
and places, except in Deborah's room, to John or to
Joe, to Rover if they were absent, to the clock or the
bird-cups if Rover refused to wake up, she raged at
the absent Stephen. The household furniture became

294

his " whipping boy." The clothes in the tub, the
hens round the door suffered vicariously for him.

"You nasty blackguard!" she apostrophized
Rover one day, shaking the dolly at him so fero-
ciously that he ran whimpering from the kitchen
and never stopped till he reached the end of the
Leasowes pastures, while the sheep bunched and
regarded their awful Deity in this new guise with
prim satire.

When Eli looked in on the morning of Christmas
Eve to ask John's help with some ewes, she turned a
wrathful face on him.

"Dunna come prying here!" she said. "It's all
your fault."

"What is?"

"You know right well. And if I had him here I'd
tear him inch-meal, so I would."

"Who?"

"Glad enough you'll be! For you smell out
trouble like a blow-fly smells a carcase, and you'd
liefer see tears than beer!"

"Well, cough it up, 'ooman. Let's hear the worst.
In the hand o' the Lord there is a cup."

"In your ears there'll be a singing if you dunna
stop your texes," said Patty. "I canna hear myself
speak."

John came down to stop the tumult, in his stocking
feet.

"Well, a happy Christmas, John," said Eli.
"Leastways a righteous and repentant 'un, and some
wadding for your ears. Who's dead? Cow with
the hoost?"

"There's none dead by the mercy of Him whose
name is Love. But my poor girl's in sore trouble."

"Heh?"

"She'm laying only just outside the shadowy gate,
and it's quiet feet and soft voices and a hand in the
dark for us in this house."

" Cottage," said Eli mechanically. " What ails the wench? She's a lusty, strapping young 'ooman enough."

" Eli," said John, " though sixty-five summers and winters have gone o'er you, they've not learnt you as there's ills beyond the ills of the poor flesh, that turn the heart to water, aye! and make life a bit of a trampled berry. When love's cut we drop down from God."

" To hear a man of your age talking of love's disgusting," said Eli; " no wonder you're poor in this life and 'll be poorer in the next—for you'm nought but flimsy words, and no eye to business neither in cows nor religion. What's took the girl, as you're so beside yourselves? "

" Stephen's left her."

" Didna I say so? Didna I say he was a gallus young scoundrel? He took my Bible and miscalled me. He's got no fear of God in him, nor the devil nor yet me. Well, good riddance—so long as he left her the cottage and furniture."

" Money's nought and bread's nought when the heart's dying, Eli. And she's burnt the furniture."

" Burnt the furniture? The new chairs and the table, as had a good market value? What a wicked 'ooman! "

John looked at him with pitiful scorn.

" Chairs and tables and all such," he said, waving his hand, " is for use in the meetings and partings of man; and the hills is for man to climb; and the stars to light him up'ards. But ne'er a one of 'em is ought to do with man hisself. For the end of man's life is love—to give it and take it—and if he dunna, he met as well be dead."

" Well, burn my ricks if you binna mad, John! Gobbling ' love, love, love,' like a crazy turkey."

" God is love, Eli." John turned on his heel.

" Well, you met as well come and love my sheep a

296

bit," said Eli; " for they'm got fut-rot, and it takes
two to dress 'em."

" When Deb's better I'll come."

" Not afore ? "

" No."

" Well, I'm surprised at yer. Selfish to the bone !
Their market value's going down every day."

" Dear sakes ! " John was as near to exasperation
as he ever was. " You talk as if the 'orld was nought
but pounds, shillings and pence."

" So it is, and the sharpest gets 'em."

" I'd liefer lose 'em."

" Well, that you surely will, lief or no," said Eli,
as he stumped out.

Meanwhile, Patty had seized the opportunity to
steal up to Deborah's room and ensconce herself with
much creaking in John's chair by the bed, with the
Bible he had been reading on her lap and a pathetic
imitation of his contemplative attitude. But stillness was unnatural to her, and to read the Bible on
working days was, as she put it, against the grain.
So she began to amuse herself by fortune-telling with
the Bible, by letting it fall open and putting her
finger on a text with her eyes shut. The sudden
little slap and rustle at regular intervals awoke
Deborah from her uneasy doze, and wearied her
exhausted nerves. Mrs. Arden had no idea of the
fact. When John came back, she said—

" Now, dunna come disturbing her ! I'm sitting
with her."

" There's a bit of a smell in the kitchen as if summat
in the oven met be ketched," said John.

" Laws me ! "—she let the Bible fall—" it's the
mince-pies ! "

John sat down calmly, and went on reading from
where he left off. The feverish flush on Deborah's
face slowly subsided. In an hour she was asleep again.

" Fidge, fidge, fidge in her room from morning to night," said Mrs. Arden to Lily next day. " She'll ne'er get right if he dunna give me a chance to nurse her."

Neither she nor Lily knew that to some natures all the conventional precautions are so much poison, and only the strong, invisible tendance of the spiritual, the unpractical, unscientific, is of any use at all. For there are times when it is not the deft hand, the skilled brain, the accumulated knowledge of centuries that can bring a human being back from the dark, but only the unskilled hand of a lover, the timeless gaze, the care that knows nothing of precaution or precedent.

The room sank deeper into quiet; Deborah slipped from her waking numbness into complete oblivion; the darkness thickened. John sat pondering for the hundredth time as to what could have made Stephen go. He looked daily for the postmaster from Slepe, who was also the grocer, and who received the letters from an " oxiliary," who in turn received them from an old man with a broad gold band round his hat and a faithful " V.R." on the back of his cart. But when the postmaster came, looking, as he toiled up the snowy valley, like a fly in a sugar-scoop full of fine, white sugar, he only brought a Christmas card from Lucy Thruckton.

Suddenly the grey peace of the room was rent by shrill children's voices, singing outside in the cold air. It was the Shakeshaft children. They were an embodiment of the urgent life of the world, which will seek joy, no matter who lies dying.

John crept to the window.

" Do you little 'uns know ' Lead, kindly Light ' ? "

" Aye—leastways, a verse and a bit."

" Well, you sing that, then, my dears, for nights be dark."

The three little voices sang with unruffled blitheness the frantic appeal out of a gloom of which they had never dreamt.

Deborah awoke into the pathos of it, and wished that her father's light and the faint remembrance of the hymn had not brought her home. She would never have the courage now to walk out of her father's ken into Lostwithin pool. That night she could have done it. She felt that the lamp on the stairs had been treacherous to her, taking advantage of her exhaustion to undermine her resolve. Now the future rose before her like the black rocks of Lostwithin. She remembered how the cranberry flowers had looked like tears, when she was listening to the rock-crusher on that day in August. She had no tears now. Stephen made no more demands on her. With the wild self-reproach of generous natures she thought that she had been cold and selfish. It was agony to remember any moments but those few in which she felt that she really had given him all she could. Any thought spent on others seemed to her now a crime. It had been dreadful to her not to know how he was faring down at the mine; the present complete silence left her mind a blank.

The children galloped through the hymn, and finished off with a rush " —and lost awhile. A merry Christmas." Something in the hymn's merciful way of treating loss as merely finite, recovery as infinite, brought the long-frozen tears to Deborah. It was not that she definitely expected anything; she did not; for even if Stephen came back, now that she was sure he did not love her, living together would be worse than nothing. Yet the optimism of the hymn was sweet after the iron horror of that black night above Lostwithin.

" Father," she said suddenly, " can I have the map of the 'orld ? "

" A map, my dear ? "

" Aye, the old school 'un, as Joe and me learnt on."

John went down to look for it, and found Patty giving the children mince-pies.

" Not as you'm earned them," she remarked, " for a more miserable vexatious ditty than that there yearning thing I never listened at on Christmas Eve. You was used to sing nice peart things, like ' I saw three ships.' Sing it now, loud—and not stand craiking, like turkey poults in the rain ! "

" Not ' The Ships,' " said John.

Mrs. Arden was inarticulate with rage.

" Well ! " she said at last, " to think as I've worked and scratted and saved and bore you two chillun, and now you up and say in my own kitchen as I munna hear talk of my favourite carol."

" Stephen's gone in a ship."

" Stephen, Stephen ! I'm fair sick of the name. I can understand right well now them wold fellows as stoned that Stephen in the Bible. By the way you din about him he met be some one as died respectable and left money, instead of enjoying himself among the buffaloes. And all along of him I canna hear a bit of heartening song from chillun as I give their first wash to, all three ! "

" There ! " said John, " to-morrow we'll have a tuthree carols, mother."

" Is Deb awake ? "

" Aye."

" Why didna you tell me ? There's her broth been ready this hour. A more forgetful man I never see—forget to eat, forget to sleep ! If it had depended on you, you'd have forgotten to be born."

She disappeared upstairs, making the most of her practical qualities, since John had all the others. John fetched in the holly, and began to arrange it round the pictures as a little surprise for her.

Then he sat down to " lap up " his Christmas presents in various bits of ornamental paper saved during the year; fastening them with some copper wire that he had by him, and writing on them after long, pleasant cogitation.

XLVIII

FAINT tinklings—quick and small as a robin's
" chink-chink "—came up the dark slopes above
Slepe on Christmas evening. The handbell ringers
were coming Christmassing, as they did every year
when the weather allowed them.

Joe and Lily had just arrived, and they were all
having tea, Deborah apart in an armchair by the
fire, withdrawn in heavy unconsciousness. She had
got up at John's entreaty. It had taken her hours
to dress—so hard was it to fix her attention on
anything—and, once downstairs, she sank again into
stupor.

Joe, not having seen her since her illness, tiptoed
across the kitchen with the air of a hop-scotch player
and a great scratching of hobnails on tiles.

" When you'm quiet, Joe, you make more noise
than when you'm noisy," said Mrs. Arden.

" Well, Deb," said Joe, in the ventriloquist whisper
that he kept for invalids and the " Amens " in
chapel; " how be you ? "

" I be all right," Deborah spoke slowly. " Aye,
quite all right."

" Our Deb's a good-plucked 'un," said John, with
tears in his eyes.

Lily kissed Deborah.

" Well, Deb," she said, in the rather patronizing
tone that she used to the sick or unfortunate; " I
hope you'll soon be well."

"Aye. Soon be well," said Deborah, without raising her eyes.

Joe sat regarding her with awe. What had come over her to make her a stranger to him? She was only "our Deb," a good sister and pleasant spoken— but nothing out of the common. He was puzzled by her remoteness, her dignity. For the chlamys of grief, though it does not create, brings out hidden greatness. Deborah, in her silence, her unalterable grief, her tragedy which to many would have been no tragedy, had the bearing and presence of a queen of some vast, unknown land.

"Damn his eyes!" said Joe suddenly, with passion, banging his closed hand on the table till the cups rattled, and quite forgetting his invalid manner.

Mrs. Arden opened her mouth for reproof, but realizing who he meant she remarked instead—

"I says the same!"

"Well, mother!" said John.

"I wish, if you must swear, Joe," complained Lily, "you'd swear genteel."

"Damn who, Joe?" asked Deborah, coming halfway out of her reverie.

Joe was, to use his own expression, "put about." He stared helplessly at Deborah.

"Damn who?" she repeated, in level tones.

At this moment a tinkle was heard outside.

"It's the Slepe handbells!" cried Lily. "What a treat!" Handbells, and such festivities, had never come to Bitterley.

Joe welcomed the diversion. "Aye, there they come," he said, "Cadwallader an' all."

"Damn who?" said Deborah.

"Best say summat, Joe," murmured John anxiously.

"Cadwallader, Deb," said Joe. "Damn Cadwallader and his missus and his kid," he repeated, with great relief at having found a lamb for the sacrifice.

Deborah went back into her stillness.

The gate clicked and John went to the door.

" Well, neighbours ! " he said, " you're kindly welcome. What'm you going to give us ? "

The postmaster, as head of the band, and bass bell, said he'd thought of " Ox and ass," which every one knew to mean " Good Christian men, rejoice "; though why the ringers always named it after a line in the second verse, no one asked.

" And a very suitable 'un," said Mrs. Arden, " for if we 'anna got an ox we'n two cows, and our Joe's an ass if ever there was one."

When the merriment subsided they grouped themselves in a semicircle, Job Cadwallader having been urgently entreated to come in at the right moment and not half a note too late as he always did; the postmaster cleared his throat and said in the tone of one inciting a mob to evil-doing—

" The chime."

Obediently, under the large stars on their black velvet, the chime of eight bells rippled out—with one dotted note occasioned by Job.

" You did it agen ! " said the postmaster, in a grieved voice.

" I did me best," said Job; " but when I'm expecting 'im to waggle he dunna, and as soon as I've giv up expecting he does it sudden-like."

" You're not master of your bell," said Shakeshaft solemnly.

" Ca'waller ain't mas'er of his missus nor hisself, so it ain't likely he'd be master of anythink as determined as a bell," said the blacksmith, who had taken a good deal of refreshment.

" If you'm Christmas peart when you'm on'y done the Parson's and the Squire's and two more, what'll you be when we'm through?" asked the postmaster.

The blacksmith subsided.

"Now! The chime again and into the hymn right off."

The antique tune, sweetly and emphatically uttered by the bells, slipped out over the great plateau, pearl-tinted in the light of stars and the rising moon. The sense of the words was in the air—they were so well known by all—and they brought the strange joy with which some old Christian hymns touch the human heart, a joy alien to those here—and to most human beings—who are pagan at the core.

Even John's Christianity was earthy, fuller flavoured than any formulated creed can be—but perhaps not fuller flavoured or as natural or as rich as the Gospel story, if we knew it in its entirety. This was John's favourite carol because it brought in the animal world.

"Ox and ass before Him bow."

"Aye!" he murmured; "the dumb things know."

Mrs. Arden tapped her foot to the tune and found no trial of faith in the words; for every birth to her was wondrous, and she was only a little less thrilled by the coming of this marvel two thousand years ago than by the coming of a neighbour's child to-night.

Lily rocked idly in the old rocking-chair. If her rather vague and muddled ideas could have been unravelled they would have resolved themselves into a kind of pity for a woman who had the pains of maternity without the ameliorations of wifehood.

Joe sat contentedly drinking in the picture of childhood and cattle and mangers; for these were things he knew, friendly and homely. But there was not in him or in any of those present the sense of sinfulness implied in the carol—for that sense is an artificial product of civilization, and though it

305

may be both beautiful and necessary in some environ-
ments it is not so among simple people living normal
lives.

"What a dot-an'-go-one chap you are, Job," said
the postmaster. "What ails you, hopping on the
note like that?"

"I done my best," said Job. "I fixed my eye
on the clapper three bells afore my note, and I puts
me tongue out and I thought I should catchen 'im,
but I didna. Belike I will some time."

"When bit-bats sleep yeads up'ard and women
sleep alone," piped a small man who rang the treble
bell. He was dapper as a robin, and wore a per-
petual smile, as if he had thought of a splendid joke
in babyhood, and had never yet told it. He was
the wit of the party; there was much mirth and
covering of large mouths with large hands at his
remarks.

"Will!" said the tenor bell, who was parish clerk;
"such speaking's not convenient."

"Nor yet sleeping alone bain't!" said the blacksmith, who had an enormous voice, which gave to
his remarks (all broad in humour) a kind of shame-
lessness.

"Now, now," said the postmaster, finding his flock
rather unruly; "manners afore ladies, men! We'll
play 'As Joseph was a-walking.'"

Afterwards John asked for "Lead, kindly Light,"
with a sorrowful glance at the silent figure by the
fire.

"Oh! laws me!" said Patty, "that gloomy thing
agen! What a man! What do we want wi' en-
circling gloom and angels' faces, when we'm just
going to sit down to Christmas beef an' pickle?"

"And beer," said the blacksmith, outside, in tones
that would have been persuasive if they had not been
stentorian.

" Ringing first," said the leader firmly.

They played, and Deborah sat with the map on her knee. She had drawn a line from Liverpool to New York across the Atlantic. But no pencil line, nor anything else—letters, cables, photos—can soften the tragedy of distance. She had suffered so much that she was numb, as people are after intense physical pain. She looked worn, but this added to her beauty, for the spirit shone more clearly. The younger men among the ringers, looking into the mellow firelight of the room and seeing her there, aloof from the rest, beautiful and silent, thought Stephen a great fool. They also, seeing Lily's sunflower of a head going to and fro in the rocking-chair, thought Joe a lucky man; which thought Lily divined, and smiled intoxicatingly at them all.

" Well, thank you kindly ! " said John at the end. " And now come you all in, and have a drop and some pies."

They came in, shuffling, broadly smiling. The blacksmith was in high feather.

" Well, Joe ! " he shouted. " What's one and one make ? "

" Two. What a soft riddle ! " said Joe.

" Three ! " roared the blacksmith, with depths of meaning, and the less discreet laughed.

" Very mild for the season," said the postmaster, to cover this remark. " A mild, dropping time."

" I thought it was a black frost," said Deborah, in a low desolate voice; " a long black frost."

Every one in the room grew still. A kind of fear gripped them. Mrs. Arden wiped her eyes. Joe stared at his boots. Lily looked impatiently at Deborah, angry with her for dimming the revelry. The ringers stood with mugs and pies suspended. John put down the jug he was carrying and went over to her.

"In the black frosses," he said, "there's green and reds down under, and summer in the making."

He sat down by her and stroked her arm gently.

"I hear tell," said Cadwallader, who was not noted for tact and who had been following a train of thought, "as they're all sixens an' sevens at the mine, since he's gone. The manager canna get the men in hand no more'n a babby. *He'd* got a way with him, they say, though he was young, and they durstn't go agen' him. What'n you treading on my foot for so heavy, Mr. Shakeshaft?"

Deborah turned to Job with the first faint look of interest that she had worn since the twenty-first.

"All sixes and sevens be they?" she said, with pride.

"Aye, missus," said Job, taken aback.

"Canna get on 'ithout him?" she asked eagerly.

"No danger, missus."

"Aye!" she said, with such a fire of love in her eyes that the men watched her open-mouthed.

"Aye, they'll miss him! They'll not find his like. Not in all the 'orld can they find the like of—my Stephen."

It was the first time she had said his name. She was immediately overcome with such terrible weeping that Mrs. Arden was alarmed, and helped her upstairs.

The blacksmith, tears rolling down his cheeks, advanced in boxing style upon poor Job.

"I'll gie you a black eye for tarmenting of her!" he shouted in a bass voice which was rather spoilt by its unsteadiness.

"I didna!" Job retreated. "I only said——"

"Listen at him! 'Only said!'"

"Now, now, Jim!" the postmaster interposed, "shooing" his ringers out as he would "shoo" fowls.

"Good-night all," said John. "Dunna take on, Job, for tears is a balm."

The ringers disappeared, scattering faint silvery tinklings that fell on the night like drops of water. Through them could be heard the blacksmith's infuriated bellowings.

XLIX

AFTER a January of blinding snow and almost
unbroken frost, February came with the first minute
white points of snowdrops pricking through the soil
of the warm valley gardens.

It was lambing time, and John was busy, night
and day, with his flock, often sitting up till dawn in
the fold-house where the sheep were.

Deborah would stand at her dark window on the
nights when she could not sleep, and watch his
lantern—an old-fashioned octagonal one with horn
slides—dance to and fro across the fold, like a depend-
able will-o'-the-wisp, when he came and went to the
house, fetching oil or bringing a lamb to warm by the
fire. It comforted her as the sense of a watcher
comforts a sick man, as vivid faith in God comforts
the dying. She was sick with a great self-weariness.
She wanted Stephen and had only herself. She had
lived outside her own personality, and now to be sent
back into it was like returning to some small village
after travelling across the world. She was paralyzed
in emotion, her heart slowly dying. On her face
began the subtle misting-over of expression that
ends in a look of torpor and means stagnation of soul.

On the nights when sleet drove like a tide against
the small, leaded panes of her window she would
look across the fold at the yellow, homely glow of the
unglazed window behind which her father dozed or
tended the lambs. He was her one link with sanity;
for him she still had some living love, which had somehow survived the desolation of her life. When the

310

unanswerable questions, " Where is he ? " " Why doesn't he write ? " came upon her more urgently than usual, and her love groped in the darkness of ignorance for some small clue of her beloved; when the thousand ills that might befall him came on her with sickening agony, and the deadly remembrance that she would not be near him, could not get to him, whatever might happen, however he might want her, tried her almost to madness—then she would follow John about, pitiful in her purposeless existence as the young lambs that bore her company. And John, with his tall, bent figure, his clear, noble profile and far-seeing eyes, became to her in these benighted months a symbol of the Flockmaster who understood all and healed all. As he went to and fro on his daily duties, impeded at every step by the small creatures that loved him, followed silently by Rover, hilariously by the hens, wistfully by the ewes that still waited their hour, importantly by those that were shadowed by one or two black-faced, black-legged lambs, he soothed her by his endless patience, his large humour that had room for all.

He could not cure her nor take away any of her pain, but he could strengthen her by the beauty of his personality, as the hand of some one deeply loved can help those in physical agony.

Mrs. Arden, looking sometimes from the kitchen window, bright with pink and red geraniums, would stamp with jealousy at seeing Deborah following him all day and herself not needed. Then, in a revulsion of feeling, she would wipe away the tears and say—

" Well, he deserves it an' I dunna. To see him now ! all clustered up with a throng of lambs and fowl, and them soft ducks, and Rover—as is getting softening of the brain—not to speak of the cows an' pigs an' ewes as ought to know better—and he never kicks one of 'em, though he's forced to go like walking on eggs, and as slow as a tortoise's funeral."

Then she would go to the door and shriek across the yard that tea was nearly ready, and go in again to concoct some dainty.

On a night towards the end of February, with a sharp frost, she called them across the darkening yard.

" Coming, mother," cried John.

" Always coming, you are, like summer butter, and never come ! " replied his wife, with asperity. For cold nights " ketched her chest," as she put it, and she was sorrowful for Deborah, and felt the bitterness of those who desire to comfort and have no skill in it. In the west there was still a red gash that stained the dusky tops of the shippen and the house and the shed at the back with reflected light. A scent of hay came from the little stack on the sharp air, with the warm smell from the shippen where John had just finished milking. A blackbird " craiked " from the small kitchen garden where he had found a warm roosting-place, and was settling for the night. In the shed the sheep stirred and stamped. Whitefoot pulled down hay from his cratch and chumbled it contentedly. The small world of creatures under John's care was at peace. Within, against the close-drawn blind and the shutters, the geraniums stood up fresh and bright in their brick-red pots.

The furniture shone, the tiles glowed, and above the crackling wood-fire bubbled the usual saucepan of potatoes. Tea was laid, and Mrs. Arden took up her knitting till John and Deborah should come in. She was making socks for the two new-comers into the family. She made socks for all the babies in the neighbourhood; but as she talked all the time she knitted, she never knew how many stitches she had started the first pair with, so they were inevitably of different sizes—a difficulty she conquered by hoarding them all and then sorting them into large, medium and small.

The large she put aside for Deborah, attaching

such generous bows to them that Lily's had to have merely rosettes. In this way she expressed her sympathy. She was also very busy at present "doing up" the cradle with pink glazed calico and muslin. This was kept locked in the attic.

She finished off a small boot, sewed the bow on, and looked up as John opened the door.

"Where's Deb?" he asked anxiously.

"How'd I know, when I never set eyes on my own child from sunup to sundown, with you 'ticing her off in the bitter cold to get her jeath?" replied his wife.

"I thought she was in an hour ago. I missed her."

The two old people gazed at each other with growing anxiety.

Unspoken fears were in both their minds.

"I'll go and bang the tray," said Mrs. Arden at last, taking refuge in practicality.

"It unna be no manner use," said John. "If she's anywhere in the place she'll be in the buildings, and she'll answer when I call." But no answer came to his anxious, wistful calls, and he lit the lantern and went out again.

Patty followed, struck silent by fear, and having the same air of dependence on him as all creatures had in trouble.

As they turned disconsolate from the old threshing-floor under its round roof to the stable and the loft over, a stumpy figure came through the gate.

"What'n you lost?" he queried, his hoarse voice hoarser with the cold; "money or sense? You'm none to spare of neither."

"We'n lost our Deb," said John, his voice trembling.

"Oh! well, she'll come in at meal-time."

Patty rushed at him and administered a stinging box on the ear.

"I'll learn you, you callous little nut without a kernel," she cried, beside herself with anxiety.

313

" Now, now, Patty ! " said John.

Eli was amused, surprisingly and pleasantly. Any one who braved him amused him and gave him a pleasurable thrill; and human emotion—especially the emotion of love which led people into such incalculable doings—amused him as much as anything had power to do.

He therefore received the box on the ear with more blandness than he ever showed when people were pacific.

" I'll look along of you," he said. " An' then you can gie me a drop of your sheep oil, John, for I've got none."

He found it convenient never to have any of these things, drawing his supplies from John.

" Han you looked on the rick, up the ladder ? " he asked.

" Well, of all softness——! " said Patty.

" It's where I'd go, if I wanted to be out of the clickety-clack of a tongue like a wold wind pump, never still day nor night."

John climbed the ladder slowly, his lantern in one hand. Halfway up he stopped.

" Mother, you go and put the kettle on," he said, " in case she'm bad and wants tea and that."

Patty obediently trotted off.

" Eli," said John, " you can go and help yourself to that oil."

Eli seized an opportunity that he did not often get.

John went up on the ladder, having succeeded in his object—to be alone if he found Deborah.

The top of the stack, under its corrugated iron roof, was dark. John turned the lantern-light on it. There was something dark at the end of the stack. He groped his way along.

" Deb ! " he said.

She sat crouched, white, silent. In her hands— blue with cold—were Whitefoot's reins.

" Deb ! " he said.   " Deb, my dear ! "

In his voice were all the low notes of tenderness.

He put his arm round her, and warmed one of her cold hands between his, talking softly of small things in tones of infinite love.

He sometimes talked to the sad-eyed ewes and young lambs in tones like these, and they would look lovingly at him, understanding what he meant, though not what he said.   Deborah looked at him now, across leagues of thought, out of a far country of despair.

" What ails you, Deb, dear heart ? " he asked. " Tell your old dad what ails you."

She looked at him dumbly.

" See, Deb, my pretty," he went on winningly, " mother and me, we've been fair crazy with sorrow, looking you in every place.   And the cold ketches mother summat cruel.   Wunna you come in now ? I'm cold, too," he added artfully.

" Aye, it's cold—cold as death," said Deborah. Her words were shaken with her long shivers.

" There's no need to talk of death," said John. " We'm well and hearty, thank God."

" It came on me," said Deborah, looking at him with horror in her eyes, " sudden-like, when you went for the cows, as Stephen "—she stopped.

" Yes, my dear ? "

" As Stephen met be—dead," she went on, in an expressionless voice.   " Dead and lonesome.   It came on me as he met be.   And though he dunna love me, nor yet didna want me in the full of life, he met be lonesome and wanting me if he was low in the cold grave—wanting me, and me not there."

" Aye, I see, Deb," said John.   " Well ? "

" And so," said Deborah, " it seemed to me as I met go to him, if he was dead, though I couldna live with him in life—for he dunna love me and 'ouldn't want me.   And so I fetched the reins.''

315

"Aye."

"And come up here, and——"

"There, there!" said John. "Dunna go on, lass! I'd sooner you didna."

He was sick with horror and suffering for her sorrow. He knelt by her on the hay, searching for comfort to give her, staring out at the black sky. As he gazed, a line of light came up over the little wood, and the moon rose, majestic, leisurely, changing the massed clouds to ingots of silver and the high cirrus to an ivory filagree. The house and shippen sprang into being, bright-roofed, black-shadowed. A cock crowed, and the sound came through the clear air with the peculiar sweet pathos it has at night.

John knelt, tranced, his eyes on the moonrise, his soul caught into one of its visionary moments.

"Deb," he said, in a voice quite different from his usual one; "he inna dead. He'm maybe in sore trouble; but he inna dead."

She looked at him with the penetrating look of the stricken, and knew that it was not just a facile phrase to comfort her. She was convinced as she could have been by nothing else.

"How d'you know?" she whispered.

"I know," said John, "as whimbrels know the way to the upper pastures and frogs the way to a far pond. It came o'er me like it does now and agen, quick as lightning, and quiet as an owl."

From the house came the voices of Patty and Eli, raised in altercation, for Patty had seen in the bright moonlight how generously Eli was helping himself.

"He inna dead," John repeated pleadingly. "He met come back at long last."

"It wunna be any use. He dunna love me."

"But he met be ill, and want nursing."

"Aye. He might," said Deborah reflectively.

"He'd want you then," John went on, persuasively and wistfully.

316

" Only for a while."

" Aye. Maybe. But you'll not like him to be asking for you to nurse him, and you not there ? "

Deborah got up stiffly and with difficulty, for she was half frozen.

She stood up in the white moonlight and stretched her arms westward.

" I want him ! " she said, with a controlled passion that shook her. " I want him as is the 'orld and all to me. And I canna find him——"

" ' I sought him whom my soul loveth, I sought him and I found him not,' " said John, quoting the beautiful words with the tender cadence he kept for such things. " ' It was but a little time . . . but I found him whom my soul loveth : I held him and would not let him go.' "

The words fell like April rain on her seared heart.

" Aye, I could find him—out of the 'orld, and keep him in the face of death and hell," said Deborah, " if he'd lief be found and kept : but he'd liefer not."

" We must live in good behopes," said John. " And we'll talk a bit of him now and agen, you and me, Deb, what a fine chap he is and all, and how hard he worked and how they miss him. And now we'll come in to poor mother, as is that anxious——"

" She's scolding Eli," said Deborah, with the lambent humour that came to her in tragic moments. " She dunna want me. There's none wants me, only you, father," she went on, and broke into bitter weeping.

" But I want you so bad," said John, " that there inna no sun, moon, nor stars 'ithout you, my lass. So you'll come whome with me now, wunna you, Deb, and let mother tuck you warm in bed, and I'll kindle a bit of fire in your room, and light the lamp, and we'll talk about Stephen."

So he persuaded her in homely phrases that breathed a god-like love.

They got down the ladder with difficulty, she was so numb with cold and grief.

Patty heard them coming over the frozen yard and ran out.

She had conquered her fears by preparing for Deborah's return, and had kept her thoughts off dread possibilities by scolding Eli.

"Listen what I'm going to tell you!" said Eli, who was almost bland, and had decided to go before John found out how much oil he had taken.

"You'm a passel of fools. But you keep a plenty of things—I'll say that for you—and it'll bring you to the House."

L

Mid March came with a week of spring weather.
The hoar frost slipped from the brilliant, pointed lilac
buds and the stout, brown chestnut buds as soon as
the sun was up. After tea, in the fresh, vivid fields,
blackbirds sang in the clear evening light, and
through the mild darkness afterwards the lambs cried.

"The days be drawing out," said John, coming in
with a primrose for Deborah.

"Too long they be," said Deborah.

John looked at her worn face, and came to a
decision long pending.

"I'm going to market, Saturday, mother," he
said.

"Market? With one cow dry, and the other near
it, and the garden stuff done, and eggs as scarce as
charity, till not a hen can look me in the face? What
in the name of softness for?"

"Oh, tuthree things I want."

On Saturday John called at the office of the county
weekly, and asked for the editor.

"Engaged," said the boy.

John sat down, took out his New Testament, and
put on his spectacles.

In due time the editor appeared, and John, dreamy
from his favourite passage in Revelations, pulled out
a sheet of paper.

"Will you please to read it, sir?" he said.

"If Mr. Stephen Southernwood will write to this
office he will hear something to his advantage and
oblige."

" Yes, that's quite clear."

" You think it'll fetch him, sir? Or had I best explain a bit? "

" It sounds inviting," said the editor. " Money, I suppose? "

" Well, no."

" Land left? "

" No."

" What then, if I might ask? "

" A little 'un—soon," said John, as if that were the best that could befall any man.

" Good Lord! " said the editor, who had half a dozen children. " No—don't explain, if you want him."

" And it'll find him, certain sure? " asked John, looking at the editor over his spectacles. " In America? "

The editor struggled between truth and the credit of his paper.

" Well," he said, " of course, America's a big place, and although we've a large circulation, he might not see it. Why not try a cable, if you know his address? "

" I dunna," said John. " I mun try a different sort of cable."

" Eh? "

" A bit of a prayer."

When John got home, Mrs. Arden was throwing hay to the sheep.

" And I hope you've done gallivanting for a bit," she said, " for I canna do all. There's Deb slaving, day in, day out, to stop thinking, and Lily, as wunna do a hand's turn, and me up and down between 'em like a bird in a cage. If I go down and get Lily to take an airing, when I come back there's Deb scrubbed both the floors. And you off to town, as if you wunna going to be two grandfathers in a month. And never a ' thank you ' from Lily! And there's Deb, worth

320

six of her, and met be a widow for all the good that Stephen is to her."

, " Well, we mun do our best, mother."

" Hark at him ! *We* mun do our best—and him going off and enjoying himself ! It's long work and short words as gets through trouble, not them as stand and blaat like lambs."

Within, Deborah sat in the fading light, weary after too hard a day. She always exhausted herself in an instinctive desire for mental torpor. There was no light of coming motherhood in her eyes. She was not interested in her child. If she ever thought of it, she felt intense pity for it. For the rest, her thoughts followed Stephen, and she had none to spare for herself. She had no eyes for the things around her—the Devil's Chair stirred no fear in her, the Flockmaster's signpost gave her no comfort, except that she remembered her dream of him with Stephen's face. The ordeal before her brought no terror, the future no curiosity. She was like one asphyxiated. For if the thing that is the spirit's breath of life is taken away, its life stops. All that she did was mechanical. Because she was strong, she fought her thoughts by work; because she was naturally un-selfish, she made clothes for Lily's child as well as her own. Lily took full advantage of this. She did not feel sorry for Deborah—she was so sorry for herself. Hers was not one of the natures from which sorrow strikes out a vast pity for all the world.

John looked at Deborah, tragic in her white silence. He thought of what he had done, and rubbed his hands in childlike joy, never doubting that he would have a speedy reply.

" If you must rub 'em, rub 'em with the soap in 'em, and get washed, for goodness' sake ! " said Patty. " And have your meat—for it's as late as good luck."

"Maybe I'll bring good luck," said John, through suds, from the wash-house.

"Maybe you'll do a lot, but if I didna poke you and prod you, you'd go to sleep standing, like Whitefoot in the shafts. Now, Deb, my dear, draw up to your tea," she went on, with a drop of three notes in her voice and a tenderness that none but the sick ever heard from her. "A bit of thin bread-and-butter, now?"

"Anything, thank you, mother," said Deborah, as she always did.

"That's a good girl. I only wish Lily 'd say the same. So frangy as she is, and my cooking's too rough, seemingly, though she canna cook herself, not if it's ever so. There she sits, snivelling in the armchair, eating sugar till she feels sick, and then refusing good food, and Joe having to go down on his knees, as clumsy as a load of coals, and feed her by spoonfuls, and him looking at me—as had done a morning's washing for her—as if I was a black convict-criminal! Only saints have the patience as she calls for, and I'm not a saint, thank God!"

Outside in the dusk a thrush sang with poignant sweetness, possessing the silent pastures with its fresh voice. John listened, his spoon arrested in stirring, the music plucking at him like a hand on a harp. He listened so long, while the song slipped into the clear, primrose west, that Mrs. Arden was irritated.

"What's eggs?" she rapped out.

"Eggs?"

"Yes. Dunna you know what 'e-g-g' is? What be they now?"

"I didna ask."

"And butter?"

"I didna ask."

"Well, of all the——"

322

Words failed her. She put her feelings into cutting bread.

John said nothing. He was accustomed to silence, for in success or failure the seer knows the impossibility of explaining himself.

"Can you loan me a few turmits?" said Eli's voice at the door. "My sheep's finished theirs—greedy beasts!"

"You didna put in enough," said John. "I was afraid you'd be short."

"He wanted to be short!" cried Patty with perspicacity. "You've never asked after Lily yet, Eli."

"Why should I? Spent breath's gone and wasted."

"You unnatural, grudging little bantam!"

"If you was my wife——"

"If I'd been so crackbrained as to be any such thing, I'd maybe've ended by making you summat *like* a man—working overtime at you."

"Best come for the turmits, Eli," said John.

"Taking the turmits out of our very mouths," said Patty wrathfully. "And you soft enough to give 'em."

"Give and it shall be given to you, mother."

"Not in this life!" Patty spoke with the scepticism of those who toil for their daily needs. "And in the next we met not want turmits."

She turned and surprised Deborah silently crying. She was much concerned. With her, visible grief meant much, hidden grief little. She suddenly realized how Deborah had been feeling all this time. She shyly stroked her arm.

"He'll be sure to come soon," she said.

"Never no more. Besides, away or not away's no different now. He dunna care about me."

Mrs. Arden gave it up.

"I canna make Deb out," she said to John later.

"Cut love's hard to mend, mother. But if so be

323

he'd come back, there met be things to be said for him as we dunna know."

"If so be he'd come back," said Mrs. Arden, "and I could get my tongue round him real proper, I could say ' Lord, now lettest thou thy servant depart in peace.' "

LI

IT was early June, and Deborah was out-of-doors again, taking slow walks with her baby in her arms. On the green, lonely hills the sheep grazed with their lambs, and the air was never empty of their sweet, sad calling. In the warm plain the May hedges were already in flower, and the thorn trees that clustered by the valley streams like wide-skirted children, or climbed the steep hillsides, were opening their hard green buds and breaking softly into white. Looking at them, Deborah remembered how she had said to Stephen, " The thorn blows late." Once more the bracken pushed out soft fingers, and cuckoos cried from orchards at the foot of the cwms. The snipe summoned his love from his airy circles, and curlews ran along the hilltops with their forlorn, elfin music.

" The seynty tree's gold over ! " cried Mrs. Arden one day, when the little family came back from Slepe, where the baby had been christened. She plucked a spray for Deborah, and another for Lily, who had come up for the christening party. Lily had insisted on calling her boy Stephen, to Joe's great bepuzzlement. Deborah would not call her child by its father's name. She blazed into hostility at the suggestion. The very idea made her almost regard her own child as an interloper.

" None shall be called by my man's given-name ! " she said. " I'd be minding me, nights, when I called the lad whome, of the days that's gone, the shiny days, and the ways of him as I call whome never no more. And when it was only the lad that came, and

Y   325

not my Stephen, I'd come nigh to hating the poor child."

So he was called John.

After tea Deborah went with her baby along the bright ribbon of turf that led through the heather to the shepherd's signpost. She found Lily's presence irksome. Lily was so untroubled, so approved of, so cold. Deborah did not know that her sense of injustice was the age-long feud between storm-tossed greatness and sheltered littleness.

Low on the opposite ridge, the larch woods still kept their breathless May freshness, reaching up wistfully toward the gaunt, unchanging heights and the Devil's Chair. Among them the fir-trees reared their tarnished blue-green—sullen, archaic, sentinels of death in a world of immaculate, indomitable youth. A soft, strong wind blew from the west, quick with the year's promise, brimful of meadow and mountain scent. Large clouds continually came up from beyond the Chair, darkened it, swept over the valley, and suddenly disappeared like conjured ghosts as the warm air struck them.

Deborah sat down beneath the signpost, exhausted with a weariness that even the tiny shell-pink fingers, so determinedly fastened on her thumb, could not lift. She looked down at the golden spray of laburnum on her breast, drew in its curious sharp scent, and began to sing in a low voice—

" Some were sobbing in the gloom
   When we found it, when we found the golden arrow—
   Wand of willow in the secret cwm."

She looked across at the Devil's Chair—dark and shining as a night-sapphire. It seemed to her that there was no hostility now between the two ranges, between the towering throne and the small white

cross. Always before, she had superstitiously regarded the Chair as wholly evil, the Flockmaster's
signpost as wholly good. Now she saw good and evil
mingled, and felt a slumbering terror in the protecting
cross, a hidden beneficence in the inimical stronghold
across the valley. Beyond both, behind light and
shadow, under pain and joy she felt a presence—too
intangible for materialization into words, too mighty
to be expressed by any name of man's. Intuitively
she looked at the dogmas she had been taught, and
in the fierce light that her experience had lit in her
she found them wanting. She had nothing definite
to put in their place, only a conception as vague and
volatile as light or scent, and without the anæsthetic
quality of those creeds that affirm God to be love and
goodness only. She was naturally religious, and she
felt an almost mystical comfort and rapture in the
peace of the Flockmaster's green pastures, and in
the presence that dwelt there for her as well as for
her father. But away in the black night, among the
tomb-like rocks, in the glare of her burnt happiness,
she had heard devils laugh, had felt a dark power
brood on the crag. Instinct told her that the two
visions were one. She was content with the balance
of life as she found it, being dimly aware that the terror
and the beauty intermingled in something that was
more wonderful than beauty.

" The thorn blows late," she murmured, with the
patience of one that has come through tumult and
found peace.

She thought how Stephen had failed her; then,
quick as light on water came the remembrance of her
dream, when Stephen appeared to her as the Flockmaster, holding in his glance infinite, godlike love
and pity. She looked down at her child. Life had
given her this gift, for which she had not asked,
denying her the gift she desired. Yet, bent above

the sleeping face—clear and sweet as a pale-tinted wild rose—she acquiesced, though sorrowfully, in the decree. She had love to give still, in large measure, and here was one of love's little beggars.

She gazed into the distance while the slow, honeyed loveliness of evening intensified toward its climax. Above the blue ranges rose bluer mountains of cloud; against this background the swallows, yet more brilliantly blue, darted with the half-gay, half-panic-struck frenzy of creatures aware of their endless capacity for joy and of the tragic brevity of their day. With such wild, despairing haste do natures like Stephen's seize the gleaming moment.

The Devil's Chair had a light behind it from the setting sun; rays came from it as if it had a heart of warmth. Suddenly, in the grave silence of all things at sundown, Deborah turned sharply as if at a cry.

LII

NOTHING had stirred; but far away, from the direction of Wood's End, a man appeared walking with the difficult haste of one eager but exhausted.

Deborah put the child down and stood up.

Stephen came on, dragging after him a gigantic shadow. Deborah stood waiting, numb, joyless, since for her the meaning had been struck from all meetings. The shadow of the cross barred her dress.

Stephen said nothing. He looked at her with a dumb, haggard gaze that had nothing of his old self in it. New lines were in his face—lines too deep to be accounted for by physical suffering alone. He was gaunt; strangers would have considered before they spoke of him as a young man. His lip trembled. He sat down on the mound at the foot of the signpost and looked up at her, absorbed, silent.

" You'm tired, lad," she said, with quick concern.

" Not now. I was. But now I'm home."

In the last sentence, with its wild, pathetic rapture, were reflected all his forlorn days of absence. For the intensity of present joy is the gauge of past grief.

His " I'm home ! " by its triumphant security, told that he had been in hell. In his voice were the tones of the world's homesickness—the nightmares of children in the dark, the blind groping of lover for lover, the sob of humanity cast out of Eden.

But Deborah did not understand.

Too much pain had left her bewildered. She

only felt, in a dim way, the pitiful irony of his words, since she was his home no more.

"You look as if you met have been poorly, lad," she said practically.

"Yes, I had typhoid. I was in hospital for months. That was why I didn't come. And the minute I knew I couldn't come, I wanted to more than anything in this life or any other. I was off my head for a long time; I couldn't remember anything except your name. It was awful. I couldn't get to you, and I couldn't live without you."

"Poor lad. You allus liked to do things sudden-like."

She had not understood. He became aware of the change in her. Terror flashed into his face.

"Deborah," he said, standing up; "Deborah, I want to kiss you."

"You'd liefer not, I know," she answered. "It's only for my sake. Thank you kindly all the same, Stephen."

"Liefer not?"

"Aye."

"But I've come half across the world for it!"

He did not mention that he had worked his way home on a tramp steamer, sick and ill and scarcely convalescent. He did not mention a score of things that might have aroused her. Trouble that happened to himself had ceased to be worth either mention or thought in his estimation.

"Aye," said Deborah. "But first you went."

"I know. Good God! I know. Was any man ever such a blind fool? But I felt—then—that going was the only way to keep sane. These ranges—they got hold of me——" He faltered. By the new light in him he saw how meaningless his reasons must appear to her. He knew that now neither the wilderness nor dark weather, devils, nor the infinite void, mattered to him in the least. His love for

330

Deborah made him impregnable to terror, gave him a grasp of truth deeper than reason. He had found the golden arrow, to his own agony and ennobling.

"There's no ill-will, lad," Deborah went on, in the toneless voice that was natural to her now. She was anxious that he should not reproach himself, for a moment's pain for him was more than she could bear.

"I understand all about it," she went on, sitting down and laying a motherly hand on his hair as he flung himself at her feet. "Aye. All about it. You thought—as folk will—as you loved me best in the 'orld, and then you came to see it different."

"I didn't know—I didn't understand. But now I do. I love you—oh! what's the good of words? You can see!"

"See what, Stephen?"

"That I love you better than myself."

"You was used to say that," said Deborah, with terrible, unintentional cruelty; "but you didna."

"But I do now! I do now! How can I show you? Can't you believe it, Deborah, my darling?"

"Never no more."

Suddenly, in her eyes—her emotionless lips, he learnt the agony she had endured. He covered his face with his hands; hard sobs shook him.

"There, there!" she said, patting his shoulder. "Dunna take on, lad! There's nought amiss."

He groped for her hand.

"Poor child," he said brokenly.

Deborah, a year ago, would have known from the very simplicity of his words, and their selflessness in the midst of his own misery, that he loved her now, if never before. To-day she did not know. She was a woman of one fixed idea—that he did not want her. So he must not be allowed to sacrifice himself out of kindness.

"There, there!" she comforted him. "It's nought."

"I'm like a man that kills himself in his sleep," he muttered. "Tell me about it—that night."

"The longest night," she said, like a child repeating a well-learnt lesson."

"Don't, don't!" he cried, flinching.

But she was back by the Devil's Chair, in a horror of darkness, and she had forgotten him.

"The devils laughed down the spinney and called me a kept 'ooman, and so I was—ring or no ring. For there's nought can hallow a man and an 'ooman as lives together if they dunna love each other; and if they can abear to be apart, and if they can do 'ithout the little ways each of other——" She paused. "Oh, well!" she ended, with a hint of cold pride; "then the 'ooman's a kept 'ooman and the child's baseborn."

"The child—?" Stephen questioned. He had not noticed the white bundle, frail as the cotton-grass down that wandered from hill to hill, a poor white waif blown along the steep, dark mountains.

"Aye, Stephen! your child." She was suddenly anxious that he should enjoy to the full the pride of fatherhood—the joy she had wanted for him. She took the child up and parted the shawl.

"There!" she said. "The only thing I've ever done for you, Stephen."

She sat with the child on her knee.

He knelt and examined it, anxious not to hurt her by any seeming indifference—but thinking only of her.

The sun had gone. From the thickets of colour in the west, as from an orchard of ripe, falling fruit, the red and yellow softly passed. In the subdued light the little group was like an austerely imagined Holy Family.

"It's very—" said Stephen gropingly, "very small, isn't it? And a bit broad for its length?"

The child began to cry, frightened by the tear that fell on its face as Stephen bent over.

"All that too!" he muttered, and shook his head in a kind of helplessness. "All that pain—for me."

"He's only broad because of his wraps," said Deborah, kindly explanatory; "and he's big for his age," she added, quoting her mother with detachment.

The baby cried louder. He was hungry, and had inherited from his father the axiom, "Here and Now!"

"I mun take him whome and give him his supper," said Deborah.

"What does it have?" asked Stephen, catching at trifles in the desperate way of those in a great crisis.

"He's breast-fed," said Deborah.

"Then need you—?" began Stephen, striving to keep her with him. "I mean, can't it be fed here?"

"No."

In her proud, aloof glance he read the death-sentence of his hopes. He was a stranger. He looked round him like a man lost on the ranges in a snow-storm.

"I'd better go," he said. "It's all I can do. You hate the sight of me. I don't wonder."

"You know I love only you out of the 'orld, Stephen!"

"Well, then—!" he cried, with a rush of joy. "Can't you believe that I do? How can I make you believe?"

"You canna. You told me you did afore, and you didna. I canna believe anything agen."

"Deborah! Live with me once more—just for one week, one day, at home yonder above Lost-within. You'll understand then," he cried frantic-ally; "you'll know without telling when you see how I'll take care of you!"

"There inna no whome there now, for I burnt the things. And the cattle go to and agen by the hearth. And there's none to stay the wind and the rain driving in o'er the thrashold."

"I'll make a new home; I can'!" He flung his head back with his old, unconquerable look.

"Thank you kindly, Stephen, but I'm well enough as I be. It's only your goodheartedness, I know. But I dunna need to be beholden to any one."

"But it's I that would be beholden, Deborah. I'm asking it as a favour, the greatest in the world."

"Afore, when you asked, I gave you all I had—such as it was; and you flung it back in my face. I've no ill-feeling, Stephen. Only I've no more to give."

Stephen stood up. On his face as he looked down at her was the lambent beauty of those who find the Golden Arrow and clasp it to their hurt and glory. His face was the face of her dream. In the dusk, tall and deep-eyed beside the little signpost, he was the incarnation of the Flockmaster.

Worn, world-battered, despairing, he stood there in a grandeur that had not been his before — the splendour of perfect manhood. All the passions of his eager nature were quelled before this new, burning force in him. All his old readiness of tongue, his old poses, were gone.

He felt nothing of his own tragic beauty as he said gently—

"The dew's falling, Deb, you two should be home. Good-night."

"Good-night, Stephen," said Deborah, not realizing the parting any more than the meeting; "and may the kindly light be along with you."

From the cwms rose white wraiths of mist, slipping along the hillsides, ascending, torn by the sharp buttresses of the rocks, touching the hills to a strange, grieved beauty.

From the westward side two of these wraiths came slowly, detaching themselves with soft determination from the physical world of rock and tree, and sweeping high over the plateau on the wind, like spirits too delicate and too eager for the limitations of a material world. They faded in the dusk.

At last Stephen turned and went a few steps in the direction from which he had come. He looked back, and she waved her hand; then she also turned to go.

As soon as he was out of sight, all power of movement left Deborah. There was no room in her mind for anything but the sense that her fingers had touched his hair, and now did not touch it. Slowly, as life comes back to a paralyzed limb, she awoke to the knowledge that he had been here and was gone. What did it matter whether he loved her or not, whether she was a " kept woman " or not, whether he left her again some day? She wanted him. Everything else was washed from her brain by this primæval, ungovernable passion for the reassurance of touch.

She hastily put the child in the heather, though it was wet with dew. Even motherhood was swept away. She ran along the path calling " Stephen ! Stephen ! "

But no voice answered. Around her were only the inscrutable hills, the night sky — intolerably secret, remote, vast. The child wailed, and its cry pierced the solitudes like the eternal lament of humanity with its limitless desires, its weak, small hands.

Away at High Leasowes a little light moved in widening arcs, as John searched for Deborah, coming slowly nearer in a small aura of warmth along the hill in the cold gloom.

But Deborah gazed away into the vague night, for she knew that somewhere in the huge folds of

335

the hills a light was passing from her—a light which shone, now that it had ceased to flicker, with a large glory even more beautiful than her father's. It had smitten her new-found quiescence and destroyed it, wakening her to life. It could, she knew, circle her in from all uproar, all grief and gloom, though she dwelt in the starless cwms of pain and death.

LIII

In the rosy kitchen at High Leasowes, Deborah and her mother sat by the fire, tensely silent. John had taken the octagonal lantern and was away on the hills.

"If he's to be found by mortal man, father 'll find him for certain sure, so ease your heart, Deb, my dear," said Mrs. Arden; "wunna you put on that gown with the poppy-sprig?"

"No. I'll take nought for granted," Deborah replied. Like all who have lived with sorrow and looked below the surface of life, she had a shivering sense of its irony. She sprang up, the child in her arms, and sank into her chair half-fainting, when she saw that only Eli stood at the door. He had come to borrow the sheep-shears, having broken his own.

"What a time of night! Borrowing's allus in season seemingly," scolded Mrs. Arden. "You'll go round in your bones to borrow your coffin, Eli! Now as you *be* here, you may's well look what a fine boy Deb's got."

Eli advanced upon Deborah and stood grimly contemplating the baby.

"Well?" queried Mrs. Arden, thirsty for admiration, from however unpromising a quarter.

But Eli was lost in frowning study of the child, which was met by a composed blue gaze—fearless, eager, wilful as Stephen's.

Suddenly Eli leant forward and shook his fist at the child.

" Where's my Bible ? " he shouted.

Deborah stiffened. Through the uncurtained window she had seen, very far away, a small light. While it was only a point in the darkness there was a sound outside of a man running. They all listened.

In the breathless quiet the footsteps acquired a strange significance. It was as if humanity ran blindly down the steep, hastening with unquenchable longing toward some mystery that the night cradled.

Stephen stood in the doorway. He came in. Mrs. Arden tiptoed through the door and went down the path.

Stephen looked at Eli.

" Get out ! " he said.

And Eli, in an unaccountable, awed silence, went. Stephen shut the door.

" Well," said Eli, stealthily unglueing himself from the window, and startling Patty nearly out of her wits, " if the young fool wants to go down on the floor like a struck bullock, why canna he go down to the Lord A'mighty, and not to an 'ooman as is nought but his wife when all's said ? "

He slammed the gate after him.

" If he was my son— ! " he said, and faded in the dim, soft night.

John came up.

" The lad outstripped me, mother," he explained. " I'm thinking it's the shippen for you and me to-night, while cut love's mending."

They sat on the straw, in an aura of light from the lantern.

" Shanna I kindle a bit of fire for 'em, and light the lamp ? " asked Patty.

" There's no need, mother. D'you mind the tale of them that found the Golden Arrow, and went with apple-blow scent round 'em, and a mort o' bees, and warmship, and wanted nought of any man? There's no need of fire or can'le for them, my dear, for they'm got their light—the kindly light—and the thorn's white over."